Neil Broadfoot worked as a journalist for fifteen years at both national and local newspapers, including *The Scotsman*, *Scotland on Sunday* and the *Evening News*, covering some of the biggest stories of the day.

His Stirling-set series, which begins with *No Man's Land* and features close protection expert Connor Fraser, has been hailed as 'tense, fast-moving and bloody' and 'atmospheric, twisty and explosive', with a 'complex cast of characters and a compelling hero'. *No Man's Land* was longlisted for the 2019 McIlvanney Award.

As a father of two girls, Neil finds himself regularly outnumbered in his own home. He is also one of the Four Blokes in Search of a Plot, a quartet of crime writers who write stories based on suggestions from the audience. The Four Blokes have appeared in England, Spain and Scotland, including at the Glasgow International Comedy Festival.

Also by Neil Broadfoot

No Man's Land
No Place to Die

Neil
Broadfoot

The Point
Of No
Return

CONSTABLE

CONSTABLE

First published in hardback in Great Britain in 2020 by Constable

This paperback edition published in 2021 by Constable

A CIP catalogue record for this book
is available from the British Library.

ISBN: 978-1-47212-764-8

Typeset in Minion Pro by Initial Typesetting Services, Edinburgh
Printed and bound in Great Britain by Clays Ltd, Elcograf S.p.A.

Papers used by Constable are from well-managed forests and
other responsible sources.

Constable
An imprint of
Little, Brown Book Group
Carmelite House
50 Victoria Embankment
London EC4Y 0DZ

An Hachette UK Company
www.hachette.co.uk

www.littlebrown.co.uk

For Fiona and Alex. Now and always.
And in memory of Ali Logan. Your time came too soon.

CHAPTER 1

Free is a four-letter word.

The thought strikes me suddenly, and I'm forced to swallow down the unexpected laughter that tickles the back of my throat like champagne bubbles. Laughter at this moment would draw attention, and what I need right now is dignified composure. So I strangle it, force my face to take on a neutral expression. Nod at the appropriate times, cock my head when points are made. To the casual observer, I am sombre, attentive, following proceedings intently.

The truth is far simpler.

I am fucking elated.

Free. I am finally free. After fourteen years – fourteen years of confinement, restraint and denying myself – I am finally free. Free again to hunt, to roam.

To kill.

The revelation sends dull sparks fizzing across my eyes, the colours of the day suddenly becoming hard, dazzling things that seem to leap out at me, as though the contrast on the world has suddenly been dialled all the way up. I feel as though I'm having an out-of-body experience, drifting untethered, disconnected as bureaucracy grinds its way through seconds and minutes before finally, finally, it's over and I'm released.

I stagger out into the day, blinking like a newborn as cameras flash and questions are shouted. I put my arm out, wrap it around

1

the person next to me, pull him close. I suppose it could be seen as a gesture of comfort, support.

Honestly? I'm clinging on for dear life.

Finally the noise and chaos is behind us and the world takes on its former soft focus. We walk silently, falling into step with each other, no words needing to be spoken. After all, we've had more than a decade to consider this day. What more needs to be said now?

I am free. Finally. Free to choose where I want to go and what I want to do. And what I want to do is very, very simple. It is the same thing I've wanted to do for the last fourteen years. A tingle of anticipation flashes from my stomach to my crotch at the thought.

Free. Free to do what I want.

And *where* I want to do it is obvious. After all, they say home is where the heart is.

And my heart has always been in Stirling.

CHAPTER 2

The sound of the mirror exploding filled the room, the noise as jagged and sharp as the shards of glass that hit the floor in an almost musical tinkle of static.

So much, Connor Fraser thought, for a quiet assignment.

He was in Stockbridge, one of the more gentrified areas of Edinburgh's New Town, all granite buildings, leafy streets, artisan wine stores, exclusive restaurants and, of course, boutique salons where hair could be cut, nails could be buffed and appearances could be maintained. And the salon Connor stood in at that moment was one of the most exclusive. Linklaters was renowned for having the most discerning clients – footballers, politicians and even a few well-kent faces from TV were known to be shorn and groomed by Stuart Linklater or his wife, Audrey. They had appeared in style magazines, hosted a TV makeover show, embarrassingly called *The Missing Linklaters*, were regulars on the society pages and at all the best parties across central Scotland.

All of which went part of the way to explaining why Stuart Linklater was now lunging towards Connor with a pair of scissors in his hand, perfectly bleached teeth almost glowing as he pulled his perma-tanned features into a sneer. 'Move Connor, *now*!' he hissed, a faint Highland burr softening some of the menace in his voice with a singsong quality Connor almost found funny. 'I swear to fuck, I'm going to gut that cheating hoor!'

Connor staggered forward a half-step as Audrey slammed into his back, trying to get around him.

'Come on, then, you fuck!' she hissed as Connor stood his ground and pushed back. 'You think I'm scared of you?' A sneer of laughter, as sharp and cold as what was left of the shattered mirror. 'You're about as threatening as my last shite, Stuart, and it had more backbone. I only brought Connor here because Grant recommended him but, believe me, I don't need him to deal with a limp-dicked little prick like you!'

The moment the name had been uttered, Connor knew what was going to happen. Grant. As in Grant Lucas. One of the Linklaters' regular clients, a perfectly coiffed and manicured presenter on STV's late-night current-affairs programme. And it was current affairs that had led to here, when Audrey had announced her love for Grant and her intention to leave Stuart, taking with her half of their business and the empire they had built up over the last twenty-five years.

All of this flashed across Connor's mind in the split second it took Stuart to react. He jerked once, as though the name had somehow electrified him, then lunged forward again, bringing up the scissors, his face a mask of well-moisturised hatred, his intention to cut straight through Connor to get to Audrey glinting in his eyes.

Connor took a half-step back, Audrey giving a startled cry as he sent her sprawling, then stepped forward, ducking low and into the arc of the scissors. He punched upwards, into Stuart's exposed armpit, sending him off balance. With a startled cry of pain, Stuart collapsed to the side, crashing into a barber's chair and tumbling to the floor. Connor swept his foot, trailing Stuart's path, a quick stamp to the wrist of the hand holding the scissors, which skidded away across the exposed wood floor.

'Stay down, Mr Linklater,' Connor said, as he took in the room. Audrey was picking herself up theatrically from the floor, eyes darting between the scissors and her soon-to-be-ex-husband, who was cradling the wrist Connor had just stood on and folding in on himself like a beaten puppy.

'Don't, Audrey,' Connor said slowly, making sure his eyes conveyed the message. 'Just collect what you came for and let's get out

4

of here, OK? Stuart's not going to give us any more trouble, are you, Stuart?'

'You almost broke my fucking hand!' Stuart yelped, an edge of tears in his voice now, all bravado gone.

Connor considered this. 'You came at me with scissors, Mr Linklater,' he said, feeling anger rippling across the back of his neck in slow, cramping waves as he spoke. 'If I'd wanted to, I could have hit you hard enough to dislocate your shoulder instead of just throwing you off balance. And I could have easily smashed your wrist. Under the circumstances, I've been a model of restraint. So keep that in mind, will you?'

He turned as Audrey bustled towards him, a large, ugly glass sculpture that looked vaguely like a kid's Play-Doh rendering of a pair of scissors cradled in her arms. Connor sighed internally. Of course, he thought. I should have known. So much for the simple assignment.

She swept past him, heels crunching on the glass from the mirror shattered by the phone Stuart had hurled into it when they arrived. 'Let's go,' she hissed, her face twisting momentarily as she passed the prone figure of Stuart. 'You,' she whispered, 'will be hearing from my fucking lawyers.'

Connor followed her out, got in front of her to block her access to the Land Rover parked outside the salon.

She looked up at him, rearranging her face into a grateful smile. 'Thank you, Connor. As you can see, Stuart has always had a temper. I should have left him years ago.' Her voice was a low drawl, little more than a whisper. Christ, did she really think he was that stupid? Maybe she did, after his performance just now.

'Mrs Linklater, Audrey,' Connor said, keeping his tone neutral. 'Please, don't try to play me. Yes, Stuart was out of line just now, and yes, I maybe went a little hard on him. But don't pretend it wasn't exactly what you wanted. We're both better than that.'

'Why, I don't, I mean I . . .' she blustered, suspicion puncturing the mask of civility she wore.

Connor locked his gaze with hers, suddenly tired. He had better things to do than this. 'You asked me to escort you here to retrieve some essential items. I agreed because Mr Lucas is our client, and he

5

is keen you receive the best care, especially since Mr Linklater can be somewhat, ah, unpredictable. But what you came here for was a worthless Salon of the Year award. You knew Stuart would be here. Wanted to bait him with me around to look after you. What was it you said to him? "You'll be hearing from my lawyers"? All well and good, Mrs Linklater, but trust me on this. If your lawyers contact me, I'll deny anything happened here today. I don't like being played, Mrs Linklater. I'm here to protect you, not become a pawn in your tug-of-war with your husband.'

Audrey's mouth moved silently for a moment, as though she was speaking but had been put on mute. Emotions scudded across her face like fast-moving clouds. Shock. Outrage. Spite. Connor could see the calculations playing across her mind: what could she do? How could she avenge this outrage? He found he didn't care.

Stepped aside, opened the door of the Range Rover for her.

'Have a nice day,' he said. 'I won't include any of this in my report to Mr Lucas, but if you feel he would benefit from a personal conversation with me, just let me know.'

She glared at him for a moment longer, then slipped into the car. The award was tossed into the passenger seat like the afterthought it was, and then she busied herself with her belt, muscles fluttering in the side of her jaw as she clamped down on her anger.

Connor swung the door shut gently, took a step back as the car roared into life and squealed away from the kerb. He glanced back up at the salon, considered going back in to check on Stuart Linklater. The decision was taken out of his hands by the buzzing of his mobile in his pocket. He pulled it out, saw Robbie Lindsay's name on the caller ID.

'Robbie, what's up? I'm just heading back in now,' he said.

'Glad to hear it, boss. We've had a call – you're getting a visitor.'

'Oh?' Connor said. Curious. He had cleared his diary at Sentinel Securities for the afternoon to deal with the Linklaters, and Robbie knew better than to drop appointments into an afternoon Connor had blocked off. 'Who's looking for me?'

A moment's pause on the line, a slight clearing of the throat. Robbie was shaping up to be a good operative, but there was still this nervousness when he was delivering news he didn't think Connor was going to like. Something to work on.

'It's DCI Ford, sir,' Robbie replied. 'Says he needs to see you to discuss an urgent matter.'

'Ford?' Connor felt a ripple of unease in his guts. He had worked with Malcolm Ford on two cases now, both of which had seen people die and Connor put in harm's way. He respected the man and, as a former police officer himself, knew how difficult the job could be. But Ford's patch was Stirling and Central Scotland. Why would he be venturing into Edinburgh to request a meeting in person?

'How long have I got?' Connor asked, heading for his car, which was parked a block away.

'He just called ten minutes ago, boss. Says he'll be here in an hour.'

Connor glanced at his watch. Calculated. The Sentinel offices were on the outskirts of the city, in an industrial estate not far from the airport. Even in Edinburgh's treacle-like traffic, he'd make it back in plenty of time.

'OK,' Connor said. 'I'm on my way. I take it Ford didn't give any clue about what all this was about?'

'No, sir, afraid not. But I took the liberty of doing a little digging, and I think I may have an idea. I can send a package to you now if you like?'

Connor smiled. Yes, Robbie was shaping up to be a very good operative. A former call-handler for Police Scotland, he had left the job when the pressures of sending officers from Inverness to an armed robbery in Paisley became too much for him. Connor's predecessor, Lachlan Jameson, had found Robbie a couple of months later: a shy, nervous man with a talent for research, planning and logistics. An asset that could be used, a talent that could be exploited.

And Jameson had been all about the exploitation.

'OK, send it over. I'll see you shortly. Nice work, Robbie,' Connor said, then killed the call.

His phone beeped with an email as he approached the car. Connor opened it, found links to news stories there and a single line from Robbie: *Think it could be something to do with this boss. Kind of hope I'm wrong. R.*

Connor clicked on the link. Felt the world slow and cool around him as he read the contents. He knew the story, of course – everybody in Scotland his age did. But that didn't lessen the impact, or the revulsion he felt.

And in that moment he found himself agreeing with Robbie. He hoped he was wrong. Knew in his gut that he wasn't, and that he was about to step into a nightmare.

CHAPTER 3

The call came in just as Connor pulled up in front of the Sentinel offices. He grimaced as he read the name on the dashboard display, struck by the irony that the contact was as predictable as it was unprecedented. He stared at the red-brick façade of the office in front of him for a moment, considering.

'Fuck it,' he whispered, thumbing the answer key on the steering wheel. 'Dad, you OK? What's up?'

A moment of silence, then Jack Fraser's voice filled the car, the prickly undercurrent of static emphasising the sharpness in his tone. 'No, I'm not OK, Connor. I'm just back from visiting your grandmother. What's all this crap about you upsetting her with some old school reports? You know her condition. The last thing she needs is you trying to get her to remember things from years ago.'

Connor bared his teeth at the dashboard, bit back the surge of anger he felt caress his back. After his mother had died, it was Connor who had arranged for Ida Fraser to be transferred to a residential home in Bannockburn. It was Connor who had spoken to the doctors and specialists, made sure everything could be done to ensure the flame of Ida Fraser's identity wasn't completely snuffed out by the encroaching tide of confusion and dementia slowly overwhelming her mind. And it was Connor who had arranged the sale of her home to fund her care, Connor who was now living with his gran's life carefully boxed away in his flat. So to have his father call him now to berate him after what had been an all-too-infrequent visit to see Ida . . .

Hold on. Good point. Why the sudden concerned-son routine?

'Dad,' Connor said, keeping his tone even, businesslike, 'I didn't mean to upset her. You should know well enough the specialists encourage dementia patients to try to remember things as long as it doesn't disturb them. I found that old report card when I was going through Gran's stuff from the house. Wanted to ask her about it, that was all . . .'

(Because there's no way I could ask you.)

'. . .Didn't realise it would upset her the way it did.'

He remembered the moment all too clearly. They were in the small, self-contained apartment Ida now lived in. It was like a caricature of the house she had once called home in Stirling – the same dark furniture, floral curtains and obsessive neatness, but boiled down and reduced to fit the new three-roomed, panic-button-and-grab-rail-infested reality. Connor couldn't decide if he loved the place for the comfort it brought his gran and the memories it triggered for him, or loathed it for what it had reduced her to.

She had been busying herself in the kitchen area as they spoke, serving Connor the scones she had made for his visit, along with jam, cream and tea so strong it could have been used as an industrial cleaner. He had settled across from her, watching for the darting eyes, shallow breaths and small hand-wringing gestures that told him it was a bad day and she was more in the past than the present. But on that day she had seemed fine, her eyes bright, smile relaxed.

She was just pouring tea when he produced the report from his pocket. Little more than a rectangular of cheap card, a teacher's fading handwriting scrawled over it, detailing the progress of Jack William Fraser, who was in secondary school at the time. But two things had caught Connor's attention. One was the content of the report, which was almost the polar opposite of the man he vaguely knew as his father. The other was the dark brown stain on the top corner of the card, which spread like a careless water mark. He had seen enough crime scenes in his time to know exactly what made a mark like that.

'I found this in some old papers,' he said, pushing the card across the table to his gran. 'Wondered if you could tell me a little about it. I had no idea Dad was into the arts and English. Thought science was always his thing.'

Ida's eyes flicked to the report card, the teapot jostling in her hand, tea sloshing into Connor's saucer. He stood quickly, got his hands on her wrists, steadying the pot. Felt her pulse thrum beneath thin, waxy skin.

'Sorry, son,' Ida said, something Connor didn't recognise dancing in her eyes. 'It's the arthritis, you see. I forget it can make picking up the pot difficult. Can you finish pouring for me?'

'Course,' Connor said, taking the pot from her as she eased herself into her seat. She sat back slowly, hand inching towards the report card then retreating, as though it was somehow as hot as the tea she had just spilled.

'Sorry, Gran, didn't mean to surprise you,' Connor said, guilt flashing through him. 'Just something I found, is all. Nothing important.'

'Hmm,' she said, as though waking from a dream. 'Sorry, Connor. Yeah, your dad was a bit artistic in his youth. But he found science not long after that, I think,' she jabbed a gnarled finger at the card, 'and that was it, never looked back.'

Connor nodded. One thing they could agree on was that Jack Fraser never looked back. Forging a career as a successful doctor, he had never been one to second-guess his decisions, consider his actions. Including, that seemed, keeping Connor at arm's length all his life.

'Anyway,' Ida said, lifting her cup, steam fogging her glasses and masking her eyes, 'enough about the past. What's the latest with you and this girl you're seeing? Jennifer, isn't it?'

And so the afternoon had worn on, Connor keeping his answers as brief and circumspect as he could, all the while assuring his gran he was 'acting like the perfect gentleman'. But all the time they spoke, he had watched her eyes dart back to that card, as though it had a magnetic pull all of its own.

'. . . don't you think?'

The words filled the car, bringing Connor back to the present.

'Sorry, what was that, Dad?'

An all-too-familiar sigh of impatience filled the car. 'I said,' Jack repeated more slowly this time, 'that perhaps you should stop trying to take your gran on trips down Memory Lane. You know how upset she gets when she can't remember things, Connor.'

'Yeah, I do,' Connor replied. And a lot fucking better than you do, he thought.

'Good. Well, then . . .' A pause on the line as Jack Fraser considered the wilderness in front of him. He had said what he needed to say to his son. What was next?

Connor seized on the moment. 'You around this weekend at all, Dad?' he asked. 'Maybe we could get a pint, catch up.'

Guilty pleasure as he listened to Jack cough and squirm at the other end of the line. He had known what the answer would be before he had asked the question. Since his wife had died, Jack Fraser had had little time for his son, who had delivered the ultimate insult years before by forgoing a career in medicine for a short-lived career as a police officer, then transitioning into private security.

'Well, I . . . I, ah, I'll check my diary, get back to you.'

Connor caressed the end-call button with his thumb, suddenly wanting this over with. 'You do that, Dad. And I'll pop in to see Gran tonight, tell her you're asking for her.'

He cut the call halfway through his dad saying goodbye, sat in the silence of the car for a moment. Maybe his dad was right, that he had been stupid and selfish trying to get his gran to remember something from decades ago merely to satisfy his own curiosity about a man who couldn't have cared less about him.

Let it go, Connor, he thought. Just let it be. After all, there were more immediate problems to deal with.

He sighed, heaved himself out of the car, seized by the sudden need to move. Surveyed the car park, didn't spot DCI Ford's vehicle in any of the bays. Good. That gave him just enough time to track down Robbie and get himself ready for what was going to be a very long unpleasant afternoon.

CHAPTER 4

The gun was stripped down on the table in front of him, a surprisingly innocuous jumble of springs and slides and metal; a lethal jigsaw just waiting to be assembled.

He set about inspecting the parts and cleaning them as necessary, pausing only to savour the one measure of whisky he had allotted himself for the task. The peaty aroma combined with the surprisingly sweet tang of the gun oil and sour afternote of gunpowder in his nose. It somehow intensified the pleasure of the whisky, he thought. Then again, he could be deluding himself, telling a story to make the experience more profound, give him an excuse to fall deeper into the bottle and wash away the cold hard truth of what he was doing right now.

He thought back to the day he had bought the gun, all those years ago. Unlike in the TV series, the films or the books, there had been no clandestine meeting in an abandoned, shadow-dipped building in Glasgow or Edinburgh, no rendezvous on a desolate stretch of waste ground that looked out onto the cold, grey waters of the Clyde or the Forth. No, he had driven to a farm in the Borders, been welcomed by a ruddy-cheeked, white-haired man who had a belly as full as his laugh, and shown to a warm outhouse where the aroma of horse manure hung in the air. Money had been exchanged and the gun had been produced – an immaculate SIG Sauer, still in its box, nestled there with three extra clips. The farmer had happily given his full name, then taken an hour to show him how to use the weapon.

Of course, he could have got that training at work, but what was the point of raising suspicions?

He had driven home, using the time to contemplate what he had just done, persuade himself that he had, ultimately, had no choice. Once home, he had placed the weapon in a pre-selected hiding place and then, like an insurance policy, he had forgotten about it. Until, that was, the next headline or TV programme brought everything flooding back, and he found himself retreating to the attic and pulling the weapon from behind the insulation panel where it waited for him. For today.

Satisfied with his cleaning, he began to reassemble the weapon. After all these years it was an act as natural as tying his shoelaces or making a cup of tea, yet today his hands shook slightly, the components rattling like loose teeth as he clicked them together. He took another swig of the whisky, resisted the urge to pour another glass.

When the gun was assembled, he laid it on the table, leaned back and surveyed his work. And as ever, in that moment, a third option occurred to him, as alluring as the whisky bottle sitting on the table beside the gun. Just pick it up, chamber a round, flick off the safety. Feel the chill of the barrel against his chin, close his eyes. Pull the trigger. Let God or the Devil or whatever was waiting for him judge him. He didn't fear that judgement. He knew what he had done. Knew the price he would ultimately pay.

His hand strayed forward, hovered over the gun for an instant, then settled on the whisky bottle. He topped up his glass, swallowed it in a swig, told himself the tears nipping at the back of his eyes were caused by the acidic burn of the alcohol, nothing else.

It was time. Finally, after all these years, it was time. Time to finish what had been started one cold, blood-soaked night more than a decade ago, when he had discovered that monsters could be found in the most prosaic of places and that there were horrors in this world that could barely be contained in a rational mind.

He picked up the gun, the sound of a round being chambered a blunt insult to the silence of the room. Wondered how long it would be until he unleashed that bullet into the world, and which monster it would be aimed at when he did so.

14

CHAPTER 5

When Ford arrived, Connor was waiting in Sentinel's fourth-floor conference room, contemplating the view. The day had darkened, sky fading to an apathetic grey, as though it wanted to rain on the world but was too lethargic to share its misery. Connor wished Ford felt the same way.

He stood up when Robbie showed Ford into the room, extending his hand as he walked towards the gaunt policeman. 'Sir, good to see you,' Connor said, wincing at the involuntary 'sir' that his time in the Police Service of Northern Ireland had trained him to call Ford. He was out of the police now, but a senior officer was a senior officer. And looking at the man in front of him now, at the tousled grey hair and lines that seemed to dig into his pale skin like trenches, Connor thought Ford looked about as senior as he had ever seen him.

'Fraser,' Ford mumbled, taking Connor's hand and giving it a firm shake. Connor could feel sinewy strength in that shake. And determination.

He broke the grip, gestured to the table that stood next to the back wall of the room beneath a massive TV that was bolted to the wall. 'Can I offer you some coffee? Tea?' he asked.

Ford held up a hand. 'No, thank you. Look, thanks for seeing me at such short notice.'

Connor waved this away, nodded toward the slab of mahogany that was the conference table, indicating Ford should sit as Robbie

15

beat a stealthy retreat. 'No problem at all, though I was slightly surprised that you wanted to meet here.'

Discomfort and irritation played across Ford's face. 'Yes, well . . . I'm not here in a totally official capacity,' he said, picking his words deliberately, as though they were rocks that would lead him across a fast-flowing stream. 'You see, Fraser, something's come up, and I need your help.'

Connor nodded. Suspicion confirmed. 'Not surprising, sir. I suspect that where Colin Sanderson is concerned, you're going to need all the help you can get.'

Ford's eyes narrowed as he knotted his hands in front of him. Connor could see the fingers go white as he squeezed. 'And how the hell did you know this was about Sanderson?' he asked.

'Actually, it was Robbie who figured it out,' Connor said. 'Though I should have twigged myself. After all, Sanderson's face has been plastered across every TV screen and newspaper in the country for the last week.'

Ford made a noise that was halfway between growl and affirmation. A week previously, at the Court of Appeal in Edinburgh, the quashing of Sanderson's life sentence for the murder of two students at Stirling University had seized the media's attention. Of course it had. Back in 2006, the murders, and the sheer brutality that had been displayed, had captivated and horrified in equal measure. The victims, Rhona Everett and Jessica Kristen, had been strangled, beaten and sexually assaulted before being mutilated and dumped, Rhona on the grounds of the university, in a scrub of bushes not far from Airthy Loch in the heart of the campus, Jessica on a farm road east of the university that led to Gogar Loan. Reports from the time lingered on every detail: the women's last movements, the fear that had settled like a shroud over the university and Stirling, the haunted looks of the women's parents as they made an appeal for information, the frantic hunt for the killer. A hunt, it transpired, that ultimately led to Sanderson, who had been a labourer on a renovation site at the campus at the time.

During the trial, Sanderson had remained an aloof, even amused figure, smiling in court as details of the murders were read out for the jury. This earned him the nickname 'The Beast', along with a swift and unanimous verdict – guilty. The Beast had been sent to Hell – or the Scottish penal system's equivalent of it – for the rest of his life. Justice was done. Case closed. Until, that was, a year ago, when new information came to light, which suggested that the chain of custody on the evidence linking Sanderson to the crime had been incorrectly logged, tainting the prosecution's case. This, in turn, led to an appeal, and Sanderson's conviction being quashed.

Connor remembered the last line of the Sky News report Robbie had sent him, a report written by his friend, Donna Blake. It was a brief statement delivered on Sanderson's behalf by his lawyer, Carl Layton, an odious little shit whose nickname was 'Lazarus': 'Mr Sanderson is glad this ordeal is over and his innocence has been proven. He now wishes to consider his next move in relation to compensation from the authorities, and he will do so while reconnecting with his family in more familiar surroundings.'

Which, in this case, meant home. Stirling.

'So, what can I do to help?' Connor asked reluctantly. He had an oily, unpleasant feeling he knew where this was headed.

Ford wrestled his gaze from his still-entangled hands, glanced across at Connor. Sighed. 'It's been kept out of the press, but Sanderson has received a few death threats since he was released. Nothing too specific, but enough to have his team worried.'

'Team?' Connor asked, resisting the urge to look up at the ceiling for the other shoe that was about to drop on him.

Ford's face curled in disgust. 'Oh, yes, Mr Sanderson has been a very busy little boy. Lined himself up a nice little book deal with a London publisher to detail his ordeal. There's talk of a TV series too. So, of course, they don't want their latest golden goose to come to any harm, but there's a snag given Sanderson's, ah, fraught relationship with the police.'

Connor closed his eyes, leaned back in his seat. 'They want private security,' he whispered, more to himself than Ford.

'Precisely,' the policeman said. 'In about an hour or so, you're going to get a call from the PR company handling him, asking you to take the contract. And I'm here to ask you to do just that.'

Connor leaned forward, fixed his gaze on Ford, asked the question he already had the answer to. 'How do you know I'm going to get the call?'

Despite himself, humour arced across Ford's eyes, like a flash of headlights in the dark. 'Because I recommended you when he refused police protection,' he said. He paused, looked away, as though what he had to say next was knotted up with his fists.

'Look, Fraser. Connor. I remember the case, OK? What he did to those girls, I mean.' He looked up at Connor, pupils suddenly magnified by moisture. It wasn't a sight Connor enjoyed. 'Connor. This man is a fucking animal. I don't care what any smart-talking lawyer says. I worked the case, reread the files when he was released. He fucking did it. And if he's coming back to my patch, I want him watched by someone I can trust. Not for his safety, but for everyone else's, OK?'

Connor pushed aside the irrational stab of pride he felt at the compliment. 'You think he'll try to kill again?'

Ford leaned down to the briefcase he had stowed beside his chair, producing a large manila file. He stared at it for a moment, then slid it across the conference table to Connor. 'You never saw this,' he said, 'but it's a copy of the case file on the murders. Read it, then you tell me. He's a killer, Fraser, plain and simple. I don't care what that appeal found or how Sanderson's legal team managed to wheedle him out of Barlinnie. He's got the taste and, after so long inside, he'll kill again. He won't be able to help himself.'

Connor considered the file in front of him. He knew Ford put pragmatism over procedure, but to share confidential police records with a civilian? It told Connor everything he needed to know. 'OK,' he said, drawing the file towards him. 'I'll look at this. And I'll take the assignment. But if this smells bad, or it's just a PR stunt by Sanderson's people to drum up a few more headlines, then I'm out.'

'Fine,' Ford said, his shoulders slumping. 'But if it's a PR stunt, it's a very sick one. No, I think someone is very serious about doing Mr Sanderson some serious harm.'

'Oh?' Connor said, something cold churning through his gut. 'How can you be so sure?'

Ford jutted his chin towards the file. 'It's all in there. But the first threat was delivered to the Sanderson family home in Cambusbarron two days ago. It was a picture of Sanderson coming out of the court with his lawyer. The picture had been pinned to the corpse of a large rat, with a note saying, "This isn't the only beast that will die.'"

Connor whistled breath through his teeth. He felt the sudden urge to push the file back to Ford, then call Jen and tell her they were going away for a long holiday. Anything to get away from all of this.

He was startled from his fantasy by Ford standing and picking up his briefcase. 'Read that, listen to the offer, give me a call if you need to,' he said as he clutched Connor's hand in his again.

Connor agreed, not liking the look in Ford's eyes. He had seen the man furious. Seen him contemplative. But until that moment, he had never seen him scared. He buzzed for Robbie, had him show Ford out. Then he turned back to the conference table and flipped open the file.

If he was to meet The Beast, the least he could do was learn its origins.

CHAPTER 6

Donna Blake scanned the page of notes in front of her, the irrefutable proof that the call she had just taken was real, not just a figment of her imagination. After all, things like this didn't just happen to her. Did they?

She had been at home, an all-too-rare day off after seemingly endless weeks covering the Scottish political desk for Sky after the usual reporter, Fiona Banks, had been wooed away to a big-paying job with one of the US networks. Donna didn't mind the work, or the pay bump that went with it, but it had rankled that the shifts she was doing meant she had missed out on the Colin Sanderson acquittal case.

She smiled as she looked again at her notes. Not any more.

When her mobile had chimed, she had earned a typically sour look from her mother, who was busy playing with her grandson, Andrew, across the room. Irene Blake made no effort to disguise her disapproval at Donna's choice of career, especially when it intruded on the oh-so-precious time she had with her son.

Donna had flashed a smile and retreated with the phone to the small spare bedroom at the back of the flat, which she had converted into a study. 'Debbie,' she said as she answered the call. 'This is a surprise – what's up?'

'Hi, Donna, yeah, been busy, sorry it's been so long. How you doing? I see you whenever I turn the news on. Looking good.'

Donna smiled. She had worked with Debbie Maitland at the *Westie* in Glasgow, when they were both general reporters. As with a lot of journalists, Debbie had seen the writing on the wall when the cost-cuttings started and jumped ship, taking a job with Frontline PR, one of the larger marketing and PR consultancies in Edinburgh. It was a well-worn path for journalists to take – after all, they knew what worked as a story, and the PR companies were glad to have them on their side of the fence instead of trying to take their clients down. From the bubbly good cheer in her voice, Debbie had taken to the move easily.

'So, how can I help you?' Donna asked, already dreading whatever puff piece Debbie was going to try to sell to her.

'Well, actually,' Debbie said, her voice taking on a cloying edge of smugness, 'I think I might be able to help you. I take it you know the Colin Sanderson story?'

'Who doesn't?' Donna had said as she scrambled around on her desk for a notepad and a pen. 'But what's that got to do with Frontline PR?'

Debbie gave a laugh as genuine and natural as her bottle-blonde hair. And then she offered Donna the opportunity of a lifetime.

She scanned the notes of the call again, feeling excitement prickle the base of her skull. Frontline had been hired by RedBrick Books, which had snapped up the rights to Sanderson's story. And to pique interest for the book, they wanted to keep Sanderson in the media spotlight, exploit the 'innocent man who lost more than a decade behind bars' angle for everything it was worth.

'So, naturally,' Debbie had said, 'I thought of you. After all, Sanderson is back with his dad in Cambusbarron, and you're based in Stirling, aren't you?'

The plan was simple. Debbie was offering Donna an exclusive interview with Sanderson. And it was no-holds-barred, no topic off the table, questions wouldn't be screened beforehand. The only condition Debbie had placed on the deal was the location. It had to be somewhere that was recognisably Stirling, a location that Sanderson himself would choose.

Donna had struggled to keep the grateful excitement she was

feeling out of her voice. This was huge. An exclusive interview with the man just cleared of one of the most horrific crimes in the last twenty years? A sit-down with The Beast? Fuck politics. This was the big-time.

She had agreed to contact her editor, then get back in touch with Debbie to make the arrangements for the interview. And that was when Debbie had dropped the second bomb, the one that had literally taken Donna's breath away. Her eyes drifted back to the two words she had written, two words underlined several times with a hand that wasn't quite steady.

Ghost write.

'You see, Donna, there's one other thing. RedBrick are looking for someone to help Colin write this story. Ideally they'd like a journalist, someone who can dig into the real story and get the best from Colin. If the two of you hit it off, I'd say the job is yours if you want it. And with the money they're talking about paying, you're going to want it almost as badly as I want the finder's bonus for getting you to sign up.'

Donna leaned back in her chair, stared up at the ceiling. An exclusive interview. The chance to write the definitive book on two murders that had transfixed and horrified the country. The chance to do some old-school interviewing, and satisfy a lifetime ambition while she did it. Donna wasn't uncommon among journalists in her desire to write a book, but with Andrew and her job, the thought had drifted off into a distant horizon of what-ifs and might-have-beens. But now here it was, front and centre.

She forced thoughts of book deals aside, concentrated on the job in hand. First step, contact Caroline Spiers, her editor on the Sky news-desk, tell her what had just happened. And then she would do some digging. Find out what else RedBrick and Frontline had planned for Colin Sanderson – and what she could do to be a part of it.

CHAPTER 7

Untangling himself from the twisted snarl of traffic that turned the roads around the Gyle into a slow-moving sludge of cars, Connor headed west out of Edinburgh, past Linlithgow and on towards Bannockburn. He opened the Audi up as soon as he hit clear road, letting the act of driving occupy his conscious mind and give him time to think. And after reading the file Ford had left him, Connor had plenty to consider.

Most of what was in the police report was in the public domain, thanks to the blanket media attention the Sanderson trial had garnered at the time. But what had been missing from those reports, thankfully, was the detail of what he had subjected his victims to.

Rhona Everett and Jessica Kristen had both been students at Stirling University back in 2006 – Rhona studying politics and history, Jessica sport and exercise science. They were popular students, expected to go far. But other than their academic excellence, there was little to connect them – Jessica came from a wealthy family in Perthshire, Rhona from a council scheme on the west side of Glasgow. And while Rhona was dark-haired and olive-skinned, Jessica was marked out by her pallor, hair so red it looked dyed and a slender frame that spoke of grace and power. They weren't known to be friends: there was no record of them attending any of the same university clubs or even frequenting the same pubs in Stirling or the surrounding areas. Just another two strangers who happened to study at the same university. Rhona, perhaps unsurprisingly, was known to be active in student politics and had helped with a local MP's constituency surgeries, while Jessica was forging an off-the-track reputation as an actor, having joined an amateur dramatics company in Stirling and appeared in several productions. Typical students with their lives stretching out in front of them.

Until, that was, Colin Sanderson had come into the picture.

He was hired as a painter and decorator, working on a refurbishment of some of the fitness suites in the main gym complex on the university campus, which had earned Stirling the grand title of Scotland's University for Sporting Excellence. From the files Ford had given Connor, a picture of Sanderson emerged that raised questions about how he had ever got onto the campus in the first place. His record was a litany of escalating crimes, from thefts and assaults to one instance in which he had been accused of attacking a woman who was too drunk to know what was going on. All too predictably the case had been thrown out, Sanderson's lawyer claiming that what had happened was consensual and, after all, 'the victim has a history of promiscuity and sexual adventurism fuelled by alcohol'. Reading those words, Connor had wished for a moment that he was still a police officer in Belfast, where the alleys were dark and the staircases were steep. A place where a man like Sanderson was bound to have an accident at some point.

Unfortunately, Sanderson was in all-too-robust health when he'd arrived at the university. Rhona had been the first victim, disappearing between Stirling and the campus one night, her body found two weeks later, abandoned at the side of a farm road not too far from the university. The police had kept the details out of the press, partly to shield her parents from what had been done to their daughter and keep the press away from them and as a way to help them track down whatever animal had done this to her.

And Connor was in no doubt. It was the work of an animal.

According to the post-mortem report in Ford's file, Rhona had been subdued by a blow to the head, then bound and gagged – the marks from the ropes that had bitten into her wrists and ankles stood out like livid scars in the pictures he had seen. She had been beaten, her body reduced to little more than a sack of meat tattooed with purple and green bruising, then raped. But not satisfied with this humiliation, the killer had gone one further and mutilated her. Connor felt a sick roiling in his guts as he remembered one line in the coroner's report: 'blood pooling around the wounds, coupled with lividity and the presence of petechial haemorrhaging would indicate the victim was alive while these wounds were inflicted'.

The police reaction had been swift. Officers flooded the university, canvassing students for any information that might have given a clue as to who had killed Rhona. TV appeals for information were broadcast, Rhona's family dumb and pale and raw-eyed as they blinked into the barrage of camera flashes directed towards them.

And then, a fortnight after Rhona was taken, Jessica was found, naked, mutilated and violated in the same barbaric fashion as Rhona. The papers at the time reported the discovery as a 'humiliation' for the police, with the killer 'taunting the authorities by taking a victim right from under their noses'. One tabloid, which Connor refused to read because of its slurs on a particular football-related tragedy, went a step further and interviewed a criminal psychologist, who opined that two killings in such a short period of time pointed to an extremely dangerous individual. And, in a final flourish, added that 'the number of murders to be classed as a serial killer is three, and the aggressor here seems to have every intention of attaining that goal.'

Fortunately, it never got that far. Forensic inspections found fibres on both bodies that were matched to a heavy-duty fabric that had been spattered with paint. A trawl of campus CCTV footage revealed the painting and decorating van used by Sanderson had been there at the time of both girls' disappearance, while interviews of students turned up a witness who had seen Sanderson talking to Jessica on the campus the evening she disappeared. From what the witness had said, the confrontation had not been a civil one, with Jessica storming off and Sanderson laying down a slick of tyre rubber as he screamed out of the campus. With a suspect identified, the police moved in, matching the fibres found on the bodies with sheets found in Sanderson's van, where they also found blood spatters from both victims. Coupled to Sanderson's criminal record, he was quickly charged.

All well and good, Connor thought. They had a credible suspect, with forensic evidence tying him to both victims. The lack of DNA evidence on the victims was an annoying chink in the prosecution, but the fact that condoms had been used during the rapes could almost explain away the lack of trace evidence either on the victims or on Sanderson, while the lack of defensive wounds showed he had bound his victims as soon as he had struck them, meaning they had no way of injuring him.

Almost a watertight case, Connor thought. Almost.

The case had gone quiet until two years ago, when a high-profile defence lawyer, Carl Layton, who had acquired the nickname 'Lazarus' for his ability to reanimate old cases, took an interest after a true-crime documentary turned the spotlight back onto The Beast's crimes. Layton dug in, finding that witness statements had been incorrectly taken, the chain of evidence on the drop sheets in the van tainted. After almost a year of work, he had secured Sanderson an acquittal. Which was where Connor came in.

He pulled himself from his thoughts, unconsciously raised a salute to the massive twin steel horse-head sculptures that reared up on the horizon before him as he passed: the Kelpies. He had always found the sculptures, designed to commemorate Scotland's use of horses in industry, vaguely unsettling. But today they were a welcome distraction from the horrors he had read in Ford's file and the thoughts that were churning through his mind.

Sanderson had returned to his parents' home in Cambusbarron, a small village to the west of Stirling. He had, perhaps understandably, refused police protection when the death threats had come in, opting instead for private security. Connor had to admit that the terms of the contract Frontline PR had sent over to him shortly after Ford's visit were generous, which only fuelled his suspicion that the threats on Sanderson's life were some kind of PR stunt to generate more interest in the forthcoming book.

But still, there was Ford's warning: *He's a killer, Fraser, plain and simple. I don't care what that appeal found or how Sanderson's legal team managed to wheedle him out of Barlinnie. He's got the taste and, after so long inside, he'll kill again. He won't be able to help himself.'*

Connor was forced to agree. In his experience, once a killer started they rarely stopped until forced to. And if Sanderson was the killer the original trial had decided he was, then Connor wanted to be close by. After all, a predator is never more dangerous than when it has been starved in captivity and suddenly released.

He forced the thought from his mind as he took the turn-off to Bannockburn, slipping his mind off autopilot to throw the Audi into the twisty A-roads that led to his gran's care home.

He was just pulling into the driveway, the gentle crunch of gravel almost like a sigh of relief from the car, when his phone rang.

He read the name on the dashboard display. Of course, he thought, he should have been expecting this. It had been inevitable from the moment Ford had walked into his office.

He glanced up at the care home, thought of his gran in her room. Would she recognise him today? Forgive him for the confusion he had wrought on his last visit? Or would she just give him the patient, fragile smile she had perfected for the days when she recognised no one and waited for them to introduce themselves? Found he wanted to put off the discovery for a few more minutes, thumbed answer on the steering wheel.

'Hello, Donna,' he said.

CHAPTER 8

Duncan MacKenzie put the phone down gently, almost reverently, as though it was a piece of delicate cut crystal rather than a chunk of moulded plastic. Leaned back in his seat, looked up at the ceiling, the weight of the call he had just taken seeming to bear down on him, as irresistible and devastating as the car-crusher at the back of the yard.

Fuck.

The door opened and Paulie King lumbered into the room in his standard dress uniform – crumpled suit that barely contained his massive shoulders and gut, tie pulled squint and loose, skull glinting beneath the bristle of his close-cropped hair. 'Problem, boss?' he asked, a look that a stranger would almost mistake for concern contorting his bulldog features.

MacKenzie sighed, exhaling his thoughts like cigarette smoke. Christ, what he wouldn't give for a cigarette right now. But he had made a promise to Jen not long after her mother had died of cancer that he would give them up. And he had. No nicotine gum. No sucking smoke from something that looked like a fucking mobile phone, no patches. Just cold turkey and willpower. For Jen. Because she had asked him.

And promises mattered. Especially now.

He gestured for Paulie to sit opposite him at his desk, the chair squealing a gentle protest underneath the man's bulk. They were in the head office of MacKenzie Haulage, which occupied a large industrial yard on the outskirts of Stirling, halfway between the city and Bannockburn. Late-afternoon sunlight streaked through the Venetian blinds, painting the room with slats of darkness and light. Unsurprisingly, Paulie was sitting in shadow, his dead eyes on MacKenzie. No uncertainty, no shifting in his seat, no small-talk to try to fill the silence. But, then, that was why MacKenzie kept him around. Paulie was a mechanism, happy to idle on standby until fresh orders were received.

The question MacKenzie was asking himself was what, in light of the call he had just received, those orders should be. 'You had the TV on much today, Paulie? Seen any news?'

Paulie's forehead creased. Not the opening he had been expecting. 'Naw, boss,' he said. 'Been out all morning, dealing with that little, ah, supply problem with Derek.'

MacKenzie nodded. The problem in question was Derek Jackson, who had, until his meeting with Paulie that morning, been a driver for MacKenzie Haulage. Unfortunately it had come to Duncan's attention that, due to an affinity for class-A substances and the company of women who charged for their companionship by the hour, Jackson had been inflating his mileage claims, while some of his deliveries had come up short, the documents and reports doctored. It hadn't taken Paulie long to discover the missing whisky, meat and electrical goods Jackson had acquired – the stupid bastard had given them to his brother to sell at the Sunday market in East Fortune. So Paulie had paid him a little visit to teach him about the error of his ways and deliver his P45. From the rust-coloured spot on the collar of Paulie's shirt and the scrapes on his mangled knuckles, Duncan could tell the delivery had gone well.

'Good,' he said, getting up from his chair and fiddling with the overly complicated coffee machine Jen had insisted on buying him a couple of years ago. 'Well, do me a favour, and keep an eye on the headlines, will you? Just had a call. There's going to be a story running shortly that we'll take a bit of an interest in.'

'Oh?' Paulie leaned forward, scooping up the cup that MacKenzie had placed in front of him, massive hand dwarfing it.

'Yeah, seems like an old acquaintance is on his way back into Cambusbarron, and we're going to keep an eye on him.'

'Cambusbarron,' Paulie rumbled, his voice as dark as the coffee he had just been offered. 'Haud on. You don't mean that little fuck . . .'

Duncan held up a hand. The last thing he needed was one of Paulie's expletive-fuelled rants. 'Yes, that's exactly what I mean, Paulie. I thought this was done and dusted, but it seems like there's more to do. No good deed and all that. And we always honour our debts, don't we, Paulie?'

Paulie's eyes hardened into cold marbles of hate and MacKenzie could see memories fuelling that rage, could read them in the hunching of his shoulders and the whitening of his knuckles around the coffee cup. 'Yes, boss,' he hissed. 'We always do. And this is one debt I'll be happy to collect with interest.'

CHAPTER 9

Watching her was exquisite torture, the pain as bright and sharp as the stab of a needle into the puckered, broken flesh of a junkie's arm. The knowledge was the same as, well – Here is Heaven. And the only price you have to pay is a descent into Hell.

I was too far back for her to see me, yet still I kept my glances short, furtive. It was perverse: like an alcoholic sipping whisky after some tragedy has forced them to crash off the wagon in a tangle of broken limbs. But, as ever, my perversion had a purpose. If I had let myself look too long, linger at all, she might have known I was there, my gaze triggering the fight-or-flight response we all have, that primitive call-back to our ancestors that tells us when a predator is near.

And I am undoubtedly a predator.

The afternoon sun turned the grey water of the loch into a sea of jewels, winking and glinting like a promise. And there was promise in that moment, undoubtedly. After all, we were in a place where futures were crafted and lives were built.

And sometimes ended.

I admit I was surprised by how little the campus had changed. Yes, the trees were taller, the flowerbeds more lush, filled in by time, but the core of the place was still the same, manicured grounds and concrete paths connecting blocky, harled-faced buildings studded with large plate-glass windows, as though to allow those inside to drink in the vision of the future the architects were so sure of when the place was built in the sixties. It's been described as one of the most beauti-ful universities in the world, and with its rolling lawns, the backdrop of the Ochil Hills and the Wallace Monument glaring down at the campus like some kind of Gothic sentinel, it's hard to argue.

But there's no beauty without ugliness. And maybe that was why I was there.

I caught my quickening pace, forced myself to be calm. Patience. There was time. The realisation sent a flash of heat racing through me, heat that became an electric jolt in my groin. Time. The gift of time. Time to plan. To consider. To ensure that the moment is perfect when it arrives. And it will. As inevitable as the crash after the heroin high or the guilt after the deed itself, it will come.

The sudden feeling of freedom this revelation brought was almost as exhilarating as the sight of her as she made her way towards the student union building, head high, long dark hair sleek and glisten-ing, like oil in the sun. Of course, I didn't need her to turn around to know her face – I had seen it every night in my dreams for the last fourteen years.

I tightened my grip on the knife in my pocket as she disappeared into the student union, her radiance swallowed by the shadows of the building. I know that soon she will step into a purer darkness, a more welcoming one.

And, in that darkness, we will be reunited at last.

CHAPTER 10

Even with Bach in his ears and a heavy dumbbell in each hand, Connor was unable to banish the nervous unease that jangled in his guts like some twisted echo of the searing pain in his biceps.

If he was being honest, Donna's call wasn't that much of a surprise. Since they'd first met two years ago, she'd proven to be a resourceful and tenacious reporter, letting nothing get in her way when on the hunt for an exclusive. She'd seen dead bodies – including that of her former boyfriend, Mark Sneddon – and drawn the not-inconsiderable ire of DCI Malcolm Ford along the way. So it was no real surprise that, with the news the man just acquitted of two of the most brutal murders in Stirling's history was coming home, where he would fall under Sentinel Securities' protection, Donna Blake would be getting in touch. What had surprised Connor was the almost breathless excitement in her voice as she spoke, telling him about her exclusive interview with Sanderson, and how his PR company had enlisted Sentinel Securities to protect their client.

'So, you going to confirm this for me? Maybe give me a statement?' she had asked.

'And why would I do that?' he replied, grip bearing down on the steering wheel, the pressure detonating dull pulses of pain in his forearms. 'You already know that we're involved, and you know there's nothing operational I can share publicly.'

'Fair enough. Profile piece on Sentinel Securities it is,' Donna said, the giddiness in her voice blossoming into glee now. She had him. And she knew it. 'Good colour for the article, especially with the local connections, thanks to Jameson and the shitshow Blair Charlston's little event created at the Alloa House Hotel last year.'

Connor closed his eyes briefly, the sickly sweet smell of burning flesh filling his nose as the memory of crazed eyes set in a face engulfed by flame flashed across his mind. 'Come on, Donna,' he said. 'We both know you're not going to do that. You got enough mileage out of the Charlston case and Mark's death at the time, didn't you? No need to be raking all that crap up again.'

There was a moment of silence on the line, time enough for Connor to regret his words. Donna had scooped everyone with the exclusive on Mark being found hanging from a tree in the grounds of the hotel, his entrails hanging from his body like grotesque gore-streaked streamers. Connor knew Donna regretted breaking the story, no matter how much good it had done for her career. After all, how does Mummy explain to her son that the first thing she did when she heard Daddy was dead was to turn to camera and say, 'Action'?

'OK,' she said slowly, the giddiness gone from her voice now. 'Maybe just a light overview, then. Unless . . .'

'Unless what?' Connor asked. Useless question, really. He knew what she was about to say.

'I know you've already got people watching Sanderson's place, and you're scheduled to meet him tomorrow morning, go through arrangements. So, I was thinking, why don't we meet him together? That way we can compare notes on the man afterwards, see what we think.'

And you get to see how he reacts to an authority figure who won't take any of his shit, Connor thought, and smiled. Typical Donna, always thinking. 'And, in return, you keep Sentinel and me out of the story?'

'Cross my heart,' Donna said. 'You'll be mentioned only as a "prestigious private security firm".'

Connor paused a moment, considered. The last thing he wanted or needed was his name in the press again. And having Donna there might prove useful, let him probe a little deeper than he could if he was the sole focus of Sanderson's attention.

'OK,' he said. 'Agreed. But you leave first, and I speak to him privately about any security arrangements we make. You want me to pick you up, or are you happy to make your own way there?'

'Oooh, the VIP package,' Donna said. 'Does Audrey Linklater get the same personal service?'

Connor felt his mouth drop open. 'How the hell did you . . .?'

'Contacts,' Donna said, laughter dancing behind her words. 'Always good to keep an eye on the local celebs – you never know when they might turn into something juicy.'

Connor gave a growl that might have been mistaken for the revving of the engine, then arranged to pick Donna up from her flat at ten the following morning. He killed the call and concentrated on driving. He'd skipped visiting his gran on the road back, opting instead to call the home to check on her, then head straight for the gym and try to clear his head with a workout.

Unfortunately it wasn't working. The thought of Donna being involved with Sanderson so early on in the operation rankled, and he found himself constantly glancing at the TVs mounted on the walls of the gym, half expecting her to appear on Sky to break the story. And then there was the file Ford had left with him. Something that was nagging at him that he just couldn't quite pinpoint.

Something . . .

His thoughts were interrupted by movement in the floor-to-ceiling mirror. He watched as she approached from behind, moving with the fluid grace only those who spend a lot of time in the gym and on the yoga mat possess. She smiled as she spotted his gaze, flashing a set of teeth so perfect they might have been shipped in from Hollywood. Connor returned the smile, felt a rush of heat that was nothing to do with his workout as he dropped his weights and popped out his earbuds.

'Hey, Jen,' he said, leaning in to give her a light kiss, suddenly conscious of how busy the gym was.

'Hey, yourself,' she said, after returning his kiss. 'How you getting on? See you're taking it light today.'

Connor glanced down at the weights, gave an embarrassed smile. He hadn't even noticed he had gone for the heaviest dumbbells on the rack. He had just come into the gym, grabbed weights and started lifting. It was purely subconscious, a habit bred into him by long years of training with his grandfather in Northern Ireland. Jimmy O'Brien had been an amateur bodybuilder in his day, and he had instilled in Connor a love of the gym and the belief that the way to calm the mind was to punish the body. So when Connor had to think, or was about to start a challenging assignment, he made his way to the gym.

But in this gym, which sat just off Craigs Roundabout on one of the main roads into the town centre, he had found something, or rather, someone, else. He had met Jen MacKenzie about six months after he had returned to Stirling after a disastrous stay in Belfast and a short-lived career as a police officer. They had flirted, evaded and finally succumbed to the inevitable. There were challenges, not least being Jen's father Duncan and his pet sociopath Paulie, but they were managing, taking it one day at a time.

At least, Connor was.

'Yeah, busy day, wanted to work some stress out,' he said, lifting his towel and draping it around his shoulders.

'Oh? How so?' Jen asked, tucking a strand of blonde hair behind her ear.

'Ach, nothing, really, just work. Got an assignment starting tomorrow, think it might be a bit of a tricky one.'

Jen stiffened slightly, the smile fading from her face. Not long after she had met Connor, bodies had started to appear in tourist destinations around Stirling. A year after that, a man had doused himself in petrol then thrown himself into a bonfire at a self-improvement weekend in a spa hotel, an event for which Connor's company was providing security. It hadn't scared her off, perhaps the opposite, but it had made her wary.

Connor shook his head, put a reassuring hand on her shoulder and was struck, again, by the strength he could feel radiating from her slender frame. 'Nothing to worry about, just a bit complicated, got a bit of history, that's all.'

The smile brightened, but Connor could tell by the way she leaned away from him slightly that she was putting on a show for his benefit.

'Anyway, we still on for dinner tonight?' he asked, hoping his attempt to change the subject was not as clumsy as it sounded to his ears.

'Yeah, sure,' Jen said, posture relaxing as she spoke. 'Your place or mine?'

Connor smiled. 'My place,' he said. 'I can't be bothered fumbling around your kitchen tonight.'

She laughed, punched him gently on the shoulder. It was a running joke with them. Connor liked to cook, found the monotony of following a recipe step by step soothing. But to do so, he needed to know where all his ingredients and utensils were. And while his own kitchen looked like it had been ripped from a Michelin-starred restaurant, Jen's approach to cooking was more haphazard. Everything was cleaned and squared away, but not always in the same place. When it came to organising her cupboards, she was firmly in the out-of-sight, out-of-mind camp.

'OK,' she said. 'How much longer you got to go here?'

Connor glanced up at the clock on the wall, calculated. 'Say half an hour. What time do you get off?'

'Seven,' she said. 'So I could be at your place for, say, eight thirty?'

Connor raised a quizzical eyebrow. Interesting. 'No problem,' he said, drawing the words out to form the question he wanted to ask.

Jen smiled, genuine this time. 'Dad,' she said simply. 'He called earlier, said he wanted to see me after work so I'll pop to his before coming to yours.' She paused, her brow creasing as she started to chew her bottom lip. 'That's weird,' she said softly.

'What?' Connor asked.

Jen started slightly, as though woken from a daydream. 'Oh, nothing really,' she said. 'Just a funny coincidence. Something you said. See, Dad was talking about something with a bit of history as well.'

CHAPTER 11

Malcolm Ford wasn't a man known for regrets. He lived his life on a simple basis – make a decision, act on it, take responsibility for the consequences. It was an outlook instilled in him by his father and reinforced by a lifetime in the police, where there was often no time for introspection or second-guessing.

But occasionally, just occasionally, regret nagged at him, like the ghost of pain from a long-healed injury.

And tonight the regret that Ford felt was for the lack of children in his home.

The decision hadn't been his or Mary's – it was a simple fact imposed on them by Ford's genetics. He remembered the day the doctor had told him, after months of tests, that there was 'little likelihood that you will be able to father a child'. A moment of silence followed as one vision of his life splintered and fractured, as though it was a sheet of stained glass and the doctor had just lobbed a boulder through it. And then there was the new reality he and Mary were faced with. They had considered adopting but decided against: as a junior officer, Ford knew there would be long periods during the adoption process that he would have to leave Mary alone to shoulder the majority of the stress, and he felt he had been selfish enough already.

But their lives had been full and, despite Mary's increasing criticism of his job, happy. They had their jobs and their interests – one of which, a book club, had taken Mary out of the house that night.

They holidayed when they could, enjoyed each other's company and lived comfortably. But occasionally Ford would feel the absence of a larger family in their home, the possibility of what might have been haunting the silence, giving it weight and form.

And tonight, with Mary out and the house still, he felt it all too keenly. After all, if the house was full of children – hell, maybe even grandchildren by this time – he wouldn't have room for the dark thoughts that crowded in on him like a fast-moving storm front.

He grunted a humourless laugh, hoisting himself out of his chair and across to the sideboard where the whisky sat in its decanter. Topped up his glass, then made for the dining-room table, and the open file that lay there.

He had waited till Mary was out before retrieving it from his brief-case. She had heard about Sanderson's release, knew about Ford's connection to the original case, and he didn't want her worrying about him when she was out. He felt a vague snarl of guilt as he looked at the file – wondering again about his decision to give a copy to Fraser. But the moment he had heard about Sanderson's release, he had known he had no choice. After all, a promise is a promise. And this was one vow Ford had no intention of breaking.

He had still been in uniform when the murders had been committed, recently transferred from Edinburgh. But while he wasn't officially assigned to the case, he had made a point of getting as close to the investigation as he could. His reasons were purely personal: Mary had not long started a job at the university, working in the IT department, and the campus was only ten minutes from their home in Bridge of Allan. Whoever had killed the young women had done so on Ford's doorstep, in a place where his wife should be safe.

He kept his enquiries discreet at first, picking up what he could from the internal update bulletins that were circulating around the force and watching closely the manpower requests that were being sent to Lothian and Borders Police from the old Central Scotland Force, which had existed before the advent of Police Scotland. The main fact he picked up was the sense of urgency behind the investigation, which was led by a DCI called Dennis Morgan. Ford knew

Morgan only by reputation – he was a Glasgow officer, recently transferred to Central Scotland after a stint in the Pitt Street CID unit in Strathclyde Police, during which he had built the case that had brought down Bobby 'Brickhouse' Barnes, then one of the most feared gangsters on the West Coast.

Ford made a point of sticking close to the CID room at Randolphfield police station in the south of the city, an ugly brick of a building with pebbledash walls that looked like scar tissue, and too-small windows that seemed to squint at the day with suspicion. He volunteered for overtime, joined the search parties that combed the grounds of the university and the remote scrubland at Gogar Loan, where Rhona Everett's body had been found. Keeping his head down and his work rate up, Ford soon became the investigation's uniformed gofer, ferrying messages back and forward, collecting case files, securing chains of custody for evidence relating to the inquiry.

And it was on one such errand, late at night when the station was quiet and gloomy and the lights took on a yellowing, miserable hue, that Ford met DCI Dennis Morgan.

He was dropping action reports into the CID room for the following day's case conference when he paused in front of the huge whiteboard that dominated the far wall. Some officers called it the murder wall – a space where information relating to the case was displayed for all to see. Ford recognised the locations in the pictures, felt something cold twist in his guts when he spotted the walkway around the university loch that he had strolled along with Mary only a month before. And then there were the other pictures. Two women, faces bleached grey and cold by the harsh flare of the pathologist's camera flash. Eyes closed, the livid greens and reds and purples of bruises across their flesh like grotesque tattoos that told a story of pain and suffering.

'What ya think?'

Ford started as the voice pierced the silence. Whirled around to see a man emerging from an office off to the side of the main space of the room. In his late forties by the look of it, shirt sleeves rolled up to expose thick arms carpeted with a mat of dark hair. He was taller than Ford, which put him at more than six feet tall, but there was a solidity about his frame that made him look shorter. He approached, waving at the board with a mug that Ford could tell from the man's bloodshot eyes was holding something a lot stronger than coffee.

'Sorry, sir,' he said, straightening his back. 'Just dropping off the action reports and got caught up. Sorry, I'll be on my way.'

Morgan held up a hand, a thick watch glinting in the overhead lights as he did so. 'Stay where you are, Sergeant . . .?'

'Ford,' he replied, feeling his cheeks redden. 'Malcolm Ford.'

Morgan nodded, as though satisfied by this. 'So,' he said, as he stood beside Ford, 'what do you think?'

'I'm not sure, sir,' he said, swallowing a twist of awkwardness. 'I mean, I've read what was in the news, tried to keep up with the investigation, but I'm not certain what more I can add.'

Morgan studied him for a minute, cold dark eyes unblinking. 'Good,' he said finally. 'First step in this game is admitting what you don't know, and working from there. We've got two victims, and a perpetrator who is almost unspeakably savage. And that's all we've got. He's strong – must be to overpower them quickly – brazen to take them from the university but careful at the same time. We don't have a murder weapon, and there's a distinct lack of trace evidence. So what does that tell us?'

'He's not a rage killer,' Ford said. 'And he's going to do this again.'

'Oh?' Morgan asked, something almost predatory flashing in his eyes. 'And why is that, PC Ford?'

Ford turned back to the wall, the thought bleeding through his mind, like dye into a fresh stream. 'Because two victims in such a short period of time shows he's got a taste for it now. And two victims is only one away from three.'

'And that means what?' Morgan asked, his voice low, almost eager now.

Ford felt the words tumble from numb lips as the thought solidified in his mind. 'Three victims is the threshold for describing an offender as a serial killer, sir. And if our man is as meticulous and violent as you suggest, then he fits the profile for a repeat offender. Which means he can't stop, even if he wants to. Which he doesn't.'

41

'Very good, Ford,' Morgan said, draining his mug.

Ford searched for something to say in reply, found nothing. 'Jesus,' he whispered.

'Got fuck-all to do with him, Ford,' Morgan said, a sharp edge of anger cutting through his voice. 'This is all on us. We need to find this bastard. Now,' he paused for a moment, studied the bottom of his mug. 'Go on, get out of here, go home,' he said at last.

'Sir,' Ford said, then left the room. He finished up his shift and headed home, detouring past the university, the memory of his conversation with Morgan clinging to him like a half-remembered dream.

The next morning, he turned up at Randolphfield for his shift, and was summoned by the duty sergeant, who informed him he'd been assigned to the university murders case.

'Seems you made a bit of an impression on DCI Morgan last night,' the sergeant, a wizened old career officer called Carlyle, told him. 'He asked for you specifically.'

And that was how Ford's path towards CID and becoming a detective began. He shadowed Morgan, did the grunt work on the case, watched as they put together the pieces of the puzzle that led to Sanderson, even when some of those pieces had to be a little forced to expedite matters.

After the case and the trial, Morgan retired and faded from Ford's thoughts. Until, that was, Sanderson was acquitted at the High Court. Ford had known the call was coming the moment he had heard the appeal judge's verdict.

'You know it was him, Malcolm,' he whispered into the phone, voice stretched thin and coarse by the passage of years and a stubborn refusal to give up either the whisky or the cigarettes. 'We both do. But it's on you now. You remember what we did back then, you have to keep an eye on him. After all, two is only one away from three.'

Ford looked up from the file, staring into the middle distance. Was that why he had given Connor a copy of the case file? To have him verify what he and Morgan had found all those years ago? To show that they, not the appeal judges, were right and Sanderson was a killer after all?

He shuddered suddenly, another memory rising up. The hard, blunt thud of wood on flesh, screams of pain echoing off cold stone walls, the hot, metallic smell of blood in the air as it splattered onto a concrete floor. And a word, a single word, repeated like a twisted mantra, laden with malice and hate.

'*Again.*'

Ford shook himself, drained his whisky as he forced down the memory, and the guilt that came with it.

They had been right. Sanderson was a killer. The most depraved Ford had met in his long career. And now Connor Fraser was watching over him. And, just behind him, Ford would be there. Waiting.

Again.

CHAPTER 12

The next morning, Jen had an early appointment with a client for a personal training session, so Connor gave her a lift to the gym, using the trip as an excuse to get in some cardio. He didn't really need the exercise, but he liked watching Jen as she worked. Her client was a middle-aged man afflicted by the standard problems those years brought – an expanding gut, a receding hairline and a steadfast belief that he was an expert in everything. And yet, as Connor watched in one of the mirrors in front of the exercise bike he was on, Jen laughed and joked with the man, correcting his form on machines and demonstrating how everything worked. She had a patience and an ease with people that Connor at once admired and coveted. He found meeting new people mildly stressful at the best of times, the doubt always nagging that he would say the wrong thing or unwittingly cause offence. But not Jen: from what Connor could see, she was working through her client's doubts, her tips being greeted with warm smiles and enthusiastic rapport.

Connor wondered if it was a trick he would ever master.

After his session, he went back to the flat for a shower and a change. Then he headed for the car, pulling the Audi up in front of Donna's block in a new-build estate on the road out of Stirling to Cambusbarron. He texted her when he arrived, declining the offer to come up for a coffee. The last time Connor had visited, Donna's mother had buzzed around him like an over-eager moth, and he had been handed Donna's infant son, Andrew, to hold. Neither experience had been particularly soothing, and he was keen to avoid a repeat performance if at all possible.

He was dragged from his thoughts by the clunk of the Audi's passenger door being opened and Donna folding herself into the car. 'Morning,' she said, as she fiddled the belt into position, then rested her bag on her knees. Sharp business suit, hair scraped back into a tight ponytail, just enough make-up to accentuate her high cheekbones and piercing blue eyes. Interesting.

'So, who's being interviewed here anyway?' Connor said as he fired the engine. 'Sanderson or you?'

'What?' Donna asked, defensiveness cooling her gaze. 'What do you mean by . . .'

Connor jutted his jaw towards her. 'Come on, Donna,' he said. 'No camera crew today, yet you're wearing a brand new suit and look ready to go on air nationally. You're out to make an impression. So I'm guessing this isn't the prelude to a one-off interview, but the opening gambit for something else, maybe a series of interviews after what you said about mentioning Sentinel in the piece. Not much use in a one-off "wrongly imprisoned man returns home" piece, but if you're going deeper and profiling him for something more in-depth . . .'

She glared at him for a moment, before a smile played across her lips. 'Not bad, Fraser,' she said. 'Yes, there's a chance of more work in this for me, if today pans out.'

Connor got the car moving, concentrating on the road, letting the silence pose its own question.

'OK,' Donna said. 'Look, this is off the record. But there's a chance of a book deal for Sanderson, and some of the PR folk he's working with think I could be a good fit for that.'

Connor nodded, Ford's words in his ears. *He's a killer, Fraser, plain and simple. After so long inside, he'll kill again. He won't be able to help himself.* 'You sure you want to get that close to this guy?' he asked.

Donna opened her mouth, closed it. Looked out at the road, then back to Connor. It was a fair question, which she had asked herself more than once after the euphoria of Debbie's offer had receded. Yes, the man had been acquitted and released on a technicality, but he was still no angel. The details of his previous crimes, released after he was found guilty of the university murders, revealed a man with a pattern of escalating violence. But, then, she hadn't got into journalism just to report the puff pieces. This was news. This was her job.

'You think I can't hack it?' she asked.

Connor held up a hand. 'Not at all,' he said. 'It's just that, after everything you've already been through, maybe . . .' He trailed off, an image of Mark Sneddon hanging from a tree dancing across his mind. Yes, Donna had seen her fair share of death and violence. The question was, did she want to see more?

'It's the job,' she said at last. 'And if this works out, there might be more writing gigs in the future. This could be good for Andrew and me, very good.'

Connor murmured agreement, turning his focus back to driving, following the twisting road that threaded its way through farmland on the way to Cambusbarron. It was a small village, only a mile or so from Stirling, and typical of any number of dwellings dotted across Central Scotland. Solid, blunt-faced buildings hewn from sandstone or granite, grey slate roofs and white-framed windows. Neatly trimmed hedges bordered the roads, contrasting with the pink of cherry blossom or the burgundy red of the maple trees that dotted the landscape like sentries.

He crawled along the main street, watching the satnav. Turned right onto Sanderson's street when indicated to do so, counted the house numbers in his head until he found the one he was looking for – an unremarkable sandstone bungalow wedged between two tenement buildings. Connor pulled in across the street from the house, killed the engine. 'Like I said, we go in together. But when you're done, I need to speak to him alone about the job I've been hired to do. I can either call you a taxi back to town, or get one of my guys to drive you.'

Donna looked around. 'Your guys? You mean?'

He nodded. 'Robbie's inside at the moment, got another couple of guys in the area. So you're covered for a lift back if needed. OK?'

He saw a moment of indecision in her eyes, knew she was considering arguing the point. Being told what to do had never been Donna's strong suit, and they both knew that, if she wanted to, she could push the point with Sanderson and get him to ensure she stayed in the room.

'OK,' she said, after a moment. 'Let's go and meet Mr Sanderson, shall we?'

***

He clicked the gun's safety on and off: a metronome counting off the steps as the man walked around the car to join a familiar-looking woman and headed for the Sandersons' home. He was big but lithe, moving with a wariness that marked him out as a former copper even more clearly than the file currently sitting on his lap.

Connor Fraser. Former officer with the Police Service of Northern Ireland, currently a director at Sentinel Securities. He grunted at the name. Sentinel. A soldier posted to stand watch. Well, at least he and Fraser had that much in common.

He waited for a moment as Fraser and the woman disappeared into the house, then cast another glance around the street. He had seen one car cruising the area in the hour he'd been there, carefully anonymous, two suits squeezed into it, most likely driving a slow loop around the block, looking for anyone who didn't fit in, anyone who looked like they might send a rat through the mail to Sanderson and his family.

Luckily, he didn't fit those criteria. And he was practically invisible anyway. He should be. After all these years, it was a reflex action to blend in.

Satisfied, he flicked the safety back on the gun for a final time, stowed it beneath the passenger seat. Started the car and slid out of his parking space slowly, just another suburban driver heading out on another pointless errand. As he passed Fraser's car he committed the licence plate to memory – it would come in handy later on for tracking down Fraser's home address.

Yes, he and Connor Fraser were going to need to have a long talk at some point. Just the two of them, sentinel to sentinel.

***

47

The door was answered by a small, stooped man who looked as though he'd been beaten down by both age and life, the wrinkles on his face like scars from the passage of years. He looked up at Connor, eyes dancing between him and Donna, then offered a hand. 'Donald Sanderson,' he said, in a voice that was heavy with the ghost of cigarettes and whisky. 'Take it you're here to see my son.'

Connor took the outstretched hand, surprised by the strength in the grip. 'Yes, sir,' he said. 'Connor Fraser, Sentinel Securities. And this is—'

'Donna Blake,' Donna cut in, offering her hand to Sanderson. 'Your son is expecting me.'

'Oh, yes, the journalist,' Sanderson said, as he stood aside and gestured for them to step into the hallway. 'Yeah, Colin did say something about that. Come on away in, then, get this over with.'

Connor and Donna followed Donald down a small, narrow hallway. The walls had been white once, covered with the textured wallpaper that was the hallmark of industrial seventies council-house chic. Now, though, they were dulled to a dirty beige, the smell of the cigarettes that had stained them hanging sourly in the air. On the left of the hallway, a staircase traced a path to a small landing, the faded red and black pattern of the carpet transforming the stairs into some kind of diseased tongue sticking out from the mouth of the first floor.

At the end of the hall another door opened into a surprisingly large kitchen, which looked out onto a plain square of neatly tended lawn, surrounded by a high leylandii hedge. In the middle of the room sat a large kitchen table with two people sitting at it.

Robbie stood as Connor entered the room, nodding slightly. 'Sir,' he said. 'Good to see you. This is . . .'

'Colin Sanderson,' the other man said as he rose, chair scraping off the lino of the kitchen floor. 'And you must be the man they've decided is going to babysit me.'

Connor offered his hand, taking a step forward. He knew from the files Ford had provided that Colin Sanderson was in his late forties. But while his father looked as though he had been in a bare-knuckle fight with time and lost every round, Sanderson junior looked as though he had thrived on the battle. His skin was tight and pale, grey hair cropped close to his skull above a face that was dominated by a thick, slanted nose and lips that had obviously been burst open more than once. He was, like his father, compact, but the kind of compact that spoke of wiry strength and solidity. Connor found himself wondering idly what it would be like to punch the man.

'Connor Fraser,' he said. 'And, yes, as I'm sure Robbie no doubt explained, we've been hired by Frontline PR to arrange security for you at this, ah, delicate time.'

Sanderson grunted, waved a hand. 'Waste of fucking time,' he whispered. 'Some hero sends a bit of hate mail and everyone gets their knickers in a knot. Fuck 'em. They've got a problem with me, let them come to the door. I'll show them what the fucking score is.'

'Colin,' Sanderson Senior said, stepping forward. 'Mind your bloody manners. There are women present.'

Donna let out a laugh. 'Don't worry, Mr Sanderson, I've heard worse in the newsroom. Colin, I'm Donna Blake. I believe Debbie mentioned me?'

Something flashed across Sanderson's eyes, making the blue there sparkle coldly. Then he twisted his face into a smile that showed off small, even teeth that were as stained as his father's hallway. 'Ah, yes, Ms Blake. Debbie did mention that you would be visiting today. But ...' eyes flicking back to Connor '... why did you come with Mr Fraser? Surely you don't think you need a bodyguard to speak to me?'

Connor winced internally. He had been so focused on containing which way Donna reported this that he hadn't considered how the two of them arriving together would look to Sanderson. Sloppy.

'Not at all,' Donna replied, eyes not leaving Sanderson's. 'I just wanted to have a quick word with Mr Fraser as background for the interview we're going to do. My producer is keen on doing some location shots around Stirling, and with Frontline insisting on security for you after the threat, it made sense to discuss this with Mr Fraser on the way here.'

Nice recovery, Connor thought. Bullshit, but nice.

Sanderson waved towards the table. 'I don't need babysitting,' he said, eyes on Connor as he gestured for Donna and Connor to sit. 'I'm only playing along with this shite as the publisher insisted. Now, you two want tea while I tell you how this is all going to play out?'

CHAPTER 13

The air was sour with the smell of drying blood and fresh sweat. Looking around, Paulie could see the meagre crowd was cheering and urging him on, but he couldn't hear them for the hammering of his heart in his ears.

He ducked as his opponent lunged forward, aiming a left hook at his jaw. Twisted and pivoted up, crashing his fist into the man's midsection, feeling ribs shatter as the blow lifted his opponent off his feet. He staggered back, hand grabbing his side, eyes wide, searching Paulie's face. And then there was that moment, the moment Paulie lived for. It was like a candle being snuffed out in their eyes – the instant the other fighter knew it was over, that nothing could save them from what came next.

Paulie hawked back and spat a wad of blood-streaked phlegm onto the cold floor. Then he marched forward, as inevitable as dawn, closing in on his prey. The man danced around the makeshift ring, trying to move away, trying to flee. 'Fuck, Paulie, enough,' he said, his voice a grating counterpoint to the hammering in Paulie's ears. 'Enough. I quit, OK?'

'OK,' Paulie said with a shrug. Then he surged forward, lashing out, bone stabbing into his knuckles as teeth splintered and flesh parted. His opponent staggered back, suspended in a frozen moment, as though his body was buffering the information Paulie had just delivered with his fist. Then his knees buckled and he crashed to the floor, a spray of blood pluming from his mouth as the concrete drove the breath from his lungs.

The crowd exploded in wild cheers, an almost physical force that washed across Paulie like a wave. He took a half-step forward, vision focusing on the other man's exposed temple. Felt a sudden twitch in his right foot, some deep impulse whispering to him to lash out again, drive his heel into the man's temple. And it would be so easy.

So, so easy . . .

Paulie shook his head. Stepped forward and dropped to his knee, checking on the man he had just knocked out. He was just a kid, really. One of the labourers on the site who loaded the trucks. Big and healthy in the way all those models in the fucking men's health magazines were, overly keen and overly cocky. So when the chance to go up against Paulie in a friendly bare-knuckle match came up in return for a few extra quid, the kid – what was his name again? Liam? – was all too keen to oblige.

Too bad for him.

Paulie looked at the crowd, spotted the yard foreman, Michael, whose gaze was flicking nervously between Paulie and a large wad of notes he held scrunched in his left hand. The fight had been profitable at least.

'Mon tae fuck, Michael,' Paulie called. 'Fight's over. Boy needs help. Get a couple of guys to clean him up, check he's OK. And make sure he gets some of that' – he indicated the ball of notes Michael was holding – 'for his trouble.'

Michael nodded eagerly, gestured for a couple of other men to help him. Paulie watched them for a moment. Then, satisfied, he turned and made his way from the warehouse, the remaining members of the crowd parting before him as though he was a ship cutting through waves.

Stupid, he thought, as he stepped out of the warehouse, the cool of the afternoon air making a chill shroud of his sweat. Stupid. After all, it wasn't the kid's fault that he was pissed off. No, once again, that honour went to Connor Fraser.

When MacKenzie had told him about the situation in Cambusbarron, the involvement of Fraser had almost become inevitable, like the punch line to a bad joke at Paulie's expense. He was, grudgingly, forced to admit that Fraser was capable of looking after himself and, more importantly, Jen, and there was no doubt he had balls of steel – he had proven that the night he had handed Paulie a loaded gun, then turned his back on him and walked away. But, still, there was unfinished business between Connor and Paulie – business that dated back to their first meeting, and an altercation that had resulted in Paulie suffering some broken fingers. And while the fingers had, like so many other wounds, healed over time, the memory of that indignity glowed like a hot coal somewhere in Paulie's gut. He had, so far, stayed his hand out of deference to the boss and Jen.

But now there was this. Cambusbarron. The stirring of old ghosts, the opening of old wounds. Paulie grunted, headed for his car, which was parked at the far end of the site, away from the spit of gravel and plumes of dust kicked up by the trucks that sped in and out of the yard and the jealous glances of the other lorry drivers.

The Merc sat waiting for him, pristine in the waning afternoon sun. Paulie gazed at it for a moment, letting the cool perfection of the paint job and the immaculate gleam of the polished alloys soothe him. He prided himself on the car – in a world as chaotic as his, its appearance was one of the few things he could control.

He plipped the central locking and folded himself into the vehicle, the springs sagging slightly beneath his weight. Then he fired the engine and punched an address into the satnav. The boss had asked him to take care of old business. Business that would, Paulie knew, turn bloody at some point. And in situations like that, there was always collateral damage.

And if some of that damage just happened to find its way to Connor Fraser's door, then so be it. It would be poetic justice. And finally Paulie would have the last laugh.

CHAPTER 14

Connor had the rev counter buried into the red, the car's engine screaming its protest at him. He short-shifted, feeling as though he was going to kick his foot straight through the floor as he hammered the clutch and threw the car into top gear. Vehicles blurred past him, some flashing their lights as he darted by.

He didn't care. All that mattered was getting there.

The call had come in just as he was trying to decide how much trouble it would be to toss Colin Sanderson through a window and deal with the paperwork later. After he had made a pot of insipid tea, Sanderson had done everything he could to assert his dominance in front of Donna. It was, Connor knew, a typical jail-time trick. Get the seat in the corner, then control the room, prove you're in charge. Which, in Sanderson's case, meant either ignoring Connor and Robbie completely or flatly observe that he didn't need 'no fucking babysitters following me around everywhere'.

The only thing keeping Connor in the room at that point was loyalty to Donna. He had no doubt she could look after herself, and he doubted that even Sanderson was stupid enough to try anything, but there was something about the man, something in that almost predatory gaze and the way he casually leaned forward every time he spoke to Donna, that bothered Connor. And then there were Ford's words: *The man is a fucking animal.*

Connor was considering the point when his phone beeped. He

pulled it out, felt his world grow cold as he read the caller ID. Nodded his apologies to Donna and gave Robbie a look that told him to take over. Strode into the hall. 'Connor Fraser,' he said, silent prayers thundering through his mind as he spoke.

'Mr Fraser? Mr Fraser, it's Isla Kennedy at Carson House. It's about your grandmother, Ida.'

'Yes,' Connor said, lips numb. In his mind he was back in Belfast, knuckles stinging as a man's blood dried on them, pint in hand, answering a call from his gran the night she had rung to tell him his mum had cancer and he needed to come home.

'First, don't panic. She's OK – but she had a fall earlier on today. Seems she was trying to get to something in one of her wardrobes, climbed up on a chair and took a spill. She lay there for a little while, but managed to activate her panic button. She's resting now.'

Connor felt a black band of pain tighten around his head. Forced himself to release his clenched jaw. 'Have you called a doctor?' he asked, his mind filling with formless nightmares shot through with words like 'concussion' and 'blood clots' and 'fracture'.

'The on-site medical team have looked at her and she's fine. Resting comfortably in her room now. But you're listed as her primary contact in cases like this so I thought I should call you.'

'Yes, quite right. Thanks for letting me know,' Connor replied, his voice an afterthought now, his mind already turning to next steps. 'Tell her I'll be there in ten minutes.'

He cut the call before Isla could say anything else, then turned back for the kitchen. Snagged Robbie and filled him in on what had happened, then stepped back into the room.

'Mr Sanderson,' he said, talking over Donna. 'I'm sorry but something's come up. I've got to leave but my associate here will go over the last of the security arrangements with you when you're finished with Donna. I'll call in later to confirm you're happy.'

'Connor, what—' Donna began, something halfway between curiosity and concern passing across her face.

'Just a personal matter,' Connor said, his voice a bullet point in the quiet of the room. 'Robbie will make sure you get a lift back to town. I'll call you later on.'

She nodded, something in his tone telling her not to push it any further.

Out the front door of the house, cursing as he slammed it too hard. Into the car, engine on. Then off, down the back roads that led from Cambusbarron to Bannockburn, like the arthritic branches of some ancient tree. He tried to remember the nurse's words as he drove – *She's fine, resting comfortably.* Found they did nothing to calm him.

Growing up, Connor had been estranged from his father. His childhood was a place of awkward family dinners, hushed arguments bleeding up the stairs as he lay in his bed at night, and a low-level aura of disapproval radiating from his father. His mother had done as much as she could to shield Connor from this, but it was his gran, Ida, who had given him the support and understanding he needed. In many ways, Connor thought, she was the third parent who actually raised him, the one who understood the man he was slowly becoming.

If only she knew who that was today.

He pushed aside the thought, concentrated on the road. It was only a ten-minute drive from Cambusbarron to Bannockburn, but Connor cut it to seven. The Audi slewed to a halt in the car park at the care home, gravel spraying up and pinging almost musically off the underside of the car. Connor jumped out, his momentum slowed only briefly by a sight that gave his guts an extra twist even as he moved.

In the corner of the car park sat another car. A BMW estate, a classic or a clunker now, depending on what you thought about cars with more than a hundred thousand miles on the clock and owners who refused to get rid of them. Connor didn't need to go across to the car to know there would be the ghost of a small dent in the bumper on the offside. He had put it there when he was learning to drive and misjudged a parallel parking manoeuvre. It had been repaired, but not to Jack Fraser's exacting standards.

His dad had shouted at him that day. Told him to concentrate, that this wasn't a game. The memory ringing in his ears, Connor jogged up to the main door of the care home, wondering what fresh insults his father would have prepared for him today.

CHAPTER 15

If the last fourteen years have taught me anything, it's patience. The ability to let events unfold around me while I wait for the tide to turn and circumstances to inevitably move in my favour once more. And while that last hour was maddening, it yielded something else, a benefit I was not expecting.

It brought me her.

I recognised her the moment I saw her, of course. Donna Blake, a reporter for Sky News. I'd watched her for a while, been impressed by her poise on camera. From what I witnessed, she had it off camera as well. From the perfectly tailored suit to the long dark hair that looked as though she had just stepped from the salon, she was perfect. She moved with a certain determination and fluid grace, though anyone would look graceful next to the lumbering hulk that accompanied her. I was glad to see him leave.

But now the dilemma. The need, the hunger, urges me on, whispering in my ear to give it free rein, strike now. But to do so would have consequences – it would mean keeping *her* waiting at the university, and I want to see her again so very, very badly.

But then Blake. The hair. The poise. I remember watching one report she made last year, from a luxury hotel just outside Stirling, when a man had thrown himself onto the bonfire. I was impressed by her professionalism, could see the trauma in her eyes and the steely determination not to let it beat her as she spoke into the camera.

I went to bed that night wondering what it would take to make Donna Blake scream.

The knife was in my hand before I was aware of reaching for it, as though my body had made the decision before my conscious mind.

No. Patience. Planning. Control. This plan was years in the making, crafted detail by detail in the endless nights when release seemed impossible and freedom was little more than a dream. I did not go looking for Donna Blake or a distraction from my work, but Fate delivered her to my doorstep.

But no, I argued with my hunger, made the decision to resist. Finally, after all these years, I have time. So I will be careful. Modify the plan. Prepare. Be patient.

And when I learn what it takes to make Blake scream, the sound will be the sweetest music I have heard in the last fourteen years.

CHAPTER 16

Connor sat at the table, tapping his fingers against his coffee mug, forcing himself to remain calm. On reflection, caffeine was probably a bad idea. The last thing he needed just now was a stimulant. No, what he needed was to hit the gym.

Or just hit someone. Period.

As expected, his father had been waiting for him when he arrived at his gran's flat, full of that mix of righteous fury and weary disappointment that he had bestowed on Connor his entire life. 'This is all your bloody fault,' Jack Fraser hissed as Connor passed him, kneeling in front of his gran.

'You OK, Gran? What happened?' he asked, taking her frail, bird-like hand in his, trying not to concentrate on the purpling lump that was swelling on her forehead.

Your bloody fault, he heard his father whisper in his mind.

Ida Fraser smiled down at him, and Connor was torn between the sudden need to laugh and cry at the same time.

'I'm fine, son,' she said, patting his hand with hers. 'Just my own stupid fault. Wanted to get, ah, something from the wardrobe, just overbalanced and cowped over. Stupid, stupid old woman.'

'What were you looking for?' Connor asked, the question out before he had consciously thought it. He felt his father's eyes on him in that moment, ignored it, even as he saw his gran's eyes dart to her son and then back to him.

'Och, nothing. Just some old photies I wanted to have a look at. Couldn't find them in the end.'

'They might be among the stuff I've got at my place. Want to tell me what you're looking for? I can have a look, bring them to you?'

Again, a moment's pause, the air in the room growing heavy as Ida glanced across at Jack. 'Ach, just some old photies from when your dad was a bairn. Nothing important, son, you just forget it.'

Connor studied his gran's face a moment longer. Saw the twitching at the corners of her mouth, the paling of her lips as she clamped them tighter. Ignored a flash of shame as he snaked a finger around her thin, brittle wrist and felt her pulse hammer against her skin.

'But you're sure you're all right?' he asked, keeping his voice soft even as questions charged through his mind.

'She's fine,' Jack answered, stepping forward. 'I checked her out myself. I am a doctor, in case you'd forgotten, Connor.'

Connor bit back the answer that burned in his mouth like acid. Not here. Not now. Not in front of Gran.

He smiled at her again, stood. 'Well, if you need anything, you just let me know, OK? I've got to head off now, got a job on. But I'll call back in later on, make sure you're all right and not trying any more acrobatics.'

Ida let out a laugh that could almost have been mistaken for genuine. 'I'm fine, son, just an old woman's stupidity. You go and do your work. And don't worry about me tonight. Take that wee lassie of yours out instead.'

Connor smiled, ignoring the quizzical look his father shot him. He hadn't got around to telling him about his relationship with Jen. Hardly surprising. It was questionable whether he would tell his father if he had been diagnosed with terminal cancer. 'OK, will do, Gran,' he said, bending to kiss her cheek, lingering a moment as he leaned in to inspect the bruise on her forehead again.

Your bloody fault.

He excused himself, grunted a goodbye to his father, then headed for the door. Got about halfway down the corridor when he was stopped short by a voice, like an unruly student being brought to a halt by a stern teacher.

60

'Connor,' his father called. 'Just wait a minute. I want a word.'

Connor turned, watched his father approach, again struck by how little in common he had with this man. He was shorter than Connor, maybe just a little over five foot eight, and where Connor was broad, Jack Fraser was wiry and slight. It was like a flyweight approaching a heavyweight.

'Not here,' Connor said, glancing over his father's shoulder towards his gran's room to convey the message. 'Outside.'

They walked in silence, Connor struggling with the mixture of guilt and anger churning inside him. It was always the same when he was with his dad, especially when he was being criticised. A lifetime of unanswered slights and absent parenting rose to the top of his thoughts, like scum on a poisoned lake, the boy who had been robbed of a father by his medical career crying out for retribution.

They reached the car park, Connor making for his car and checking his phone. He thumbed in a quick message to Robbie asking for an update, then turned to his dad. 'Can we make this quick, Dad?' he asked. 'Only I wasn't kidding, I do have work to get done.'

Jack Fraser shook his head slowly, as if he had somehow tried to impart ancient wisdom and Connor had been too slow to understand. 'This won't take long. You know it was you and that bloody report card that caused all this, don't you? You come here waving that around, and she gets some stupid idea into her head to start digging around for old pictures of me. You do realise she's seventy-eight years old now, Connor, that she could quite easily have broken her neck in that fall?'

Connor had taken a step forward before he knew it, his shadow falling over his father. 'I honestly didn't think I was doing anything wrong,' he said, voice a strained whisper. 'I found the report card in some boxes I'm storing at my place. It told an interesting story about you and I wanted to ask Gran about it. After all, you'd hardly be in a hurry to talk to me about it, would you, Dad?'

Jack flinched for an instant, his face slackening with some deep sadness. He looked away, then back to Connor, defiance in his eyes. And something else. Something Connor had not seen since the night his mother had died.

Fear.

'Connor, I . . .' He paused, back stiffening. 'Look, Connor, please, just leave it, OK?' He sounded tired now, the way he sounded when he would come back from a nightshift at the hospital when Connor was a boy. They would exchange words over the breakfast table as Connor got ready for school, his father not really there, just a lump of exhausted flesh going through the motions with a son he barely knew.

'Dad, I'm sorry,' he said. 'I didn't mean for this to happen. Last thing I'd want is for Gran to get hurt.'

'Aye, fine. Just leave it, though. You keep poking about in the past, God knows what she'll start asking for. And we don't want her upset, do we?'

Connor had murmured agreement, headed for his car. Not sure what else to say, the look his father had given him running a loop in his mind. And something else he had said, something that nagged at Connor like toothache even as he'd urged the Audi faster, faster back to Stirling and a hastily arranged meeting with Robbie.

That bloody report card—

Connor was startled from his memories by the sound of the café door opening. He looked up, saw Robbie weaving his way through the tables towards him. Bit back a smile as he watched him move. Gifted at research, background checks and logistics, Robbie had struggled a little to assert himself in the more practical areas of personal security. But after last year, and the death of a colleague at the hands of a knife-wielding madman, he had started to take the physical aspects of his job more seriously. He had taken up self-defence classes, sought Connor's advice on working out. Now, walking towards him, Connor could see that Robbie was still trying to navigate the world in a body that was bigger than he was used to – there was uncertainty in his movements, as though he was a toddler trying to get used to walking.

'Boss,' he said, as he reached the table and placed a hand on the back of the chair opposite Connor.

Connor nodded. Permission granted. Robbie took a seat.

'You want a coffee?' Connor asked.

'Does it come with a whisky?' Robbie murmured, eyes widening slightly as he realised he had spoken aloud. 'Sorry, boss, I didn't mean . . . It's just that, well . . .'

Connor waved aside his excuses, caught the eye of the waitress behind the counter. 'Don't worry about it,' he said. 'I take it you mean Sanderson was a delight to be with after I left?'

Robbie let out a sound that was halfway between a cough and a curse as he shrugged off his jacket. 'Well, he's not going out of his way to make our life easy, that's for sure.'

They paused for a moment as the waitress arrived at the table and Robbie ordered a coffee. Black, no sugar. Interesting, thought Connor. Two months ago, he was a three-sugar latte man. He was obviously taking his training seriously.

'So, what's the issue?' Connor asked, a vague suspicion creeping across his thoughts.

'Well, Mr Sanderson is not at all happy about us being assigned to keep an eye on him,' Robbie replied. 'He insists that he can look after himself and his dad, seems quite keen on whoever sent him the rat taking another shot at him so he can even the score. Insists that we keep our distance, no perimeter surveillance and no following him if and when he leaves the family home. "I didnae swap one fucking prison for another," was the way he put it.'

'Tough,' Connor said. 'Our contract is with his publishing company. Not him. We'll keep an eye on him for the moment, quietly. At least until he does his interview with Donna Blake. I can only imagine whoever sent that little message is going to have something to say after they see Sanderson on the TV.'

Robbie nodded his agreement. 'I've assigned Sarah and Jamie to a perimeter patrol for the moment, boss, but we're going to have to up things a bit when it comes to the interview.'

Connor raised an eyebrow. Suspicion confirmed. 'Go on,' he said, as the waitress returned with Robbie's coffee.

'I'll say this for Ms Blake, she knows how to handle Sanderson,' Robbie said, over the lip of his mug. 'She wants to do the interview somewhere outside, a . . . What did she call it? Oh, yeah, a "walk and talk" somewhere familiar, somewhere identifiably Stirling.'

'Oh, Christ,' Connor said, leaning forward, 'you don't mean . . .?'

Robbie smiled. 'No, sir, that's what I mean about Ms Blake being good. When she mentioned it, Sanderson jumped on the idea, was all for getting in the car and heading for the university campus there and then. But she managed to talk him down, convince him that wouldn't be the best way to win the public over to his side, by flaunting himself at the very place two women were killed.'

Two women Ford is still convinced Sanderson killed, Connor thought.

'OK, good. So where did they settle for in the end?'

Robbie's smile grew wider, more relaxed, as he jerked a thumb over his shoulder. 'Just up the road, sir, at Mar's Wark.'

Connor couldn't help but smile back. Mar's Wark. It was the skeletal remains of a mansion house dating back to the 1500s. Designed to be the home of the keeper of Stirling Castle, the building had served as a barracks during the Jacobite Rising before falling into disrepair. Today, it was another sandstone-hewn piece of the architectural puzzle that made up the historic heart of Stirling, where the streets were stone canyons and a doorway to the past seemed to be only one cobbled side-street away.

'So, let me guess,' Connor said, 'they do a walk up the hill towards the castle, passing the Wark on the way?'

'Exactly, sir. Which means . . .'

'Which means if they start at the right spot they have to pass the entrance to the Old Town Jail on the way up the road,' Connor said. 'And I'll bet you Donna gives the cameraman very specific instructions on how to frame that shot.'

Robbie raised his coffee mug in a toast. 'I thought so, sir,' he said.

'When's this meant to be happening?' Connor asked.

'Plan is to do the recording tomorrow afternoon. Ms Blake thinks the interview will go out the day after that, give Sky enough time to promote it, ensure an audience.'

Connor nodded. Made sense. Also presented a problem. 'Did she make any other arrangements to see Mr Sanderson again?' he asked.

'They spoke about finding a place to have a meeting after the filming tomorrow, sir, though Ms Blake didn't give any further details about what that could be about.'

'OK,' Connor said. No doubt they were going to talk about the possible book Donna had mentioned. But the fact she had suggested meeting Sanderson somewhere public was interesting, and Connor made a mental note to follow that up with Donna later that day.

CHAPTER 17

Jack Fraser was no drinker. He hated alcohol, the smell of it reminding him of his father, Campbell, and those all-too-frequent nights when he had sat slumped on the sofa in their home, his tie pulled down, whisky balancing on the couch arm, the silence seeming to coalesce around him, as though the house was holding its breath, waiting to see what his next move would be. Would he scream or whisper? Rant or weep?

On the night of the report card, he had decided to scream. And the echoes of that scream were stirring.

Jack muttered a curse, drained the brandy from his glass. Shuddered at the unfamiliar, cloyingly bittersweet taste. Thought of Connor looming over him outside the care home. Physically, he was as far from his grandfather as it was possible to be, but there were deeper echoes of the Fraser bloodline if you knew what to look for. Jack saw it in those eyes of his – chips of cold jade that sparked and flashed with an almost primal rage. Jack had seen that rage too many times over the years, felt it snarl in his own mind more than once. But he had fought with it, controlled it. After what had happened, he would never let it be free again. Never give his father that final victory.

He crossed the room to the drinks cabinet, topped up his glass. Paused at the picture that sat on top of the cabinet. It was a family picture of Connor, Jack and his wife, Claire. It had been taken on one of their visits back to Newtownards to see Claire's parents. Connor was about fifteen at the time, all legs and arms. But what struck Jack as he looked at the picture was how like his mother Connor was. The fine, almost delicate nose, the high cheekbones and, of course, the eyes. There were almost no visual clues to his paternity.

A fact that Jack Fraser was grateful for. Especially now.

He knew Connor resented him for the childhood he had endured. Jack had worked long hours at the hospital, specialising in oncology. As the years passed, Connor had become a stranger to Jack, most of what he knew about his son learned from whispered conversations with Claire at night after Connor had gone to bed. He knew that was partly behind Connor's decision to go off to Belfast and study psychology rather than following in his footsteps and doing medicine in Edinburgh. It was a means of revenge, of killing the visceral hopes and dreams of a father who had never shown him any attention as a child. It also explained why Connor was so close to his gran and his grandfather over in Northern Ireland: both of them had given him the time and encouragement Jack had never been able to.

If only he could tell Connor why.

Jack felt the heat prickle the nape of his neck as his fingers tightened around the glass. He bit back the sudden urge to smash the fucking thing against the wall, knew that if he did, he would unleash a maelstrom that would not be satisfied until the whole room was destroyed.

Instead, he closed his eyes. Forced aside the sudden memory of a bottle smashing, the hammering of a body on wood as it crashed downstairs, concentrated on controlling his breathing.

Connor had nothing, Jack told himself. Just an old report card. His mother knew enough to keep her mouth shut, not try any more stupid stunts like today's. Stunts that would attract attention. Stunts that would pique Connor's curiosity.

The sting of the tears on his cheek was a revelation, dousing the anger as violently as a fireman's hose on a disposable barbecue. Jack reached up and swiped the tear aside, painfully aware that his hand was shaking as it moved.

It had been decades since he had last shed a tear. He hadn't cried when Connor had been born, hadn't even been able to bring himself to show what he was feeling when Claire was diagnosed with cancer and he watched it eat away at her from the inside out. He hadn't been able to cry since *that* night. Yet now here he was. Crying because of his father and what had happened all those years ago.

Crying for his son and the life they could and should have had. If not for that night. And that fucking report card.

CHAPTER 18

The sky was a bruise, staining the world with a jaundiced hue as the sun rose on a day that promised sullen squalls of rain punctured by stabs of bright sun. Just enough to taunt the tourists and those who ventured outside with the prospect of what could be if the Scottish weather threw off the perpetual sulk that passed for late spring.

Standing on the small patio beyond the French windows that led off his living room, Connor breathed in the morning air, using it to try to wake himself up and slough off the residual warmth of the bed, which hung around him like a tempting blanket. At the far end of the garden, a bush quivered, attracting his attention. He smiled as a tortoiseshell cat emerged warily from it, stopping at the border of the lawn.

'Morning, Tom,' Connor said, raising his mug in salute. The cat had started visiting the garden a couple of months ago, warily watching Connor as he indulged in his morning coffee. Connor knew nothing about it, had never got close enough to know if it was male or female, stray or collared. But there was something about the morning meetings he enjoyed so he had taken to opening a can of tuna and leaving it on the patio whenever the cat appeared. It had never deigned to come and eat with him still standing on the patio, but whenever Connor went back to check on the dish, it had been licked clean.

He stepped back into the flat, made up the bowl and laid it on the patio, Tom still watching from the other end of the garden, like a sentry observing enemy troops taking up position.

'Enjoy your breakfast,' Connor called, then stepped back into the flat and headed for the kitchen. Glanced down the corridor to the bedroom door, checked his emails for reports from the team observing Sanderson the night before, then busied himself making poached eggs and fresh coffee while Jen stayed in the bedroom and went through an elaborate morning exercise routine that made Connor wince at the thought of it.

She'd asked him to stay with her as she stretched, offered to show him some moves she promised would help him, but he'd excused himself and left the room. Even though they had shared a bed the night before, he couldn't shake the feeling that watching her morning routine was an intimacy too far. He didn't know what that said about him, or his feelings towards her, but his gran would have a field day with it if he ever told her.

He turned his attention to the mental checklist of tasks he had to complete that day. After his meeting with Robbie, he had checked in with Donna, confirmed that she would be filming the Sanderson interview at Mar's Wark near the castle at eleven. It was the perfect time. The streets would be busy but not overly so, lowering the chance of someone recognising Sanderson and deciding to have a go at him. As an additional precaution, Connor had Robbie organise a car to pick Sanderson up and take him to the interview, then wait nearby in case he had to be hustled out of the area in a hurry. He checked his texts as he cooked, just in case he had missed any updates to the action reports from the team he had stationed at Sanderson's home the night before. Sanderson wouldn't like it if he knew Connor was having the house watched – he had made it clear to Robbie that he neither wanted nor needed any protection – but Connor didn't really care. Let Frontline PR pick up the bill. As far as Connor was concerned, his client was DCI Malcolm Ford.

Christ, he thought, Ford as a customer. How the mighty had fallen. He grunted a laugh as he plated the eggs with wholewheat toast and poured fresh coffee. Called through to the bedroom to tell Jen it was ready, then paused as he looked at the small dining table and the meal he had prepared. How many times, he thought, had his father made breakfast for his mother like this? How many times had he done the same for his son? The thought left him with an ache as hot as his coffee.

Jen walked into the room, cheeks flushed, a light misting of perspiration glistening on her brow. She hesitated for a moment, then leaned forward and kissed him on the cheek. He could feel the heat from her body ripple across his face, smell her sweat as she leaned in. Although she was wearing one of his old T-shirts, which had all the tailoring of a tarpaulin, he was acutely aware of the shape of her body close to his, and felt his breath grow short with arousal and unaccustomed embarrassment.

'Thanks for this,' she said, sitting down at the table. 'I'm starving.'

Connor smiled at that, again marvelling at how much Jen could eat. He had made a massive curry the night before, enough that he was still feeling stuffed, yet here she was, ready to tuck in all over again. The joys of having a job in fitness and the metabolism to eat whatever she wanted.

'So,' she said around a mouthful of egg, 'you going to drop in to see your gran before you start work today?'

Connor sipped his coffee, considered. They had talked about it last night, Jen trying to assure him that his gran's accident at the care home had not been his fault. And yet there was something in the way Ida had exchanged glances with his dad, something almost furtive, that nagged at Connor. He remembered his dad's words – *This is all your bloody fault.* But was it? And how far was he prepared to push it to find out?

'Yeah, probably,' Connor replied. 'I've got a bit of time before my first appointment, so I should probably make sure she's all right.'

Jen smiled, her face becoming a thing of dimples and perfect teeth. Connor felt a sudden urge to kiss her. 'First appointment,' she echoed. 'You do play the man-of-mystery part when it comes to your work, don't you?'

Connor shrugged, self-conscious. He knew it was an outmoded, even sexist attitude, but some less evolved part of him, the part that clubbed animals to death and dragged them back to the family cave, wanted to shield Jen from any contact with Sanderson. From his initial meeting with the man he had formed a powerful dislike of him, despite his own professional involvement, and he wanted to keep Jen as far away from him as possible.

That he would also be spending most of the day with Donna Blake was entirely coincidental.

'Yeah, well,' he said, busying himself rearranging his breakfast. 'Anyway, you never said what your dad wanted to talk to you about. You said it was "something with a bit of history".'

She frowned at him, nose crinkling, as though his clumsy attempt to change the topic of conversation was giving off an odour. 'Nothing really important,' she said at last, her tone telling him she was on to him, and not impressed. 'Just that he's got some old business that's going to keep him busy for a wee while, and he wondered if I could help him out at the yard. Paperwork and the like.'

Connor kept his expression neutral, forced himself not to look over at the couch in the open-plan living room. The couch where, a year ago, Duncan MacKenzie had lain, his back slashed open, Paulie tending the wound, like a nightmare version of Florence Nightingale. Two more people he wanted to shield Jen from. But how?

'Ah, OK,' he said. 'You going out there after your shift? I might have time to—'

He was cut off by the sudden chirping of his phone, the vibration jangling the cutlery on the table slightly. He gave Jen an apologetic nod, picked it up and turned it over. Felt his stomach give a greasy lurch when he read the caller ID. 'Chief Inspector,' he said, the false cheer in his voice grating on his ears and giving his stomach another cold stir. 'Early start for you this morning. How can I—'

'Tell me your people had eyes on Sanderson last night,' Ford said, his voice cold as a wet gravestone.

Connor rose from the table, turned towards the patio doors. Got walking. Felt Jen's eyes on his back, ignored them.

'Yes, why?'

'Your people didn't report anything? Him leaving the house, anything like that?'

Connor felt the room contract around him, as though the air pressure was being turned up, making it an almost tangible thing. He forced himself to breathe. Knew there was no way of avoiding the question he was going to have to ask.

'No, nothing in the action reports from the evening that I've seen.' A moment's pause. 'Why? What's happened?'

Silence on the line, long enough for Connor to wonder if Ford had hung up. And then the policeman's voice, a thin whisper laced with anger, disgust and sorrow. 'A body's been found,' he said. 'Airthrey golf course. Reported by the greens keeper. He found her when he was taking his dog out and checking the course.'

The word hit Connor like a slap. 'Her,' he said, voice low, acutely aware of Jen sitting behind him. 'Was she . . .'

'Yes, Fraser,' Ford replied, exhaustion staining his voice now. 'She was strangled and mutilated. Not got the full post-mortem results back yet, but I'm told the wounds are strikingly similar to those inflicted on the Stirling University victims.'

Connor stared out of his patio windows to the jaundiced world outside. 'Fuck,' he muttered. 'I'll double-check with my people now, but I didn't see anything in the reports from last night. Which means . . .'

'Which means,' Ford said, voice hardening, 'either I was wrong all those years ago and Sanderson wasn't the killer after all, or you've just given a killer an alibi. Now tell me, Connor, which option do you prefer? Because at the moment, I'll be fucked if I know.'

CHAPTER 19

Airthrey golf course was part of Stirling University, tucked away from the central campus behind Airthrey Castle, an eighteenth-century building of sweeping curves crafted from beige stone turned grey by the passage of time. It was close to Ford's home in Bridge of Allan, merely a five-minute drive. The proximity was one of the reasons he and Mary had chosen to move to the village in the first place – it was convenient for Mary to get back and forth from work. But that morning Ford wished the university was on another continent.

The day had made good on its threat of rain, which drummed on the roof of the SOCOs' tent like background static, accompanied occasionally by the bass snap of the tarp as the wind picked up and yanked at it. Ford stood outside the tent, which had been given an almost ethereal glow in the dour day by the heavy spotlights trained on it. He didn't want to go in there, confront the nightmare. Felt, again, the sudden urge just to turn and leave, head home and write his resignation, post it along with his warrant card. He was coming close to retirement age anyway, and hadn't he seen enough horror for one man to endure?

The hard, blunt thud of wood on flesh, screams of pain echoing off cold stone walls, the hot, metallic smell of blood in the air as it splattered onto a concrete floor. And a word, a single word, repeated like a twisted mantra, laden with hate and malice.

'Again.'

Ford's back stiffened against the memory, and a sudden chill that had nothing to do with the wind or the rain. Steeled himself, took a step forward. He deserved this. He needed to see what was in that tent.

After all, it could have been his fault.

He was stopped in his tracks by a huge figure emerging from the tent. Even swathed in a white SOCO suit, Jim Dexter was unmistakable to Ford. He had worked with the crime-scene technician for years, developed a friendship grounded in black comedy and casual callousness that those who worked close to death fostered as a coping mechanism.

'Morning, Jim,' he said as the big man pulled down his protective face mask, revealing a ginger beard that was rapidly retreating in the face of an onslaught of white whiskers and ruddy cheeks that always made Ford think of some kindly uncle.

'Aye, mornin', Malcolm,' Jim replied, his watery eyes staring directly into Ford's. 'Hell of a way to start a day.'

'Bad?' Ford asked, a sliver of ice tracing its way down his spine.

Jim's gaze didn't waver, but the pinching of his lips and the creasing around his eyes told Ford everything he didn't want to know.

'Take a look for yourself,' he said at last, his voice thin. 'But, aye, it's bad. Female, early twenties I'd say. Blunt-force trauma to the head and upper body. Lacerations across the upper chest area, stomach and lower abdomen.'

'Lacerations?' The word was bitter ash in Ford's mouth. 'You mean?'

'Aye,' Jim said, his Highland roots expressing themselves in the word. 'She was mutilated, Malcolm. Breasts. Genitals.' He sighed, drew a hand across his beard. It wasn't steady. 'It's a real fucking mess, Malcolm. Whoever did this is one sick bastard.'

Morgan's voice in Ford's head now, low and insistent. *You know it was him, Malcolm.*

He took a breath, steadied himself. 'OK, better go take a look. Just give me a minute to nip back to the ops van and I'll get a suit on, then—'

'Sir? DCI Ford?'

Ford turned to see Detective Sergeant Jason Troughton jogging across the grass towards him. Even at this hour, in this damaged and sullen day, he managed to look awake and eager, ready for duty in a way Ford was sure he had never been. Again, the thought of just writing the letter called to him. He could be home in five minutes . . .

'Yes, Troughton, what is it?'

The detective sergeant held up a mobile phone then offered it to Ford, as though they were in some perverse relay team and it was his turn to carry the baton.

Or the can.

'Sorry to interrupt, sir, it's just, well . . .' he gestured forward with the phone again '. . . it's the chief, sir. Says he tried calling you on your own phone, got sent to voicemail.' Troughton gave the statement the same gravity he would give a death knock to a bereaved parent. 'He says he needs to speak to you. Now.'

CHAPTER 20

After Jen had left, Connor checked in with Robbie and the team covering the Sanderson house. As he'd suspected, they reported that Sanderson had gone out with his dad to a local pub, stayed for a few hours, then returned home. Given Sanderson's insistence that he didn't want round-the-clock security, Robbie's team hadn't kept an eye on the house all night, but had instead made check-in patrols every hour, while insisting that Sanderson call them if there were any problems at the property.

So, Sanderson could have slipped out during one of those windows when the team was not on patrol. But, Connor thought, would he? And even if he had, could he have been the killer? The university was a twenty-minute drive from Sanderson's home in Cambusbarron. Assuming that the killer's victim was taken from there, there was still the small matter of grabbing her, killing her, then getting the body across to the other side of the campus and the golf course. All of which, Connor calculated, would take a couple of hours. So if it had been Sanderson, he would have returned home, slipped out when the house was unwatched and his father asleep, killed the girl, then slipped back in without being detected.

Possible, Connor thought. Schrödinger's Killer. While the house door was closed, he was both guilty and innocent.

Connor leaned back in the couch, looked to the ceiling as he felt the frustration prickle and build in him. Ford had promised to call him once he had visited the crime scene, check what the Sentinel teams had to report, which gave Connor time to write up an official statement for Ford's investigation. Problem was, what was he meant to say? 'We surveilled the client's property but, per his instructions, not on a round-the-clock basis. The window of opportunity exists for him to have left the family residence unseen and later returned to it. Our logs show no unusual activity on the street or in the locus of the property during the time window in which we assume the victim was attacked and murdered. Sorry, Chief Inspector, but flip a coin on this one.'

With a sigh, Connor pushed aside the laptop. It was only then that he noticed the item on the coffee-table, propped up against a candle-holder, a Post-it note stuck to it.

He leaned forward, picked it up. The report card he had found, with a note from Jen: 'Check on your gran. It'll give you peace of mind, make you less of a bear to deal with tonight. Thanks for breakfast. Jx.'

He peeled the Post-it note from the report card with a smile, looked at it. He hadn't intended for anything serious to develop with Jen but, increasingly, he felt the lines between their lives blurring and merging. After what had happened in Belfast with his ex, Karen, Connor wasn't sure he was ready for another serious relationship. But what say did he have in the matter?

He dismissed the thought, concentrated instead on the report card. Rubbed the grainy, russet-brown splodge at its corner with his thumb, his dad's words echoing through his mind. *That bloody report card.*

Question was, had he been talking figuratively or literally?

He sighed, laid the card aside. Too many questions. Not enough answers.

One thing at a time, Connor, he told himself. He dropped to the floor, started doing press-ups, letting the pain from his muscles burn away his thoughts, allow him to focus. He was up to seventy-five when he heard the phone chitter on the coffee-table. He picked it up, fully expecting to see Ford's caller ID on the screen.

Gritted his teeth when he read the number. Shit. Should have known. 'Morning, Donna,' he said.

CHAPTER 21

She was perfection.

After all these years, after all the fantasies and plotting and waiting, I had feared that the reality would somehow be hollow or would disappoint. That it would pale against the fantasies I had painted on those seemingly endless nights when I lay awake, wondering if I would ever be free.

I shouldn't have worried. It was everything I had hoped. And more. From the look of terrified surprise in her eyes the moment I took her, to the scalding heat of her panting breath on my hand, to the first glorious red eruption as my knife parted flesh, it was perfection.

I know they must have the body by now – I left it in an obvious enough place. I could have hidden it and, in many ways, it would have been wiser to do so. But I have taken precautions. Besides, what is the point of great art if it is not to be seen and appreciated? And last night was art. I admit that some of my strokes were hesitant and rusty, and I rushed in my excitement after all these years, but art is art. And this was only my first draft, a sketch of the masterpiece I will craft.

Blake will no doubt have questions. Let her ask them. It's all part of the game. A game that will truly begin the moment I see her reporting my work on television. And she will. After all, this is her story to tell.

What she doesn't know yet is her central role in the story. But that's fine. There is time. Finally, after all these years, there is time. And when I come to crafting my masterpiece, it will be sculpted from Donna Blake's blood and tears.

CHAPTER 22

Ford sat in his living room, pen in hand, paper in front of him. He had poured himself a large Glenfiddich, only a glance at the clock telling him it was not yet nine a.m. stopping him downing it in one gulp.

He felt another wave of anger scald his thoughts, cursed himself for not predicting what was going to happen. After all, Chief Constable Peter Guthrie had won his job as much for his political acumen and ability to solve embarrassing problems as for any practical policing experience he possessed. He was a new breed of copper, recruited from university and put on the career fast-track to the top. One who placed budgets and bureaucracy over proper on-the-street policing, who was more concerned about positive headlines than the mechanics of getting the job done. Which was why he had called Ford.

'Look, Malcolm,' he said, his voice dripping with a false sincerity that set Ford's teeth on edge. 'I know you're on scene now, and I'm sorry to do this, but there's no way I can have you associated with the investigation of this murder. There's just too much baggage with your connection to the original Sanderson inquiry.'

Ford took in a deep breath, focused on the SOCO tent as it flapped and twisted in the wind. 'Sir, with all due respect, I think you've got this backwards. My familiarity with the original Sanderson inquiry makes me the perfect choice to be senior investigating officer on this murder. No one knows the Sanderson case better than I do. If this was him, I'll know it.'

A sigh on the line. 'I'm sorry, Malcolm, but that's the point. We've already got a bloody nose from his acquittal and the review we're having to conduct because of it. You on this case just adds to our problem. And, be honest here, Malcolm, can you tell me, hand on heart, that you would be a dispassionate investigator? That your past experience with Sanderson wouldn't colour your view of this case?'

Ford opened his mouth, closed it as a memory rose up in him like bile.

The hard, blunt thud of wood on flesh, screams of pain echoing off cold stone walls, the hot, metallic smell of blood in the air as it splattered onto a concrete floor. And a word, a single word, repeated like a twisted mantra, laden with hate and malice.

'Again.'

He blinked, forced the memory away. Not now. Not when a girl was lying dead less than twenty feet in front of him, her body violated in unspeakable ways. Later. He could feel guilt later.

'Sir,' he said, through clenched teeth as he unconsciously snapped to attention. 'I can assure you that I will approach this case with the same professionalism that I apply to all my work. From what the forensics team tell me, there are obvious similarities between this murder and the university killings back in 2006. Guilty of those crimes or not, Sanderson is a link here. Which makes me part of this, one way or another.'

'Yes, yes,' Guthrie said, weary boredom seeping into his tone, as though Ford was a child he had told repeatedly to tidy away his toys without success. 'Look, Malcolm, I'm sorry, the decision is made. You're right, you are involved in this, so you'll act as liaison to DCI Alan Ross's team and offer them every assistance.'

Ford bit back the curse he felt his tongue curl around. 'Sir, with all due respect, DCI Ross is—'

'Is a dedicated and proficient police officer who will be leading this investigation. He's already at Sanderson's home, verifying his movements last night. I expect you to give him every assistance, DCI Ford. Is that clear?'

'Crystal, sir,' Ford had replied, tone as cold as the rain.

'Very good. I expect your handover report shortly,' Guthrie said.

'Oh, and, Ford, keep your phone on the next time you visit a crime scene, will you? Last thing I need is to be chasing your subordinates to find you.'

Ford had muttered a response, then killed the call. Handed the phone back to Troughton as he passed him and headed for his car. The drive home was a blank spot in his mind: one minute he was at the golf course, the next he was rattling his front-door key into the lock.

And now he sat at his dining table, ready to write the letter Mary had wanted him to write for years. Tell Guthrie to take his job and stuff it, take almost three decades of policing and turn it into another statistic, a pensioning-off of more senior officers to trim the budget and make way for new, cheaper blood.

He grabbed for the whisky, raised it to his lips. Felt the peaty tang of the liquor bite at his nostrils, tempt his tongue. Nine a.m. But it was dinner time somewhere in the world, wasn't it? And, besides, this was a special occasion: it deserved a toast.

He was about to drink when he was interrupted by the ring of the doorbell. He frowned, put the glass down. Padded through to the front door, hoping it was a Jehovah's Witness or a politician out canvassing. Someone he could vent his fury at.

He swung the door open, felt his legs go weak and his head spin as a ghost from the past stared back at him.

'Hello, Malcolm,' DCI Dennis Morgan said. 'Hope you don't mind. Desk sergeant at Randolphfield told me you were home. Mind if I come in? I think we need to talk.'

CHAPTER 23

Donna sat huddled in the front seat of the broadcast van as her cameraman, Keith, worked in the back, packing up his camera and microphones, humming a tuneless dirge that unsettled her almost as badly as the cold that seemed to have seeped into her bones.

She glanced at her watch: 9.10 a.m. and she had already gone live with an exclusive on the discovery of a body at Airthrey golf course. A quick glance at her phone showed that the story was starting to dominate the domestic news schedule, other media outlets scrambling to catch up on her work. She smiled at that despite the cold. Donna Blake, landing the big stories first. Again. Look at me now, Mum.

The call had come just after seven, as she was getting Andrew ready for pre-school. He went three days a week, his care the rest of the time Donna was working split between her parents and Sam, one of the carers at the pre-school who was grateful for the extra money. Donna's mother hated the arrangement, moaned that her daughter was working too hard and that her grandson shouldn't be left with strangers so often. But Donna shrugged off these complaints. After all, she knew first-hand what type of damage too much time in the care of Irene Blake could do.

'Yes, Mr Sanderson,' she said, trying to keep the exasperation out of her tone. When she had given him her number, she hadn't expected wake-up calls from the man. 'How are you this morning? Looking forward to talking to you later on.'

'You might want tae talk to the polis about that,' Sanderson had replied, words punctuated by a soft sucking sound that told Donna he was smoking.

She froze. 'Police? Mr Sanderson, what do you mean, police?'

'Just had a visit from a copper. Some lassie's been killed and, of course, they wanted to know where I was last night. It's harassment, Blake, and I want to get that on the record. Now.'

Donna felt the world lurch around her, a thousand thoughts crowding and colliding in her brain. 'You're telling me a woman was murdered last night? Where?'

'Fucking pig wouldn't say, but they asked if I'd been around the university last night, so I'm assuming it was somewhere close. And because I was fitted up for the other murders, they're trying to pin this one on me as well.'

Donna paused, forced herself to breathe. Felt a rush of relief as she heard a key jangle in the lock of her front door – her parents arriving to take Andrew to pre-school. She moved into the hallway, gave her dad an apologetic smile as she gestured to the phone, then pointed to the living room, where Andrew was happily playing amid a rabble of toys on the rug.

'Go on, Mr Sanderson,' she said. 'What happened?'

'Nowt more than that,' he said. 'Some copper called Ross turned up at my door, asked me to account for my whereabouts last night. Told him I was out with my da for a couple of pints, then back haime. Fucking harassment, Blake. I'm an innocent man.'

'Have you spoken to your lawyer yet, told him about this?' she asked.

'Gonnae call him as soon as I get off the phone with you. I want to get on the TV today, Blake, tell my side of the story. Get in front of this. I'll no' be called a killer again.'

Donna bit down on the excitement that surged up her throat. She needed a moment to think. Would the police let Sanderson go on air when a body had just been found? More importantly, could they stop him? Probably not, but what did this mean for the interview planned for later in the day, or the book that was meant to come from it?

No, she told herself. Stop. Focus. One thing at a time. Tell the story in front of you now, not the story two hours from now. 'Look, Mr Sanderson, I'll check up on this now, get back to you as soon as I can. In the meantime, call your legal team and tell them what's happened. I'll be speaking to them later as well.'

She ended the call, then focused on making sure Andrew and her parents were organised. Ignoring the disapproving looks from Irene, she explained the situation, then retreated to her makeshift study. Her first call was to Keith who, thankfully, was already heading to Stirling from Sky's Edinburgh office 'to make sure I beat the traffic'. She redirected him to the golf course, then checked the news wires and her emails, unsurprised to see there was no official release from Police Scotland on the discovery of a body. Which meant the story was hers.

It took only three more calls for everything to fall into place. The first was to Danny Brooks, a journalist turned police press officer she knew from her time at the *Westie* in Glasgow. Thanks to that relationship, and her knowledge of Danny's fondness for settling gambling debts with doctored expense claims, it didn't take her long to convince him to share what he knew about the discovery of a body at Airthrey golf course in the early hours of the morning. After that, it was a call to the newsdesk at Sky to tell them what she had and request a live slot in the morning news line-up. The last call was the one she was both looking forward to and dreading, the one she knew she couldn't avoid.

'Connor, how you doing this morning?' she asked. 'Take it you've heard the news?'

'News?' Connor replied, tone noncommittal.

'Come on, don't give me that. Police have already been at Sanderson's place, checking on his whereabouts. No doubt they've checked in with you as well to see if you've got any record of him leaving his house last night. Which brings me neatly to why I'm calling you.'

'Donna, we've been through this. I can't discuss operational matters with you. Sanderson can tell you what he wants, but I can't get into specifics.'

'But the police have been in touch with you?'

'No comment,' Connor replied, the barest hint of humour lifting his voice.

'Fair enough,' she said. 'I'm heading out to report on the story, but then how about we meet up for a coffee? This story's going to run for a while, and I don't know how it's going to affect our plans to interview Sanderson later on today.'

'OK, call me when you're done,' Connor said, distracted now, almost as if she had reminded him of something.

He ended the call before she had the chance to ask him what that might be. Frustrated, she got moving, heading for the golf course. Felt the familiar thrill when she saw two police cars stationed at the entrance, two pissed-off uniformed officers standing guard in the wind and the rain. Keith arrived five minutes later, by which time she had managed to squeeze the barest of facts out of the Police Scotland press team. Yes, officers were called to Airthrey golf course at six this morning after a report of a body being found in scrubland bordering the first tee. No, no identity for the victim had been established yet. No the death was not being treated as accidental. Yes, the victim was female.

Donna made notes, then got herself ready, dread rising in her stomach, sour and choking, as she thought about going on live television. She let Keith get her ready, adjust her earpiece, frame the shot, and started talking when he waved her into action.

As ever, she remembered nothing of what she said during the report, but Keith assured her that it was fine. Now, sitting in the van, watching the story explode across the wires and social media, she knew it had been.

'. . . breakfast?' Keith asked.

Donna pulled her attention from her phone. 'Huh? What?' she said, turning to him.

'Breakfast?' he said. 'Do you want to go and get some breakfast before we meet up with Sanderson later on?'

Donna flashed back to the last time she had eaten with Keith, a lunch in the centre of town. On that occasion, she'd guessed only about 40 per cent of his meal had made it to his mouth, the rest of it finding a home on the T-shirt that was stretched tight over his pendulous gut. It wasn't an experience she was keen to repeat. 'No, thanks, Keith,' she said. 'I've got to meet a contact in town anyway. Why don't you get something to eat, then recce the shooting site at the top of the town? I can give you a buzz when I know what's happening.'

'Right,' he said, the sudden disappointment that flashed across his pale, acne-encrusted face almost making Donna feel sorry for him. Almost.

She said her goodbyes, then headed for her car. Plipped the locks and got the engine running. Pinged Connor a quick text to tell him she was heading for Cambusbarron, and they could find a coffee shop there to compare notes before she went to see Sanderson. She was just putting the car into gear when she got a single-word reply: *OK.*

She smiled. Connor Fraser. Man of a thousand words. Fine. She didn't need him chatty, she just needed him beside her. Because, for reasons she couldn't quite explain, she didn't want to meet Colin Sanderson without Connor at her side.

CHAPTER 24

Ford invited Morgan in, hastily clearing the stationery and whisky from the dining table as he gestured for his old boss to take a seat. Instead, Morgan stood in the centre of the living room, taking it in. Ford didn't mind – it gave him a chance to do the same to the man in front of him.

Morgan hadn't changed much. The years had faded his hair to a dusky grey and etched itself into his features, which were slacker than Ford remembered, but he still had an air of solidity and strength about him that was somehow both reassuring and disconcerting.

'Coffee, guv?' Ford asked.

Morgan turned to face him. Held up a hand that was twisted and gnarled with arthritis. 'Enough of that for a start,' he said. 'I retired years ago and, besides, we're the same rank now anyway. So Dennis, OK?'

'All right, Dennis,' Ford repeated, the name alien in his mouth. 'So, coffee?'

Something hardened in Morgan's eyes. 'No, thanks, Malcolm,' he said. 'You know why I'm here, of course?'

Ford took a seat, waited for Morgan to settle himself on the couch opposite him. 'I take it it's about the murder up at Airthrey this morning.'

'Yes,' Morgan said. 'I saw the report on the TV, knew it was only a matter of time. I told you, didn't I, Malcolm? He's an animal. A predator.'

The hard, blunt thud of wood on flesh, screams of pain echoing off cold stone walls, the hot, metallic smell of blood in the air as it splattered onto a concrete floor. And a word, a single word, repeated like a twisted mantra, laden with hate and malice.

'Again.'

Ford blinked away the memory, shifted in his seat, saw Morgan stare at him expectantly. 'I'm not sure what to say. The officers investigating are checking on Sanderson's movements now, but my understanding is that he may have an alibi.'

Morgan nodded. Then: 'Hold on, what do you mean "officers investigating"? Tell me you're SIO on this, Malcolm, for God's sake.'

Ford shook his head, the thought of the paper and pen rising in his mind again. ''Fraid not. With my links to the initial investigation of Sanderson, the chief feels I'm too much of a risk for this case. So he's replaced me with DCI Ross. I'm to offer every assistance.'

'Christ's sake!' Morgan barked. 'What the fuck is that little wanker thinking of? You're the ideal man to lead this investigation and pin that bastard Sanderson to the wall once and for all, show that fucking judge how wrong he was.'

Ford took a deep breath. 'With all due respect, sir, we don't know this was Sanderson. I agree it's a huge coincidence, and I'm told the victim was mutilated in a similar way to the original victims but, as I said, he may have an alibi for last night. Which means . . .'

'It means nothing,' Morgan said, anger and defiance darkening his tone. 'He did it, Malcolm. All those years ago. And now. We both know it. For fuck's sake, you were there.'

Ford stood, seized by the impulse to move, as though he could escape the memory that was crowding into his thoughts like an old nightmare. 'Yes, sir, but we both know we, ah, cut a few corners. What if we were wrong? What if it wasn't him at all and the judge was right? What if there was another killer then and now?'

Morgan gave a bitter laugh. 'Oh, come on, Malcolm,' he said. 'Sanderson is put away for more than a decade. Then he gets out and a couple of days later a woman is found murdered in exactly the same way as his victims were? Give me a break. I told you back then he's an animal. He got the taste for it and now he's free to get back to killing.

And, trust me, he's not going to stop this time. You have to put him away. Now.'

Ford wandered to the fireplace, frustration building. 'I'm not sure what you want me to say. I'm off the case, chief's orders. I'm only a liaison to give them background on the Sanderson investigation you led. Other than that—'

'Well, use it,' Morgan said. 'Tell this – what was it? – Ross what you know. Make sure he sees Sanderson as we saw him back then.'

And, Ford thought suddenly, keep him away from some parts of the investigation that we don't want anyone looking at too closely. The parts that lead to chairs and warehouses and planks of wood and blood. Is that why Morgan was here? To make sure his reputation went untarnished? To keep their secrets in the shadows? Made sense. 'I'll do what I can, sir,' he said at last. 'But I can't promise anything. It's not the same force as it was back in your day. It's all action reports, spreadsheets and budgets now.'

Morgan gave another sneer. 'Fuck that,' he spat. 'You're a copper, Malcolm. You'll do the right thing.'

The right thing? Ford thought. I thought I was doing that fourteen years ago. 'You want that coffee now?' he asked, suddenly unsure of what else to say and wanting to veer the conversation away from any more unpleasant recollections.

'Aye, go on,' Morgan said, glancing at his watch. 'Michael said he'd pick me up in an hour, so I've got time.'

'Ah, Michael,' Ford said, recognition arcing across his mind. 'How is he? Was I mistaken or did I see him with you at the hearing where Sanderson's conviction was quashed?'

Morgan's face tightened, the memory obviously unpleasant. Couldn't have been much fun seeing his case dismantled in front of him like that. 'Yeah, he was with me,' Morgan said. 'Moral support. He's a good lad, working in Edinburgh now, making the big money as a politics lecturer at the university.'

'Really?' Ford said, unable to keep the surprise out of his voice. He had only met Michael Morgan a couple of times, but the stories his father told were of a sporty, active kid who was more interested in going out with friends than studying. But then, he thought, remembering the young sergeant he had been all those years ago, people can change.

Morgan gave a prideful smile, and again Ford wondered what that would feel like. To watch your child grow and exceed your own accomplishments, see them fulfil the dreams you had not even imagined. And in that moment he thought of Mary, and the sacrifice she had made to forge a life with him. She deserved better.

He clapped his hands together. 'Right, coffee. How do you take it, sir? Still black, one sugar?'

'Still sharp, Malcolm,' Morgan said. 'Very good. Yes, please. But do me a favour and add a dram of that whisky you were trying to hide, will you?'

CHAPTER 25

After a text from Donna informing him that *There's no café open in Cambusbarron after all*, Connor picked up some takeaway coffees and arranged to meet her in a car park that was adjacent to the village's community centre just off Main Street. He spotted her car as he drove in, flashed his lights. The rain was heavier now, tap-tapping on the windscreen and smearing his view of the world as he parked. A gust of cold air invaded the car as Donna swung the passenger door of the Audi open and dropped into the seat. 'What a sodding morning,' she said as she accepted the coffee he offered her.

'You talking about the weather or the way the day's going?' Connor asked. 'Nice work on the report, by the way. Bet that pissed off the police no end.'

Donna smiled around her coffee cup. 'Thanks. Slightly surprised, though. I thought DCI Ford would have left at least three sweary rants on my phone just now, but so far, nothing.'

'He's probably got his hands full,' Connor replied, deadpan. He had seen this in Donna before, a habit of putting the story she was working on at the centre of her universe and everyone else's. Who cared if Ford had a murder investigation to co-ordinate? That was only a minor inconvenience. What mattered was how he reacted to Donna's report. And how she could use that reaction to play him.

'So, how do you want to do this?' Connor asked. 'You know I can't tell you anything related to our security arrangements for Sanderson.

I can work with you to secure the location of the filming, and give best advice, but I can't go into anything outside that.'

Donna lifted a hand, swatted away his objection. 'Doesn't matter, he'll tell me anything I want. You should have heard him on the phone this morning, Connor. The man is desperate to prove he's innocent, and he's going to cry police harassment from the top of his lungs until he gets everyone to listen.'

And you're going to give him just the platform to do that from, Connor thought. 'So, where have you decided to do the filming?' he asked.

'Still going ahead up at Mar's Wark – you know, next to the castle,' she said. 'I thought maybe the weather would mess things up, but it's quite atmospheric, don't you think? Wrongly convicted man walking the rain-swept streets, talking about the injustice he's suffered?'

Connor bit back a sigh. The story. Always the bloody story. 'I'm just there to advise,' he said. 'It's a public space, which increases the danger for Sanderson. That's assuming he can talk to you today. The police might take a dim view of that with an active murder investigation going on. An investigation he's linked to, one way or another.'

'One way or another?' she asked, turning in her seat to face him fully for the first time. 'You don't really think he did this, do you?'

Ford's words now. *He's an animal, Fraser. He did this.*

'I don't know,' he replied, looking out of the windscreen, as though the answer lay there, beyond the veil of rain. 'On the one hand, it's a hell of a coincidence that he's freed and a woman dies a few days later. On the other, would he be that stupid? He would know he'd be the first person the police would look at for it. Would he really risk going back inside? Bottom line, I don't know, Donna. But either way, we're both tied up in this mess, so we'd better make the best of it.'

Donna nodded, drank some more coffee. 'OK,' she said. 'Here's what I'm thinking. We go to Sanderson's place, make arrangements for the interview. You make whatever suggestions you want regarding his security, but I think we both know he's not going to like it. Then we take it from there.'

'And what about the police?' Connor asked, thinking again of Ford. 'They're not going to like this at all.'

'Tough,' Donna said. 'Unless they've charged him with anything, he's a free man with as much of a right to tell his story to the press as you or I.' She paused. Considered. 'Speaking of which, you changed your mind about giving me that interview?'

'Absolutely not,' Connor said, a warning tone creeping into his voice. 'I told you, Donna, keep me out of this. I'm not the story here, Sanderson is.'

She gave him a smile that told him she had been teasing. 'OK, let's go. Think it's safe enough to leave my car here? I really don't want to get lashed by that sodding wind and rain again before I see Sanderson.'

'Fair enough,' Connor said, stowing his coffee in the centre console's cup-holder and firing the engine. He turned out of the car park, following the main street until he hit Sanderson's street. Didn't take long to find a space: most of the residents had left for work, leaving plenty of gaps next to the pavement. He drove up to the top of the street and turned, wanting the Audi pointing towards the main road. Wasn't even a conscious decision on his part, just training. Always have your vehicle positioned for the fastest possible egress from a location. Turning the car around would take precious seconds.

He pressed a button on the dash, disabling the proximity sensors. If he wanted to, he could have let the car park itself. But he disabled the sensors for the same reason he never used cruise control and always drove a manual. There were some things a machine just could not and should not do. He was reversing into a space, arm slung over the back of Donna's seat as he peered out of the back window, when he spotted it. Further up the hill, nose nudging out of a side-street, just enough so the driver could watch the house Connor was now parking in front of. A black Mercedes, immaculate even in the gloom of the morning rain. Connor didn't need to see the driver to know who it was. He could picture him, sitting squeezed into the driver's seat, shirt sleeves rolled up as he chewed on the stub of a cheap cigar he refused to smoke in the car in case he tainted the fresh smell of the leather.

He finished parking, checked Donna was ready, kept his face casual. Didn't look up the street when he got out of the car and headed for Sanderson's door. But even as he knocked, his mind was already on Paulie, and the conversation they would have as soon as this meeting was over.

CHAPTER 26

After Morgan's son had picked his father up, Ford made a decision. He packed away the stationery and the whisky, then headed out to the car to retrieve his case files. Technically, it was a breach of procedure to keep any in a car, even one that was locked and in a secure driveway, but it was an unwritten rule Ford had made when he became a police officer – nothing connected with that life would cross the threshold of his home any time Mary was in the house. He wanted to keep her as far away as possible from the world he was forced to live in. Which explained his decision. The first victims had been taken from Stirling University, a short drive from here and Mary's place of work. If the killer was following the pattern and this morning's victim had been taken from the university as well, Ford wanted to stop him.

No one hunted around Mary. No one.

He retrieved the file from the boot, spread its contents across the dining-room table. It was the same as the file he had given Fraser, everything that had been collected on the original university murders back in 2006. It was the case they had built against Sanderson, brick by brick, statement by statement, fact by fact.

He paused to make himself another coffee, then picked up his phone. Hesitated for a second, then berated himself for putting off the unpleasant task like a petulant child. Dialled the number and waited, eyes strafing the case file as he did.

'Ross.' The answer came in a clipped, precise tone.

'Alan, it's Malcolm Ford. I thought we should talk.'

'Ah, Malcolm, thanks for calling. Yes, the chief told me you'd be assisting on this one when he got me up to speed.'

Assisting? Ford swallowed back the insult. He knew Ross only by reputation – a detective transferred from the Borders when Police Scotland was created, he was known to be more of a bureaucrat than a beat cop. He ground his way through cases, like an accountant totting up columns on a spreadsheet. His clearance rate was like everything else Ford had heard about the man: mediocre. But he followed procedure and never made waves. Which was why he was perfect for Guthrie's needs. After all, why worry about finding a murderer when there was a reputation to protect?

'So, what have you got so far?' Ford asked.

'Not a lot at this stage. Body has just been sent to Dr Tennant for the post-mortem examination. I'm due to meet him at one o'clock to discuss the results.'

'Any preliminary findings?' Ford asked, Jim Dexter's words flashing through his mind. *It's a real fucking mess, Malcolm. Whoever did this is one sick bastard.*

'Couple of things, ' Ross said. 'And this is where your expertise might come in useful. The victim, we've yet to identify her, was heavily mutilated. Stab wounds to the chest and lower abdomen. Sound familiar?'

Ford closed his eyes, pushed back the images strobing across his mind. Rhona Everett, her flesh turning grey and marbling as death atrophied it, accentuating the violent wounds inflicted on her body. They stood out like scarlet explosions on the chest, which had been reduced to little more than a mound of minced meat. It was as if an animal had got to the body before they had found it. In some ways, Ford thought that was right.

'All too familiar,' he said, his voice a whisper through clenched teeth. 'That's consistent with the injuries inflicted on the victims we had, until recently, attributed to Colin Sanderson. Speaking of whom . . .'

'Ah, yes, Mr Sanderson,' Ross replied, his voice betraying a note of disgust that gave Ford a strange kind of hope for the investigation. 'I met with him first thing this morning. His father corroborates his alibi for last night, that they were at the pub then home without going back out. Not that that's anything concrete – he could have slipped out of the house while his father was sleeping. Though I believe you know the man who's providing security for him through the PR firm that's working for him?'

'Yeah, Connor Fraser at Sentinel Securities. I had a brief conversation with him earlier. I know they were running some sort of surveillance around Sanderson last night, though I'm not sure how close it was or whether it'll be any use to us.'

A pause on the line, just long enough for Ford to realise his mistake. 'Us?' Ross said finally. 'You know you're only advising on the historical aspect of this, Malcolm? The chief was explicit that you play no part in the active investigation.'

Ford ground his teeth again, thought suddenly of the whisky he had poured for Morgan earlier. 'I'm only trying to help, Alan. I understand the chief's reluctance to have me involved but, bottom line, there's a killer out there and, if I'm right, this is only the start.'

Morgan's words now. *Two is only one away from three.*

'Understood,' Ross said. 'Well, let's hope Tennant can give me something to work on. In the meantime, if you could supply me with the contact details for this Connor Fraser, I'd be grateful.'

Ford thought about offering to contact Connor himself, dismissed the idea. It was clear that Ross was going to toe the line on this, do it by the book. Just like the chief wanted. He agreed to text Connor's contact details to Ross, arranged a meeting with him at Randolphfield that afternoon for the 'official case handover'. What Ross didn't know was that Ford would be taking an indirect route to the meeting, one that would just happen to put him in Dr Walter Tennant's office. Then he killed the call, turned to the folder on the dining table and dived into his own past, looking for something, anything, he might have missed all those years ago.

CHAPTER 27

The rain had beaten a reluctant retreat by the time Connor drove into Stirling, but it had done its work, staining the buildings dirty greys and tired beiges to match the colour of the sky, making the cobbles glisten like dark, slippery jewels in what little light there was.

The plan they had agreed on with Sanderson was a simple one. They would drive from Cambusbarron in a convoy to Stirling, using the Stirling Highland Hotel at the top of the town as a makeshift base of operations. Connor had called ahead and agreed the use of parking and a conference room with the hotel manager, who owed him a favour. Sanderson would travel with Robbie, Donna in her car trailing them, Connor bringing up the rear. He made the sequencing of the cars seem casual, almost random, but spent the entire trip searching his rear-view mirror for any further sign of Paulie.

Once they reached the Highland, they met Donna's cameraman, Keith, a kid who, to Connor, had the complexion of a pizza and a body that looked like it had been sculpted from a wad of cookie dough. He made little effort to hide his enthusiasm for his work and Donna, raving about the 'brooding light' and the 'fantastic backdrop for the filming'. After clipping portable microphones to Donna and Sanderson, they ventured out onto the street and walked back down the steep hill a little towards the entrance to the Old Town Jail. From here, they would shoot what was called a 'walk and talk', Donna and Sanderson walking up the hill towards the skeletal remains of Mar's

Wark, Keith filming, lots of expressive hand gestures, sympathetic nods and looks of deep empathy and understanding from Donna. It was, like most of TV, a trick. The full interview would be done in the conference room at the Highland, the footage from the street spliced in by Keith during the editing process.

Connor watched as they went through the timetable of events, wondering if they would get to do the interview and how much, if any, of what was shot today would be used. On the drive there, he had had a call from a DCI Ross, who explained he would be taking the lead on the murder inquiry launched that morning. Connor had felt a strange mixture of confusion and relief. While he wasn't sure why Ford wasn't calling him as arranged, he was more than happy to tell Ross of the planned filming. Suspect or not, there was something about Sanderson going on camera while a murder investigation was kicking into high gear that bothered him, and he half hoped that Ross would make good on his threat to have the whole set-up shut down before it ever hit TV screens.

'You ready?' Donna asked Sanderson, who was shuffling from side to side now, shoulders slumped, his dismissive attitude briefly punctured by the presence of the camera and the prospect of telling his story. In that moment, in the snatched, nervous glances at the camera, Connor saw a different man from the one he had previously encountered, the one Ford's briefing had conditioned him to expect. Instead of a hardened, cynical man, who had been left twisted and embittered by more than a decade in prison, he saw a tired middle-aged man who had adopted defiance as a survival mechanism. He had spent years screaming into the void and now here he was, about to tell the story he really wanted to tell. The question Connor was forced to ask was, what if that story was true? Had Ford and his colleagues been wrong all those years ago? Was the man standing in front of him now a miscarriage-of-justice victim after all?

Or was he something else? Something altogether worse?

Connor raised a hand, telling Donna to hold on for a moment. He clicked on the mic in his shirt sleeve, pushed the earbud deeper into his ear. 'Comms check,' he said. 'Alpha Tango to Charlie One. You there, Robbie?'

'Copy that, boss. We're here and in position. Ready when you are.'
Connor looked up the street. The arrangement was simple, and the
best they could get Sanderson to agree to. Connor would follow him
and Donna as they did their filmed walk, with Robbie waiting in a
car opposite Mar's Wark, ready to scoop them up in case there was
any kind of problem. Connor doubted there would be: the weather
had mostly emptied the streets, leaving only pedestrians who were
too focused on getting to where they were going and out of the cold
to worry about what was going on around them. But, still, there was a
job to do, and Connor hated leaving anything to chance.

'Copy that, moving now,' he said, then cut the line.

He nodded to Donna who, after a brief glance at Keith, touched
Sanderson gently on the arm and they got walking. Connor held
back a couple of steps, just enough to give him a wide view of the
street around them and who might be ahead. But even as he walked,
his thoughts were turning back to Paulie. He felt a fleeting pang of
doubt, crushed it. No, it wasn't paranoia on his part. He had seen that
car trailing Jen often enough to know it when he saw it. No, Paulie
was keeping an eye on Colin Sanderson, either on the orders of Jen's
father, Duncan, or on his own initiative.

The question was, why?

He realised they were passing the entrance to Cowane's Hospital
and the entrance to the Church of the Holy Rude. Felt an old pain
whisper in his leg as he walked past the gates, the sudden memory of
a blade being sunk deep into his thigh flaring across his mind. Had it
really been only three years ago that he had confronted Amy Hughes
there, in the grounds of the church? It felt like a lifetime.

He turned away, concentrated on the task in hand. Saw that
Donna and Sanderson had opened up a little more of a lead on him
and quickened his pace to catch up. They slowed as they arrived outside Mar's Wark, the ancient skeleton of the palace seeming to brood
over them in the rain-strained light of the morning. Connor kept
walking, up to the junction of the street, where Mar Place split off
to run up to the castle or back into the centre of town. Turned when
a sudden burst of swearing filled the air, watched as a man wrestled
boxes out of an old Transit van and into a restaurant in what looked

like an old Georgian townhouse at the corner of the street. One of the boxes had burst, bottles of condiment now rolling down the cobbles, staining them with reds and greens and oranges, as though a child had been asked to colour in the drab, rain-soaked picture of the day. A second man emerged from the restaurant and slipped on the cobbles, repeating the trick that had obviously caused the problem for the van driver. More swearing, a pinwheeling of arms, the driver moving with a surprising grace, catching the other man by the arm and propping him up against the van. The other, probably a chef from the whites he was wearing, swatted the driver away, took a moment to catch his breath. Looked towards Connor, then away. Did a double take. No doubt, Connor thought, embarrassed by his almost-fall.

Connor screened it out, turned his attention back to Donna. She and Sanderson had stopped now, Sanderson framed against the stone backdrop of the building, Donna in front of him, holding what looked like a massive black feather duster at waist level. Connor knew it was a more powerful mic than the clip-ons she and Sanderson had been using during their walk but, still, the image was strangely comical.

What's she going to do? he thought. Tickle him to death?

More shouts from across the street now. Connor turned, curious. He hadn't heard another box of supplies hit the ground, had the . . .

His brain was still processing what he was seeing as he got moving. Across the street, marching in a straight line, eyes locked ahead, was the older man in the chef whites. In his hand, winking in the weak light of the day, was what looked like a meat cleaver. It didn't take a genius in geometry to figure out where he was going: he was going to cut through the gardens that made up the top of the junction, heading straight for Colin Sanderson.

'Charlie One,' Connor said, into his wrist mic, as he broke into a run, 'crash the primary. Repeat. Crash the primary.'

With that done, he broke into a sprint, shouting a warning to Donna as he did so. Watched as she turned and backed off, confusion collapsing into panic and terror. To her left, Keith took a step forward, putting himself between Donna and the attacker, while Sanderson tried to claw his way around Keith. Connor felt something

103

nag at his mind in that instant, mentally shrugged it off. He could analyse it later.

He got to the man when he was halfway across the road, putting himself between him, Sanderson, Donna and her cameraman. Caught sight of Robbie coming up behind him, car door open, ready to bundle Sanderson inside.

'Sir,' Connor said, voice calm and even. 'No need for that. Please, just turn around now. We don't have to take this any further.'

The man's face contorted into a sneer of rage. He was older than he looked at a distance, maybe mid sixties. Pale skin that hung in melancholy jowls around his neck, dark eyes that snatched glances between Connor and Sanderson. He raised his arm, confirming Connor's suspicions. It was a meat cleaver he was holding. And, from the look of the blade, it had already tasted blood that morning.

'That fucking cunt killed those wee lassies!' he spat, his voice native Stirling, flattening out the consonants. 'Mah Abbie knew one of them, Rhona. And now this cunt is here, large as day? Fuck that! He deserves this!' The cleaver rose higher, a perverse exclamation point to the man's statement.

''Mon then, you fuck!' Sanderson roared from over Connor's shoulder. 'You want me, come and fuckin' get me!' Connor didn't turn, but he heard the staccato drum of feet on stone, prayed Robbie was doing his job and would get Sanderson the hell out of the way.

Too late. The man with the cleaver surged forward. Connor grabbed for the outstretched arm. Felt sinewy strength there. Made sense: if the man was a chef, he spent his life splaying meat from bones. That took focus. And strength.

'Look, sir, I really don't want to—'

The wad of spit hit Connor's face like a slap, blinding him momentarily as it seeped into his eyes. Reflexively, he eased his grip on the arm with the machete, just enough for the assailant to prise himself free. Connor wiped at his eyes, swallowing the white-hot, bilious rage that surged into his mouth like battery acid.

'Fuck off!' the chef hissed. 'I swear to fuck. I don't want you, but I will gut you to give that bastard what he deserves.'

'Not fucking happening,' Connor whispered. He blinked, looked over his shoulder, took in the scene. Robbie manhandling Sanderson into the car. Donna backed up against the wall. Keith with the camera trained on him. Fine. He was going to take the blade. If he had to break this man's arm to do it, so much the better.

The man feinted left, following the path of Sanderson and Robbie. Connor surged forward, not going for the blade this time, instead aiming an elbow strike at the man's side. He hit him as though he were a punch bag, elbow leading, swinging his forearm out for the follow-through. Registered the dull shudder of bone hitting bone, felt the man's weight shift. Pivoting with the movement, grabbing him by the neck then hauling him back, the man giving a sudden 'URK!' as though he was a cartoon character being pulled offstage. Still moving. Connor got a hold of the wrist of the blade hand, put all his strength into his grip. Heard a sudden gasp of pain as he felt bones flex beneath his fingers. Grasped tighter.

'Fucking drop it,' he whispered into the man's ear, the smell of drying blood and sweat burning his nose and making his gut lurch. 'Drop it or I'll start with your wrist and break every bone in your fucking arm.'

One last squeeze to confirm his promise, then the clatter of metal on stone as the cleaver was dropped. Satisfied, Connor whirled the man around and grabbed him by the shirt. Frogmarched him across the road and slammed him into a wall hard enough to drive the breath from his lungs in one foetid gasp.

Looked around, saw Donna staring at him, something between horror and excitement dancing across her face. 'Do me a favour,' he asked, ignoring the man's breathless moans of pain. 'Get that knife off the road, then call the police, will you? I get the feeling they'll want a word with Mr Masterchef here.'

CHAPTER 28

Since I first saw him, Connor Fraser represented a question. He was like the one crossword clue you just couldn't solve to complete the grid, the unknown that danced just beyond your grasp. Don't get me wrong, he certainly looked the part and, on paper, his credentials were impeccable. But, still, I've seen enough fakes over the years to never take anyone at face value. In all my long years of waiting, I became a student of human behaviour. I've seen muscle-bound monsters reduced to quivering wrecks at the first hint of violence, sinewy scraps of men fight until they were little more than bloody smears on concrete. So the question remained.

Until now. Now I have all the answers I could want. From the way he moved to tackle the attacker to the flash of rage when he was spat upon and the brutally efficient way he disarmed the man, Connor Fraser passed the final exam with flying colours.

There is only one small, lingering problem. That moment. That one split-second look that passed between Fraser and Donna Blake. Almost like a shorthand between them. *Here comes trouble. Step out of the way, I've got this.* And then, in the aftermath, the admiration on Blake's face. It was fleeting, and she hid it well, but it was there.

Which makes me wonder. How much of a problem is Connor Fraser going to be? I will have Donna Blake, of that there is no doubt. It is Fate. Inevitable. But how to deal with the problem of Connor

Fraser? Get Blake alone, take her when he is far away and distracted? Or something else, something more definite?

The thrill in my chest and the tightening of my grasp on the knife is all the answer I need.

Fine. Let it be a game of chess. Blake is my queen. And I will take her. But first I need to clear the board, make sure Fraser can neither intervene nor seek retribution after the fact. And he would, of that I have no doubt. With the delights I have planned for Blake, he would raze the world to ash seeking revenge. So I will secure my future by sacrificing his.

And then I will make Donna Blake my masterpiece. And finally, finally, after all these years, the world will understand my message.

CHAPTER 29

One of the few advantages of not being the SIO on a murder investigation was being able to skip the post-mortem examination of the victim or its immediate aftermath. Sitting in Dr Walter Tennant's office, chemical smells as harsh as the lighting triggering a kaleidoscopic montage of memories of past horrors he had witnessed there – bodies flayed open, the wet slap of organs as they were dumped into cold steel bowls to be weighed, the harsh bark of a bone saw as it bit into the skull, the soft, almost liquid pop as the top was lifted away to expose the brain – Ford felt a chilled weariness settle on him. He had seen it in other officers before him: burnout, the point at which they could not take any more, like a chalice overfilled with horror.

He knew he was close to that place now, the hours he had spent reading old case files before coming here pushing him ever closer to that point of no return. But not yet. Not until he had his answer, not until the doubt was put to rest.

He was startled from his thoughts by the sound of Tennant bustling into the room. He was a huge man, built for strength and certainty. Ford often thought he would look more at home on the rugby pitch than in the morgue, but he knew the dedication Tennant gave to his work. He was an artist with the scalpel, deft and assured, and there was something in the grace with which he examined and dissected the bodies sent his way that filled Ford with both disgust and admiration for his friend.

'No, no, don't get up,' Tennant said, placing one large, warm hand on Ford's shoulder and pushing him gently back into his seat as he rose to greet him. 'You want some coffee?'

'No, thanks, I'll pass,' Ford replied, his stomach giving a sour clench at the thought. He had made a pot at home while he had been reading, was now running on an unpleasant mixture of caffeine and questions.

Tennant shrugged, busied himself at the Nespresso machine that sat on a small shelf behind his desk. The spitting grind of the machine filled the room, then Tennant turned and settled himself in his seat across from Ford, hands forming a barrier around the steaming coffee cup.

'So, Malcolm,' he said at last, peering through the thin wisps of steam snaking lazily from the cup. 'What brings you here today? My understanding was that DCI Ross was SIO on this case. He was here earlier by the way, for the post-mortem. I don't think he enjoyed the experience too much.'

Ford was unable to mask the smile he felt twist his face. Gallows humour. Always Tennant's way.

'Look, Walter, I know I'm not here in an official capacity, and feel free to tell me to piss off if you feel I'm putting you in an awkward position. But you know the history here. My history. If there's anything you can tell me that will either help me connect this to the original university murders or otherwise . . .'

Tennant nodded, pale eyes fixed on Ford's. 'Understandable,' he said at last. 'You were on the original Sanderson case, weren't you? The one Dennis Morgan was leading on. So this either proves you were right and Sanderson was the killer, or it proves you wrong.'

Ford shifted in his seat, uncomfortable, stifled grunts of pain as wood slammed into flesh echoing in his ears.

Again.

'Yeah, something like that,' he said, his tone neutral. 'I'm liaising with Ross, offering him insights into the original case, seeing if there are any similarities that could verify things one way or another. But I wanted to talk to you, just in case there was anything that Ross might have missed.'

Tennant flashed a row of teeth that seemed too small for the maw of a mouth that held them. 'I see what you mean. DCI Ross does have a reputation for being somewhat, ah, pedantic in his endeavours.'

'Yeah,' Ford said, not wanting to disagree but not wanting to be seen criticising a fellow officer, even to Tennant. 'So is there anything. Anything at all?'

Tennant sipped his coffee, leaned back in his chair, studied the ceiling as though looking for an answer there. Then he rocked forward and opened his desk drawer and deposited a manila folder on the immaculately tidy desktop. 'It's a bad one, Malcolm,' he said, flipping the file open. 'Seems the victim was subdued with a heavy blow from behind, inflicted with a heavy implement of some kind. Fractured the skull. There's evidence that she was bound and the body moved before being severely mutilated, including her left ring finger being removed. Cause of death was exsanguination which, given the extent of the wounds inflicted on her, is no surprise.'

Ford looked up. One paradox of Walter Tennant was his ability to be clinically detached in his work, yet still have a need to humanise those whose deaths he had to study. It meant that if he had the victim's name, he would use it during their discussions, meaning . . . 'Hold on, "her"? So Ross hasn't been able to identify her yet?'

'No,' Tennant said, a trace of sorrow darkening his tone. 'There was no identification on the body, and no one matching her description has been reported missing yet, from what Ross told me. We're running a DNA sample and dental records now to see if we can get a match, but it's unlikely we'll have much luck unless she's got a criminal record.'

No identification, Ford thought. Interesting. And an anomaly. Both Rhona Everett and Jessica Kristen's bodies had been found with their personal items discarded nearby, like sweet wrappers tossed aside by a thoughtless child. 'I didn't get to see her before I got the call from Guthrie,' he said. 'What was the description?'

'See for yourself,' Tennant said, selecting a picture from the file and sliding it over the table to Ford, who took it, forcing down the familiar cold dread he felt as he did so.

It was a standard post-mortem picture – all harsh light and dull, muted colour. It showed the face of a young woman, no more than twenty-one or twenty-two, Ford guessed. The dappling grey of her skin made her look like a grotesque caricature of beauty, the full lips, elegant nose and dimpled chin turned into cruel taunts of life. Purplish smears of bruising ran under her closed eyes, like a child's experiment in mascara, and there was a welt on her forehead, which was surrounded by a crown of dark, almost black hair.

Ford studied the picture for a moment, a vague memory stirring. This woman, whoever she was, looked nothing like either Jessica or Rhona, but there was something, some familiarity, that nagged at him like a half-remembered song.

He pushed the picture back to Tennant. 'You get a chance to compare the case files?' he asked.

Tennant flashed a you-know-better smile. 'Briefly,' he said. 'Yes, there are similarities between the injuries to this poor girl and to both Jessica Kristen and Rhona Everett. The mutilation of the chest and groin areas, for example, the blow to the head. But it's nothing conclusive, Malcolm, as I pointed out to DCI Ross in my official report.'

Ford looked up at the barb, smiled. 'I know, Walter, I'm not on this. I appreciate what you've told me. If you get anything else from the blood work, could you possibly . . .?'

Tennant held up a hand. 'Off the record, yes,' he said. 'But I want you to do something for me, Malcolm.'

'Oh? What's that?'

Tennant's expression darkened as he dropped his hand onto the folder on the desk, dwarfing it. 'This was savage. Whoever did this will not stop. Don't get blinded by the past, help Ross find whoever did this. If it doesn't lead to Sanderson, so be it. But if it does . . .'

Ford let the silence draw out for a beat, felt it crowd in on him. 'If it does, what?'

'Deal with it,' Tennant said, his words as blunt and harsh as the strip lighting. 'Prison is too good for whoever did this, Malcolm. And if it was Sanderson, this shows he's learned nothing. So deal with it. For me. And for them.'

CHAPTER 30

Connor stood beneath the shower, willing the pulsing spray to soothe his body as he tried to clear his mind. So far, the water wasn't having much effect on either.

After his confrontation with the cleaver-wielding chef, who, Connor now knew, was called Jonathan Clarke, the owner of the restaurant, events had unspooled in a predictable pattern. The police had arrived, two cars, one carrying armed police just in case. Clarke had been bundled into a vehicle, quiet now, defeated, no hint of the murderous fury that had propelled him across the street. It was as though he had expected failure, and this was merely the way of things after it. Connor had spoken to the officers, agreed to take Sanderson back to the conference room at the hotel where they could give their statements. Donna had balked at this, citing press freedom and the right to file her story, going as far as to ask, in an almost clichéd fashion, if she was being charged and detained. When the officers at the scene confirmed she wasn't, she flashed them a smile that was almost predatory, then stalked off back to the hotel, where the satellite van was waiting.

Connor watched her go, unease unfurling in his gut. He knew Keith had filmed him taking Clarke down, and the last thing he wanted was to be seen on the TV news, especially not when he was threatening to break an older man's arm.

His father's voice whispered in his mind: *You've got the Fraser temper, son. Keep a lid on it. I have.*

A plain-clothed police officer arrived ten minutes later, introducing himself as DCI Alan Ross. Connor wasn't sure what to expect of Malcolm Ford's replacement, but this wasn't it. He was a short man, what had been a ginger hairline retreating as his gut expanded, a side effect of the gravitational pull of middle age. His face was unnaturally smooth, as though it was a balloon that had been over-inflated, an impression only magnified by the hectic patches of colour on his cheeks. But despite his appearance, there was nothing over-inflated about his manner. He spoke softly, choosing his words with an almost clinical precision, as if English was a second language he was still trying to navigate.

'And you'd never seen this man before?' he asked when he had Connor alone, Donna and Sanderson taken to other rooms to give their statements.

'No,' Connor said, remembering the naked hatred on the man's face as he marched across the road for Sanderson. He paused. Something about that. About the crashing of boxes onto the street before Clarke had appeared . . .

Something . . .

'You say Clarke said he knew one of San– one of the university victims from 2006?' Ross asked, dragging Connor from his thoughts.

Connor nodded, remembering Clarke's words. 'Yeah. He said his daughter knew one of the victims, ah, Rhona. Rhona Everett. And then he made for Sanderson. At which point I intervened.'

'Yes, I saw the footage Ms Blake's cameraman filmed,' Ross said, irritation colouring his voice just enough for Connor to make a *go on* gesture with his head.

'Oh, just that footage,' Ross said. 'I can't technically stop her broadcasting it but, still, it's maddening. The last thing any of this needs is the oxygen of publicity.'

The same thought had occurred to Connor. Footage of Sanderson as large as life on the streets of Stirling would enrage those who still believed him to be guilty of the original murders, let alone last night's.

Original. The thought hit Connor's guts, like a jab. He knew the latest victim was yet to be identified, Ford had sent him a text telling him as much, but still . . .

'Christ,' he muttered. 'Have the parents of the 2006 victims been told about all this?'

Ross had the good grace to look embarrassed. 'They were informed when Sanderson's case was quashed, of course,' he said. 'And we've offered them support services. But the problem is they're not local any more. Jessica Kristen's mother is in Portree, her father died of cancer two years ago. And Rhona Everett's parents moved to Newcastle not long after Sanderson was convicted.'

Another thought snagged in Connor's mind, an image of the file Ford had given him darting across his thoughts. Then it was gone.

The rest of the interview was perfunctory, almost routine. Connor promised to keep Ross informed of any security arrangements surrounding Sanderson, and to email him an official report on his movements from the night before. With the interviews concluded, he drove the same convoy back to Sanderson's home in Cambusbarron, minus Donna, who had said she was going to head for the Sky newsroom. Something in her look told Connor something else was going on, but he opted not to pursue it. He had enough to deal with.

With Sanderson dropped off, with the usual curses to 'let any fucker try it', Connor instructed Robbie to set up a patrol perimeter around the house, then get some rest. Then he headed home, deciding he wanted some peace and quiet and the chance to prep some ingredients for the meal he was to make for Jen that night.

But even as he chopped and boiled and blended, thoughts buzzed around Connor's head. Something about the file Ford had given him, Clarke's words: *Mah Abbie knew one of them, Rhona. And now this cunt is here, large as day? Fuck that! He deserves this!* and the clatter of bottles on cobbles. And then there was the thought of Paulie's car, sitting like a coiled predator up the road from Sanderson's house. Why was he there? What did he – or Duncan MacKenzie – have to do with Sanderson?

He finished his prep work, headed for the shower, frustrated. Took his time, turning up the heat as high as he could bear, hoping it would scald out some of the questions in his mind. It didn't. Frustrated, he grabbed his car keys and headed out to pick Jen up from work.

As they drove back to his flat, Connor half expected to see Paulie's

Merc in his rear-view mirror. But the drive was uneventful and they were soon back at the flat. Connor feeling a momentary jar of unreality as Jen wandered in and made herself at home, heading for the kitchen, retrieving a bottle of white wine from the fridge and two glasses. And again the thought hit him – where was this going? It had started casually and yet now, here they were, spending cosy nights in, Jen knowing her way around the flat almost as well as he did, leaving him little notes reminding him to check in on his gran. Was this what he wanted?

He was startled from his thoughts by the doorbell. Connor frowned, returned the confused look Jen gave him. He wasn't expecting anyone, and few people knew where he lived. So who?

The thought flashed across his mind suddenly, putting him on alert. Paulie. He hadn't been following them because he was already watching the flat, waiting for them to return. Connor felt his muscles tense, his jaw tighten, even as excitement began to tingle at the base of his skull. Whatever Paulie wanted, he would give Connor some of the answers he desperately wanted.

'Why don't you take a seat? I'll see who it is,' Connor said, his voice surprisingly relaxed in his ears.

'Sure,' Jen said, folding herself onto the couch with the relaxed elegance Connor had always admired. Satisfied, he headed to the door. Thought briefly about how he was going to deal with it. Take it outside or invite Paulie in, have it out with him in front of Jen?

No. Outside. He would open the door and keep moving, force Paulie to back off. And if he didn't? Well, Connor had an answer for that as well.

He swung the door open, took half a step forward and stopped. Confusion flushing away the adrenalin coursing through him.

'Evening, Connor. Sorry to drop in unannounced but I saw the report of what happened in town on the TV, wanted to make sure you were OK. Mind if I come in?'

Connor scrambled to regain his composure, a thousand thoughts and possible answers churning through his mind. 'Sure, Dad,' he said, after a moment. 'Come on in.'

CHAPTER 31

At that moment, Donna was having parental issues of her own. After filing her report and rescheduling her interview with Sanderson for the following day, she had headed home, looking forward to nothing more than a glass of wine and something mindless on the TV to crowd out the memories of Connor wrestling with the cleaver-wielding chef.

Her mother had different ideas.

After making a show of checking on Andrew, who was happily passed out on his bed after an afternoon at pre-school, Irene bustled into the living room and stood in front of Donna, who could tell what was coming by the uncomfortable way her dad was shifting around in the seat opposite her.

'What?' Donna asked, wanting to get this over with.

'You know fine well what,' Irene replied. 'We saw your report, Donna. A man with a knife attacking you? It's not fair. Not on us, or on Andrew. He's already lost one parent, such as Mark was, and we don't want him losing another.'

Donna looked up, felt the anger rising in her throat as the skin around her neck prickled. She blinked back the image of Mark, Andrew's father, who had been killed the year before at a hotel just outside Stirling.

Not killed. Butchered, she thought.

'Look, Mum,' she said very slowly, her voice glacial, 'it's the job.

The man wasn't attacking me, he was going after Colin Sanderson. And if you saw my report, you know he was dealt with. I was never in any danger.'

Irene Blake threw up her hands, glanced over her shoulder to her husband for support. 'No danger? Give me strength! Donna, since you've been working for the TV, how many people have died around you? That poor boy at the radio station, Mark, the man you used to work with at the newspaper, and now this? It's no job for a mother with a young son. No job at all.'

Donna felt her jaw clench, the first echoes of a headache snarling through her mind. 'It's the job I chose, Mum,' she said at last. 'I know you don't like it and, yes, there have been some, ah, problems. But that's the job. I'm not reporting on bloody knitting classes, you know.'

Irene flinched, her eyes hardening as Donna's barb hit home. Irene had been the stereotypical stay-at-home mum when Donna had been growing up, giving knitting lessons and taking commissions for items of clothing to make a little extra money. Donna wondered if it had been enough for her.

'Well,' Irene said, 'don't expect us to pick up the pieces. Really, Donna. What happens if you get hurt? Or worse? What happens to Andrew?'

Donna opened her mouth. Closed it. It was a good question. What would happen to Andrew? She had never seriously considered that she might be badly hurt on this job, always assumed she would make it home at the end of the day.

But would she?

'Look, Mum,' she said, suddenly tired, 'I'm being careful. Sometimes these things happen. But it's the job. Sanderson is a big story, and I'm doing this for Andrew as much as me.'

Irene gave a dismissive snort, as though Donna had just offered to sell her the Forth Bridge at a bargain price. 'And there's another thing, this Sanderson. What on earth are you doing with him anyway? He's a killer, Donna. Why are you giving him the time of day?'

Donna felt her headache kick up a notch. 'He was cleared of those murders, Mum,' she said slowly. 'And I'm giving him the time of day because he is news. He was inside for fourteen years. Wrongly convicted as it turns out. You don't think that's newsworthy?'

'I remember those murders, and the trial. Even if he didn't do it, Sanderson was hardly a paragon of virtue. He deserved to be inside, one way or another. And the last thing you should be doing is helping him profit from those girls' memories now.'

A thought stirred in Donna's brain, punching through the headache, like sunlight through rainclouds. She stood up, gave her mum a smile. 'You know, Mum, you're absolutely right. Everyone's been so busy looking at Sanderson and what happened today to look at the girls from the original murders. So that's exactly what I'm going to do.'

CHAPTER 32

They stood in the living room, Connor, Jack and Jen, like three points charting a Bermuda triangle filled with lost conversations and connections that were never truly forged.

Jen got moving first, sensing the unease that was settling into the room like thickening ice. 'Hi, Mr Fraser, I'm Jen MacKenzie,' she said, shooting Connor a glance. 'Nice to meet you.'

Jack took Jen's outstretched hand, a practised, reassuring smile falling into place on his lips. 'Yes, ah, likewise. It's good to meet you, Jen, I'm sorry for intruding on your evening like this. It's just that, after seeing what happened on the TV, I—'

'You're not intruding,' Connor said, voice sharper than he intended. The truth was that his father, who had never shown any interest in his life, was intruding. On his home. On his time with Jen. On his thoughts. 'Can I get you a drink?'

'Oh, no,' Jack said. 'I just wanted to drop in on my way home, check you were all right.'

Connor made it to the fridge, retrieved the bottle of white wine. Paused. He didn't want any, so he took it out and topped Jen's glass up instead.

'Ah, go on, Mr Fraser, join us for a drink,' Jen said, motioning to the couch. 'You can tell us how your mum is. Connor was worried.'

Something flashed across Jack's face, dimming the wattage on his smile, like a fleeting power cut. Then it was gone, composure restored.

'Thank you, Jen, but no. As Connor will tell you, I'm not much of a drinker, I'm afraid. And I'm driving. So I'll pass. Just wanted to check in on Connor after his heroics today.'

Connor looked at his dad. It was like he was listening to him read a script someone else had written for him. The words were all there, but nothing sounded genuine. Three years ago Connor had been stabbed in the leg while fighting for his life, and his father had barely raised an eyebrow. So why now, after a fairly minor skirmish in which it was clear Connor was never at any real risk of injury? A line from the report card suddenly flashed across Connor's mind, unbidden: 'Jack is a sensitive and empathetic pupil, with strong communication skills and a striking maturity in his art. He cares deeply for his classmates . . .'

Cares deeply. Connor thought. Right.

'So how is Gran, anyway?' Connor asked. 'With everything that's happened today, I've not had the chance to check in on her.'

'Oh, she's fine, fine,' Jack replied, moving towards the couch and hovering, not willing to sit down. 'Nurses say she had a good day, and it doesn't look like her fall did any lasting damage.'

'That's good,' Jen said, sipping her wine as she sat back down, tucking her legs beneath her. 'Connor said she was looking for some old photographs. We've got a load of them here, so if there's anything you think she might want . . .'

We? Connor thought, again hit by the sudden realisation that this relationship was moving, evolving, developing.

'Thank you, Jen, that's very kind,' Jack said, eyes falling to the coffee-table. 'I'll be sure to let her know. But anyway, I'm sorry I intruded. Connor,' he straightened, looking at his son square on for the first time, 'I'm glad you're safe, son. But please, be careful, OK?'

'Part of the job,' Connor said, moving past his dad to the coffee-table, and the item he had seen his father's eyes fall on, like those of a bargain hunter spotting a diamond in a jumble of cheap costume jewellery. 'Here,' he said, lifting the report card and handing it to his dad. 'You might want to give this back to Gran. Or destroy it for the trouble it seems to have caused.'

Jack's hand jerked up slowly, as though the motion was independent from his thoughts. He flashed Connor a weak smile, eyes darting between him and Jen, before taking the report card. He held it gingerly between his fingers, as though it would scald him if he grasped it too tightly, an almost painful sorrow hollowing out his eyes.

'Thanks,' he said, stuffing it into his pocket. 'I'll see she gets it back.'

Aye, right, Connor thought. That thing's going straight in a bin or a fire. Question was, why?

'Right, I'll leave you to it,' Jack said. 'Jen, it was a pleasure to meet you. Don't let this one take advantage.'

'If anyone's going to be taking advantage, it'll be me, Mr Fraser,' Jen said, an unexpected coldness seeping into her voice. 'But don't worry, I'll take good care of him.'

Jack flashed another smile, then got moving, Connor following him. He opened the front door, stepped out into the night, turned.

'Look, Connor, I . . .' he started. Then stopped. Coughed. Tried again. 'I really was worried about you today, son.'

Connor felt something like a smile tighten his lips. 'Nice to know,' he said. 'But this place isn't on your way home from either the hospital, your place or Gran's home. Look, Dad,' he softened his voice, forced himself to stoop a little, look less intimidating, 'I don't know what's going on, but if there's something I can do, something you or Gran need, I . . .'

Jack Fraser held up a hand, a sad smile on his face. 'No, son, no. There's nothing. Just check in on your gran, make sure she's fine. And take care of yourself. I saw that look in your eyes today on the film. You were ready to take that bastard's head off, weren't you?'

Drop it, or I'll start with your wrist and then break every bone in your fucking arm.

Connor blinked the sudden memory aside, swallowed the hot tang of rage that accompanied it.

'So like Campbell,' Jack said. 'It's the Fraser temper, son. You've got to watch for it. Please.'

Connor didn't know what to say. Instead, he just nodded, then retreated back into the flat, closing the door slowly. Stood there for a moment, considering. Then turned and walked back to the living room, Jack's words ringing in his ears.

It's the Fraser temper, son. You've got to watch for it.

Jen looked up as he came in. 'Well,' she said, flashing a smile up at him from the couch, 'I've had worse introductions to a boyfriend's parent, but not many. Tell me it wasn't just me, but that was weird, right?'

'Yeah,' Connor said, distracted. Another Bermuda triangle was forming in his mind now. Three points that were loosely connected, one of which might hold a possible answer.

'OK,' he said, clapping his hands together. 'How about I cook you my famous teriyaki salmon with sticky rice? I'm doing a Baileys chocolate mousse for dessert.'

Jen's smile widened. 'Sold,' she said, unfurling herself from the couch and walking towards him. 'And what do I owe you in return for such a feast?'

Connor put his arms around her, pulled her close. 'You can help me with my family tree,' he said.

CHAPTER 33

Donna pushed away from her desk, let out a deep breath of frustration, then listened to the silence of the flat. Her parents were gone and Andrew had, mercifully, slipped off to sleep quickly, leaving her free to work.

The problem was, there wasn't much to work with. At least, not to get to the story she wanted to tell.

After speaking to her mother, Donna had resolved to go back and look at the original university murders, see if there was something that connected the victims, something that might either exonerate Sanderson of this latest murder or link him to it. She had left a message with Danny, her contact at Police Scotland, telling him she would be extremely grateful for anything he could give her on the body found at the golf course but, so far, there had been nothing.

She had started online, finding the press reports from the time. The case had been a national sensation, the killer dubbed 'The Beast' for the sheer savagery of the crimes. Donna wondered about that. With the amount of invective spilled onto the pages of the newspapers and on the TV from the time, how difficult would it have been for Sanderson to get a fair trial?

She waded her way through the stories, all variations of the same facts. Rhona Everett and Jessica Kristen had both been students at the University of Stirling, and had been taken mere days apart, their bodies horribly mutilated, then dumped with little care paid to hiding them. Either the killer was careless or, more likely, he was somehow proud of what he had done, and wanted the bodies to be found, his work to be seen and admired.

Donna felt a twist of disgust at the thought, her mum's words scampering through her mind. *This is no job for a mother with a young son.*

The police had, understandably, thrown up a wall between the victims' parents and the press after an initial appeal for witnesses, and those students who were persuaded to give a comment by the media were so vague in their platitudes they could have been reading from a script.

Jessica was one of a kind. I can't believe anyone would do that to her.

Rhona was such a caring, loving person. Life of the party. It's unbelievable. Who would do such a thing?

The investigation was run by a DCI Dennis Morgan, who looked to Donna as though he had been freshly pressed from the seventies-era hard-cop mould especially for the case. He was compact, heavy-set, with dark features and a scowl that did not endear him to any of the cameras that were trained on him at the press conferences. The newspaper reports detailed his pleas for information and witnesses, and vow to find the killer quickly. It was, as it turned out, a vow he made good on, the link to Sanderson and his work at the university quickly established.

But, still, it didn't tell Donna what she needed. It was as if the victims had been reduced to walk-on parts in their own tragedy – she knew their names, knew they had gone to the university, but nothing else. There was nothing in the coverage that told her who those women were beyond the headlines. Was there something that connected them, some commonality that bound them together, made them irresistible to the killer? Or, more horrifying, were they chosen completely at random, killed because they were just in the wrong place at the wrong time? Either way, Donna wanted to put a face to them, give them the voice they had been deprived of in their deaths. She would make it a condition of her writing the Sanderson book: the victims would be seen. Donna felt a pang of guilt as she studied the printouts strewn across her desk. Her desire to do this was, ultimately, a selfish one. After all, when Mark had died, strung up and gutted in a cold, isolated patch of woodland, she had done exactly the same – turned him into a story, a statistic, a headline, and forgotten the man along the way.

Again, her mother's voice – *It's no job for a mother with a young son.*

She pushed the thought aside, booted up her laptop. A couple of years ago, before she had landed the Sky job, Donna had supplemented her income by tutoring journalism students at the university. Her schedule with Sky had forced her to give that up, but she was still friendly with some of the faculty staff, and she was sure she could persuade one of them to let her have access to whatever files there were on Rhona and Jessica. Yes, she was on dubious moral ground asking for confidential files, but after she explained why she was asking, and how it was all for the greater good, surely someone would help.

She logged into her email, scrolled through, absently deleting the staff memos and pointless updates she had received over the course of the day. But then, two emails from the top, there was a message that stopped her in her tracks. An address she didn't recognise: Stir-ed666@gmail.com, and the message description: *Sadism to the fore. Want to peek?*

She glanced up, the shadows of the room suddenly deepening. Chastised herself when she felt the sudden urge to check the door. It was probably nothing. Working on high-profile stories always brought the nutcases out of the woodwork, those who claimed to be a killer, or who knew for a fact that it was all an insidious government plot.

Still, she hesitated before clicking on the email, which she spotted had an attachment.

It opened to three simple lines of text. Three lines that made Donna's heart race even as pins and needles, fibrous and harsh like spider's legs, scuttled up and down her spine.

It's no job for a mother with a young son.

Donna, this is my latest work from the golf course.
Thought you'd like it.
I'll be seeing you VERY soon.

She rocked back from the laptop, her mind screaming just to close it down, get away from it. Get to Andrew, then phone someone (Connor, her mind whispered), tell them what she had received.

Instead, she reached forward, her fingers feeling fat and alien as she double-clicked on the first attachment.

In the instant it took Donna's mind to make sense of what she was seeing, the world froze. She jerked back, hands flying to her face, nails digging in as she clamped her hands over her mouth and the scream that was scrabbling to get free. Knew that if she started screaming, she would never stop.

Andrew, she told herself, even as the horrified tears began to scald her cheeks. Think of Andrew. Be strong for him. Don't scream. Don't scream. Don't scream.

The picture was a close-up of a wicked-looking knife, the type that would be used in a kitchen for cutting meat. Its handle was wooden, the gleaming blade dappled with blood and darker clots of purplish-green matter that brought rancid bile to Donna's throat. Beside the knife was a single finger, chipped red nail varnish made grotesquely vibrant by the pale, greying flesh of the rest of the digit, which had been severed from its owner at the last knuckle, just above where a ring would sit.

I'll be seeing you VERY soon.

Donna leaned forward, crashed the laptop screen down, the sound like a thunderclap in the charged silence of the room. Got moving on legs that were heavy with adrenalin and fear. Stumbled to the front door, double-checking the locks, then into Andrew's room, eyes straining the darkness, searching for . . .

For . . .

I'll be seeing you VERY soon.

She fought the renewed urge to bundle Andrew into her arms and run, some part of her punching through the terror, refusing to be driven from her home. Reluctantly, she went back to her office, found her bag. Got her mobile.

Felt the world lurch and sway on its axis, something fundamental wrenching and untethering in her mind as she read the text message that had been sent less than ten minutes ago from an

126

unfamiliar number: *Hope you enjoy the email. I'll be seeing you VERY soon.*

Donna's control snapped. She fell into the couch, buried her head in a cushion.

Screamed.

CHAPTER 34

Ross slid a cup of coffee over the desk towards Ford, who took it with a weak smile. He hated police coffee, but found it a necessary evil, just like this meeting.

'So,' Ross said, settling into his seat again, 'that's what we've got so far. No identification yet. From what you've said, the mutilation of the body is similar to that found in the 2006 murders, though the severing of a finger is a new addition. So the question remains, is it the same killer coming back for more or someone new? And how does Sanderson tie into all this? It's hardly coincidental that he comes home and, less than a week later, a young woman is found dead.'

Ford sipped his coffee, grimaced. Set it aside. 'To be honest, Alan, I'm not sure what to make of it. You say that Fraser's team can't give Sanderson a hundred per cent alibi, so it could conceivably be him. But would he be reckless enough to start killing again this quickly, drawing all that attention to himself? And then there's the chef you told me about who went for Sanderson in the street – Kent? Clarke? Seemed handy with a meat cleaver from the report. Just the type of thing you'd need to chop off a lassie's finger.'

Ross sipped at his own coffee. Smiled as though at some private joke. 'Unfortunately, he's got an alibi for the most likely time the girl was taken. He was in his restaurant all night, along with his wife, whom he then drove home and stayed with. No window of opportunity. Oh, we're looking into him but it seems what he told the officers who arrested him stands up – he saw Sanderson and just lost it.'

Understandable, Ford thought. He seemed to have that effect. 'Any other witnesses, suspects? Anything that might help?'

Ross opened his mouth, closed it. Took another gulp of coffee, as though it was mouthwash to rinse away a bad taste. Then he put the cup down, leaned forward, lacing his hands together. 'Look, ah, Malcolm, I'm sorry,' he said, addressing his words to the table, not looking Ford in the eye, 'but I can't tell you any more, probably shouldn't have told you as much as I have. The chief was insistent. You're not to have any active part in this investigation. I'm grateful for your historical input on the 2006 killings, but I really can't go any further than I have. Especially now. This afternoon's little fracas has put Sanderson right in the media spotlight, and I can't have you anywhere near that.'

Ford murmured understanding, felt his jaw ache as he started to grind his teeth. Fucking Guthrie and his 'reputation management'. A chef goes nuts and starts swinging a meat cleaver around in the centre of town. A young girl is found slaughtered. A once-convicted killer is freed and heads home. But *noooo*, fuck possible links and actually finding the bastard responsible for butchering those poor women. Let's make sure the optics are right.

'Speaking of media,' Ford said, 'how are you finding Donna Blake?'

Something flashed in Ross's eyes, dark and cautionary. 'Difficult,' he said. 'She's hardly the most co-operative type. Insists that she's free to talk to Sanderson at any time, that we can take it up with his lawyer if we're going to stop an innocent man speaking to the press.'

'She been sniffing around for background on the latest murder?' Ford asked.

Ross shrugged. 'I'm not sure. She's on the mailing list for the press releases we send, but we've had no official queries in from her to the press office if that's what you mean?'

Ford shook his head, suppressed the smile he felt threatening on his lips. 'Blake's not one to go the official route,' he said. 'But keep an eye on Danny Brooks in the press office. He used to work with Blake in Glasgow, and I know he's thrown her more than a few tips in his time.'

'Noted,' Ross replied. 'Now if there's nothing else, Malcolm, I really . . .'

Ford rose, glad of the excuse to be leaving the coffee unfinished. 'No problem, I'll get out of your hair. I'm not assigned to a case at the moment, drowning in paperwork instead, so if there's something else I can do to help . . .'

'Thanks, Malcolm. If there's anything you can do I'll be in touch,' Ross said, offering Ford his hand. He took it, the shake as insipid as the man's tie, then turned to leave.

Almost got knocked off his feet by DS Troughton, who knocked on the door, then swung it open without pausing.

'Troughton! What the . . .?' Ford began.

Colour rose in the young officer's cheeks, eyes darting between Ford and Ross. 'Sorry, sir, sirs, but I thought you'd want to know. We just took a call from Control in Bilston. Seems there's been an incident out at Alloa. They're treating it as attempted murder.'

'Alloa,' Ford echoed, an ugly equation being solved in his mind. 'That's Dennis Morgan's neck of the woods.'

Troughton's expression darkened, colour bleeding from his cheeks. 'Yes, sir, it's DCI Morgan. Officers were called to his house a short time ago. He's being taken to hospital now but it looks bad, sir. Officers at the scene say it looked like he'd been stabbed. Repeatedly.'

CHAPTER 35

'You know, Donna, the police would have been a better call than me.'

They were in Donna's study, Connor looming over her computer, Donna curled into a chair, nursing a drink, eyeing the laptop as though it was some sort of half-tamed animal that might decide to leap on her at any minute.

The call had come just as Connor was managing to find some sort of equilibrium after the unexpected visit from his father. He had cooked, then he and Jen had relaxed into the evening, talking about nothing more than what was happening at the gym, the new classes Connor should try. The questions still buzzed around Connor's head, angry and insistent, but he'd managed to screen them out, focusing on the mundanity of cooking, setting the table, eating.

When they had finished they had ventured into his spare room, and the boxes of his gran's life that were packed up there. The visit from his dad had left Connor with questions, and Jen was happy enough to help him find answers. He was again struck by a moment of discomfort at the new level of intimacy that letting her delve into his family history created, but he dismissed it. She was here. She was willing to help. He was glad of the company.

He could deal with the bigger issues some other time.

They were on their third box, sifting through old pictures and documents, when his phone chimed from the living room. Connor stalked through, wondering what fresh interruption was conspiring to screw up his night.

His anger dissipated when he heard Donna's voice. He knew the tone all too well, had heard it from her before, on the night Mark Sneddon had died. Grim defiance in the face of horrified shock, her voice was a flat, dull thing of dead consonants and anaemic vowel sounds.

She explained what she had been sent, asked Connor to go over. He made his apologies to Jen and, for reasons he couldn't explain to himself, forgot to tell her where he was going, just that it was 'part of the assignment, won't be long'. Jen, who was lost in the pictorial history of the Fraser clan, gave him a distracted smile, kissed him on the cheek. Asked him to grab another bottle of wine on his way back if not too late. She held his gaze when making the request, both of them knowing what it meant. Another night with him, instead of at her own flat. That made how many this week alone? Two? Three?

He got to Donna's place in under ten minutes, texted her from his car so the buzzer wouldn't wake her son. Watched as she warily opened the door to him, then followed her through to the study, and the horrors on the computer.

He banished his revulsion at the image, tried to focus on the facts. Called Robbie and asked him to run a trace on the email address that the image had been attached to, got Donna to give him her IP address and router codes so he could check on her end as well, see when and where the email had been sent from. Then he forwarded the email and attachments to Robbie and deleted that from sent items. Probably futile, the police's digital forensics team had taught Robbie everything he knew, but still, the last thing he needed was a 'tampering with police evidence' charge around his neck.

'You want me to put someone on the flat?' Connor asked, as he read the message again. *I'll be seeing you VERY soon.*

Donna looked up at him, some strange blend of guilt and defiance etched on her face. In that moment, she looked tired to Connor. A single mum with a tough job and little in the way of support. Yet she refused to give in to it. Refused to take an easier path. And in that moment, Connor realised why he admired Donna so much. In the face of everything, she marched on, refused to quit, refused to compromise. Just as his gran had done after her husband had walked out on her and Jack Fraser.

'Hmm? No. No. Thanks, Connor. I'll call the police soon, tell them what's going on. We'll stay here tonight as Andrew is settled, then I guess we'll head to my folks' place tomorrow. I'll make some crap up about the heating or something. Won't be a problem.'

'And then what?' Connor asked. 'That police officer, Ross, isn't going to like this, Donna. It looks very much like the killer is reaching out to you. That being the case, the last thing he's going to want is you near to this or Sanderson, if he's involved.'

Her gaze hardened, the old defiance rising like a shield. 'Fuck him,' she said. 'This changes nothing. If anything, it makes it all the more important that I stick close to Sanderson, make sure I tell his story.'

'Oh, how so?' Connor asked, trying to work the maths in his head as he spoke and failing.

'Think about it,' she said. 'Either everyone got this wrong and Sanderson is and always was the killer, which means he's trying to show off to me. "See you very soon" could be a reference to our meeting and interview tomorrow. If so, he's hardly likely to do anything when you and Keith are there, and I'm giving him his platform to roast the police, is he? And if he's not the killer, then whoever is will be somewhere nearby, probably watching. In which case, you'll be there.'

She shuddered again, curled herself around her drink more tightly.

'You're putting a lot of faith in me,' Connor said, a pang of discomfort stabbing his guts, cool and clear. 'And it's a hell of a risk to take either way. Maybe you should step away from this one, be with Andrew until this is all sorted out.'

Anger in her eyes now, making them hard, dead pools of blue. Connor felt the urge to shrink away from that gaze. Fought it.

'Fuck that,' she said, voice dropping to a whisper. 'I'm not being scared off this story or my job by anyone. You don't think you can handle it, fine, I'll do it myself. But I'm not backing down from this, Connor. Not for a minute.'

Connor held up his hand in a *whoa* gesture. 'OK, OK. Far be it from me,' he said. 'Look. Call the police now, tell them what's happened. I'll wait for them to get here, make sure you're not alone. And I'll get one of the team on Sanderson's place to do a drive-by when they come off shift, make sure no one's lurking around, yes?'

Her eyes warmed a little. 'Thanks, Connor,' she said, staring into her drink. 'It's appreciated.'

'No problem,' Connor said. 'You can repay me by making sure we have somewhere nice and public for the Sanderson interview tomorrow. Like you said, either it's him and there's safety in numbers, or it's someone else. Someone who will stick out in a public place.'

A question flashed across Donna's face, then vanished, unuttered. Connor understood what it was. How could he know who might be a killer in a crowd of seemingly normal people? The simple answer was instinct. Some part of him that had hunted and killed, some regressed part that knew predators from prey and reacted accordingly.

Donna fished around in her bag, produced a business card with Ross's phone number on it. Sighed, then dialled. As she spoke, Connor turned back to the laptop, and the message there. Clicked on the image, studied the finger and . . .

. . . and—

He was interrupted by the buzzing of his phone in his pocket. Jen: *Make it two bottles of wine*, the message read. *I'm on later tomorrow so I can have a lie-in and, besides, you owe me.*

Connor frowned, a vague concern that he'd messed up dinner flashing across his thoughts. *How so?* he texted back, again hating how awkward he felt communicating by text.

The answer came almost instantly. She had been waiting for this moment. Waiting to celebrate her victory with him. *Found something in the boxes*, the text read. *Something you're definitely going to want to see x*

134

CHAPTER 36

The news that Dennis Morgan had been attacked had a paralysing effect on Ross, almost as though he was trying to process too much information at once. He stood in the room, blinking between Troughton and Ford, his thoughts almost visible in the contortions of his features.

Ford felt a brief flash of sympathy for the man. Strangled it. Later.

'Troughton, get a car. You can take me to the hospital. Alan?' Ross blinked up at him, regaining his composure. 'I suggest you stay here, co-ordinate with the local station in Alloa, see if they can free up any bodies for a door-to-door.'

'Yes, agreed. But again, Malcolm, the chief . . .'

Ford bristled, sympathy replaced by anger. 'Fuck the chief,' he said, the words out before he knew he was going to say them. 'Dennis Morgan is a friend. A guv. He was at my house earlier this morning and now someone's tried to carve him up. I'm going to see him. If the chief doesn't like it, he can fucking tell me so himself.'

The shock of Ford's words seemed to galvanise Ross. 'OK,' he said. 'Take Troughton, check on Morgan. But Troughton takes any and all statements, clear? I don't want your name attached to one scrap of official documentation on this.'

'Fair enough,' Ford grumbled, the thought of that piece of paper and the letter he should write rising in his mind again. With his outburst about the chief, had he just penned the first line?

He met Troughton in the car park and they drove east, heading for the Forth Valley Royal Hospital in Larbert. Ford didn't speak on the trip, just let Troughton get on with the job of driving as he tried to order his thoughts, take a step back from the clamour of events that threatened to overwhelm him and see the big picture. A body was found at the golf course behind Stirling University, mutilated in a similar way to the 2006 victims. Then Dennis Morgan turned up at Ford's house, urging him to keep the focus on Sanderson, convinced he was the killer. Just hours after that, Morgan was found near death, having been repeatedly stabbed in his own home. Coincidence? Ford didn't think so. But again . . .

'Troughton, what time did the call come in from Morgan's home?' he asked suddenly, breaking the silence in the car.

To his credit, Troughton didn't even take his eyes off the road. 'Eh, about two thirty p.m., sir. His son found him, called the police at that time. My understanding is he's at the hospital with his father now.'

Ford nodded, adding this to what he knew. Two thirty. After Sanderson had been attacked at Mar's Wark, which made him a potential suspect. What were his movements after that? Had the attack in town triggered him, forced him to seek revenge on the man who had put him in prison in the first place?

Ford grunted as he realised what his next move would have to be.

He dug his phone from his pocket, scrolled through the contacts until he found Connor Fraser's number. Hesitated for a moment. Had it been a mistake bringing him into all of this? Fraser was a talented investigator and, with his background as a police officer, he understood the game better than a civilian, but still . . .

Ford shook himself clear of the thought. Was about to hit dial when another thought hit him. Instead flipped over to the web app on his phone, fiddled with it and called up Google maps, charting three locations: Alloa, Stirling and Cambusbarron.

He was still working on this when they arrived at the hospital. Found the A and E and asked for Morgan, who, it transpired, had been transferred to the critical care unit. They made their way there, heels squeaking on the floors, the antiseptic smells of the hospital and the enforced silence crowding in on Ford's senses. He had never liked hospitals, a feeling made worse over the years as he had begun to associate them with a trip to Walter Tennant's morgue.

They found the critical care unit, were led to a small, gloomy waiting room. Michael Morgan stood there, looking blankly out of a window. Ford could see the echoes of his father in Morgan's dark complexion and heavy brow. But where Dennis Morgan was small and compact, his son was tall and broad. For an instant, Ford was reminded of Connor Fraser, and he wondered if, like Fraser, Morgan put in a lot of gym time.

'Michael,' Ford said, crossing the room and offering his hand, noticing the drying, pinkish-brown blotches on his rolled-up sleeves even as he did so. Made a note. If he had found his dad and called the police, the forensics team would normally have asked for his clothes, to rule him out of their enquiries. Routine procedure. This hadn't happened.

Why?

'I'm so, so sorry,' he said, coming back to the present. 'How's your dad?'

Morgan blinked down at Ford, as though confused. Then he nodded to himself, eyes clearing. 'Oh, yes, Malcolm, of course. I picked Dad up from your place earlier on.'

Ford saw Troughton's quizzical glance. Ignored it. 'That's right,' he said gently. 'How is your dad, Michael? The officers who took the call say you found him.'

Michael's face drained of colour, eyes glazing as he looked into the past. 'Yeah, that's right,' he said, voice low, unsteady. 'After I picked him up from your place I dropped him home, then went and did a couple of errands. You know, shopping for Dad, that kind of thing. Got back and found . . .' He coughed, eyes now watering. Turned away, embarrassed.

'It's OK, Michael,' Ford said. 'Just tell me what you can. DS Troughton here can take your official statement later.'

'There was just so much blood,' Morgan whispered. 'The front door was open – I thought maybe I hadn't closed it right when I left. Went in and found Dad in the kitchen, slumped against the breakfast bar. He was – was—' Morgan broke off and gestured at his chest with a hand, marking the locations of stab wounds. 'There was blood everywhere. It looked black, Malcolm, so black. I don't remember calling the ambulance, but I must have because the next thing I remember was being in the ambulance with Dad. They've got him sedated now, say it's fifty-fifty if he'll recover. I had to get out of the room for a minute. Jesus, the blood . . .'

Michael lost himself again, washed away by what he had seen. Ford took a step back, awkward, giving the man space to process. To grieve. One question answered. The forensics team had yet to process him: he'd come straight here with the ambulance carrying his dad. He made a mental note to ensure Troughton made the appropriate arrangements, then focused back on what else Michael had said. If the door was open, not forced, had Dennis known who had attacked him? Opened the door for him? Welcomed them into his home? Police officers had caution of house guests trained into them, so who could that be?

Sanderson, a voice in Ford's mind whispered. He'd know Sanderson. Might even open the door for him, confront him. Get it done.

Ford shrugged internally. Conjecture. What he needed were facts. 'Michael, would you mind if I popped my head in on your dad while you speak to DS Troughton? I'll only be a minute.'

'Of course,' Michael said, trying and failing to give a reassuring smile. 'He's just down the hall, third room on the left. Though it's not . . .' a hitching breath '. . . not a pretty sight.'

'Understood,' Ford said, reaching out and giving Michael's arm a reassuring squeeze. It was like grasping stone.

He found Dennis Morgan's room with no problem. Steeled himself, then stepped inside. Dennis lay in the middle of a nest of wires and tubes, the damage evident in the bloodied bandages and dressings that tattooed his chest in a patchwork of pain. His chest rose and fell rhythmically, each breath punctuated by the sigh of a machine that was attached to the tube that had been forced down Dennis's throat. He looked so small, Ford thought. So fragile.

He took a half-step forward, tried to see the man he had known beneath the medical equipment that was now keeping him alive. Felt his eyes prickle with sudden hot tears, even as impotent fury seared his thoughts, drowning out the memory of another time, another room, and the sound of wood hitting flesh.

'I'm sorry, guv,' he whispered. 'This is my fault. All of it. But I'll find whoever did this, I swear. And if it was Sanderson, I won't stop this time. I swear to God.'

Morgan gave the only answer he was capable of giving. The ventilator hissed its approval.

CHAPTER 37

After making sure that the police had everything in place for Donna's safety, and telling Robbie to organise a drive-by of her flat, Connor headed home. He made the journey on autopilot, mind working through the events of the day. And there was something in Ross's manner when he arrived at Donna's flat, some nervous distraction as he asked his questions and informed Donna they were going to take her laptop away for analysis, that told Connor more bad news was waiting out there for him.

He parked outside the flat, fished his phone out of his pocket. Considered calling Ford to tell him what had happened, maybe get a lead on what was bothering Ross. Looked at the stairs leading down to his front door. No. One thing at a time. Jen said she had found something. He reached into the back seat, grabbing the bottles of wine he only vaguely remembered stopping to buy. Then he headed down the steps.

Jen smiled up at him as he walked into the living room, the coffee-table buried under a drift of photographs, albums and pictures. 'Hiya,' she said. 'Everything OK with work? I see you've brought your offerings.'

Connor looked down at the wine bottles he was holding. 'Yeah,' he said, crossing to the couch, planting a kiss on her forehead, then heading for the kitchen to chill the bottles. 'You want a top-up just now?'

'Nah, I'll wait. Had a few glasses while I was looking through your gran's stuff so I'm good just now.'

Your gran's stuff. The words brought Connor up short. How would his gran feel, knowing a woman she had never met was pawing through the mementoes of her life? How did he feel about that? And what did it say that he was allowing it to happen?

'OK, gimme a minute to get changed, then you can show me what you've got,' he said, heading for the bedroom.

He emerged a few minutes later, suit swapped for a T-shirt and jogging bottoms. Jen was still in her spot on the couch, but her glass of wine had been joined by a glass for Connor. Whisky. A big one.

'So,' he said, settling into the couch, 'what have you got for me?'

'Couple of things,' Jen replied, absently brushing her hair back as she leaned forward to grab a handful of photographs and papers from the coffee-table. 'Your dad seemed awfully keen to get that report card and, from what you said, it's what caused your gran to go looking for something in her flat. So it got me thinking, was there anything else from your dad's schooldays lying around?'

Connor made an approving noise. Sound logic. Jen would make a fair investigator if she ever got tired of the gym life. 'And I take it you found something?'

'Couple of things,' Jen replied, a small frown furrowing the smooth skin of her forehead. 'No more report cards, but there was this . . .' She passed him a piece of paper, yellowed and brittle. 'It was jammed in the back of an album.'

Connor took it, unfolding it as gently as he could. It was an old newspaper clipping, from the *Stirling Observer*. A page from the local round-up, back in the days when newspapers featured articles on the achievements of the schools in their area, and not just pictures from graduations or charity days.

'Stirling Pupil Gets to the Art of the Matter,' the headline read, above a black-and-white picture that at once made Connor want to smile and wince. His gran stared back at him, a young woman, vibrant, undamaged by the years or the dementia that was now robbing her of herself. In front of her, smiling awkwardly, was a boy, all long legs and unruly hair, school tie tugged defiantly askew. Connor had never seen much of himself in his father, but looking at a young Jack Fraser, he could almost be looking at a fifteen-year-old version of himself. But it was the third figure in the picture who fascinated Connor most, the one who drew his attention. A stern-looking man, tall and rangy, his suit doing nothing to hide his almost skeletal frame. He had one hand placed on Ida's shoulder, the other on Jack's. There was something stilted in that pose, almost proprietary.

Campbell Fraser, Connor thought. Pleased to meet you, Granddad.

He glanced at Jen, smiled, then read the article. 'Local lad Jack Fraser has had his first brush with the big-time, after coming third in a national art prize. Fraser, 15, who is a pupil at Stirling High School, was praised for his imaginative and sensitive use of colour and technique in his painting, *For This Land*.' Connor's eyes slipped to the middle of the page, and the crude black-and-white reproduction of a landscape painting, instantly recognisable as a view of the Wallace Monument, which had been rendered like some kind of Gothic monolith stabbing into the sky. Again, Connor was reminded of the report card: 'Jack is a sensitive and empathetic student . . .'

Who was this man?

He forced the question aside, focused back on the article. 'Jack's parents, Ida and Campbell, said they were particularly proud of their son, who told the *Observer* he now wants to pursue a career as a painter. "Obviously we're proud of him. To come third is no mean feat. However, art doesn't pay the bills, so we'll see what happens next. He wanted to be a mechanic last week," said his father, Campbell.'

Connor skimmed the rest of the article. The message was clear. Jack Fraser had talent as an artist. So what the hell happened?

'OK,' Connor said, putting the article aside, hand hovering for a second at the whisky. 'Interesting. Dad never mentioned anything about this, and Gran never told me he harboured any ambition to be a painter. Certainly, by the time Campbell left, he seemed pretty focused on medicine from what Gran's said in the past.'

'Hmm, that might explain this,' Jen murmured, reaching for another picture. It was in colour, the same trio, this time outside. They were standing in a Chinese pagoda, wood painted red and green, rich, lush foliage behind them, punctuated only by chunks of dull granite, like they were in a gorge. They were dressed casually, making Connor think they were on holiday. The only thing that shattered that illusion was the ungainly cast encasing his gran's left arm. He flipped the picture over, saw a scrawl of writing he instantly recognised as Ida's. Less shaky, more confident, but hers nonetheless: 'September '69,' it read. 'Campbell showing us around his home town and childhood haunts in Pittencrieff Park, Dunfermline. Jack has been brilliant helping me with my arm. The boy has healing hands.'

Connor looked up at Jen, who frowned when she saw the question form on his face. 'What?' she said. 'It's one of the few pictures of your grandfather I could find. Thought the note might have explained your dad's shift in interest. You know, got a kick out of helping his mum get better, got a taste for looking after people.'

'Maybe,' Connor said, distracted. More questions now. Unwelcome ones. 'But there's just one problem.'

'Oh? What's that?' Jen asked.

'This note. It doesn't make sense. My gran always told me that when Campbell walked out on her and Dad, he went back home, took up with another woman, started another life.'

'Yeah, so?' Jen asked, confusion seeping into her own voice now. 'He went home to Fife. Couldn't be that hard for you to track him down if you wanted to. Do you?'

Connor shook his head. 'That's not it, Jen. Gran always told me Campbell came from Inverness, went back there. But this note says otherwise. So the question is, why would she lie to me about that?'

CHAPTER 38

I have cultivated patience over the years. I pride myself on it, have made it the guiding principle of my life. The ability to wait, to allow events to unfold as I remain watchful for opportunities. Take my latest work at the university: a masterpiece of patience and restraint until the perfect moment.

Predictable, then, that *he* would make me cast all that aside.

I hadn't meant to lose control, I swear. But seeing him there, so smug and confident in himself, the same calm conviction that he was right and the world was wrong, that the course of action he chose was the right one, I was unable to help myself. I lunged for him, pushing forward, surprised that a man of such presence could be so ephemeral and easily moved. We crashed through the house, him stumbling backwards and falling. I swear I only landed on him because he dragged me with him. I tried to get away, but his hands were on me. Strong, grasping, clawing. Just as they were all those years ago.

The knife was in his chest before I knew it, stabbing the air from his lungs in a spray of blood spatter that misted the air in front of me. I caught the iron tang of it in my nostrils, felt the heat of it on my cheeks and, in that moment, I was gone.

I don't know how many times I stabbed him. The truth is, after the first slash, I lost the ability to care. I just kept on moving the knife until he went limp and silent, the blood pooling around him like some slick, obscene aura.

In that moment, as I came back to myself and realised what I had done, I saw the opportunity in this. That finally this man, who had held me back for so many years, stopped me being me, had finally given me something. A gift I could use.

The police officer, Ford, would no doubt want to look into this, find out who had attacked his friend. And to do that, he would certainly have to contact Connor Fraser. And, after seeing Fraser in action, I know the man will be compelled to act. Especially in light of the message I sent Blake, which she will undoubtedly share with him soon enough. I saw that in the look she gave him in Stirling as the cleaver swung. She trusts him. Believes he can protect her.

And, ultimately, that will be what destroys them both.

CHAPTER 39

The next morning, Connor rose early, leaving Jen to sleep off the previous evening's wine, and went for a run, in an attempt to order his thoughts and set out his plan for the day.

He tried to block out thoughts of his gran, his father, Sanderson, Ford and Donna with Bach in his ears and his breath scalding his lungs. But still images churned and crashed through his mind. His gran in the photograph. The email sent to Donna. The newspaper clipping. The cleaver flashing in weak daylight as Clarke charged him. All posing questions without answers. Problems to be solved.

He ran his normal five-mile circuit around the King's Park area, watching as the houses stirred, cars sliding from driveways and people walking dogs as they settled into their day. He sprinted the last half-mile, pushing himself as hard as he could, craving the endorphin hit and the calm that strenuous exercise brought him. He knew it was an addiction, that he was perilously close to overtraining, but it was, he reasoned, better than some of the other addictions he could have picked up. He didn't drink much, but when he did, he found the measures got a little too large a little too quickly. No. Better to exercise himself to exhaustion, get high on natural chemicals and ease his mind that way.

Back at the flat, he did a set of press-ups then showered and made coffee. Stepped out onto the patio with Tom's breakfast, popped his head in on Jen, who was still snuggled down under his quilt, then got down to the business of the day.

And that day, business was bad.

His first call was to Robbie, who reported a frustrating lack of progress in tracking down the source of the email sent to Donna. The account itself was a generic web-based one that could have been set up by anyone, anywhere, and a study of the headers and IP addresses it came from showed that it had been sent, unsurprisingly, from somewhere in central Scotland. The best guess Robbie had, so far, was that the sender had used a smartphone with email and camera, snapped the image, composed the email and hit send. If they had any sense, they would have used a pay-as-you-go SIM card. Simple. Convenient. Relatively anonymous.

Connor grumbled his understanding, moved on to an update on Donna. Robbie reported all had been quiet around her flat the night before, almost as quiet as things had been around Sanderson's home in Cambusbarron where, on Connor's instructions, the teams had been on the look-out for a black Mercedes-Benz, and reported nothing. Connor considered this. Was he wrong? Had Paulie been following him and not Sanderson? Possible but, if so, how had he known Connor would be heading to Sanderson's home and been there waiting for him?

Another question. Another problem.

He thanked Robbie for the update, held back on giving him the task he had thought of on his run. Instead he told him to keep coordinating the security around Sanderson and try to think of another way to trace whoever had sent Donna that email. It was probably an exercise in futility, and one the police would also be undertaking, but, still, something in that email niggled at Connor. Something . . .

He ended the call with Robbie, turned his attention to Donna. She snatched up the phone halfway through the first ring, snapped a hello down the line.

'Bad night?' Connor asked, reaching for his coffee and feeling the first after-effect of his workout bite into his shoulders.

'Bad morning,' Donna replied. 'Take it you've not heard about what happened to Dennis Morgan yesterday?'

'Morgan? You mean the detective in charge of the Sanderson inquiry back in 2006?'

'One and the same,' Donna said, the sound of keys clattering in the background. 'Turns out someone attacked him yesterday. Being treated as attempted murder. He's in critical care at Forth Valley now.'

Connor felt these facts click together in his mind. Donna pissed off. Morgan attacked. 'They've cancelled your interview with Sanderson this afternoon,' he said.

'Yeah,' she replied, weary resignation in her tone now. 'Just got a call from his lawyer. They're going in to Randolphfield later to give a statement on his whereabouts yesterday. Means the interview gets bumped. Annoying, but I might get to doorstep him anyway.'

'Doorstep? How?'

'Ross has called a press conference at ten a.m. at Randolphfield,' she replied. 'No notes on details or subjects in the press call, but it's easy to see why. A murder, a cleaver attack and now this, all in the space of twenty-four hours? Makes it look a lot like the mighty Police Scotland can't keep things in order. Chief constable won't like that. And neither will his political bosses.'

Connor could see her point. It wasn't a good look. Especially since Ford had told him Ross had been brought in to calm the situation down and avoid any adverse headlines. Later. He had more immediate concerns. 'Look, Donna, I have to go. If Sanderson's being taken to Randolphfield, I'll have to liaise with his legal team on that. They should have called me to let me know.'

'I did mention you to them,' Donna said, slightly defensively. 'Carl said he was going to get someone from the office to call you and let you know what was going on. Guess they've just been busy trying to get everything ready for Sanderson's interview.'

'Maybe,' Connor said, irritation prickling his skin. Carl Layton treated those handling personal security, especially those employed privately to do so, as an inconvenient fact of life. After all, he was a QC with a legendary arrogance, and a supreme belief in his own untouchable status, he tended to forget that mere mortals didn't live in the hermetically sealed bubble of the police-protected court room.

'Any luck with the email?' Donna asked, interrupting his thoughts.

Connor filled her in on what little he had discovered from Robbie. It echoed what she had been told by the IT experts at Sky, who had similarly studied the problem. Conclusion? Unless the police found something, whoever sent that email would remain anonymous until they chose to be otherwise. The thought wasn't particularly comforting.

'Listen, Donna. I know I can't stop you being at the press conference, but be careful. If you want someone to give you a lift, let me know.'

She gave a snort. 'Turn up with a security detail? Christ, how would that look? No, thanks. Keith is picking me up and we'll head there together. Besides, I get the feeling whoever sent that email will be too busy watching the press conference to do anything about his threats.'

The message flashed across Connor's mind. *I'll be seeing you VERY soon.* Was that what the sender had meant? I'll see you on TV soon?

He looked up at the sound of the bedroom door opening, Jen padding into the room wearing one of his T-shirts. Smiled, raised a hand in a hello.

'Donna, I'm going to get going,' he said. 'We'll talk later, see if there's going to be a rearranged interview with Sanderson, figure out how to handle it.'

'Oh, there's going to be an interview all right,' Donna replied. 'Trust me on that.'

He said his goodbyes, ended the call, looked up at Jen. 'You want some coffee?'

'Yeah, please,' she said, leaning over him and planting a kiss on his forehead. 'You OK? Early start?'

'Yeah, just a lot to do today. Seems like my schedule has changed a bit.'

Jen frowned down on him. 'You still going to have time to talk to your dad?'

Connor felt a flash of discomfort in his guts. It had seemed so clear last night, with Jen beside him and a couple of whiskies down. Ask his dad outright about the note on the picture. Now, in the cold light of day, he wasn't so sure. 'Maybe,' he said, noncommittal. 'I'll see how the day goes.'

She held his gaze long enough to tell him he wasn't fooling her.

Shrugged. 'I'm going to get a shower. Got time for breakfast before you head out? Cisco's?'

Connor nodded. It was a small café on Port Street, not far from the gym. A handy place to refuel after a workout, he had been there a few times, enjoying the comfortable anonymity the place offered. And, being close to the centre of town, it was handy for the next task Connor had to attend to. 'Sure,' he said. 'I'll make a couple of calls while you're getting ready, then we'll head out.'

She murmured agreement, made for the bathroom. Connor scrolled through the contacts in his phone, waited until he heard the sound of the shower running before he hit dial. After all, conversations with Paulie could be unpredictable. And the last thing Connor wanted Jen to hear was anything . . . unpleasant.

CHAPTER 40

The incident room had the abandoned, still feel of a suddenly emptied home. Coffee cups and plates lay strewn across desks piled high with paperwork and forms, the bureaucratic jet trails left by a large-scale investigation. But now, at nine twenty a.m., with the main ops meeting of the day held, assignments handed out and Ross locked into talks with the chief constable about the upcoming press conference, the place had been emptied out.

Except, that was, for Malcolm Ford.

He stalked around the room, picking at the odd folder, glancing back at the murder wall, which had names, headshots and maps stuck to it. Technically, he shouldn't have been in there. After all, he was only an adviser on the case. No, he should be a good little DCI and scuttle off to his office, deal with the admin hell the chief had made sure would keep him out of the way.

Fuck that, he thought. Fuck that all the way to Hell.

He made one final lap of the room, then collapsed into a chair in front of the murder wall, sipping coffee as he absorbed the silent horror of the tableau in front of him, his eyes falling on the golf-course victim. There had still been no success in identifying her, but there was something in that headshot, something that nagged at Ford, like the ghostly ache of a once-broken bone on a cold day.

He took another sip of his coffee – real stuff, not the muck Ross had forced him to endure the other day – then smiled, realising it was the coffee that had given him a plan for the day.

He had arrived at the station early, wanting to see if he could persuade Troughton to give him any more information on the deceased or any leads they might have developed on who had attacked Morgan. After leaving the hospital, he'd given Michael Morgan his phone number, told him to call any time he wanted. Michael had made good on this, ringing Ford just before midnight to tell him there was no major change in his dad's condition, but the doctors were guardedly optimistic. 'I thought you'd want to know,' he had said. 'Thought it might make you sleep better.'

Ford smiled at the memory now. A considerate gesture. Pointless, but considerate.

He had collared Troughton just after the morning ops meeting. Hauled him aside and tasked him with his usual job of 'nipping out to get some real coffee'. Troughton had initially seemed hesitant, until Ford had pressed a ten-pound note into his hand and told him to grab a latte for himself as part of the deal.

He had returned to Ford's office fifteen minutes later, two Starbucks balanced in his hand as he shouldered the door open. Ford took his coffee, kept his tone casual. 'What you assigned to? More follow-up on the Morgan stabbing?' he asked.

Troughton opened his mouth, closed it. Ford could almost read the instruction from Ross playing through his mind. *DCI Ford is not part of this investigation. Do not discuss this with him.*

Ford sat quietly, letting the silence and Troughton's own sense of loyalty do its work. Didn't take long.

'No, sir,' he said at last, talking around his own coffee cup. 'That's been assigned to DC Jefferson. I'm following up on the Donna Blake lead.'

Ford sat forward. Blake? 'Go on.'

'Well, sir,' Troughton said, voice dropping, as though they were in a library, 'it seems the murderer sent her a picture last night. Of the woman killed up at the golf course. Or, more accurately, a piece of her.'

Ford nodded, Dr Tennant's words floating across his mind. He took a sip of the coffee, found it suddenly unappealing. 'A finger,' he said. 'He sent a picture of a severed finger.'

'Why, yes, sir,' Troughton said. 'Anyway, I'm following up with the IT guys, and then I'll be at the press conference to talk to Ms Blake.'

Ford had let the silence work its spell again, then told Troughton to leave. Waited for a few minutes, making sure the murder room was empty, then drifted in and started picking around. He wasn't sure what for, but he'd know it when he saw it.

His eyes drifted back to the murder wall. To the pictures of three women, fourteen years apart.

Two is only one short of three, Malcolm, he heard Dennis Morgan whisper.

Again, the feeling of familiarity, of something obvious being missed. Could Sanderson really have done all this? After re-reading the original files, Ford was sure he had been the killer back in 2006, the extra evidence Morgan and he had 'found' notwithstanding. What had he said to Fraser? *He's a killer, Connor. And he'll do it again.*

Two is only one short of three.

He shook off the thought, drained the cup. Looked up at the murder board again, then away, planning his day. Coming here had been a waste of time: there was nothing in the room for him. Back to Plan A: kill time, keep his head down, then slip into the press conference and wait for Blake to . . .

He stopped in his tracks, a sudden flash of cold recognition arcing down his spine.

Familiarity. Jesus, could it be that obvious?

He fumbled for his phone, got onto the news app. Scrolled through Sky until he found what he wanted. Hit play, then pause. Turned back to the murder wall, feeling as though worms were coiling, glistening and oily, in his guts.

The hair. Jesus Christ. The hair. He marched back to the murder wall, found what he was looking for. The crime-scene picture of the latest victim, lying pale and abandoned on cold, wet grass. The headshot was stark, brutal, all heavy flash and bled light. But it showed enough. The woman's head. What had Tennant said? She had been subdued with a heavy blow to the head. Gagged, murdered, dumped.

Yet the picture in front of Ford now showed a woman whose hair was much neater than it should have been. Styled so it was parted at the side, revealing a trickle of blood and a greying flap of skin, one lock of long, dark hair falling across her right eye.

Just the way Donna Blake wore her hair in the image frozen on Ford's phone now.

CHAPTER 41

Paulie had grudgingly agreed to meet Connor at Beechwood Park, a large public area comprised of walkways, children's play areas, a BMX track and a football pitch. The grass was neatly trimmed, the area interspersed with high trees that swayed gently in the wind. Connor vaguely remembered his gran telling him that some of the trees in the park, which had been originally built, like much of Stirling, to service a large family home, dated back to the eighteenth century. It was an interesting aside, but Connor didn't think Paulie had chosen the place for its horticultural merits.

No. Paulie had chosen Beechwood Park for its location. Sitting just off Randolph Terrace, it was only a two-minute drive from Randolphfield police station. And Connor could guess one reason Paulie wanted to be close to it on that particular morning.

The question he had was why.

He was standing at the entrance to the park, watching a short blonde woman being dragged along by an over-enthusiastic beagle, when he saw Paulie lumbering towards him. Connor had heard the expression 'built like a tank' many a time, but he had never seen the embodiment of it until he'd met Paulie. He was a small, squat man, with silvering hair that had been buzzed ruthlessly down to the skull. He moved with the top-heavy, lumbering gait of someone who was badly overweight, arms out to his sides, head tipped back, gut thrown forward. But Connor had seen Paulie in action, knew that, when he wanted to, he could move with the type of fluid grace you usually saw in sharks as they struck their prey. And, like a shark, Paulie's size was not to be dismissed. Yes, the gut was prodigious, straining at the trousers of his rumpled suit and fighting valiantly to be free of his jacket, but there was nothing soft in that stomach. Like many of the most dangerous men Connor had ever met, Paulie wore his weight like armour.

And he knew how to use it.

He stopped a few paces in front of Connor, the aroma of cheap cigars and sweat cutting through the smell of grass and leaves. Small, beady eyes darted across Connor like a strobe, checking posture, hand position, stance. Since their first meeting, Paulie had always approached Connor as if he were expecting violence at any second. What Connor didn't like to admit to himself was that he was curious to see what would happen if that ever did take place.

'OK, I'm here. Whit?' Paulie said.

'Nice bit of make-up,' Connor said, jutting his jaw towards a fresh graze that ran up Paulie's cheek to his eye socket.

Paulie's hand rose to his face, one blunt, sausage-like finger scratching the graze absently as he shrugged shoulders that looked like two boulders squeezed into Armani. 'Job-related injury,' he grumbled. 'It happens. Now, we gonna stand here aw day or are you gonna tell me what the fuck you want? Got things to do today.'

'Aye,' Connor agreed. 'Like heading up the road to keep an eye on Colin Sanderson at the press conference later on? How'd you hear about that anyway, Paulie? Don't strike me as the type with friends in the press.'

A smile curled its way onto Paulie's lips, thin and cruel. Amusement flashed in his eyes. I know something you don't know, the look said. 'Dunno what you're talking about,' Paulie said as the smile faded. 'Look, I agreed to this because I owe you, Fraser, but dinnae push it.'

'No problem,' Connor said. A year ago, Paulie had given him some information in confidence that had helped him solve three murders in Stirling. Paulie had done it to keep Jen safe and, in return, Connor had kept the source of the information confidential, which, in Paulie's twisted morality, meant he owed Connor something. Problem was, with Paulie that could mean anything from a pint down the pub or a bullet between the eyes.

'I'll keep it simple,' Connor said, drawing his hands from his pockets and fighting the urge to ball them into fists. Just in case. 'I just want to know why you're keeping an eye on Colin Sanderson. See, I had thought maybe it was me – maybe Duncan was worried that working with Sanderson would somehow wash up at Jen's door. But then you agree to meet here this morning, right before the Sanderson press conference. So, as much as it pains me to admit it, it's him you're interested in, not me. So what gives, Paulie? You watching him on Duncan's orders, or your own?'

The humour faded from Paulie's face, leaving only the cruelty behind. Again Connor was reminded of a shark: the empty black eyes glaring at its prey.

'Fuck off,' Paulie whispered. 'I didnae come here for this. See you later. Make sure you treat Jen right,'

Connor raised his hands, placatory, ignoring the comment about Jen. Their relationship was none of Paulie's business. And, besides, what the fuck did he think Connor would do? Lock her in a closet every night? Tie her to the bed?

'Paulie, please,' he said, deciding to take a risk. 'You know I'm working security for Sanderson. Doesn't mean I have to like it. And if the guy did have anything to do with those murders back in 2006, or the girl up at the golf course yesterday, I'm in the best place to find out. And you know I'll deal with it if I do. But I can't do that if I don't have all the facts. So tell me, what's going on? Please?'

Paulie's face changed again, softened. From killer to kindly uncle in the blink of an eye. It reminded Connor of how dangerous the man in front of him truly was.

'Aye, I heard about the lassie being found up at the university,' he said, head shaking. 'Hell of a fucking thing.'

'Then help me,' Connor said. 'One way or another, Sanderson is tied up in this. Help me understand how.'

Connor could see the calculation run in Paulie's eyes, cold and smooth. Tell him? If so, how much?

'Aye, all right,' he said, fishing into his pocket and pulling out the stub of a cigar so thick Connor mistook it briefly for a tree branch. ''Mon, we'll walk and I'll have a smoke. Tell you a story. But, Fraser, this does not get back to the boss. Clear?'

'Understood,' Connor said, again fighting the urge to clench his fists and raise his guard.

Paulie dipped his chin. Terms agreed. 'Right. 'Mon. Let's see if you can keep up. But before we start, you're no' as clever as ye think ye are.'

'Oh, how so?'

The cruel humour reappeared on Paulie's face, spreading like sun over a battlefield and revealing the horror of a man who took pleasure only in the misery of others.

'Well, see, you're right. I was watching Sanderson. But it wasnae him I was looking for.'

CHAPTER 42

Donna sat in the second row of seats that had been arranged in the basement room used for press conferences at Randolphfield, her mind on the past. The last time she had been in that room for a formal press conference with the chief constable of Police Scotland, she had been working for Valley FM, the local radio station. On that occasion, she had been forced to stand at the back, and her questions were roundly ignored by DCI Ford and the chief constable. She felt a sting of melancholy as she realised Mark had been at that press conference as well. Mark, with whom she had once thought she would have a life. Who had run back to his wife and his dead-but-convenient marriage the moment she'd told him she was pregnant.

Mark, who had gasped his last breath hanging from a tree, entrails sliding from his belly as he thrashed and twisted on the rope.

Donna blinked away the image, swallowed the sour saliva that flooded her mouth. Was her mother right? Was she taking too many risks? She had covered murders, seen people close to her killed, and now a murderer was sending her notes and pictures. *I'll be seeing you VERY soon.* And if she was a target, what did that mean for Andrew? He had already lost his father. Was she taking too big a risk by sticking with this?

She straightened in her seat, focused her thoughts on the present, angry with herself and her mother, who had placed the seeds of doubt in her mind. It was irrelevant now, anyway. The damage was done.

She had come to the attention of a killer or someone with a very sick sense of humour. Either way, running would help nothing. The only way to resolve this now was to see it through, find whoever it was. Make sure they were caught and exposed for what they really were.

And after that? Well, that was a question for another day.

There was a flurry of activity and three people filed out of a door at the far end of the room: Chief Constable Peter Guthrie, DCI Alan Ross and a woman in a business suit whom Donna didn't recognise. She saw Ross scan the room as he took his seat, his eyes falling on her. He had called her earlier that morning with a simple message that was somewhere between a warning and a threat. As a member of the press, she had every right to attend the press conference, but if she mentioned anything about the email or the picture she had received, she would be charged with hampering a police investigation, and Sky's press privileges with Police Scotland would be cancelled.

Donna had reluctantly agreed. It suited her to keep the email to herself anyway. For now.

The woman Donna didn't recognise headed for a lectern at the far end of the stage, looked around the room. She was tall, with long dark hair scraped back into a sleek ponytail. The suit she was wearing was elegant, tailored, and Donna found herself wondering how well communications roles in Police Scotland paid these days.

'Good morning,' she said, her voice cool, clipped. Edinburgh, Donna thought. Somewhere in the New Town. No one else managed bored efficiency in quite the same way. 'My name is Victoria Gilson. I'm the new director of communications for the Central Division of Police Scotland. I'm looking forward to working with all of you. We've called this press conference to address some recent incidents in Stirling and the surrounding area. DCI Ross and Chief Constable Guthrie will both give short statements, and there will be time for questions after that, which I'll chair. If you're asking a question, please identify yourself and your publication or broadcast outlet. Thank you. DCI Ross?'

Gilson moved back to her seat, heels clicking on the floor as she passed Ross, who was glancing nervously at the press pack as he approached the lectern. Donna smiled. She had thought DCI Ford was the most uncomfortable man she had ever seen in front of the press, but Ross seem determined to give him a run for his money.

'Ah, good morning,' Ross said in a hesitant voice, eyes darting between the notes he had placed on the lectern and the assembled reports in front of him. There was a soft murmur of camera clicks, Ross flinching slightly as the flashes hit him. Donna glanced at Gilson, whose face was set, eyes stony. She knew his discomfort wouldn't be a good look.

'As you know, a member of staff at the Airthrey golf course reported the discovery of a body on the grounds yesterday morning at approximately six thirty a.m. Ah, following investigations and post-mortem examinations, we can confirm this morning that the death was suspicious in nature, and we are appealing to members of the public for any information they may have. We have yet to formally identify the victim, but you will find a full description in the media packs that we are distributing and we would be grateful if you could run these in full in your reports. You may also be aware of reports that a man was attacked in his home in the Alloa area yesterday. Investigations are ongoing, and we will be releasing further updates on this in due course. However, I would like to stress that such in-home attacks are rare, so the people of Alloa and the surrounding area should be reassured that this type of event is the exception, not the rule. Thank you.'

Donna sighed as Ross shuffled back to his seat. He had just given a textbook no-comment comment. The police had nothing new to say, but they had to say something. Brilliant.

A moment's pause, punctuated by the polite clearing of throats, as Guthrie made his way to the lectern. He was everything Ross hadn't been, confident, assured. His back was ramrod straight, his head high. When he got to the lectern he paused, scanning the room, letting the photographers do their work. He was trying hard to project an image of quiet authority, but to Donna he just looked like another middle-aged man playing dress-up in a faintly ridiculous uniform.

'Thank you, DCI Ross,' he said, nodding towards the detective, the magnanimous leader praising his troops. 'As you know, Police Scotland puts public safety and the swift apprehension of those who would break the law at the heart of everything we do. As chief constable, I want to emphasise what DCI Ross said. To have two violent incidents in two days is highly unusual, and will not be tolerated by myself or my officers. To that end, we are increasing patrols across the division area, and we will . . .'

Donna tuned Guthrie out. Two? Interesting maths. Unless, of course, someone being attacked by a cleaver-wielding chef didn't constitute a 'violent incident' these days. She started playing with the idea, wondering if there was a way she could make a joke about how crimes were reported to keep the stats down, when her phone buzzed on her lap. She unlocked it, toggled into the email app. Felt something cold and malignant twist around her lungs, making it suddenly hard to breathe.

The same email address as the night before: Stir-ed666@gmail. com. Topic: *Today's the day.* She clicked into it, suddenly feeling as though everyone in the room was looking at her.

Morning Donna,

Well, today's the day. I've got a bit of business first (hope the press conference is more lively than my meeting), then I can concentrate on you. I'm looking forward to it. I'll be seeing you REAL soon.

Donna scanned the message another two times, fighting back the roiling in her guts. Sanderson? Yes, he'd be tied up with the police this morning, and he knew Donna was here at the press conference. Or someone else? Someone watching her. Waiting. Someone who would see her REAL soon?

She fought back the urge to get up and get out, go to her parents' home, collect Andrew and leave. Heard her mother's voice again: *It's no job for a mother with a young son.* Grasped her anger like a life raft. Nurtured it.

Fine. Let Sanderson, or whoever it was, come. She'd be ready. And she'd have a surprise for him.

CHAPTER 43

Connor watched as Sanderson got out of the car, fiddling with his phone as he did so, oblivious to Robbie, who had opened the door for him. Interesting how quickly he had moved from being a hard-ened ex-con to a pampered wannabe celebrity. The question was, how many other personas did he have, and was a killer among them?

The sight of the phone bothered Connor. By rights, the police should have seized it as part of their investigation into the email that was sent to Donna. But with Sanderson being a sensitive subject, it was obvious the kid gloves were on and he was being given a certain latitude.

He swallowed a sudden prickle of irritation, focused on the job in hand. Make sure Sanderson got into the station safely, then ensure he knew to contact Connor when he was done for a ride back home.

'Fucking hate this place,' Sanderson grumbled in greeting to Connor, jutting his jaw towards the blunt façade of the police station.

Connor murmured agreement. Truth was, he wasn't too fond of it, or any other police station, either. Since he had left the Police Service of Northern Ireland, he had made a personal vow to stay as far away from police stations as possible. Being inside them stirred up too many ghosts, which whispered to him about regrets and paths not taken.

'Your lawyer is already in there, said he wanted to meet you at the desk, make sure you were treated properly from the moment you stepped inside,' Connor said.

Sanderson smiled, nothing pleasant in the expression. 'Oh, aye, Mr Layton is loving this,' he said. 'A chance to drag the police over the coals and the promise of a nice wee harassment case to boot. He's earning his money, and mine, while these wankers waste their time.'

'It's hardly a waste of time,' Connor said, cool disdain caressing the back of his neck. 'One man's been seriously injured, and you just about got your head taken off with a machete. The police need to be doing something about that.'

Something uglier than his smile flashed in Sanderson's eyes. 'Look, Fraser, what happened to Dennis Morgan was fuck-aw to do with me. I'll admit I'll not shed any tears for the cunt if he dies, but I didn't touch him, OK? And as for the wee incident up the road, I was never in any real danger, was I?'

Again the image of condiments and spices spilling across cobbles flashed across Connor's mind. Something . . .

He stiffened slightly as it hit him, like a word in a crossword puzzle he had been looking for. He grabbed at the thought, turned it over in his mind. Examined it.

I was never in any real danger . . .

Connor glanced at his watch. 'Press conference should just about be done,' he said, 'which means Ross will be looking for you. You get in there, Mr Sanderson, text me when you're done and I'll meet you, give you a lift home.'

Sanderson raised a finger to his temple, ticked out a brief salute to Connor. 'Right you are, boss,' he said, turning to walk up the stairs.

Connor watched him disappear into the police station, Robbie falling into position beside him.

'Charmer, isn't he?' Connor asked.

'Oh, yes, boss, a delight,' Robbie said, barely bothering to keep the contempt from his voice. 'You sure you want to drive him home when this is done? I can get him easy enough.'

'Thanks, Robbie, I appreciate it. But I've got a couple of things I need you to do for me. And I need them done quickly.'

Robbie straightened, as though being called to attention. 'Just say the word, boss.'

Connor smiled. Typical Robbie, always eager to please. Though this time, Connor wasn't sure there was going to be anything pleasant coming out of his work.

He took a breath, started talking. Told Robbie what he needed, ignoring the confusion that fell over the younger's man's face as he spoke. Then he sent him on his way and retrieved his phone. Found the contact he was after, hit dial.

No, nothing pleasant at all.

'Hello?'

'Morning, sir,' Connor said to Malcolm Ford. 'Sorry to bother you, but I'm at Randolphfield now. Yes, escorting Sanderson to his interview with Ross. Look, I just had a very interesting conversation with a contact, and I was wondering if you had time to talk.'

His phone buzzed as Ford spoke, telling Connor he would come and meet him, they could use his office to talk. Connor swallowed back his discomfort at the thought, agreed. Then killed the call and flicked over to his text messages, reading the one that had arrived while he spoke to Ford.

As he did so, he remembered Sanderson's arrival. Phone in hand. *I was never in any real danger.* Knew then that the conversation would not be between two people but three, and it was going to be a lot more complicated than Connor had initially thought.

CHAPTER 44

Donna did a to-camera piece from inside the room where the press conference had been held. As she suspected, her requests to interview either Ross or the chief constable were politely but firmly refused, leaving her with little new to add to the story.

Well, little that she could share at this stage.

After she had received the latest email, the temptation to lob a grenade at the chief constable was almost overwhelming. Stand up, hold up her phone. 'Chief Constable Guthrie, care to comment on the fact that a killer is stalking me and has made a threat on my life?'

She fought down the urge – barely. Instead, thumbed in a message to Connor. The reply was almost instant: *Going to meet Ford. Give me ten minutes then call me. I'll come find you and you can join us. He needs to hear this.*

She agreed, reluctantly. Malcolm Ford was hardly one of her biggest fans, but he was a good policeman. And, being close to the original murder inquiry, he was someone she needed to speak to.

Donna wrapped up her report, then sent Keith back to the van with instructions to send the footage to Sky for the lunchtime bulletin. He offered to stick around, but she sent him back to Edinburgh. No matter what happened, the last thing she wanted to do was put Sanderson on camera. Not yet. Not when there were questions she still needed answered.

Impatient, she glanced at her phone, checked the time. She didn't like being kept waiting, and part of her was curious to know what Connor wanted to discuss with Ford that he didn't want her to hear.

One more question to ask.

***

At that moment, Connor was sitting in Ford's office. It brought back a lot of memories from his time in Belfast – the cheap furniture, incident reports and maps tacked to the wall like cheap wallpaper, the forgotten coffee cup on the cluttered desk. Belfast or Stirling, it seemed police chic was universal.

He had filled Ford in on Donna's latest email, the policeman's face implacable as he spoke. Ford agreed, reluctantly, to the three of them speaking, as long as it was off the record, which Connor assured him it would be. 'And speaking of off the record, sir, there's something I wanted to talk to you about before Donna joins us.'

'Oh, and what's that?' Ford asked, sitting back in his chair.

Connor looked at Ford for a moment, considering his approach. Decided that straight on was the only way to tackle it. Ford wasn't a man who liked to mess around.

'Paulie King,' Connor said. 'Did you know he's been watching Colin Sanderson at the request of your old boss?'

Ford blinked, sat forward. 'What?' he whispered. 'Paulie King? Duncan MacKenzie's thug? Fraser, what the hell are you talking about?'

Connor gave an apologetic smile. 'From what I've been told, Morgan asked MacKenzie to have an eye put on Sanderson in case his son tried anything, ah, rash.'

'Son?' Wary confusion bled Ford's voice of any conviction. 'You mean Michael? What the hell has he got to do with any of this?'

'Turns out there was a bit of a run-in when Sanderson was released,' Connor said, recalling what Paulie had told him. 'Morgan's son was with him, didn't take kindly to some of the things Sanderson said about his dad to the press at the time. Seems Dennis Morgan was worried enough about it that he wanted Sanderson watched, and Paulie to intervene if his boy turned up and tried anything.'

'Michael? I don't believe it. He never struck me as the violent type. I mean, I can understand him being protective of his dad since his mum died, but still . . .'

'I did a little checking,' Connor said. 'Seems Michael has a bit of history. Back in 2009, he was cautioned for assault in Edinburgh. He claimed self-defence, said a guy came at him with a broken bottle outside a bar. CCTV backed it up, so he was let off with a strong talking-to, probably his dad calling in a few favours. An assault charge would have thrown a real spanner into his teaching career.'

'How the hell did you find this out?' Ford asked, leaning forward and grabbing a pen from his desk as he spoke.

Connor shrugged, kept his face neutral. 'Contacts sir,' he said. In truth, it had been simple. One call to Belfast and his old partner Simon McCartney, the promise of a pint or two the next time he was over in Scotland, and Simon had checked the police database, found the initial report. Not technically legal but, Connor thought, what are friends for?

Ford let the silence stretch out long enough to confirm Connor wasn't going to say any more. Absently, he raised the pen to his lips, tapped it against his teeth softly.

'Michael? Going after Sanderson? Christ, you don't think after what happened to his dad he'd . . .'

'I don't know, sir, but I've told my people to keep an eye out for him, just in case. But I thought you should know. Technically, I should report this to DCI Ross, but the last thing I want is to make things difficult for the Morgans, especially now. I don't know what deals Dennis Morgan's done with MacKenzie for this sort of service, and the last thing I want is to be dragging all that out in public.'

Ford nodded. 'I appreciate that,' he said. 'I'll have a word with Michael, see what this is all about. Now,' he grimaced as he stood up, hand going to his lower back, 'before we talk to Ms Blake, have a look at this.' He handed Connor a slim manila folder from his desk. Connor flipped it open. Felt something cold slither through his guts. A crime-scene picture of the woman found up at the golf course, pale and still.

'See the similarity?' Ford said, tapping the picture with his index finger. 'Posed. Made to look like Blake. She's in some serious shit here, Fraser. Question is, what do we do to get her out of it?'

CHAPTER 45

Paulie walked around the car slowly, admiring the way it glinted in the sun, the last of the rain clinging to its slick lines like sweat. He wondered what it would be like to drive it, to push it to its limits in a way Connor Fraser never would.

He dropped to his knees for a moment by the front wheel, attending to something he had seen. Then, with a sigh, he got up and stepped back, mind again filling with the squeal of tyres and the roar of the engine.

Maybe one day he would find out.

With one final, lingering look at the car, Paulie turned his attention to the police station that sat across the road from where Fraser had parked his Audi. From this angle, he couldn't see much beyond the bank of foliage that shielded it from the street, just the telecoms mast that poked into the sky, like the skeleton of a long-dead tree, but it was enough. And Paulie didn't need to get any closer.

Satisfied, he headed back for his own car. He had thought he was going to have to wait for Sanderson to leave but, after talking to Fraser, he had decided against that. With the number of police officers around, and Fraser on the scene, there wasn't much need for him to be there.

He dropped into his own car, took a moment to drink in the silence, the smell of polish and leather. Gripped the steering wheel. Smiled. When Fraser had initially called him, Paulie had thought it might be a problem. Despite having a grudging respect for Fraser and his abilities, Paulie nursed a hatred for the man that had been born the day Connor had put him on his arse outside his home. But that hatred was calmed, if not totally neutralised, by the fact Fraser was seeing Jen and, from the little Paulie had been able to glean, was making her happy.

So he had agreed to meet Fraser. And he had told him just enough of the truth to keep him happy, keep him where Paulie wanted him. He fired the engine, slid the car into first and got moving. He knew Jen was working at the yard today, doing some filing and clerking for her father. It was irrelevant work, they could have paid someone to do it, but with everything that was happening with Sanderson and Morgan, Duncan MacKenzie had wanted to find a way to keep his daughter close. It was a feeling Paulie sympathised with. After Duncan's wife, Hannah, had died, Jen was all he had left. And sometimes, when Paulie looked at her in a certain way or her whole face lit up with a smile, he could see the ghost of Hannah in Jen, and the urge to protect her only increased.

He felt a glimmer of guilt at what he had told Fraser. Or, more accurately, what he hadn't told him. After all, he could get hurt, badly. And that would upset Jen. But then again, that was what Uncle Paulie was for, wasn't it? He would dry her tears for Connor Fraser if something were to happen to him.

After all, the man had chosen a dangerous business. And accidents did happen.

CHAPTER 46

Connor sat beside Donna across from Ford, unable to shake the feeling that they were both naughty children who had been summoned to the headmaster's office. Since Donna had arrived, Ford had gone full policeman: stern expression, ramrod straight posture, the disconcerting stillness of someone who could and would wait all day for you to tell them everything they wanted to hear.

'I'm assuming Connor told you what happened?' Donna asked at last. Connor could hear the tension in her voice. He wasn't surprised.

'Yes,' Ford replied slowly. 'I understand you received another email. Officially, I have to tell you to inform DCI Ross of this development. He's SIO on the case. I'm merely consulting.'

Donna threw Connor a quick glance, then focused on Ford. 'I know that,' she said. 'Which begs the question, why am I here with you two, having a nice little off-the-record chat when I should be talking to Ross?'

Connor spoke before Ford could begin. 'Look, Donna. We all want to get to the bottom of whatever the hell is going on here. Way I see it, there are three options. Either DCI Ford was right and Sanderson is back to his old ways, or we've got a copycat, or this is all a massive coincidence and someone else has randomly decided to kill and threaten women, and attack a former policeman, just as Sanderson was released from prison.'

Ford grunted, a policeman's natural disdain for the concept of coincidence.

'Either way,' Connor continued, 'the three of us are closest to Sanderson, the original case and what's going on now. You've been threatened, Donna, which makes this my business. So instead of pissing around, why don't we pool our resources, see what we've got? Keep you safe, maybe even get you a story into the bargain.'

Donna's eyes flashed, telling Connor she didn't appreciate being patronised or his crude attempt to get her on-side with the promise of a story. He held up his hand in apology.

'OK,' she said after a moment, pulling out her phone, calling up the email and laying it on the desk so Connor and Ford could lean forward and study it. 'I got this while I was in the press conference. Seems like whoever is doing this is going to make a move today.'

'Could be Sanderson,' Connor muttered. 'He was playing with his phone when he arrived. But again, begs the question, would he be that blatant, that stupid, to use his own phone?'

'I doubt it,' Ford said. 'The last thing Sanderson is is stupid. Vicious, yes, but stupid, no. And it's not like him to advertise like this, not his style.'

'Oh?' Donna asked.

Ford shifted his position, and Connor could see the debate flashing through the policeman's mind. How far could he trust Donna? How far should he go? They were on shaky ground as it was, what with the diktat from the chief constable and the fact they were technically withholding evidence from an investigation by discussing this email before sharing it with Ross. So how much further?

He came to a decision, leaned forward, lacing long, delicate fingers together. 'How much research have you done into Sanderson's past for this book you might be doing?'

'A bit,' Donna said, her turn to be wary. 'I know he was no angel at the time you looked at him for the university murders. He had been done by the police for GBH, and one count of aggravated assault.'

Ford nodded. 'Yes, the aggravated assault was on a woman in the centre of town. They were in a pub, down on Barnton Street, popular place. Well, he followed her into the toilet, tried it on. Pulled a knife on her. She fought him off, he broke her nose for her trouble. He did time for that one, so he was a pro by the time the university murders happened.'

'OK,' Donna said slowly, 'but what's this got to do with these emails and what's happening now?'

'Two things,' Ford said, grip tightening on his clenched hands, as though he suddenly couldn't trust them. 'First, Sanderson's crimes were characterised by a sudden loss of control, a need to lash out, act.'

The Fraser temper, Connor heard his dad whisper in his mind.

'And, second, his lawyer at the time argued for diminished responsibility on the grounds that Sanderson had a learning disability, so was prone to frustration and the feeling that others were laughing at him.'

'Learning disability?' Connor asked.

'Dysgraphia,' Ford replied simply. 'He has trouble with writing. And whoever wrote that,' he pointed at the phone, 'doesn't seem to have that problem. Grammar and spelling correct, meaning concise and plain. Doesn't seem like Sanderson to me.'

Connor considered this. Interesting but, like almost everything in this case, hardly conclusive. And if he was right about what had happened at Mar's Wark the previous day, if he had read correctly what he had seen when the condiment bottles spilled, then Ford's assessment of Sanderson was wrong. The only question was, how wrong?

'So what do we do?' Connor asked, looking across at Ford. He had asked the policeman not to tell Donna about the body at the golf course being styled to look like her, hoped he would keep his word. She didn't need that kind of stress.

'Keep alert,' Ford said. 'Report this email to Ross, make sure you get adequate protection. See if there's something, anything that ties Sanderson to this or the attack on Dennis Morgan. Push him on that when you speak to him, Ms Blake, see what type of reaction it gets.'

Donna considered this. 'Right,' she said. 'But can I ask one question, off the record?'

Ford sighed, shoulders slumping. He knew what was coming, had known since Connor had first proposed this.

'Off the record? He did it, Ms Blake. This crap about the

chain-of-evidence custody failing is just lawyers being clever. If you'd seen those girls back in 2006. The case was solid. I know it was. Dennis Morgan didn't make mistakes like that.'

'Well, someone thinks he did,' Donna said. 'Why else would he be lying in hospital now? Like you said, it would be too much of a coincidence for all of this to be random. We're missing something. The question is, what?'

Ford looked between Donna and Connor, silence deepening.

No answer. Yet.

CHAPTER 47

The hotel was cheap and cheerful, only a five-minute walk from the rail station and close to the centre of town. When Robbie had heard about the Sanderson assignment, he had booked a room for a week, reasoning that the cost and hassle of travelling from his flat in Leith to Stirling every morning wasn't worth the effort.

Now, sitting on his bed, feet tucked under him and laptop propped on the pillow in front of him, the muffled sound of traffic on the road outside providing a white noise, he was glad to have a place to work. And think.

The boss's request was, while unusual, a relief for Robbie. He hated field work at the best of times, and the gym sessions he was forcing himself through to shape up for the boss were torture. But dealing with Sanderson took his loathing of hands-on work to a new level. There was something about the man, about his cold disdain, exaggerated tough-guy posturing and arrogant superiority that made Robbie uneasy. No, far better to be doing this, research work. It was what he was good at, what Sentinel had originally hired him for. And he was going to prove it.

The boss's instruction had been a simple one – check voter records and death certificates in the Dunfermline and Inverness areas between 1969 and now for a specific person. Robbie had known better than to ask when Connor had given the name Campbell Fraser. The birth date he had provided told Robbie he was probably looking for

Connor's grandfather, and that was enough for him. It was unusual for Connor to use company resources on anything so overtly personal, but Robbie was glad of the work, and the excuse to get away from Sanderson. Besides, he had thought, it would be a simple enough matter to check official records in both areas for that time frame. Maybe a couple of hours max, just to be thorough.

But two hours had passed. And Robbie didn't have any answers. He had accessed various databases, some public, some with backdoor log-ins he had squirrelled away from his time at Police Scotland. Not totally legal, but effective. Most of the time. But using the dates provided, running the searches with every variation of spellings he could think of . . . Nothing. No council-tax records, no links to properties, no mentions in births, deaths or marriages. Reasoning that Connor might be off on his dates, he widened the time frame, going back five years to 1964. Still nothing.

Then Robbie had decided to get creative. Inverness was known as a feeder town for oil workers, so could Campbell Fraser have worked off-shore or abroad? While he couldn't check into company personnel records, he could look at tax returns and limited companies that some of those working in the oil industry had set up at the time as a way to lessen their liabilities as the money poured in when the oil boom began in earnest, reasoning that Campbell might have followed the money at some point. But, again, there was nothing. Robbie could almost have believed Campbell Fraser was a ghost, but a check with Stirling Council's records verified he had indeed paid tax on a property there. It didn't take much for Robbie to find a birth certificate for Jack William Fraser, with Campbell listed as the father, occupation listed as property surveyor. Which gave Robbie another clue, sending him checking registered surveyors in the Highlands, Central Scotland and Fife.

And, again, the answer came back. Nothing.

Frustrated, he turned away from his computer. The boss had given him a task. He had completed it, found nothing. He could go back to him now, tell him what he had found, get back to the assignment at hand. But, he thought, doing so would mean having to deal with Sanderson again.

No. Better to be thorough. The boss wanted an answer. An address, something, Robbie guessed, to give him a lead on his grandfather.

Fine. If that was what the boss wanted, that was what Robbie would deliver. And if he had to dig a little deeper to get it, so be it.

CHAPTER 48

A text message from Sanderson brought Connor's meeting with Donna and Ford to a close. It was, like the man himself, brusque: *Dun now. Fucking waist o time. Meet ye outside?*

Connor scanned it, Ford's insight about Sanderson's dysgraphia playing on his mind. The spelling errors could indicate that, or they could indicate someone smart enough to try to cover his tracks.

Only one way to find out.

After getting assurances from Ford that he would personally take Donna to Ross, Connor headed out of the station. Found Sanderson pacing back and forth at the end of the short driveway that led up to Randolphfield, a cloud of cigarette smoke clinging to him like a rumour as he moved.

'Mr Sanderson,' Connor called, 'ready to go?'

Sanderson flicked the cigarette into a patch of the bushes that lined the driveway. 'Aye, get the fuck away from here. Waste of time.'

'I take it they were asking about what you were doing when Morgan was being attacked?' Connor asked, nodding to the main road and starting to move, leading Sanderson to his car. He had no real desire to let the man get into the Audi, but he needed him there. For now.

They got to the car, Connor feeling a vague nagging sensation as he plipped the central locking. Stopped for a second, as Sanderson climbed in, to take in the side panel and the wheel arch. Smiled as he leaned down and saw what was bothering him. A small cleaned area,

179

smooth and polished, near the front wheel arch. Little more than a blemish to most people, but to Connor, Paulie might as well have taken out a marker pen and scrawled his name on the windscreen.

Don't worry, Paulie, he thought, I'm watching you as well.

He dropped into the car, found Sanderson squirming in the seat, which was jammed tight against the dashboard and raised high enough that his head was brushing the roof.

'Fuck's sake, Fraser, you have a dwarf in here or something?' he asked.

'Sorry,' Connor said, with a smile. He'd been expecting this from the moment he had racked the seat all the way forward, had the lie already prepared. 'Nephew. Controls are just here . . .'

He leaned across Sanderson, reaching down to the side of the chair and triggering the controls, giving Sanderson just enough space to unfold himself, then letting him make the adjustments.

Step one complete. Now all he had to do was keep the man occupied. And hope.

He fired the engine, gave the car just a few too many revs as he took off, pinning Sanderson into his seat. 'So, you seeing Donna later on?' he asked.

'Aye,' Sanderson said, glancing at Connor nervously as he short-shifted up the gears. 'Coppers arenae keen on me doing any filming, what with everything that's going on, but as Mr Layton said, I've no' been charged with anything, and I've got the right to speak to whom-ever I want.'

Whomever? The word stuck out like a rogue sliver of wood on a polished banister.

'And what do you think of what's going on?' Connor asked, braking heavily as he approached a roundabout, then speeding up abruptly, rocking Sanderson in his seat.

Sanderson tried to hide his discomfort. 'Ah dunno,' he said at last. 'I'm not going to cry about Morgan, and what happened up at the golf course is a shame, but I told them what I told them fourteen years ago. It wasn't me. Maybe this time they'll listen.'

'And you managed to account for the times the girl was murdered and DCI Morgan was attacked?'

Sanderson gave a grunt that was halfway between derision and laughter. 'Aye,' he said. 'And I've got you and that bloody PR company to thank for that. With them paying for you to keep an eye on me, I've got a built-in alibi for both incidents.'

Connor tightened his grasp on the steering wheel, released. He didn't like the feeling that he was being used, and he had the growing suspicion Sanderson was using him, like a pawn, in a wider game. He forced himself to be calm, concentrate on driving. He had taken steps to discover the truth, and he would soon enough.

All he had to do was keep Sanderson occupied for the duration of the drive.

He talked, keeping his driving choppy, offering up possible alternative locations for the rescheduled meeting with Donna. The house in Cambusbarron was quickly ruled out, Sanderson insisting he didn't want his dad to be inconvenienced. Connor wondered how much of this concern for his dad was rooted in the fact that Donna had access to a conference suite at a five-star hotel in the centre of town that she could offer as an alternative.

They got back to Cambusbarron, Connor pulling in in front of the Sandersons' home. He got out quickly, checked the street. No sign of Paulie or anyone else of interest. Followed Sanderson up the driveway, got him to the door.

'Damn, hold on, forgot my iPad, need to show you something about the hotel for later on,' Connor said as he watched Sanderson step into the house, his dad waiting for him.

He got back to the car, pulled from his jacket the phone he had lifted from Sanderson's pocket when he'd leaned over him. Fished into the glove box for the item he needed, a black rectangle of plastic not much bigger than a keypad at an automated checkout. Plugged it into the USB port at the base of Sanderson's phone, set it running. A quick, guilty glance at the house, half expecting to see Sanderson emerge, patting his pockets, heading for the car. But nothing happened, only the soft ping of the device as it told Connor it had done its work.

He pocketed the phone again, grabbed his iPad, then headed back for Sanderson's house, calculations already running in his mind. Five minutes of bullshitting, maybe ten, about exits and clear paths in and out of the hotel, arrangements to get him there. Then he was free to study the information he had just gathered, and he could see exactly what game Sanderson was playing.

CHAPTER 49

Ford ignored the questioning glance Ross gave him when he escorted Donna into the man's office, found he didn't have time for it.

'There's been a development, Alan,' he said simply. 'Ms Blake here needs to talk to you.'

He left before Ross could say anything, or give voice to the warning that was playing in his eyes. Fraser's revelation about Morgan's links with MacKenzie and Paulie King had left Ford with problems of his own, and ghosts to face. Ghosts that were hidden in the pages of the case file that was currently sitting in the boot of his car.

He got out of the station, heading for the hospital to visit Morgan again. The hushed silence of the car seemed to crowd in on him, amplify thoughts and memories. Memories of a warehouse. Of the sound of wood thudding into exposed flesh, of air being forced from lungs in a bloodied, hacking cough.

Of deals with the devil and pledges of a greater good.

He reached the critical care unit and was greeted by a stone-faced nurse, who would only give him any information on Morgan's condition after he had flashed his warrant card and insisted it was 'essential to an ongoing inquiry'. The tone she took when talking to him told him she didn't believe a word of that, but was simply too tired to argue the point.

'Mr Morgan has shown slight improvement. His vitals have become stronger, and it appears he's regaining some volume in his left lung, the one that was lacerated by the blade. What we can't tell at this stage is if there's been any permanent damage.'

'Permanent damage? You mean to his lungs? Or scarring?'

'Neither,' the nurse said, resignation amplifying the exhaustion in her eyes. How many times, Ford wondered, had she stood there delivering bad news or saying just enough so she didn't give people false hope?

'You see,' she said, 'the damage to Mr Morgan's lung, and the constriction to his neck, mean his brain was starved of both blood and oxygen for a period of time before the paramedics arrived. As he's been unconscious since he was brought in, we can't be categorically sure that there's not been any lasting impairment of brain function.'

Something caught in Ford's mind, like a half-buried piece of quartz reflecting the sun on a beach. Then it was gone, replaced by a more immediate concern. 'Hold on, you're saying he could be brain-damaged?'

'Yes,' the nurse said. 'The possibility is there. But otherwise he's in good shape for a man of his age, seems strong, healthy. So we just have to wait. Now, I really can't tell you any more, Chief Inspector.'

Ford thanked her, watched as she squeaked her way down the polished corridor. Dennis Morgan had prized mental agility above all else. What was it he had said when Ford had remembered how he took his coffee? *Still sharp, Malcolm.* When he was working, he impressed fellow officers with his ability to memorise case files, recall any fact at just the right moment in the witness stand. And now he faced the prospect of living the rest of his life with some or all of that mental capacity lost to a madman's blade? Ford felt a chill creep through him as he imagined himself lying in that bed, Mary hovering over him as the machines beeped and hissed his funeral march.

Recall any fact . . .

'DCI Ford?'

Ford whirled, startled. Michael Morgan stood in front of him, a puzzled look on his face. Ford remembered the young man's father poring over case files with the same expression – brows furrowed, mouth turned down.

Ford got moving, took a half-step forward, offered his hand.

Michael took it, gave it a squeeze halfway between reassuring and painful.

'Yes, yes, sorry, Michael. Just wanted to check up on your dad, see how he was doing. Actually, I'm glad you're here. I wondered if we could have a quick word.'

'Oh?' The puzzled look intensified.

'Yes,' Ford said. 'It's about Colin Sanderson.'

Michael's eyes darted in the direction of his father's room, something darker than puzzlement casting his features into shadow. Ford had seen that same look on his father's face too. So had a few criminals. And they had come to fear it.

'Let me check on my dad,' Michael said, his voice colder now, clipped. 'Then we can go and get a coffee.'

CHAPTER 50

All Connor wanted to do was go to the gym. Grab the heaviest weights he could find and push himself until his muscles burned so badly that he thought he might be sick. It was the least he deserved for being so stupid.

He was back at the flat, laptop open in front of him. More than once he had fought down the urge to throw the computer against the wall, then upturn the coffee-table. He had managed to control himself, barely, one of his gran's favourite sayings running through his mind: *Don't shoot the messenger, son.*

No, if anyone deserved to be shot, it was Colin Sanderson.

The information he had pulled from Sanderson's phone was easily decrypted by a software package Connor had on his computer – another gift from Simon and their time in Belfast. It gave him access to Sanderson's call logs, emails and text messages. And what a tale they told.

The message was easy enough to find: in his arrogance, Sanderson hadn't even bothered to delete it. A simple text message, sent the day of the attack at Mar's Wark. *Walking up now, be there in five minutes. Be ready.* The reply, from a contact marked only as PW, was simple: *I'll be ready. As agreed.*

A quick back trace on PW's number revealed him to be someone called Phil Whittaker. It didn't take Connor long to track him down: he was a delivery driver for a catering-supply business that worked out of Falkirk. Which made sense of what Connor had seen on the morning of the attack. The condiments spilling down the street from boxes, splattering the cobbles with spices and gaudy-coloured sauces. Bottles that were spilling from boxes that should have been sealed if they were genuinely being delivered and not, as Connor suspected, opened and spilled on purpose to bring the owner of the restaurant out at just the right time to see Sanderson walking up the street.

Connor confirmed this suspicion with one final check, this time on the voters' roll, finding one of the strange coincidences Ford hated so much. Whittaker just happened to live in Cambusbarron, not far from Sanderson's home and the Foresters Arms, the pub Sanderson had gone to with his dad the night before the attack. Connor had no doubt Whittaker had met Sanderson there that night, and the plan had been hatched. Get to the restaurant, create enough of a scene to bring Clarke outside, just in time to see Sanderson, large as life, strolling up the street. What, Connor thought, had Sanderson expected? A verbal assault, the chef marching over and hurling obscenities, or something more like what had happened? Either way, he'd got what he'd wanted - to play the victim before the camera, and ramp up the story a little more.

Connor considered this. Sanderson had set himself up to be attacked, presumably hoping to get more coverage. Why? To push up the price he could ask for his book? To feed some need for notoriety? And if that was the case, was he sending the messages to Donna in order to ramp up the story even further? Connor had found no evidence of this in the data he had scraped from Sanderson's phone, but that was hardly conclusive. A man smart enough to set up an attack on himself knowing he had security to handle it (*I was never in any real danger*) was smart enough to have another anonymous burner phone to send those messages. But why target the woman who was giving him all the coverage he craved? No, there was something he was missing.

Connor pushed back from the laptop, feeling the frustration grow in his body. He needed to tell Ford about this, decide what he was going to do about the rest of the contract. He was well within his rights to cancel the whole deal, and there was a payment clause in the contract with Frontline PR that made sure Sentinel wouldn't be financially penalised if he did so. His client had lied, created a situation that had put Connor and his people in very real danger. But if he walked away, what then? He had taken this job as much to help Ford as for the money, and with the threats to Donna still coming, what would happen if he just abandoned the whole deal?

He dropped to the floor, started doing press-ups. A poor substitute for the gym, but it was the best he could do at that moment. He was just starting to get into his stride, the familiar warm ache in his chest and arms soothing his troubled thoughts, when his phone pinged on the coffee-table. He got to his knees, reached for it, his arm feeling strangely alien after the push-ups. The text was from Robbie and, for an instant, Connor didn't want to open it. Asking him to track down his grandfather had been a stupid, self-indulgent idea. After all, what was he going to do? Go and find the man, give him a hug? Hardly. From the few stories his dad had told him, Connor was more likely to hit than hug.

Annoyed with himself, he opened the message. Read it. Felt the world crowd in on him with a thousand questions as the room seemed to contract, like a vacuum-sealed bag, the air rapidly sucked out of it.

He blinked. Thumbed in a reply. Looked unseeingly around the room for an answer to the only question that mattered. Let it go or keep pushing? If Robbie was right, he had lived a lie this long, so why not go on living it? What was it his dad had said? Leave this, Connor, for your gran, please? And why not? She was as comfortable and safe as he could make her, and he visited her as often as he could. So why not just drop it, forget what Robbie had told him? It wasn't as if he didn't have enough problems to deal with.

But then there was that report card. A version of his father he had never known. And the photograph in the paper, Campbell Fraser hovering like a wraith in a tweed suit, arms proprietorially draped across his wife and son's shoulders. And then there was that stain on the report card. Old, russet-coloured, rough to the touch. Almost like . . .

. . . like . . .

His fingers had made the decision before he consciously realised it. Scrolled through his contacts, found the number. Dialled. Started speaking before Jack Fraser even had time to say hello.

'Dad, it's me. Before you ask, Gran's fine. I'm not calling about her. But we need to talk. About Campbell and Dundee. I'm busy just now, so how about later on today? We can get a drink at the Settle Inn up town. I'll buy. I think you're going to need it.'

CHAPTER 51

I've never seen the appeal of guns. They've always struck me as a cow-ard's weapon, a way of killing from a distance and never seeing the look in your victim's eyes as the life drains from them. Oh, don't get me wrong, I respect the gun's ability to intimidate and coerce, but I've always favoured a more ... intimate approach. The feel of the knife as it punctures flesh, the strange weight it takes on as it rends vital organs, the hot, thick spray of blood gouting from a wound and coating you, like a lover's promise.

But now, with the gun he gifted me, I'm beginning to see the appeal.

Nothing quite prepares you for the weight of the thing, and I don't just mean physically. There's something about this firearm, fully loaded, that drags your attention to it, like it's generating its own gravity field. I feel compelled to look at it, to lose myself in the light as it plays along the sleek barrel or catches the pattern on the grip.

But, no, I must not lose focus. Time is short. I suppose it's reckless to be carrying the thing around like this, but there's something irre-sistible in the way it sits in my pocket, the feeling that it's there, my dark, deadly little secret.

I know Fraser will have held a gun. Serving in the PSNI, he would have had to. But, I wonder, has he ever fired one? Felt it kick wildly in his hand, the shock juddering up his arm and into his head like an echo. More importantly, has he ever been shot? I chide myself, have to bite back the sudden laugh that bubbles up in the back of my throat. Like the court, this is not the time or place for that. No. This is a place for quiet reflection, silent desperation and false hope.

But there is nothing false in my hopes for Connor Fraser. And he will know what it feels like to be shot soon enough.

Anderson ... at what point that talking spirit at truth at the level I'd insist. That's another line of plot at that No. That's a little ... ... questioning despite ... politics layer.

And livest nothing false in my hope for Conrad Danoe. And he will know that I believe it. He was the conduit.

CHAPTER 52

Michael Morgan led Ford down to the main atrium of the hospital, where they found a coffee shop. For Ford, it was a jarring experience, making the hospital feel more like a shopping mall than a place of healing.

They made their order then found a table, Ford slipping into the seat at the front, forcing Michael to take the one with its back to the wall. An old copper's trick in a place like this: get the person being interviewed in the place that would be most difficult for them to make a quick escape from. Ford felt a sting of shame at putting his friend's son in that position, knew that, given the chance, he would do exactly the same again.

Michael looked over at him, hands neatly clasped in front, and, again, Ford was reminded of his father, Dennis. The disquieting stillness he had perfected, the ability to calmly sit and wait, make the person on the other side of the table play the first card.

Fair enough.

'I'm glad your dad is stable,' Ford said, leaning away from the table as a waitress arrived with their coffees – a plain black for Ford, something frothy and tall for Michael.

'Doctors say he's got about a fifty-fifty chance of waking up,' Michael said, stirring sugar into his coffee, his voice a low, contemplative whisper. 'Though it might not be a blessing if he does.'

'Oh?' Ford asked, thinking of his discussion with the nurse and the chances of brain damage. He didn't want to get her into trouble, waited for Michael to fill in the gaps.

'There might be, ah, complications if he does,' Michael said, eyes finally finding Ford's. He shrugged. 'Who knows? It's all down to luck now.'

Ford smiled, not wanting to push the issue. Besides, he had other matters on his mind. 'Look, Michael,' he said slowly. 'About what I said. Sanderson. It's been brought to my attention that you might be looking to do something, ah, rash. I just wanted to emphasise, as a friend, that we're doing everything we can to either rule him out as a suspect in what happened to your dad or link him to the attack. Either way, it's a police matter. Last thing your dad would want is you taking the law into your own hands.'

Humour flashed across Michael's eyes, as though Ford had just reminded him of an old joke. He looked down at his coffee, hunching his shoulders around the cup as though drawing heat from it. And, again, Ford was reminded of Connor Fraser. Not just in physical terms, but something else, something . . .

'Look, Malcolm,' Michael said. 'My dad worries too much. Yes, I took offence at some of the things Sanderson said about Dad after the acquittal, and maybe I said a few things I shouldn't have. And God knows I gave him a few occasions to worry when I was younger, got into more trouble than I should. But you don't need to worry. Dad trained me well. I know where the line is and I swear I won't cross it. Can you imagine how that would look? Son of shamed police officer attacks man who ended his career?'

'I'd hardly say shamed was the right—'

'Oh, come on, Malcolm, let's be honest. My dad's name was shit the moment Sanderson was acquitted. We both know it. It's just lucky he got out when he did, managed to cash in his pension. But, then, the old bugger always did have a perfect sense of timing. But we both know that this is going to taint his reputation, follow him round, especially with Sanderson taking on a new career as a media star. So maybe it's best Dad doesn't wake up at all.'

Ford stared into his face. 'You can't believe that, Michael,' he said, shocked at the bluntness of the man's words. 'Your dad's got years in him yet. He'll get better, I promise.' He wondered how much he could tell Michael about his dad's concerns, concerns strong enough to drive him to enlist the help of Duncan MacKenzie.

'I just need you to let us do our jobs, OK? We'll find who attacked your dad, I swear we will. And if Sanderson had anything to do with it, I'll nail the bastard to the wall personally.'

A smile played across Michael's lips, cold as a winter's morning, little more than a polite flexing of muscles to acknowledge what Ford had just said.

'I know you will, Malcolm,' he said. 'I know you will.'

CHAPTER 53

The Settle Inn was a small pub only a stone's throw from the castle, just around the corner from where Connor had stopped the cleaver attack on Sanderson the day before. It claimed to be the oldest pub in Stirling, dating back to the 1700s, and the bare stone walls and almost antique décor seemed to back up that claim. Connor found his dad waiting for him when he arrived, sitting at a small corner table, two glasses in front of him. Connor wasn't sure what surprised him more – that his dad was early, or that he appeared to be drinking, especially at this time of day.

He took a seat, his dad offering a weak smile as he settled into position. And as he looked at his father, he thought again of just dropping the whole thing. Have an awkward afternoon drink, fill the time with stilted non-conversation about his gran and his work, then leave. Let the past lie. What was it his dad had said? *Leave this, Connor, for your gran, please*? But then what?

'Thanks for coming,' Connor said, taking the glass his dad slid across the table towards him, raising it to his nose. Warm. Peaty. A Laphroaig most likely. Connor wasn't big on Island malts, but it would do.

'You didn't really give me much of a choice, did you?' his dad said. 'I thought you were going to leave all this, Connor. What good can it possibly do?'

Connor felt guilt prickle his guts, washed it away with a swig of the whisky. 'It just didn't make sense to me,' he said, ignoring his dad's question. 'The report card describing you as artistic and empathetic. No offence, Dad, but that's not you. Then there was the old newspaper article about some painting you did. There was a picture of Granddad in that, and I realised—'

'Don't call him that,' Jack snapped, the coldness of his words startling Connor into silence. 'That bastard has no right to be called that.'

Connor looked into his dad's eyes and, for perhaps the first time, he saw himself in the man in front of him. It was a look he had seen many times in the mirror at the gym, when he was forcing out another rep despite every fibre in his body feeling as if it was on fire. Dead, empty, his eyes almost completely blackened by something deeper than rage or hate.

The Fraser temper, son. Watch for it.

'Dad,' Connor said, as gently as he could, 'what happened? I know Gra– Campbell walked out on you and Gran, not long after the newspaper article, actually. But why has this stirred up so much shit?' He was about to ask the question he had wanted to since this had begun, knew that if he did there was no going back. Here it was, at last. The point of no return.

'Why was there blood on that report card? And why did you and Gran lie about Campbell going back to Inverness?'

Jack glared across the table and, for an instant, Connor felt as though his father might lash out at him. But then the anger abated, replaced by something that put Connor even more on edge than the threat of violence. An almost indescribable grief filled Jack's eyes. He grunted a humourless laugh, wiped his nose, almost as though doing so would turn off the tears and the memories. Shook his head. When he spoke, it was little more than a whisper.

'He was a bastard,' Jack said at last, eyes now firmly on the glass in front of him. 'I've told you a few times that he had a temper. It's the same temper I see in you, Connor. What I didn't tell you is, unlike you, he was cruel with it. He would beat your gran, you know. Oh, he was careful, never the face, only ever places you couldn't see in public. Rabbit punches to the guts, pulling of the hair, cigarette burns, that type of thing. Did it to me as well, every time your gran or I did something to disappoint him. Which was fairly often.'

Connor clamped down on the sudden fury that surged through him. The thought of his gran – his kind and gentle gran, the woman who had always been there with a hug or an encouraging word when he needed it – being beaten filled him with a rage that was as acrid and sour as the whisky in front of him. He realised he was gripping the glass too tightly, released it before it shattered.

'Anyway,' Jack said, after a moment, 'it all came to a head one night. You're right, I think I was fifteen, though I can't really remember. I came home with my report card, the one you found. Your gran raved about it, about the great future as a famous artist I would have. Then he came home, and it all changed.'

'What happened?' Connor asked, not sure he really wanted to know, afraid that he already did.

'He was all right to start with. Came home from work as normal, read the report card, brushed it aside. But I could see it was gnawing at him. And then, of course, he started drinking. That stuff.' Jack nodded towards Connor's glass. 'Whisky. It's why I can't stand it, why I stick to brandy if I do drink. Which has been all too often recently.'

'Dad, I—'

'Too fucking late now,' Jack said in a tone that told Connor this would be the last real conversation he would ever have with his father. 'Anyway. I went to bed, but I didn't sleep. You could always tell when he was going to kick off, you know? Like the way you can feel rain in the air before a big storm. Everything went still, like the house was holding its breath, waiting for him to erupt. And he did. First thing I heard was a glass shattering, then him screaming at your gran about how she had given him a "poofy little artist for a son rather than a man".' Jack gave a humourless, empty laugh. 'I ran downstairs, found he had your gran pinned against the wall, handful of her hair in his fist, the report card crammed into her face. She was bleeding from her nose, I remember that, how red the blood was against her skin, and I remember thinking he'd really fucking lost it if he'd punched her in the face.'

Connor didn't know what to say or do. He felt as though he was riding some kind of poisonous caffeine high – he was filled with pent-up energy, rage, frustration, seized by the need to lash out, to move, to act. Instead, he was pinned to his seat. 'What did you do?' he asked.

'Come on, Connor,' Jack said. 'What the fuck do you think I did? I grabbed his whisky bottle and I smashed it over the cunt's head. No warning, no hesitation. I was no match for the bastard – he was a strong man, despite looking like a corpse, and I knew he'd kill me if I got into it with him. So I brained him. He went down like a ton of bricks and, for a minute, I thought I'd killed him. But I hadn't. Unfortunately.'

Jack blinked, rocked back in his seat, wiped a hand over his eyes. 'He got up and, I swear, he was going to kill me. And he probably would have, if it wasn't for your gran.'

'What?' Connor asked, something cold slicing into his guts now.

'Aye.' Jack smiled. 'She threatened him with the one thing he was scared of. Exposure. Back then, most people turned a deaf ear to the screaming, and the police couldn't give less of a fuck, but Da-Campbell was a proud man. His reputation was everything. And she threatened that. Promised that if he didn't get out, she'd make such a scene that no one would be able to ignore it. Course, the fact she did this while she was waving the poker from the fireplace in front of him might have had some bearing on his decision to get out of the house.'

Connor felt as though the world was spinning, like he was trying to process too many images and emotions at once. He felt his skin crawl with the need to move. 'So he left?' he asked.

'Aye, left that night. And that was the last we saw of him. Got one letter from him, said he was working in Dundee. Usual crap about trying to apologise, hoping everything was OK. Your gran tossed it in the fire.'

Connor nodded. It confirmed what Robbie had found – a record for a Campbell Fraser, surveyor, who worked in the Broughty Ferry area around that time. He felt the questions clamour through his mind, pushed them down. He had all the answers he didn't want. The last thing he needed was more.

'Dad, look, I . . .'

Jack raised his glass, tipped it towards Connor. Drained it. 'Leave it, son. You wanted to know, now you do. You've got bad blood, son, that fucking Fraser temper. So watch for it. And let this alone now, OK? Your gran doesn't need any reminders of that bastard, especially now.'

'Understood,' Connor said, through numb lips.

'Good.' Jack stood, skirted around the table. 'You take care of yourself on that job, Connor. And check in on your gran, will you? She loves seeing you.'

Connor stood, torn between the impulse to move towards his dad and the knowledge that there was a fresh gulf between them which he could never cross. A gulf he had created with his idiotic need to know.

His dad nodded a farewell, then wove his way out of the pub, not looking back. Connor watched him go, something hot scalding the back of his eyes. He scanned the pub, hoping, praying for some sign of trouble, a raised hand, a sideways look. Something, anything that would give him the excuse he needed to vent the empty rage he felt crawl through him with dark, fibrous tentacles.

He was moving before he knew it, heading for the pub door, people jostling to get out of his way. He was going to catch his dad, make this right, tell him—

His phone beeped in his pocket. He scrabbled for it, the thought that it was his dad calling him rising up. Instead, it was a text. Nine simple words from an unknown number. Nine simple words that called to the anguished fury Connor was feeling, gave him a lightning rod for his rage: *Got you in my sights, Connor. Ready to play?*

CHAPTER 54

The message was like a shot of adrenalin. Every sense heightened, every muscle tensed, Connor scanned the street in front of him, feeling as though his eyes were bulging from their sockets. But nothing. No sign of anyone watching him, trying to gauge his reaction.

He mashed the call button on the phone, clamped it to his ear, struggling to keep his breath even. Unconsciously took a step into a pool of shadow created by the eaves of the pub, making sure he wasn't in anyone's direct line of sight.

The call diverted to a generic 'This number is unavailable' message, meaning the phone the text had been sent from had either been switched off or destroyed. On the off-chance it was the former, Connor thumbed in a response, short and direct and explicit. Hit send. Waited.

No reply.

He closed his eyes, forced himself to think through the urge to head straight for Sanderson's place in Cambusbarron. Burst through the door, grab the man by the throat and squeeze the answers he needed from him. Knew that, after the revelations from his dad and the message he had just received, if he started down that path, there was a very real possibility that Colin Sanderson would end up in hospital. Or worse.

The Fraser temper, son. Watch for it.

Connor took one last look around the street, then got walking, heading down the hill towards home. He had decided to walk to the pub: after all, it was only fifteen minutes from his flat and a good excuse to get some exercise. Now, after a message that someone had their 'sights on him', it felt like a double-edged sword. On the one hand, it was easier to spot a tail on the narrow, cobbled streets of old Stirling when it was so quiet, but on the other, Connor was exposed, vulnerable, especially if the 'sights' mentioned were attached to a gun.

He kept his pace steady, not rushed, not slow. Just fast enough. And as he walked, senses stretching out around him, Connor tried to put some order to what had just happened, glad of a reason not to dwell on the conversation he had had with his dad.

So what did he have? He had verified that Colin Sanderson had set up the 'attack' at the top of Mar's Wark, probably in some perverted effort to get more publicity for his story. Not long after that, Donna had started to get threatening emails, one with a picture that could only have been taken by the killer, or someone who had intimate knowledge of what the killer had done to the golf course victim's body . . .

Victim . . .

The thought stuck in Connor's mind, making him slow his pace for a moment. The victim had been stripped of anything that could easily identify her. No purse, ID or personal effects had been found with the body. And she had yet to show up on any database search or missing-person report. What did that mean? The killer was going to great lengths to keep her identity concealed, that much was obvious, but the lack of records troubled Connor. It meant something, something he couldn't quite reach, like a bottle on a shelf that's a little too high.

He got his phone from his pocket, glancing at it briefly as he thumbed in a message, not wanting to take his eyes off the street for too long: *You OK? Been a development.* Hit send, hoping Donna wouldn't take too long to reply. Technically, he should report this to Ross or Ford but, after receiving the message, Connor wanted to check on Donna first.

The message came back less than thirty seconds after Connor had hit send: *Fine. What's happened? At flat. Want me to meet you?*

No, need to see Ford. Will call shortly, Connor replied, then pocketed the phone, the exchange triggering another thought. How had his messenger got his number? It wasn't widely circulated, and the message had come to his personal phone, not the one he used for work. Again, it put Sanderson in the frame.

Connor got to his street, ears straining for the sound of footsteps behind him. It was quieter here, the huge oak and birch trees that loomed over the houses creating a natural echo chamber. But Connor heard nothing, just the gentle rustle of the wind on leaves and the hammering of his own heart.

He checked one last time at the driveway that led to his flat. Nothing. Ducked in quickly, down into the flat. Saw the abandoned paperwork on his coffee-table, thought again of Sanderson. Dialled Robbie, asked him to try to trace the number he had received the text from. That done, he stood for a moment, considering his options, pushing aside the clamour of memories from the pub less than forty minutes ago.

Later. He could deal with that later.

He read the message again: *Got you in my sights, Connor. Ready to play?* And, below it, his own response: *Ready and waiting. Come and get me, you cowardly fuck.*

In my sights.

He made a decision. Headed for his bedroom, and the safe under the floorboards. The safe where a memento of his time as a police officer in Belfast waited for him. A memento that he kept oiled and cleaned, just for occasions like this.

The sound of the ammo clip slamming home was very loud in the silence of the flat, like a harbinger of shots to come. Connor found something calming in the blunt certainty of that noise.

'Come and get me, motherfucker,' he whispered.

CHAPTER 55

It had been only a few hours but, to Connor, it felt like a lifetime had passed since he had last sat in Ford's office. He shifted in his seat uncomfortably, the weight of the day's events pressing down on him like an almost physical force. He knew he was riding a bad adrenalin hangover, the revelations from his dad and the threatening text combining into a lethal cocktail that had burned him out. Knew also that there was no end in sight.

Not yet.

He took a swig of the coffee Ford had poured for him, grimaced. Almost as sour as his mood. 'So, what do you think?' he asked.

Ford pushed the mobile Connor had placed in front of him back across his desk. Shrugged. 'Not sure. Could be something, and it definitely follows the pattern that whoever is contacting Blake has set with the taunting message. Ross will no doubt give it to the digital forensics boys, but I doubt we'll get anything from it. Whoever is doing this is too smart just to leave a forwarding number for us.'

Connor murmured agreement. Robbie had called him just before he had stepped into the police station to meet Ford, told him that the number was most likely from a pay-as-you-go SIM. It could, he said, be tracked to a degree with time, but Connor had the feeling that time was the one thing they were running out of.

'So what does it leave us with?' Connor asked.

Ford stiffened slightly in his chair, and Connor was again reminded of the lingering suspicion the policeman had for him. Yes, his experience as a police officer and his help on previous cases had bought Connor some credibility with Ford, but the man was a trained police officer and, in big cases, policemen had an unfortunate habit of seeing the world in binary terms of police and the rest of the world.

'I'm not sure,' Ford said, rearranging himself. 'I managed a quick catch-up with Ross, and he says Sanderson's alibi for the time of the attack on Morgan is almost watertight, thanks mainly to the team you put on his house. Yes, he could have slipped out and got to Morgan, but the timings are exceptionally tight. Same with the messages to Blake. He could have sent them but, again, we've no solid proof. And with the appeal judge's rebuke still ringing in his ears, the chief is reluctant to go for a search warrant at this stage as he feels it would be "unnecessary harassment of Mr Sanderson".'

Connor's face curdled into a sneer of disgust that had nothing to do with the coffee he was drinking. 'But what about his little stunt setting up that attack during the interview with Donna? Surely you can use that to get something on him.'

Ford laughed. 'Like what? Wasting police time? You had the situation dealt with by the time officers arrived. All they had to do was the paperwork. And, besides, from what you've told me, you didn't exactly come by that information by the most legal of means, did you?'

Connor let out a stifled sigh of frustration. Nothing. Again, they had nothing. Just half-formed thoughts and unverifiable theories.

'How did your chat go with Morgan's son?' Connor asked, hoping the sudden change of topic would yield some results.

'He's a good kid,' Ford said. 'Naturally worried about his dad. Says he said a few things about Sanderson that he shouldn't have to his dad, who worried given some of Michael's previous run-ins with the police. Looks like he reached out to MacKenzie and King in an attempt to keep his son away from Sanderson. After all, if Michael confronted him, big guy or not, who knows what would happen?'

Connor considered this for a minute. 'But why did Michael go to MacKenzie in the first place? And why was he, a former copper, so happy to put Paulie on Michael's tail?'

Something in Ford's eyes hardened as he leaned across his desk, making Connor feel as though he had just stumbled into a trip wire in an uncharted minefield.

'Maybe you should ask MacKenzie that yourself. After all, don't you have, ah, special access to him at the moment?'

Connor bristled, pushed it aside. The last thing he needed was to alienate Ford, especially now. 'OK,' he said, holding up a hand. He wanted to ask about the body found at the golf course, decided not to in case he tripped another booby trap. 'So I take it the next step is I meet Ross, show him what I've received.'

'Yeah,' Ford said, rocking back in his seat. 'He'll be pissed off with the delay in reporting it to him in the first instance, so say you checked in with me to verify Blake's safety after his meeting with her and I'll—'

He was interrupted by a harsh rap on the door and the sight of a silhouette shifting uncomfortably from one foot to the other beyond the pane of frosted glass. To Connor, there was something strangely comedic about the image.

'Come!' Ford shouted.

DS Troughton stepped into the office, paused when he saw Connor sitting there. 'Ah, sir, I . . .' he said '. . . I, ah . . .'

Ford waved a hand impatiently. 'It's fine, Troughton. Fraser was going over security arrangements for Sanderson with me, that's all. What is it?'

'Well, ah, that's just it, sir,' Troughton said. 'It's Sanderson. We've just had a call from his father. He's missing.'

CHAPTER 56

After her meeting with Ross, Donna headed home. She had hoped to doorstep Sanderson at the police station, but Ross was annoyingly thorough in his questioning and, by the time they had finished, Connor had already spirited Sanderson away. Being honest with herself, this suited Donna. After going over the emails and the picture with Ross, she felt she needed a breather from Sanderson and the whole situation. She pinged him a text asking him to call her when he was free to arrange their interview in town, then accepted a lift home from a patrol car.

The flat felt strangely empty when she arrived, with Andrew out for the day with her parents. She tried to keep her irritation at bay as she wandered aimlessly through the rooms, noting where her mother had tidied up, putting things away in the wrong places and rearranging shelves as she did so. Told herself that, despite everything, her mother meant well.

Or so she hoped.

She made herself a coffee, then drifted to her small study at the back of the flat. It was the one room her mother never bothered with, either fearful of Donna's reaction to her work being disturbed or as some kind of not-so-subtle protest at the work itself.

It's no job for a mother with a young son.

She settled herself into her seat, booted up the laptop she had dragged out of storage when the police had insisted on taking hers for examination. It was an ancient block of black plastic, an old PC she had been issued when she had worked on the *Westie* and never bothered to return. She listened to the hard drive cough and spit its way to life, sifting through the files and papers in front of her, reminding herself of what she had been doing when the email and picture had derailed her plans.

She shivered at the memory of the message in the email. It disturbed her more than the picture of the severed finger that had accompanied it. The picture had been a graphic display of the horror that this person was capable of, nothing left to the imagination. But that message – *I'll be seeing you REAL soon* – conjured up visions and nightmares that Donna could not escape. It took up residence in the darkest corners of her mind and whispered to her with the promise of horrors to come.

I'll be seeing you REAL soon.

She took another swig of coffee, pushed the thought aside as she read the note she had scrawled on the top sheet of paper. Rhona Everett and Jessica Kristen, the two victims in the 2006 murders. She nodded to herself, drawing the laptop closer. The arrival of the picture had stopped her contacting the university and asking for any background they could provide on the women. She opened the internet, then went to the webmail address for her Sky emails, heart racing in case another message was waiting for her. But there was nothing, just the usual work emails and spam about winning lottery tickets, horoscope predictions and how a certain skin cream could transform her life.

Yawn.

She pinged a quick message to Janice Gilhooley, a friend in the HR department at the university, asking if she was free for a coffee and a chat, hinting vaguely at what she wanted. Then she turned back to her files and went over what she knew of the girls.

Two students, both second-years. One from rural Perthshire, the other from Glasgow. One studying politics and history, the other sport and exercise science. From the little she could glean from the reports in front of her, they were strangers on the campus, moving in completely different social circles. But was there a connection everyone was missing?

Donna chewed her lip, scrolled absently around the screen of the laptop. There were old files on the desktop, half-written stories from her time at the *Westie*, a file of contacts, ideas. Looking at the files, she felt a wistful pang for that time in her life. A time before Andrew, when her life was simpler, her career was set and a life with Mark beckoned to her.

She brought the mouse to a halt on an icon in the corner of the screen. A small graphic of a filing cabinet entitled 'Morty the Mort'. She smiled at the memory. Morty the Mort was the nickname the *Westie*'s staff had given to the library that held stories from the back issues of the paper. Need a question answered? Then Morty the Mort is the man you need to see.

She hovered over the icon, wondered. Could it still be active after all this time? She clicked on it, watched as the familiar log-in screen popped up. Took a moment to remember, then entered her *Westie* log-in and password. Hit enter.

The screen dissolved onto a standard search engine – keywords and timescale. Donna shrugged. Why not? Nothing to lose at this stage. She typed in Jessica Kristen, Rhona Everett and Stirling. The search engine took a moment then spat out a list of headlines from the coverage of the murders at the time. Most of the headlines were familiar to Donna, given her research, and she had the majority of them in hard copy strewn across her desk in front of her. Nothing there.

She went back to the search dialogue box. Considered. Decided to take the names one at a time, starting with Jessica Kristen. The search came back with a few articles, ranging from obituaries or those containing the names Jessica or Kristen. Nothing directly related to the university or the murders. OK, one last try. Donna cleared the search box, typed in Rhona's name. Waited for the results, already considering what her next step should be. Do a deeper dive? Drive out to the university and try to doorstep Janice, bounce her into giving up some information?

The computer did its work, spitting out another screen of results. More of the same as the search on Jessica, obituaries, stories with the relevant names, nothing really . . .

Hold on.

Donna stopped scrolling, a story catching her eye. Opened another window, ran the search for Jessica's name again. Scrolled down the results, ignoring the cold trickle of excitement that shivered down her spine like a sliver of ice.

Yes. There. An article from October 2004. Clicked on it, waited what seemed like an eternity for the search engine to call up the story. She leaned into the screen when it finally loaded, felt her pulse quicken as she read. 'Oh, Jesus,' she whispered. A link. Finally, here was a link. All the way back to 2004, and one of the most important days in Scotland's history for centuries.

She got to the end of the copy, noticed there was an attachment with a link to a related-image gallery for the story. Clicked on it, feeling the excitement bubble in her mouth like champagne.

It was a massive group shot, all formal suits and dresses and fixed smiles. She scanned the faces, felt her mouth drop open as she spotted first Jessica and then, a few people away on the same row, Rhona. She grabbed her pad, started scrawling notes, mind racing with possibilities. Read the caption, which told her nothing, and was about to close the image when she noticed another face. A face she had seen a lot of over the last few days. Zoomed in, hands shaking now. No, no mistake at all. In the row behind Jessica and Rhona, roughly equidistant from both girls, standing to attention in a dress uniform as stiff as his expression, was Detective Chief Inspector Dennis Morgan.

CHAPTER 57

They were in the kitchen where Connor had first met Colin Sanderson, his father, Donald, at the table, hands wrapped around a cup of coffee. DCI Ross sat across from him, reviewing his notes and waiting, sending the occasional disapproving glance at Ford. He had objected when Ford had arrived until Connor had stepped in, explaining that Ford was acting as liaison for Sentinel Securities, providing information on possible threats to Sanderson based on what had happened during the original investigation in 2006. It was a fiction, but a two-edged one: it kept Ford in the room, but also put pressure on him to come up with some kind of an answer to what had just happened.

'So,' Ross said, finally tiring of waiting, 'why do you think Colin is missing? He was only dropped off a short time ago by Mr Fraser. He might just have gone out for a pint or something. After all,' he paused, a sharp glance aimed at Connor, 'it's not like he's under house arrest or anything.'

'Naw, it's not that,' Donald said, running a hand through his thinning hair. 'Colin had something to do. Said he had a Skye – skip call with some podcast or something to do, needed to be back at the house for it. He wouldnae miss it.'

'Skype,' Connor corrected softly, filing the information away. He wondered if Donna knew Sanderson was speaking to other media outlets. Might make sense if it actually was him sending her the messages. After all, if he planned to kill her, he would need someone else to give him coverage, wouldn't he?

'If you can provide us with the details of who he was going to be interviewed by, that would be very helpful,' Ross said, scribbling another note into his pad.

Donald Sanderson shrugged. 'I dinnae ken,' he said. 'He just telt me he was doing it and I know he wouldnae miss it. After all, they were paying him, and Colin wouldnae miss a pay day. But all the info will be up in his room – you're welcome to go and hae a look if you want. The boy's got nothing to hide, despite what you bastards have to say.'

Connor exchanged a look with Ford. 'Welcome to go and have a look' – the police equivalent of rolling out the red carpet, turning down the bed and leaving a chocolate on the pillow.

'Alan, why don't I go and see if I can find that information while you finish up with Mr Sanderson?' Ford said, already moving towards the door. He saw Connor push off to follow him, added: 'And you'll need to speak to Fraser, too, as he was one of the last people to see Mr Sanderson before he went missing.'

Connor flashed his teeth at Ford in a *Gee thanks* gesture as Ross mumbled sour agreement. 'Yes,' he said, as Ford left the room, a PC trailing him, 'that's a good point. What happened after you dropped Mr Sanderson off, Fraser?'

'Well, sir,' Connor said, stepping into the centre of the room and standing over the police officer, 'I'll detail all of this in my official statement but, as you said, I was one of the last people to see Mr Sanderson. I gave him a lift back here after he spoke to you at Randolphfield, came in briefly to go over some of the details for his proposed interviews with Ms Blake. Then I left. Nothing seemed untoward. Mr Sanderson,' he turned his attention to the old man at the table, 'did your son seem agitated at all after I left?'

Connor shrugged away the warning look from Ross. Tough. The policeman had invited him into this conversation, only natural he would take advantage and ask a question if he could.

'Naw, not really,' Sanderson said. 'He just said he wanted to get out for a bit, get some air. Said that all this stuff with going to the polis station then going over plans with you made him feel like he was a prisoner again, back inside. Said he was going to the shop to get some tobacco, that he'd be back in time for that Skype thingy.'

A thought flashed across Connor's mind, like moonlight on a wave, then vanished. 'And that was about an hour ago?' Connor said quickly, not wanting to give Ross the chance to get back into the conversation.

'Aye,' Donald Sanderson said, his years now evident in the flat, exhausted tone of his voice. 'But when he didnae get back, I thought I'd best call you boys. Colin comes across as the big hard man, but he's still my boy, and after what happened up the town the other day, I'm no' taking any chances.'

I was never in any real danger, Connor thought. Was that what this was? Another stunt, a way to get yet more attention? Pull a small disappearing act, get everyone worried for his safety then reappear hale and hearty with yet another story to tell? Or was there something else to it, something more sinister?

Connor had his phone out, was about to hit dial on Donna's number when he heard Ford and the PC clatter back down the stairs. Turned to see Ford enter the room, a small Jiffy-bag held up in front of him, something about half the size of a credit card lying in it. 'Think you'd better take a look at this,' he said, directing the comment to Ross, his eyes darting to Connor.

Connor took a step forward, inserting himself just in front of Ross. Leaned forward, studied the contents of the bag. It was the splinter of an ID card. The left-hand side was gone, as though the card had been snapped in half. But what remained was enough. It was a picture. The girl smiled out from the card, and what struck Connor most was how vibrant the colour of her skin was. Warm, alive, radiating youth and vitality. Not like the last time he had seen her photograph, in Ford's office. Then she had been bleached and grey, her hair unnaturally styled to copy Donna Blake's. He read the name below the picture slowly, committing it to memory.

Lucy Howard.

The girl from the golf course finally had a name.

CHAPTER 58

Donna stood in front of the wall in her office, staring at the last hour's work. After the discovery of the photograph, and the connection between DCI Morgan, Jessica and Rhona, her first impulse had been to phone Ford, confront him with what she knew. But she stopped herself, remembering the words of Donald Peters, an old journalist she had worked with at the *Westie*. 'If you've got something exclusively, you've got something else. Time. Use it. Go deep. Interrogate it. Then go ask for answers.'

So that was what she did. She dug out a roll of magic whiteboard and plastered the wall with three sheets of it, marking each with a year, then filling in the dates. The second and third sheets – 2006 and 2020 – were what she had known before: 2006, Jessica and Rhona were raped, murdered and mutilated. After an investigation by DCI Dennis Morgan, Colin Sanderson, who had been a painter and decorator on the campus at the time of the killings, was tried and convicted for the crimes. Case closed until the third panel, marked 2020, when a High Court judge quashed Sanderson's conviction due to concerns over the original trial. He was released, returned to Stirling and, days later, another woman was found dead, this time at the golf course that was part of the university.

But now Donna had something no one else had. She had panel one, which might just hold the key to what was going on. She stared at it again, reading her notes.

213

Panel one, its heading 9 October 2004. It was the official opening of the Scottish Parliament building at Holyrood. After years of astronomical cost overruns, controversy and criticism, a day for the nation to celebrate and the politicians and architects to breathe a sigh of relief that the building, which always looked to Donna like some kind of demented love child of Ikea and B&Q, was finally open for business. The official opening was presided over by the Queen, with the great and the good from civic Scotland in attendance. Another quick trawl through the *Westie*'s records told Donna that Jessica was there with her father, whose management firm in Perth had worked on the Parliament project, while Rhona had received an invitation for her 'exemplary work in the Scottish Youth Parliament, which had led to her deciding to study politics at university'. And, then, of course, there was Detective Chief Inspector Dennis James Morgan. According to the *Westie*, Morgan was being hailed as a hero and a 'super-cop' at the time, after he had led the investigation that ultimately toppled Bobby 'Brickhouse' Barnes, a drug trafficker who supplied most of Scotland with cocaine and heroin from his base in Greenock on the west coast. Only natural then, that the politicians at the time had invited this shining example of Scottish policing to the opening of the Scottish Parliament building.

All of which left Donna with questions. Yes, the opening of Parliament building was a massive state occasion, with hundreds of people in attendance, so it was quite possible that Morgan hadn't known Jessica and Rhona had been there with him. But, Donna thought, unable to keep the excitement from welling up in her, how likely was it that he hadn't made the link when Jessica and Rhona were murdered two years later? It had taken Donna ten minutes with a newspaper archive to make the connection and she found it impossible to believe that someone in the police hadn't done the same.

So, this link had been hidden, forgotten and buried. Which led to a more ominous question. Why? Why hide an obvious link between the investigating officer and the two murder victims?

Donna felt her excitement curdle into something uglier as she contemplated the thought. She tried to rein herself in, be as objective as possible, but the conclusion was irresistible: Morgan had something to hide.

She felt a shiver twist its way down her spine. What was he hiding? Had he killed the girls after all, triggered by seeing them in their finery at the Parliament? Used his position as investigating officer to cover his tracks, frame Sanderson for the crime? And then, when Sanderson was released, use that as an excuse to find another victim?

But, if that was the case, why send her those messages? Why threaten to 'see her REAL soon'? And if he had sent the messages, who had attacked him in his home?

And, more importantly, why?

Donna raked her hands through her hair. She was missing something, she could feel it. It was up there, on the wall, written in black and white, and she just couldn't see it. Yet.

Frustrated, she turned away, headed for her desk and the phone. With Morgan still in hospital, it was impossible to ask him. She toyed with the possibility of going straight to Police Scotland's press office, but dismissed the thought, knowing that if she did, she would lose the story. So who, then? Only one option really.

She hit dial, waited. Let out a sigh when the call flicked to Ford's answer phone. She hung up without leaving a message, turned back to the wall. Who else? She considered Connor, again rejected the idea. He was close to Ford, true, but what could he really add to this? No, she needed Morgan or someone close to him . . .

She got back into her seat, pulled the laptop close. Called up the phone directory in the *Westie*'s files and started typing. If Dennis Morgan wasn't available, maybe his son was.

CHAPTER 59

Free is a four-letter word.

Before, in court, I couldn't laugh. After all, appearances had to be maintained. But here, now, I can finally express myself. Release the laughter that has been tickling at the back of my throat for days. Relish the memories of my all-too-brief time with Lucy before we parted ways at the golf course and look ahead to the pleasures that await me.

I've never had much need for religion. After all, any god that would allow the horrors I have inflicted on others of His flock is either insane or sadistic. But today I gave my first confession. Sitting in the stagnant silence of that room, I admitted, for the first time, everything I've done over the years. The murders. The blood. The planning for what is about to come next. I received no reply, not that I was truly expecting one, and there was no sudden bolt of lightning to take my diseased soul. Instead, what I received was a sense of peace, of relief.

Of freedom.

And now, without Ford or Fraser or that bitch Blake watching me, I can take the next step. The messages I sent to Fraser and Blake may have made things more challenging, but that's all part of the game, and it will make the inevitable outcome all the sweeter.

A moment of decision awaits. Who first? Blake or Fraser? And, again, I am struck by the glorious freedom I have. To choose who lives or dies first before I deliver my final message.

A moment to be savoured, then, as the pendulum swings between them. The bitch or the beefcake?

The answer comes to me instantly, irresistibly, and again I am struck by the sudden urge to laugh. I stifle it, my little secret, then compose myself. And then, for the second time, I confess my plan. Again, there is no absolution, no objection, no revelation in this telling. But that hardly matters. What's important is that I have been honest.

And everything that comes after will be his responsibility to bear.

CHAPTER 60

Connor stood in front of the wall in Donna's flat, eyes darting across the notes scrawled across the whiteboard. After the discovery of the shard of Lucy Howard's ID card at the Sandersons' home, Ross had flipped into full bureaucratic cop mode, declaring the whole house a crime scene, calling in a forensics team and ordering Connor to leave, with explicit instructions not to discuss the discovery of the ID with anyone.

Connor exchanged a glance with Ford, then left. Called Donna and arranged to meet at her flat. With Sanderson in the wind, the last thing Connor wanted was Donna in the open and exposed. 'Nice work,' he said, gesturing to the wall. 'But where does it get us?'

Donna leaned back in her chair, away from the laptop she was hunched over. 'Not sure,' she said. 'We know that Morgan had a link with the original murder victims. Whether he met them or not at the Parliament opening is irrelevant, I can't believe a police officer as thorough as him didn't know about it. So, the question is, why hide it? And did someone help him do it?'

Connor gave Donna a long, hard look. He knew what she was implying. The same thought had crossed his mind the moment she had told him about her discovery of the link between Jessica Kristen, Rhona Everett and Dennis Morgan at the opening of the Scottish Parliament building. It wouldn't have taken much digging to make that connection, and if it had been hidden, had Ford helped Morgan do it?

And, if so, why?

No. Ford might bend the rules on occasion, but this, this was a step too far. Connor could not, would not, believe that the policeman would conceal evidence, even if it pointed to his boss being linked to two murders.

'I'll speak to Ford once he's clear, see what he can tell me,' Connor said. He saw an objection rise in Donna's eyes, then subside. It made sense. While Ford was suspicious of them both, the last thing he would do was talk to a journalist asking sensitive questions.

'Then what?' Donna asked.

Connor shrugged. It was a question he had been worrying at on the drive over. With the discovery of the ID card, the disappearance of Sanderson was now a police matter. He would have to do a little damage control with Frontline PR about their client getting away from him but, given the limitations Sanderson had put on the security he was provided, Connor didn't think that would pose much of a problem, especially given that a concrete link between him and a murdered woman had been found in his bedroom. So, professionally, Connor's involvement with the case was over. But, on a more personal level, it was just beginning. Donna being threatened was bad enough, but then he had received a message. He had sent a reply, but what he wanted, very, very badly, was to deliver his response in person. So he would find Sanderson and give it to him. Slowly and emphatically.

'I keep looking,' Connor said, blinking away the thought of his knuckles crashing off Sanderson's jaw. 'The fact they found an ID for the latest victim in Sanderson's room suggests he's the killer. So he's either decided to make a run for it or he's waiting to make good on his threats to us.'

'"Suggests"?' Donna asked. 'You still think there's room for doubt in this, even now?'

Connor glanced back at the wall of Donna's notes, something throbbing at the back of his mind, like the echo of a receding headache. 'I know what it looks like,' he said absently, 'but still. He was smart enough to set up that attack in front of you the other day, smart enough to send you and me messages from an untraceable source. So why get sloppy now and leave his latest victim's ID in his bedroom?

219

And then there's this.' He gestured back to the wall. 'Why has this link with Morgan never come up before?'

Donna closed her laptop, stood. Stretched. 'Maybe I can get an answer for that,' she said. 'I'm going to meet Michael Morgan, see if he can add anything to this. Want to come along?'

Connor considered the option for a moment. 'No,' he said, 'but, if you don't mind, I'll send Robbie with you. If Sanderson is out there and watching, I want you to have some cover.'

Something like relief flashed across Donna's face, telling Connor she had been thinking the same thing. She put on a brave front, and Connor admired her for it, but still he could see the chinks in the armour, the doubts and the fears. Maybe he saw them so easily because he felt the same way himself.

'So what are you going to be doing?' she asked.

Connor smiled, the memory of cheap cigar smoke suddenly filling his nostrils. 'Stirring up trouble,' he said.

CHAPTER 61

'You shouldn't be here,' Ross said.

Ford just smiled. He had been expecting this – even, if he was honest, looking forward to it. Because now, finally, he had something to beat the chief constable over the head with. And the best of it was, it was the very rulebook he was so fond of quoting.

'Sorry, Alan, but you know how it is. Chain of evidence. I found the item in question. I can hand it over to you, of course, but that means paperwork. But, hey,' he threw up his hands, 'if you want to explain my involvement in this to the chief, by all means. Or we could put all the paper-pushing bullshit aside and do our jobs. Or have you forgotten that Sanderson is out there somewhere, right now?'

Ross regarded Ford coolly, a humourless smile inflating those overly rosy cheeks. Then he looked up at the ceiling, exhaled. 'Fine,' he said. 'We keep this quiet, for now. But if we start getting awkward questions about it, you disappear. Agreed?'

'Fine with me,' Ford said. 'So, what do we have so far?'

Ross shuffled some files, pushed one across the desk at Ford. 'Lucy Howard,' he said, as Ford opened the file. 'Exchange student from the University of San Francisco. Explains why we had such a hard time tracking her down. No one had filed a missing-person report as she'd only just arrived.'

Ford frowned. 'Aye, but hold on. Even if she'd just arrived, she'd have been on Stirling's records. Surely she should have pinged up on our searches there. We gave the university a description of the victim, but nothing came back close to her.'

Ross looked down at the file, seeming to deflate somehow. 'Aye, she probably would have,' he said. 'If she was a student at Stirling.'

'What?' Ford asked, confused. 'But you just said she was an exchange student. If not at Stirling, then where?'

'Edinburgh,' Ross said. 'Politics and history.'

Ford looked up suddenly, the words burning him. 'Just like Rhona Everett,' he said.

'Exactly,' Ross replied, massaging his eyes with his fingers. 'Question is, why was she in Stirling? We're getting Lothian division to check now, see if there are any records of her movements. But she's not got a vehicle registered to her name, so she had to get here somehow. Hopefully we'll get something from a rail station or a bus company that will help us track her movements.'

'Speaking of movements, what about Sanderson?'

Another sigh, longer this time. 'Checked with the shop his dad mentioned, and you'll be surprised to hear he never made it. Seems he just went for a walk, kept on going. Could be anywhere.'

Ford nodded, understanding now what had bothered him when Sanderson's father had told them he was missing. Sanderson had said his son had gone to the shop for tobacco, but Ford had only ever seen him smoking filter-tips. So the trip to the shop had been an excuse. And a lame one at that. 'Anything else interesting turn up at his place?'

'You mean like a blood-stained knife, a burner phone, something like that?' Ross smiled. ''Fraid not, nothing at all. Place was completely clean.'

Again, this struck Ford. If Sanderson was being so scrupulous as to use anonymous phones and virtually untraceable email addresses to target Blake and Fraser, why leave the ID card lying around? It was hardly well hidden, wedged between a bedside table and the mattress of the bed, which was meticulously made in prison style. Or was that the entire point? To taunt them with his guilt and then disappear. Ford felt a strange moment of weightlessness, the burden of guilt counterbalanced by the relief of vindication. Morgan had been right: Sanderson was truly guilty, and the ends really had justified the means after all.

'OK,' he said after a moment. 'I think the best thing I can do is go back and look at Sanderson's old haunts. See if there's a place we linked him to during the original investigation that he might be using now.'

Relief played across Ross's face, re-inflating his hamster-like cheeks. 'Good idea,' he said. 'Go back to the original case. After all, it's what the chief wanted in the first place, for you to act as an adviser.'

'Aye,' Ford said. 'Let's just hope I can find something useful.'

CHAPTER 62

Connor had never been to MacKenzie Haulage's site before, but it was exactly as he had pictured it in his mind's eye. Tucked away at the back of an industrial estate halfway between Stirling and Bannockburn, it was close enough to the main arterial routes to give easy access to just about anywhere in Scotland, yet isolated enough not to get too many unannounced visitors.

It sat on a large, tarmacked plot, the surface of which was so smooth and unpitted it would have put a lot of the country's highway maintenance departments to shame. Lorries and flatbed trailers were parked with almost military precision in front of two large warehouses that bordered the plot like sentry posts, guarding the main office block in the centre of the yard. Connor knew from conversations with Jen that her father had started MacKenzie Haulage on this site nearly thirty years ago, and the office block was like a living history of the company's growth. Look closely and you could see the original pre-fab office that had housed MacKenzie Haulage at the centre of a series of extensions that had been grafted onto it over the years as the company expanded.

It was a strange, slightly off-putting sight: the ancient harled walls and flat-pitch roof of the original building sprouting modern glass and steel extensions. Connor had never taken Duncan MacKenzie for a sentimental man. Looking at the building in front of him forced him to reconsider that assessment.

He pulled into a space marked 'Visitors' and was killing the Audi's engine when Paulie came barrelling out of the double doors that led to what looked like a glass atrium at the front of the office.

'What the hell you doin' here?' Paulie asked, eyes darting between Connor and his car.

'Just thought I'd drop in and say hello,' Connor said, keeping his voice as melodious as possible. He was walking a dangerous line here. He had dropped in unannounced to put Paulie and Duncan off balance, hopefully get some answers. But the last thing he needed was to make Paulie feel threatened on home turf. Like any predator, Paulie would protect his territory. And that was one fight Connor didn't want to have unless it was unavoidable.

'Aye, well, you've said hi, so do one,' Paulie whispered. 'Jen's no' here anyway, and I doubt the boss is gonna want to talk to you.'

'That's fine, Paulie. It's you I came to see. Wanted to ask you a few questions about Sanderson.'

Paulie's eyes narrowed, cold calculations running. 'Whit?' he said. 'Look, I met you earlier as a favour. Told you everything I'm gonna, so why don't you just—'

'He's gone, Paulie,' Connor said simply, glancing over Paulie's shoulder to the office. Was that someone at the window, staring out at him from behind the barricade of the Venetian blinds?

'Whit?' Paulie asked, Connor's car forgotten now. 'What do you mean, gone?'

'I mean gone. Missing. I gave him a lift home after the police interview this morning, then he nipped out to the shop and disappeared. I know you weren't there when I dropped him off, but did you go back and check on him at any point today, or have you been here?'

'Sounding awfully like a copper there, Fraser,' Paulie said. 'You sure you're no' getting back into the pig patrol?'

Connor ignored the remark, knew Paulie was just trying to distract with outrage. The question was, why? He waited for a moment, then made to move around Paulie. 'OK,' he said, 'you don't want to talk, fine. I'll speak to Duncan. See, I'm kind of curious to know what his relationship with Dennis Morgan was that a senior police officer can pull a favour like this.'

Paulie got in front of Connor, moving with that fluid, bulk-defying grace that was so unsettling. He took a half-step forward. Connor stood his ground, unwilling to back off.

'Like I said, Mr MacKenzie is busy,' Paulie rumbled. 'I telt you already. Morgan asked the boss to keep an eye on Sanderson in case his boy tried any shit with him. I was told to get in the middle of it, make sure the boy didnae get hurt. But after his dad got put in the hospital, I figured he'd be spending most of his time there. So no, after I saw you this morning, I came straight back here. Havenae seen Sanderson since. And, frankly, fuck the murdering cunt. I dinnae want to.'

'Hold on,' Connor said. 'You're telling me you came all the way to Randolphfield just to see me this morning? I'm touched, Paulie. Thought it does kind of raise the question, why?'

Paulie's face darkened, as though a cloud had appeared overhead. When he spoke, his voice was as heavy as his brow. 'Look, Fraser, I owe you for looking after Jen last year,' he said. 'But don't push it. I telt you all I'm going to this morning. I was babysitting Sanderson to make sure Morgan didnae try anything. The boss knows his dad from back in the day when he was a copper, that's all I ken. I was asked to keep an eye on Sanderson, I did, simple as that.'

'Nothing else? Come on, Paulie, you've got to admit, using you to keep a civilian like Morgan away from Sanderson is a bit like using a machete to open a letter. Bit of overkill.'

A cold smile spread across Paulie's face, lit by some sharp and malevolent humour. 'Aye, maybe,' he said. 'Boss asks. I do. I don't know where Sanderson is now, don't gie a fuck, to be honest. Means I can get back to some proper work. And, like I said, the boss really is busy.'

Connor let the silence stretch for heartbeat, just long enough to confirm Paulie wasn't going to say anything else. 'Fine,' he said. 'But, Paulie, if Sanderson really did kill those women, he's out there now. And you don't want another woman's death on your conscience, do you?'

'Fuck off.' Paulie snorted. 'Nothing to do with me. If I hear anything, I'll let you know, OK?'

'No idea where he might have gone? Old friends, places he might go to lie low?'

'I wasnae his keeper, Fraser, didnae have the life story on him. Like I said, I'll ask around, but that's it.'

'Fair enough,' Connor said. I'll make sure I tell Jen you said hello.'

Paulie bristled, but Connor was already heading back to the car. Paulie watched him go, waited until the Audi rumbled into life, then drove out of the yard. Then turned, stalked back into the office. Walked in without knocking, soaked in the calming gloom.

'Well?'

'It's started, boss,' Paulie replied. 'And if we're lucky, Fraser is going to end up right in the fucking middle of it.'

CHAPTER 63

Consciousness came back slowly, like fingers of uncaring dawn light poking through the shroud of night. Snatches of clarity at first, a glimpse of a shattered windscreen, the smell of smoke and burned rubber, the gunpowder-like scorching of deployed airbag hanging in the air like spent napalm.

And then, of course, there was the pain. It was as if it was a living thing that had made a nest inside him, its every breath electrifying his body with waves of agony that raced to his head and detonated there, triggering a nauseating fireworks display behind his eyes.

Robbie closed them tightly, found no relief in the darkness. Felt something on his forehead, took a moment to realise it was his hand. He had no memory of raising it. Felt something hot and sticky slick his palm, didn't need to open his eyes to know it was his own blood. Wondered dimly if it had the same coppery tang of the clotted, cloying mass that was lodged at the back of his throat.

He took a deep breath, used the sudden arc of agony like a flashlight against the already-encroaching fog in his mind that told him to keep his eyes closed and sleep, just sleep. Snapped his eyes open, took in the scene in front of him as he tried to remember what had happened.

Blake. Donna. Connor had called him, told him to drive her somewhere. Where was that again? Thoughts tumbled through his mind, fragmentary and chaotic. Confetti at a wedding. He smiled at the thought, choked out a laugh that stabbed a sickening dagger into his chest. Ribs broken. Definitely.

Definitely. Yes. Yes. Be decisive. Act. Now. He grabbed for the thought. Focused again. Blake. Donna. Yes, he was driving her to Fife to see Michael Morgan, who lived in North Queensferry. They had just crossed the Kincardine Bridge – which his father called the workman's bridge when compared to the grandeur of the Forth Bridge or the new Queensferry Crossing, which gave access to Fife from Edinburgh – and were climbing a hill into the twisty A-roads that would lead them towards Dunfermline then on to North Queensferry. Another snatch of memory, an old power plant, all ugly concrete chimneys and blank glass walls, nestling in the rolling hills and farmland as if someone had carelessly discarded a backdrop from *Blade Runner* in the landscape. They were on a straight section of road, driving through a canopy of trees, when the car came up behind them. Fast, brutal, little more than a blur of headlights and dark paintwork. A sudden, violent shunt, just off the driver's side bumper, enough to send the car into a spin. A kaleidoscope of sounds and images; the flashing of greenery and tarmac as the car spun, the scream of the tyres as they bit into the road for purchase, Blake's elongated bellow of 'Fuuuuck!' as they careened towards the verge. Then a blow to the face, as though whoever had been chasing them had managed to reach into the car and punch him. Again, Robbie smiled at his own stupidity.

'Airbag fuckwit,' he whispered, biting down on the urge to laugh. Laughing would wake the pain monster in his chest. And that was the last thing he needed.

He blinked, focused. Realised consciousness was leaving him again. Fumbled at the seatbelt with numb, thick fingers, managed to unclip it. Pushed the mangled door of the car open with a strength he didn't remember possessing – all those press-ups for Connor must have been paying off after all.

He landed on the ground in a heap, the shock juddering up through his knees and coaxing another snarl of agony from whatever damage the crash had done to him. He closed his eyes, vomited what felt like battery acid onto the wet ground. Took a clump of grass, rubbed it on his forehead, using the glorious coolness to focus.

He raised his head, neck feeling like it had been filled with sand, the damage to the car filling in the last gaps in his memory. Whoever had hit them had done their job perfectly, spinning them out and forcing them to crash into a long verge that ran beside what looked like a forest that stretched away from the road. It looked so lush and peaceful. They had hit a tree stump, bringing them to a sudden, violent halt and triggering the airbags.

Robbie managed to pull himself to his knees, fumbled in his coat pocket for his phone as he staggered around the car. Stopped when he got to the passenger side. The door hung open like an afterthought, the seat empty, apart from what was left of the airbag, which hung limp and spent like a forgotten party balloon.

Robbie looked around, panic replacing the pain racking his body. But no, Donna hadn't been thrown clear of the car in the crash. She was just gone.

And then, another memory, more agonising than the pain in his side, more bitter than the blood at the back of his throat. A voice, warm and cloying like blood, whispering through the semi-conscious haze the crash had left Robbie in.

'Hi, Donna. Told you today was the day. Come on, let's get you out of here. We've a lot to do.'

Robbie got his phone into his hand. Squinted at the screen. Cracked but still working. Got Connor's number up. Dialled. Waited for what seemed like an eternity for an answer, then got talking, the picture sharpening in his mind as he spoke.

'Boss, it's me. Been run off the road just outside Kincardine. No. No accident. Whoever hit us, they took Donna.'

CHAPTER 64

It was the first time Ford had been in Connor's home and, on another occasion, he would have stopped to take in the surroundings, check out the bookcases and the photographs, picking up all those little hints and clues as to who the occupant of the property really was. But Connor was making that impossible. He stood in the centre of the room, arms folded, face as impassive as granite, eyes somehow harder. It was as if he was exerting a gravitational pull of his own, commanding all attention be focused on him.

Ford had never seen this side of Connor before, the younger man's police training installing a natural buffer of deference between this version of him and the outside world. But that façade had been stripped away, and Ford was seeing another version of Connor Fraser, a simpler one.

And he wasn't sure he liked it.

Fraser had called about twenty minutes ago, told Ford what had happened to Robbie, then told him he wanted to meet. 'We'll do it at my place,' he'd said, in a calm, empty tone that Ford recognised from a hundred interviews with so-called hard men over the years. 'I've got some questions to ask, and I don't think you want Ross to hear the answers just yet.'

Ford agreed, told Troughton to co-ordinate with the police in Fife to conduct the search for Donna and check on Michael Morgan, then got moving. The door to the flat had swung open before Ford had had time to ring the bell, and Connor had led him down the hall into the living area, where he took up position. He was standing at his full height, no attempt to make himself seem less intimidating now. The message was clear: this is my fucking show.

'You checked with the police in Fife,' he said at last, the words seeming to press and needle the pregnant bubble of pressure that was forming in the room. 'So you know that Robbie Lindsay was taken to the hospital in Kirkcaldy. Three broken ribs, broken nose from the airbag, concussion, multiple contusions. Meanwhile, Donna Blake is missing. Presumably snatched by Sanderson for whatever sick fucking game he's playing. Donna has a son, Chief Inspector, remember him? Lost his father a year ago on another case we were working. He will not lose his mother. So you and I are going to talk. Now.'

Anger pricked at the nape of Ford's neck, cold and hard. Yes, things were getting out of hand, but who the hell did Fraser think he was to talk to him like this? He was a civilian, a bystander, a—

'Did you know your old boss had met Rhona Everett and Jessica Kristen before they were murdered?' Connor asked.

Ford felt as though he had been punched in the gut. 'What?' he asked. 'What the fuck are you talking about? I—'

Connor turned to the coffee-table behind him, picked up a picture. Handed it to Ford, three faces in the group shot picked out, ringed in red.

'That's what Donna was heading to Fife for. To talk to Morgan's son about this. Opening of the Parliament building, 2004,' Connor said. 'Morgan was there, along with Rhona and Jessica. Could be coincidental, it was a massive public event, lots of people were there, quite possible that the three of them never got any closer than being jostled together by a photographer so they could smile for the camera. Except it should have been flagged in the case file you gave me. All officers would have to declare any previous contact with the deceased, no matter how fleeting, in the case decision log, wouldn't they? But there's nothing here. Why?'

Ford's mouth opened, closed. He had never seen this picture before, had never known of its existence. And even as he struggled for an answer, another thought filled his mind. The sound of wood striking flesh, like steak being tenderised, the hacking bark of breath being forced from a body, the spatter of blood on a cold stone wall. And that one word.

Again.

'Look, Fraser, I—'

Connor held up his hand. 'I knew there were things missing from that file the moment you gave it to me,' he said, jutting his jaw at the manila folder on the coffee-table. 'I just got so caught up in trying to prove you right and the world wrong that I took my eye off the detail. The list of investigating officers and career bios being one of them.'

'Look, Fraser, I don't know anything about this, really. I don't know why Dennis would try to cover this up. I know he took the case personally, wanted to get a result. Maybe he thought this would get in the way of that, stop him working on the case, I don't know. But I—'

Connor raised a hand, like a games master stopping a contestant who had run out of time. 'Doesn't matter,' he said. 'We know Morgan isn't above bending the rules – he showed that when he got Paulie to shadow Sanderson to make sure his boy didn't get hurt trying anything. And since he's lying in a hospital bed, he's hardly likely to give us any answers. So, putting aside the picture, three questions. Why would Sanderson fixate on Donna? Where would he take her? And, crucially, how long do we think she's got?'

'Kristen and Everett were killed within twelve hours of being snatched, according to the post-mortems at the time,' Ford said. 'Looks like Lucy Howard was in a slightly longer time frame.'

Connor nodded, an idea snarling in his brain, niggling away at the blank fury that had him focused on finding Donna and Sanderson before it was too late. A memory of Lucy Howard's picture, so alive and vibrant, so full of life. And then the picture from the Parliament, all formal smiles, polished uniforms and Sunday best, almost like . . . like . . .

Connor turned back to the coffee-table, found the wad of pages he was looking for, the ones Jen had dug up for him in his gran's belongings. Riffled through them, finding the newspaper article, the picture of his dad, gran and Campbell Fraser striking that same awkward pose.

You've got bad blood, Connor . . .

Thoughts crashing together in Connor's brain now, snatches of conversation and ideas bouncing off each other, forming connections. Paulie's cruel smile as he spoke: *I was babysitting Sanderson to make sure Morgan didnae try anything. The boss knows his dad from back in the day when he was a copper, that's all I ken. I was asked to keep an eye on Sanderson, I did, simple as that.*

Lucy Howard's ID. The picture Donna had found. The . . .

Connor whirled, snatched the picture from Ford. Studied it, ignoring those faces he had marked. Stopped when he found what he was looking for, ice chittering around his spine.

'You said Morgan took this case personally, yeah?' Connor said, voice calm despite the thoughts roaring through his mind. 'And the case file you gave me said it was him who found the witness tying Jessica Kristen to Sanderson?'

'Yes, why?' Ford said, a mixture of fear and caution in his voice.

'Pictures,' Connor said, looking back at the image from the Scottish Parliament. He should have seen the face sooner, recognised the haunted expression in the eyes. It was the same as the one he had seen in the picture of his dad and his parents.

'Dennis Morgan wasn't alone at the Parliament that day, was he? Sure, his wife had died, but that left someone else, didn't it?'

Ford looked down at the picture, on which Connor was tapping his finger. There, two rows back from Jessica, ironed into a picture-perfect school uniform, eyes hollow, face implacable, was Michael Morgan. He was slight, almost skeletal, a world away from the gym-sculpted man he had become.

'What if I got it wrong?' Connor said. Paulie's words echoing in his mind as he spoke. 'Morgan wasn't trying to cover up his link with Jessica and Everett, but his son's. We know Michael has a capacity for violence. Daddy dear managed to cover up the worst of it, but it's there. Christ, we've been seeing exactly what Morgan wanted us to see all this time. That Sanderson was guilty. What if he's not? What if the court was right? And what if Paulie wasn't protecting Michael but Sanderson all along, because Dennis Morgan was worried his son would do something stupid, something that might get him into trouble like he did back in Edinburgh when it got swept under the carpet?'

Ford's face drained of colour, leaving just a husk. He blinked, his eyes suddenly liquid, mouth moving soundlessly, as though the weight of what Connor had just said was crushing the air from his lungs. 'Can we sit down?' he asked at last, voice a whisper. 'And can I get a drink? There's something you need to know about Duncan MacKenzie, and the original murder inquiry.'

CHAPTER 65

Stairs.

Vaguely, she remembered stairs. Stumbling down them, being pushed from behind, arms tied. Her body a symphony of pain after the car crash, magnified by the terror she felt when she woke up crammed into a dark, claustrophobic void where an animal snarled at her from the shadows. Horror like white noise in her mind, blotting out every thought until she was brought back to herself by a juddering thud that set off a chain reaction of agony through her body.

A car. She was in the boot of a car. And the snarling monster was the sound of an engine.

She blanked out again, awoken by rough hands on her as she was manhandled from the boot, dragged out into somewhere cold. She could see nothing – some kind of blindfold had been pulled over her eyes – but she could hear the sound of birds in the distance, smell the vague warm odour of animals. Then the stairs, being pushed and shoved down them, stumbling. A large room, by the harsh echoes that her footsteps left in her wake. She was shoved again in the back, stumbled forward, unable to protect herself from the fall.

Strained her senses, listening for breathing, footsteps, anything that would give her a possible location for her captor. She was rewarded a moment later by the sound of a door slamming shut, a heavy bolt rattling home.

Alone. She was alone.

The terror rose in her again, painting pictures in the darkness behind her blindfold. Andrew. He would be with her mum now, playing. She could see him, reaching out, laughing, giggling. Heard her mother's words: *It's no job for a mother with a young son.*

She felt tears dampen the blindfold, hot and shameful. Closed her eyes even in the dark, let the void take her, carry her off like a piece of flotsam caught in the tide. Easier to rest, easier not to feel. To think.

Andrew.

A sound dragged her from her reverie. Her eyes snapped open, the gloom of the room forming vague shapes around her. The blindfold, where had the blindfold gone?

She looked across the room, a large, empty space with stone walls, a vaulted ceiling and stripped-bare floorboards. The door was open and she peered towards it, eyes straining as a figure began to emerge from the shadows.

He lumbered up the stairs, shadows falling from his face, replaced by a deeper darkness that seemed to devour the meagre light around him. Skin hung loosely around his eyes and cheeks, grey and rotting. When he saw her, his face pulled into an empty leer of a smile as he raised a hand in offering. Dripping from his fingers, glistening in the half-light, were loops of intestine, black like oil, writhing like serpents.

'Hello, Donna,' Mark whispered, his voice wet gravel being dragged across concrete.

Donna snapped awake, the sound of her scream in her ears, the staccato hammering of her feet booming like the devil's bassline.

'Sorry to wake you, Donna,' a voice said in the darkness as her blindfold was pulled from her face. 'But it's time we got to work. See, you have a story to tell. And believe me, it's going to be the biggest of your life.'

Donna looked into the eyes in front of her, realisation crashing into her, washing away the nightmare of Mark. What had come was much, much worse. A nightmare made flesh.

And from this there would be no awakening.

CHAPTER 66

Connor made the drive to Alloa on autopilot, his conscious mind processing what Ford had told him and trying to mitigate the fallout. And as he did so, one question ran through his mind on repeat, like a record needle bumping off the end of an album.

What did this mean for him and Jen?

Even as he spoke to Ford, Connor had tried to tell himself that the link to Michael Morgan was more coloured by his own recent experiences with his dad than any real deductive reasoning. After all, what did he have? A picture of a public event that Morgan and his dad had attended with Jessica Kristen, Rhona Everett and about half of civic Scotland. The kid who had got into a bit of trouble as a young man because he was too ready with his fists, whose police officer dad had helped cover up. And a favour called in with a shady businessman to keep that son away from a man who had just been acquitted of murder.

Suggestive, but hardly concrete. But then Ford had told Connor his story, and finding Michael Morgan became an absolute priority.

The problem was Dean Barrett, the witness who had initially linked Sanderson to Jessica Kristen and given the police their first real break in the 2006 murder inquiry.

'The boss was getting desperate,' Ford had told Connor. 'There were no concrete leads, nothing. With Stirling being such an open campus, people came and went as they pleased, and most of those visiting were too caught up in their own world to give us anything useful. Forensics were inconclusive, CCTV coverage wasn't as great as it is now. So we were stuck. Until, of course, we ran into Dean Barrett.'

He was just another face in the crowd, stopped by two uniformed officers who were combing the campus at the time as part of random checks to see if any students remembered anything from around the time that Jessica and Rhona disappeared. He had told the officers he vaguely remembered seeing Jessica down by the loch, talking to someone, just passing the time of day. Would have forgotten all about it if the pictures of the girl on the TV hadn't jogged his memory. But there was something in the kid's demeanour, a twitchy nervousness and a desire to get away from the officers, that made him stand out enough for them to report him to DCI Morgan.

'The boss looked like all his Christmases had come at once,' Ford had told Connor as he sat on his sofa, a whisky cradled in his hands, which hung loosely in front of him. 'He went all out on this kid, full background checks, the works. Nothing too out of the ordinary on the first pass. He was a second-year economics student, came from Aberdeen. Unremarkable grades, known to enjoy the student life a bit. But then, when we dug a little further, guess who we found?'

'Duncan MacKenzie,' Connor had said, his mind full of Paulie's words about Morgan knowing him from back in the day, and calling in a favour.

'Exactly,' Ford said, a strange sound of relief in his voice, as though this had been weighing on him too long. Maybe it had. 'Turns out Barrett did some driving for MacKenzie on the weekends, and there were suspicions that not all of his deliveries to the campus were of a legal nature.'

'So,' Connor said, feeling the pieces fall into place, 'that's how Morgan knows Duncan. He approached him about Barrett, asking for background.'

'Yeah,' Ford replied. 'Turns out Barrett was doing some side deals, using MacKenzie's delivery runs as a cover to deliver his own product. You know the stuff, E, coke, the usual pills and party poppers the kids like. But he wouldn't tell us who he was doing those side deals with for some reason. So MacKenzie arranged for us to have a little, ah, chat with Barrett. Off the record, of course.'

Ford had laid out what happened with a detached, clinical detail that almost made Connor feel sorry for the man. Almost. MacKenzie arranged for Barrett to meet with Morgan and Ford at his haulage yard. MacKenzie had taken Morgan aside for a moment, and then they were shown into one of the warehouses at the back of the yard.

'They had Barrett there, tied to a chair. And circling him was that thug of MacKenzie's, Paulie.'

Connor could have asked why Ford didn't stop what came next, but he knew the answer. Two brutal murders. An experienced cop at the end of his tether and a younger, less experienced police officer who was running on instinct and fear, desperate to help his senior officer and mentor in any way he could.

And, besides, Barrett was a drug dealer, a criminal, so the ends justified the means.

Right?

The 'interview' lasted less than an hour, Paulie repeatedly asking the same questions about who he was dealing to and if Jessica or Rhona were among the clients.

'MacKenzie,' Ford had said, downing the whisky. 'It was MacKenzie who ordered it. Paulie would threaten the kid with a two-by-four. He only hit him twice, but it was enough. The first time, the first time he started to cry. And all MacKenzie said was one word. Again.'

By the time they had finished, they had their name. Barrett was supplying students on the campus and also one Colin Sanderson, a labourer who was working on the site at the time. A little further coercion and the details of Sanderson's altercation with Jessica became clear – they had been arguing on the quad, and that was what Barrett had seen.

Two days later, Barrett amended his statement, giving full details of the row between Jessica and Sanderson. After which the case fell into place, including the discovery of Jessica and Rhona's DNA in Sanderson's van, which Morgan used as justification for the methods they had used to get the break they needed.

'We never spoke about it again,' Ford had told Connor, a pleading he had thought the policeman incapable of in his eyes. 'After all, the rest of the case was watertight. The physical evidence, Sanderson's background, the timings. All of it. It was him, Fraser, I'm sure of it.'

Connor had said nothing. After what he had done as a police officer in Belfast, he had no moral right to judge anyone. But, still, he felt something like disgust. They had forced evidence and testimony from a scared kid. How reliable was that evidence? And was this just another case of Morgan trying to get people to see what he wanted them to – that Sanderson was guilty?

The thoughts churned through Connor's head as he drove. What did this mean? And what would he do about Jen? She was hardly responsible for the actions of her father, but did he want any association with a man who had helped the police fabricate evidence in an attempt to find a murderer?

He pushed the thoughts aside, concentrated on driving. After hearing Ford's story, they had agreed that the policeman should see what the officers who visited Michael Morgan had found, then coordinate the search for Sanderson and Donna. The consequences of what Ford had told Connor could wait for another time. Donna was the primary motivation.

Connor, meanwhile, was heading for Morgan's home in Alloa. His first instinct had been to head for Fife with Ford, but he knew his presence would only be a distraction and could, potentially, slow things down. And there were too many questions hanging over Dennis Morgan for Connor to dismiss. Why had he covered up the photograph? Why had he agreed to letting Paulie loose on Barrett? If it was Sanderson who had attacked him at his home, why had he let him live?

Questions, questions, questions.

Connor pulled up a few cars away from the property. It was a typical detached villa, all red brick and white-painted window frames nestling behind a slightly unkempt privet hedge. Police tape fluttered across the front of the property, but there was no sign of any officer guarding the place. Despite himself, Connor smiled. Ford would like that – the cuts being imposed on his beloved police force were showing some positive results at last and making his job easier.

Connor got out of the Audi, strode towards the house. Head high, determined, just a man on official business. Ducked under the tape and headed for the front door. It was locked, but that wasn't much of an issue thanks to the lock pick Connor had in his jacket pocket.

Into the house, which, in the silence, felt more like a library than a home. He walked through the hallway into a large open-plan living/ dining area, made remarkable only by the seventies-style décor and the large, cordoned-off blood stain that spread across most of the floor and seeped into the cracks in the parquet.

Connor tore his eyes away. Too obvious. The problem with crime scenes where violence had taken place and blood had been spilled was that they were distracting. All the attention focused on the blood, the shattered furniture, the devastation, meaning more subtle points were lost in the white noise of destruction.

He turned away from the dining area, back to the hall. Three doors greeted him, one leading to a bathroom, one to a more formal living area and another to a small garage. Connor shrugged, decided to head there first.

It was an unremarkable space, a neat workbench taking up the far end of the room, a ladder tied to the wall above it, the other wall lined with an industrial shelving unit, which was packed with tins of paint, brushes and dust sheets.

Connor stepped into the garage, crossed to the workbench. Nothing of interest. A few tools, a scattering of screws, a spring, what looked like the guts of a clock spread out on the work surface and a small screwdriver, the type used to tighten the screws on glasses. He was about to turn his attention to the shelving when he stopped, some memory dragging his attention back to the table.

The spring. What was it about the . . .

He reached out, took the spring in his hand. Inspected it, felt something cold curl into a fist in his guts as recognition took hold.

Not a spring. Not quite. A long, tapered piece of metal, coiled like a spring.

Connor looked around, found a drawer. Opened it. Found what he hoped he wouldn't. A small wand with a rough, tapered head, like a toilet brush in miniature. He lifted it to his nose, inhaled, memories of Belfast flooding his mind even as he felt the urge to run. He placed the brush on the worktop beside the spring-like item. Reached over for the rag in the corner, knowing how it would feel and smell, placed that in a row beside the other items.

It was a cleaning kit, not dissimilar to the one Connor kept in the floorboards under his flat. A cleaning kit for an object like the one that was now strapped to Connor's belt in a pancake holster, a small, metal-and-plastic parcel of death that suddenly felt very, very heavy.

Got you in my sights, Connor.

Connor shuddered. He knew where the gun that had been cleaned at this table was, prayed he was wrong. Knew somewhere deep down that he wasn't.

CHAPTER 67

Ford was parked on the promenade at North Queensferry, looking out on the slate-grey expanse of the Forth as it crashed and roiled in front of him. The light was waning, and the only real illumination came from the spotlights that were trained on the looming red exoskeleton of the Forth Bridge, which stretched into the horizon, back towards Edinburgh.

He looked down at the laptop in front of him. Not that he needed to refresh his memory: the files had been burned into his mind the moment he had read them.

After revealing his secret to Connor, Ford had felt drained, worn out. The only thought that had kept him going was the need to find Donna Blake, and a desire to prove Fraser wrong, to show that, despite what he and Ford had done all those years ago, Sanderson really was the killer after all.

The email he had received from Troughton had effectively killed that last vestige of hope.

What was it Fraser had said? Too busy concentrating on what Morgan wanted him to see rather than what was there? Too focused on trying to prove Morgan right and the world wrong to see the facts? Turns out Fraser wasn't the only one guilty of that.

A call to Troughton was all it had taken. Christ, Morgan had given him the key when he'd turned up at the house. What was it he had said about Michael Morgan? *He's a good lad, working in*

Edinburgh now, making the big money as a politics lecturer at the university.

A quick cross-reference revealed that Michael Morgan was indeed a lecturer at Edinburgh University, specialising in international politics, the course Lucy Howard had travelled to Scotland to study. A check of Lucy's emails provided the final link in the chain – an exchange between her and Morgan relating to a cancelled tutoring session. Morgan had contacted her to explain he was visiting Stirling to see his father, and Howard had replied that she would love to see 'such a historic part of Scotland'. Further emails, which became increasingly flirtatious, detailed the arrangements they made, including Morgan offering to give Lucy a lift to Stirling and drop her off before he headed to the university for an appointment with another professor, before he acted as her personal tour guide around the city centre and its historic sites.

Did she get that look around town? Ford wondered now. Had she fallen foul of Morgan while doing so or, as his gut told him, had she never left Michael Morgan's car alive?

He slammed the laptop shut, emotions churning like the waters of the Forth. He was slow, stupid. Complicit. He should write that resignation letter now. No, fuck that. He should march into the chief constable's office and tell him everything, demand to be arrested and have charges brought against himself and DCI Morgan.

He lashed out suddenly, the horn of the car shattering the silence of the early evening as he punched the steering wheel.

No. If he did that, what would happen to Mary? She had sacrificed so much to have a life with him. He'd be damned if he'd rob her of his presence as they faced retirement and old age. Then there was Blake. She was innocent, dragged into all of this because of his own stupidity and blind loyalty to a man who wasn't deserving of such devotion.

And, last, there were Sanderson and Michael Morgan. One was a killer, the other involved in some way Ford was yet to understand. But he understood that he would not stop until he had faced these men and prised the answers from them.

Then, and only then, would he write that letter and say goodbye to all of this.

CHAPTER 68

The text message was short and to the point, Ford outlining to Connor the links between Michael Morgan and Lucy Howard. Connor's reply was equally brusque: *Find Morgan and Sanderson. Now. Donna can't be far from them.*

With that done, he headed back to the Audi, felt frustration start to seep into his bones. Morgan had lied to protect his son, gone as far as covering up his links to two murdered women. Now a third victim was connected to Michael Morgan. But still the fact remained: DNA evidence had been found in Sanderson's van linking him directly to the murders.

Connor grabbed the steering wheel, squeezed. Felt the seconds tick by as he sat there, paralysed. Finding Morgan or Sanderson was the key to finding Donna, he was convinced of that. But where to start looking? The light was fading, police were covering Morgan's home in Fife and officers had been put on alert to look for Sanderson in Stirling and around his home in Cambusbarron.

He fired the engine, punched into the satnav the route between North Queensferry and Stirling and began toying with the controls. Found the stretch of road where Robbie had been run off, next to a large public area called Devilla Forest. Connor studied the area, trying to put a timeline into place. Sanderson had gone missing after his interview with the police. Stolen a car, then followed Robbie and Donna on their trip through to Fife to see Michael Morgan, pounced when he saw the empty stretch of road. Possible, but something about that scenario bothered Connor. He was the first to admit that Robbie had his shortcomings as a field operative, but he had worked hard to address those, and spotting a tail was one of the most rudimentary skills Connor had taught him.

So what else? What . . .

He dialled the number he had scrolled to on his phone, pushed aside the pang of guilt he felt. Was just about to hang up when there was an answer, the voice thick and blurred. ''Lo?'

'Robbie, Connor. Sorry to bother you. How you feeling?'

'Ah, boss,' Robbie said, and Connor could almost picture him sitting up straighter as he did so. 'Not so bad. Nurses are treating me well. Thanks for sorting out a private room for me. Just got one hell of a headache. How's it going? Any luck tracking down Ms Blake?'

'Not yet. Actually, that's what I was calling about. Before you were hit, you didn't notice anyone tailing you, did you? Nothing untoward?'

'No, sir, nothing,' Robbie said, defensiveness creeping into his tone. 'And I was watching closely, especially after Sanderson pulled his disappearing act. Car just came out of nowhere and swiped us. Big, black, boxy. Didn't get a proper look, but it was a four-by-four of some kind. After that, it was all a blur.'

'And nothing before that, nothing that rang any alarm bells?'

'No, sir,' Robbie said, weariness slurring his words slightly now. 'Nothing at all. I picked Ms Blake up as you said, headed for Mr Morgan's home in North Queensferry. She wasn't much for talking on the trip, which was fine. Only time she spoke was when Mr Morgan called.'

'Oh?'

'Yeah. I only heard Ms Blake's side of it, obviously. Not long after we were leaving Stirling. She just said we were on the way, should be about forty minutes.'

Connor glanced back at the satnav, a thought tickling across his mind. 'OK, thanks, Robbie. You take it easy.'

'No problem, boss. And listen, if there's anything I can do to help, just let me know. They're keeping me in here overnight for observation, but I'll be out tomorrow morning, and I've got my laptop with me if needed. Least that wasn't banged up in the crash.'

'You just rest, Robbie,' Connor said, then killed the call.

He went back to the satnav, toggled again. Mind full of what Ford had told him about Morgan and his links to Lucy Howard.

Forty-two minutes. That was the estimated time the satnav was reading for a trip between Stirling and North Queensferry via the Kincardine Bridge. And Donna had called Morgan not long after they set off. Routine for her, but was it something more for Morgan? Something like triangulating? Giving him enough time to get into position, wait for them to drive past?

Connor got his phone out, opened up Google. Searched for Devilla Forest. Found what he was looking for less than a minute later. There. A small farm track, just off the main road. Designed for easy access for forestry vehicles. Or for those lying in wait for a car to pass.

He closed his eyes, tried to conjure up the image. Morgan calls Donna, gets a rough time of arrival, which gives him a timeframe of when they would be passing Devilla Forest and be most vulnerable. Plenty of time to get out and into position.

Connor reached into the back seat, grabbed his laptop. Logged into Sentinel's secured database, keyed in Michael Morgan's details. Got back a car registration a few seconds later. A 2017 BMWx5, one of those souped-up saloons with delusions of being a four-by-four that Connor hated so much. Pearlescent black. Just like the car Robbie had described.

Connor felt the hairs on the back of his neck prickle. There was something here, he was sure of it. But if Morgan had grabbed Donna, where would he take her? Anyone smart enough to engineer all this wouldn't be stupid enough to take her back to his home, so where . . .

He flicked onto another search engine, keyed in Michael Morgan's details. Skimmed through the pages the computer spat back at him, eyes darting between the screen and the satnav set into the Audi's dashboard. Stopped a moment later. Scrolled. Zoomed in. Ran the chronology of events in his mind again. There. Yes. Definitely. There.

Connor folded up the laptop, tossed it into the back seat. Leaned over to the glove compartment, opened it and pulled out his gun.

Checked it, chambered a bullet, laid it on the passenger seat. He put the car into gear, paused. He should contact Ford or someone in the police, tell them what he had found, what he suspected. But then he remembered the message he had been sent.

I've got you in my sights, Connor.

If it was Morgan who had sent that message, he had made it personal. And, if Connor was right, he now had a gun. No. Better to keep this to himself, minimise the chance of someone else getting hurt. Alone, he had a chance. If he called the police, they would storm in, all force and flashlights, and Donna might pay the price for that.

'Not going to happen,' Connor whispered into the silence as he drove off, following the satnav to his destination.

CHAPTER 69

Connor left the car in a verge at the side of the road, under the sprawl of a massive tree. Sticking to the shadows, he jogged up the short gravel path leading to the house. It was a farm steading on the outskirts of Culross, a historic village on the Fife coast, less than ten minutes from where Robbie had been run off the road. An imposing mass of exposed limestone and dark slate roofing that seemed to squat in the fading light like some kind of predator. Waiting.

It hadn't taken long to find the place – a few checks on the property register and voters' roll around the area listed it as being owned by Michael Morgan, who was registered as the director of Morgan Holiday Lettings, with the property listed as a holiday let. However, a scan of booking sites showed that the house had been withdrawn from the rental market three months ago 'for renovations'. Connor glanced up at the light that glowed in what he presumed was the living-room window, then checked his watch. Somehow, he doubted painters and decorators would be working this late.

The driveway led to the right of the house, and what looked like an awning. The light was too faint to make it out clearly, but Connor could see something under there, more substantial than a shadow. With another quick glance up at the house, he moved forward, following the verge of the driveway, staying as out of sight as possible. Got to the awning, saw Morgan's BMW tucked under there. Circled the car slowly, keeping a discreet distance. Reached the front passenger side and pulled out his phone, the light from its torch picking out the warped paintwork and scratches where the bumper had been damaged by an impact.

Connor pocketed his phone, hunkered down. So that was it then, proof. Morgan had run Robbie off the road, grabbed Donna and brought her here. Only two questions left to answer: was Donna still alive and did Morgan have the gun that was missing from his father's house?

Only one way to find out.

There was a side door leading to the awning, and Connor considered it for a moment. He had three options. Knock on the front door feigning ignorance, hope the side door wasn't locked and sneak in or find another, more unexpected, point of entry.

Fuck it. Where guns were involved, stealth was always the best option.

He circled the house, studying the walls for motion-activated lights as he moved. It was a two-storey property, with an extension grafted onto the rear. From what he could see in sneaked glances through the window, it was a large kitchen area which led to a dining room/living area. No signs of anyone at home, apart from a half-empty glass of wine that stood on a large oak dining table.

Connor made his way to the side of the house, a narrow pathway that was bordered with a thick hedge on one side. He looked up, saw that the extension was flat-roofed, with lights spilling from what were presumably bedrooms. Made sense, if Connor was right: the bedrooms would have spectacular views back down the valley to Culross and beyond.

He reached out, touched the limestone of the wall. It was cold to the touch, but dry, the stones sticking out at irregular intervals like an invitation. He grabbed one, tested it, then hefted himself up, like a rock climber. Got to the top and popped his head up, making sure no one was watching from the bedroom windows. Hoisted himself up, then dropped to his stomach, lying right beneath the windows. For a moment he remained still, ears straining for any sounds from the house. Nothing. Got into a cautious crouch, frog-walked to the closest window, breathed an internal sigh of relief when he realised it was an old-style sash that was normally locked in the middle of the frame. Easier to work those locks than wrestle with a double-glazed unit.

He tested the window, wasn't overly surprised when it slid up freely. Made sense. Isolation sometimes made people lax about their security. And if Connor was right, a loaded gun gave more sense of safety than a locked window ever did.

He eased the window up slowly, willing it not to squeal as he did so, then ducked inside. Found himself in a small bedroom, empty apart from an unmade single bed and a mattress, which was propped against the wall beside an old, heavily varnished chest of drawers. Closed his eyes for a moment, mapping out the geography of the house from what he had seen through the downstairs windows. He was above the kitchen, the living area to his right. Which meant that the staircase down to it would be out of the door and somewhere to his left.

OK.

He drew his gun, flicked off the safety. And as he did, he felt the years bleed away and he was suddenly back in Belfast, Simon McCartney at his side as they searched a property.

'Easy, Connor,' he heard his old partner whisper. 'Sweep the room, check the blind spots. Don't just rely on your eyes. Don't let the gun do all the work.'

He smiled despite himself, edged forward. Gingerly tested the door, opened it. It led to a wide landing, almost as sparsely decorated as the room he had just climbed into. As he suspected, the stairway was to his left, the banister running the length of the landing, leading to a spiral of stairs that led down to the ground floor. Connor edged forward, keeping his tread as slow and light as possible, wary of loose floorboards that could give away his presence. He moved to his right, checking the two doors off the landing: one led into another bedroom, the other to a bathroom. No one. No signs of life.

He edged back to the staircase, raising his gun. Descending into the unknown was never the preferred option, but he had little choice. Keeping his back to the curving wall, he took the stairs slowly, the ground floor of the house opening out to him as the stairs led into the main living area of the house. Unlike the first floor, this space was fully decorated, all thick carpets, expensive wallpaper and land-scape paintings on the walls of the hallway he now stood in. He moved quickly, checking the door across from the staircase – a bath-room, dark and empty. Moved forward, the front door behind him, approaching a door that his internal map told him led to the main living areas of the property.

He stopped at the door, reached for the handle. Took a deep breath, ears straining almost painfully for any sound of activity from the other side.

Nothing.

He eased the handle down, then swung the door open, retreating behind the frame to keep himself out of the line of any fire. Ducked low and entered the room, gun sweeping in front of him, covering as much space as possible as he took in his surroundings.

It was, as he'd seen from outside, a living area separated from a large kitchen by an imposing breakfast bar that looked as though it was polished granite. The living area was large and spacious, domi-nated by a huge sofa that sat in front of a TV that looked like it could double as a cinema screen. Connor glanced around, approached cau-tiously. Stopped dead when he could see over the back of the sofa, eyes drawn to the object that lay there, papers, a notepad and pens strewn across the sofa as though the bag was some kind of animal whose guts had been split open to spill its contents.

A bag. More specifically, Donna's bag. The same one she'd had with her the day they'd first met Sanderson. The papers were her notes on Sanderson, old press clippings and her own background notes. But now they were annotated with more than Donna's scrawled thoughts.

Now, they were also daubed with blood.

CHAPTER 70

Connor swallowed the searing panic that rushed over him, retreated back to the kitchen area of the room. Stopped. Took a deep breath. Forced himself to concentrate, widen his focus from Donna's bag, let the world back in. Felt something familiar tickle his nostrils and the back of his throat. Hot. Metallic, an olfactory reminder of violence and fear and pain, and the feel of something warm and tacky on his palm as it pumped from an open wound.

Blood.

He moved around the breakfast bar, quickly found the source of the smell. There on the floor, lying in a widening pool of blood, was Michael Morgan.

Connor crossed to him quickly, head swivelling smoothly as he tried to take in all the angles. Dropped to his knees, checked for Morgan's pulse. Fast but strong. From what Connor could see, most of the blood was from an ugly gash along his forehead, but he didn't want to risk moving him to check for other wounds.

Two questions. Who had done this? Where was Donna?

There was a half-open door at the end of the kitchen, and Connor could make out just enough detail to tell it was a utility room that probably led to the side door of the property he had seen.

He raised his gun, forcing himself to go slowly, not let his concern for Donna overwhelm him. Got half a step forward when Colin Sanderson stepped through the door, bottle of wine in his hand.

He came to a juddering halt as he saw Connor, face flashing into an almost comical expression of surprise even as he pawed for the gun that was tucked into the waist of his jeans.

'Don't,' Connor said, aiming his own gun centre mass, finger slipping to the trigger. 'Take it out slowly, Sanderson, put it on the floor. Kick it over to me. Fuck around and I swear I will put a hole in you. Do it. Now.'

Sanderson shook his head, a smile playing on his lips as he drew the gun slowly and laid it on the floor. 'Fraser,' he said, 'you've got a shitty sense of timing, you know. I was just about to start another of Mr Morgan's bottles. Care for a glass?'

'No,' Connor said, forcing himself to ease the pressure in his jaw. 'Put the bottle down as well, then kick the gun over to me.'

The gun skittered across the wooden floor, bounced on a knot and ricocheted off into the corner of the room. Sanderson shrugged his shoulders. 'Oops.'

'On your knees, hands on your head,' Connor said, gesturing with his gun as he started stepping backwards towards Morgan. Sanderson did as he was told, cold, empty eyes glaring at Connor as he knelt.

'Where is she?' Connor asked, the words feeling fat and alien in his mouth, distorted by concern.

A smile played across Sanderson's face, leering and cruel, as something ugly flashed in his eyes. Something predatory.

'Who? That bitch Blake?' he asked. 'Don't worry, she's nearby. You should be thanking me. Looks like Morgan was planning a fine old time with her when I got here.' He jutted his jaw towards the crumpled form of Michael Morgan. 'As you can see, I managed to talk him out of it.'

Fear, cold and electric, surged through Connor. His gaze flicked from Sanderson to the door at the end of the room. 'She through there?' he asked, his voice hollow.

Sanderson's smile widened. 'Aye, all wrapped up and ready to go. Got to say, she's got a nice set of tits. Wondered about that the first time I met her.'

Connor surged forward, slashed the butt of the gun across Sanderson's face, an arc of blood spattering onto the wall. Sanderson gave a high-pitched yelp of pain and crumpled to the floor. Connor reined back the urge to stamp on the man's head, got moving for the door, overcome now by the urge to find Donna.

A groaning sound, low and guttural, froze him in his tracks. Connor's head snapped around and he saw Michael Morgan push himself up onto his elbow, rising from his own blood, like some initiate who had just been blooded in order to enter a cult.

'Stay down, Morgan,' Connor said, 'I'll get to you . . .'

And then everything fell apart.

Morgan squinted at Connor, his gaze roving across the room. Saw Sanderson, then lowered his head and laughed, blood dripping from him, thick and viscous. 'Well, fuck,' he whispered. And then he lunged at Connor.

The unexpected force of the blow threw Connor off balance and he staggered back, arms windmilling as he fought for balance. And then Morgan was on him, teeth bared, snarling and smeared with blood, like a lion that had just raised its head from the carcass of a wildebeest.

'Said I had you in my sights,' he whispered, strong hands clamping onto Connor's gun hand, trying to release his grip. Connor grabbed his shirt, took Morgan with him, let his lack of balance work for him. They crashed to the floor, gun bouncing out of reach as the force of the impact sent Connor's hand into spasm. Morgan drove his head forward, forehead crashing into Connor's cheek. He ignored the pain, pulled Morgan close, aware of the bulk and size of the man, felt a crazed strength quiver in his muscles. Rabbit-punched him in the sides, felt ribs flex as Morgan coughed out blood-spattered breaths. Morgan reared back, like a cowboy trying to break in a steed, then drove his fist forward, aiming for Connor's throat. Connor managed to move aside, the blow only glancing his neck rather than crushing his windpipe as expected, but still it felt as though a bomb had been detonated in his throat. He bucked instinctively, managed to throw Morgan off him. Surged forward and up, slamming a fist into Morgan's chest, driving him backwards.

Got to his knees, dimly aware of movement to his side, ignored it.

Morgan had staggered back, drawing a knife from a block on the breakfast bar. Smiled as he waved it at Connor.

'Was going to use this on that bitch Blake,' he said. 'Still will, but I'll use it on you first.'

'Welcome to try,' Connor said.

Morgan lunged, aiming for the gut. Connor twisted to the side, out of the path of the blade and to Morgan's side. Brought his elbow down onto the back of Morgan's neck, hard, then kept moving, almost like a pirouette, twisting round to grab Morgan by the shirt, using his momentum, adding his weight to the man's trajectory, and hurling him across the room. Dared a glance towards Sanderson, who was scrabbling around in the kitchen.

One problem at a time.

Connor lunged at Morgan, who was trying to drag himself up the wall. He could almost feel Sanderson training the recovered gun on his back as he smashed his fist into Morgan's throat, pulling the punch at the last second so he didn't collapse his larynx and kill him. After all, it was only fair that he returned the favour.

Morgan's eyes went wide, hands scrabbling to his throat as he struggled for breath. Connor kneed him in the jaw as he fell, felt teeth splinter against bone as the man's head whipped back. Spent half a second checking he was subdued, then whirled back towards Sanderson, praying he hadn't had enough time to . . .

The barrel of the gun was very large, a gaping black maw that seemed to swallow everything in the room.

'Nice work with that cunt,' Sanderson said, as he gestured to the collapsed heap of Michael Morgan. 'Now, what was it you said to me? Oh, yeah, on yer fucking knees.'

Connor's mind raced. If he got on his knees, it was over. He needed to play for time. He doubled over, grasped for his ribs, winced at a non-existent pain. 'Gimme a minute,' he said. 'Needed to catch my breath. And while I am, maybe you can tell me why you killed those girls?'

Sanderson laughed, the sound like glass being ground underfoot on concrete.

'Me?' he sneered. 'You not been watching the news, Fraser? I'm innocent. Trial declared false. I'm no fucking killer.'

'So why all this?' Connor asked, casting his arms wide even as he took a step forward, his eyes scanning the room for something, anything, that he could use as a weapon. He spotted one item, a desperate plan forming in his mind. He edged forward.

'This?' Sanderson said, looking around the room as if seeing it for the first time now. 'This is me collecting what's mine. Call it back pay for the last fourteen fucking years.'

Back pay. Two words. Two words that unlocked the puzzle in Connor's mind, let him see what connected Dean Barrett, a faked attack with a meat cleaver and his own grandfather.

'You're not the killer,' he said. 'Morgan is. And – what? His dad framed you for it? So this is revenge? Payback?'

'Very good,' Sanderson said, the gun still trained on Connor. 'Yes, that fucker Morgan fitted me up for what that little bastard did. Sent me down. But, hey, business is business. Until the fucker tried to squirm out of the deal.'

Business. Payback. The deal.

'He paid you to keep quiet, to take the fall,' Connor said, brain racing even as he spoke the words. One more step forward, towards the breakfast bar. Close now. So close. All he had to do was keep Sanderson talking. Distracted. 'You go to prison, his son goes free. And you keep your mouth shut, right?'

'Right,' Sanderson agreed, voice empty. 'Had fuck-all on the outside anyway.'

'So that's why you attacked Morgan, because he refused to pay?'

That smile again, cruel and empty. 'Fuck off. I didn't attack the old man. Why would I? He was seeing things my way, thanks to Donna and all that book bullshit and publicity. Was terrified I'd say something, was going to pay whatever I asked. You want to find out who attacked the pig, ask number one son over there.'

Connor nodded despite himself. That was why Morgan had targeted Donna: she was unwittingly helping Sanderson put the squeeze on his dad to keep their little secret. But if that was the case, why attack his own father, the man who was trying to protect him? No. Later. Right now, he had more pressing concerns.

'Let me guess,' Connor said. 'Morgan sent you Lucy Howard's ID. That's why you came here, for payment?'

Sanderson nodded. 'Smug bastard sent it with a note – "This is your latest victim. You'll be paid handsomely for the service." Cocky fuck. So I called him, arranged to meet him here for payment, was going to take my money and run. Not so easy to extradite folk these days, so I was thinking somewhere sunny. But when I got here I found this fucker had already grabbed Blake and was planning a wee surprise party for me. So we had, ah, a disagreement, and I came away with this as a wee souvenir.'

Sanderson waggled the gun at Connor. 'Now, enough talking, Fraser. Get on your fucking knees.'

Connor started to stoop, slowly, leaning forward, feeling the tension build in his legs as the adrenalin screamed in his veins. Then he exploded forward, sweeping his arm out, catching the knife block, hurling it forward towards Sanderson even as he dived for the floor.

The sound of the gun was an explosion in the silence of the room. Connor hit the floor, rolled, sprang forward, grasping for Sanderson, rugby tackling him to the floor. He landed on top of him, grabbed his wrist. Sanderson screamed as Connor twisted the bone and broke it. 'That's for the fucking cleaver attack,' Connor whispered. Then he pulled back and slammed his fist into Sanderson's face, breaking the nose. Felt something primal call to him, part fury, part fear, as he felt cartilage bite into his knuckles. Drew back to strike again, obliterate Sanderson's features, drive his nose into his brain.

He held his fist above Sanderson's face, his dad's words echoing in his ears.

You've got bad blood, Connor. That Fraser temper. Watch for it.

Swung his fist, felt Sanderson's jaw snap as it connected and the lights went out in the man's eyes. Then stood, weaving, spent, like a boxer after twelve rounds. Scanned the floor, found his gun and retrieved it, snapping on the safety with fingers that were almost steady. Spotted Morgan's gun and retrieved that as well. Then he headed for the door at the end of the room, praying Donna was still alive at the other side of it.

CHAPTER 71

He had found Donna in the utility room, trussed up at the wrists and ankles. Saw an ugly gash on her forehead. Connor wondered if Sanderson or Morgan had done that, fought down the urge to go back into the kitchen and just put a bullet into each of them. Instead, he took his knife from his pocket, cut her bonds then removed the gag from her mouth. Put a hand on the side of her face and leaned in. 'Donna – Donna, it's Connor. You OK?'

A grunt as she stirred, then a sudden bucking explosion of action as her mind reengaged. 'Fuck, Jesus!' she said, her voice almost a scream. 'Mark, I saw . . . Connor?'

He placed a hand on her shoulder, gave it what he hoped was a reassuring squeeze. 'It's all right, we're getting out of here. I've got Sanderson and Morgan. I'll call the police now, OK?'

'OK,' Donna said, voice small and confused now, as though she was trying to shrug off the remnants of a bad dream.

The police and ambulance crews arrived quickly, blue lights stabbing into the dark and strobing across the walls of the house. Connor stowed his gun, then let them in, past the unconscious form of Michael Morgan, whom he had dragged into the hall and put in the recovery position. It was more instinct than concern on Connor's part. He didn't want the man choking on his own blood.

With both men assessed and stabilised, they were removed by the ambulance crews, police accompanying them. Connor dimly wondered if they'd be taken to the same hospital as Robbie, hoped they wouldn't.

'So,' Ross said, the room suddenly feeling very quiet now that the bustle of activity had subsided. 'You want to tell me what the hell happened here, Fraser?'

Connor exchanged a hard look with Ford, who was sticking to the corner of the room, face impassive. Made a decision.

'I was trying to ascertain the location of Ms Blake here.' Connor nodded to Donna, who was sitting on the sofa, a medical blanket wrapped tightly around, exhaustion radiating from her in waves. 'You see, my firm is providing security for her at the moment, so I was obligated.'

Donna's head darted up, face quizzical. But she kept her mouth shut.

'Anyway, I found this place, which is close enough to the location where my man was driven off the road to make it a feasible place to check, especially with some of the information I had discovered about Michael Morgan. So I came here, found Ms Blake was tied up and unconscious. I had an altercation with Morgan and Sanderson, then called you.' A white lie, but messing up the timeline of events a little gave Connor some breathing room.

'An altercation?' Ross said, looking around the room. 'That's a bloody understatement. And what do you mean about information relating to Michael Morgan? What's his part in this?'

Another hard glance at Ford. 'Look, sir,' Connor said, 'as you can imagine, this has been a draining experience. I can give you the overview now, but I think it would be better for Ms Blake and myself if we came into the station in the morning and gave our full statements then.'

Ross held Connor's gaze, considering. Then, with a shrug of the shoulders and a frustrated grunt, he said, 'Fine, but Randolphfield, ten a.m. Both of you.' He turned, pointed at Donna. 'Clear?'

'Totally, sir,' Connor said. 'Donna, give you a ride home?'

The drive back to Stirling was quiet, both Connor and Donna locked into their own thoughts, trying to process what had happened, reconcile the fact that they had both looked death in the face with the fact that they were now bulleting home in a luxury car, as though they had just been to see a movie. It was, Connor thought, the normality after violence that always brought the horror home.

He pulled up in front of Donna's flat, killed the engine.

'You going to be OK?'

'Yeah, fine,' she said. 'Worst of it will be trying to explain this . . .' she gestured to a gash on her head, just above her left eye, which had been cleaned and taped up by the paramedics '. . . to my mother. She hates my job as it is. I'll never hear the end of it.'

Connor let the silence drag out, unsure of what to say. Yes, Donna had put herself at risk tonight. But that was her choice. He admired her for it, wondered if he could do the same if he had a child waiting for him to come home. 'Blame me,' he said at last. 'After all, I'm the security expert. Should have kept you safe, should have seen what was going on a lot sooner than I did.'

'Oh, come on,' Donna said. 'Sanderson and Morgan were playing everyone for fools. Sanderson using me as a way to put the pressure on Morgan as blackmail, Morgan Junior staying in the shadows until he could use Sanderson as an alibi to kill again.' She shook her head. 'Sick fuck. Him and his dad.'

Him and his dad, Connor thought.

'Yeah, well, they'll both have difficult questions to answer,' he said, thoughts turning to Ford. How much of his role in all of this could he keep quiet? And how much should Connor tell Ross in the morning?

Donna shook her head. 'Speaking of questions, you still owe me a quote,' she said, trying for levity in her tone and failing.

'Yeah, yeah,' Connor said. 'I was ready to kill Morgan tonight, Donna. That's not something I really want to be quoted on.'

'Fucker deserved it,' she said. Then, before Connor could stop her, she leaned over and planted a kiss on his cheek. Warm and soft. 'Night, Connor. And thank you. I'll see you in the morning.'

Connor sat for a moment, watching her walk up the path to her flats, the warmth of her kiss still lingering on his cheek. Then, satisfied she was safely inside, he started the engine and drove off, mind racing. Told himself to go home, call Jen, then relax, try to rest, forget about tonight.

He was still telling himself that as he scrolled through his contacts and hit dial.

'We need to talk. Tonight. Now. Meet me at the yard. I'll be there in twenty minutes.'

CHAPTER 72

The main office was the only building lit when Connor drove into the yard, the outer atriums and extensions giving it a strange art-deco glow. Connor scanned the car park for Paulie's car, saw nothing but the Rolls he knew MacKenzie drove. Not that that meant anything: he doubted Duncan would want Paulie far away with this meeting at hand.

He walked into the reception area, then down a hallway to a door marked with MacKenzie's name. Opened it without knocking, found MacKenzie at his desk, feet up, a large tumbler of something amber in his hand.

'Evening, Connor,' he said, eyes in shadow. 'Why don't you come in, get a drink? I understand you've had a hell of a night.'

Connor pushed aside the question that bubbled into his thoughts. Only natural a man like MacKenzie would have eyes and ears in the police. Eyes and ears that would have been watching the Sanderson case very, very closely.

'I'll pass, thanks,' Connor said. 'I won't be here long. I just have a couple of things to straighten out with you, that's all.'

'Straighten out, eh?' Duncan said, humour in his voice, as though he was the class bully who had just been challenged by the nine-stone weakling. 'Look, Connor, I know you're dating my daughter, which gives you some latitude with me. But if anyone's going to be doing any straightening here, it's me.'

Connor felt anger curdle in his guts, warming like a kettle just put on to boil. His knuckles, already bruised from the evening's encounters, began to throb and itch. 'Fine, let's get to it,' he said. 'Just one little thing. I'm seeing the police tomorrow morning, giving my statement to them about what happened tonight. I spoke to Ford, who told me about the help you gave him and his boss in the 2006 murder inquiries. You know, the help that put them on to Sanderson in the first place.'

MacKenzie dropped his feet from the desk. Leaned forward. 'Now just a minute, I—'

Connor raised a hand. 'I'll keep Ford's name out of it as much as I can. From what I can see, Morgan was playing him along and he made a stupid mistake any young copper could have made. But I have just one question for you, Duncan. And it's a very simple one.'

'Go on,' MacKenzie said, caution in his voice now.

'Did you help frame an innocent man so you had a policeman in your pocket for fourteen years, or was Morgan's help just a happy byproduct of setting Sanderson up in the first place?'

MacKenzie's hands, large, blunt things, curled tighter around his glass. 'What the fuck are you talking about?' he whispered, voice as cold as the ice in his whisky.

'Oh, come on,' Connor said. 'It's late, and I've had my fill of bullshit for the evening. Ford told me Sanderson was known to be working with Barrett, doing drug deals in and around the university. Must have taken a bite out of your business. So when you arranged for Barrett to have his little Paulie-assisted chat with Morgan, how much coaching did you do with him beforehand? Must have been awfully convenient, having a rival picked up for murder and taken off the board. And who's going to ask too many questions? After all, Barrett was the only witness to the alleged argument between Sanderson and Jessica. No one was going to believe a word he said, and Jessica was hardly in a position to give a statement.'

'Coincidence,' MacKenzie said, sipping his whisky. 'Nothing less. Yes, Sanderson was a thorn in my side, but a small one, hardly worth my time.'

'I've got a friend who hates coincidences as much as I do,' Connor said. 'And then there's another thing that's been bothering me. The DNA evidence they found in Sanderson's van. See, I couldn't get that. If Sanderson wasn't the killer, how did the DNA get there? Couldn't work it out until I paid a visit to Morgan's home. Saw a lot of dust sheets there, which got me thinking about the ones they found Jessica and Rhona's blood on. And since Barrett was working for you and Sanderson, I'm wondering how much persuading he took to plant those sheets in Sanderson's van for you?'

MacKenzie became very still, studying his glass closely. 'Be careful, Connor,' he said. 'You're on thin ice here. Very fucking thin. Jen will only protect you so far.'

'Fuck that,' Connor said. 'This has nothing to do with her. I can't prove any of it, but I'm right, aren't I? What happened? Morgan found the dust sheets his boy had used, came to you and asked for help, which you gladly provided, all for the cost of him being your eyes and ears in the police. And in return you gift-wrapped Barrett, using Ford as a witness, and let a murderer walk free for more than a decade.'

MacKenzie opened his mouth to say something, closed it again. Looked up at Connor with a hatred so raw he could almost feel it heating his skin.

'I'll take that as confirmation,' Connor said. 'I can't do anything about this, Duncan, but trust me, I'll be watching you very closely from now on.'

MacKenzie drained his glass, grimaced. When he spoke, his voice was little more than a whisper. The hard man gone, the human being beneath peeking through. 'What about Jen?'

Connor stopped, suddenly unsure. What about Jen? She was no part of this, an innocent bystander. A bystander who could become collateral damage at any minute. 'I care for Jen, so I'll keep all this away from her,' Connor said at last, feeling his way through the words. 'But if I get the chance to come for you, Duncan, I will. You manipulated a friend of mine, knew a murderer was running free and could strike again at any time. You don't get a pass for that. No one does.'

MacKenzie nodded. 'You just treat her right.'

'One thing you never have to worry about,' Connor said.

MacKenzie stood at the window, watching as Connor's tail lights dwindled into the night. Turned slightly when he heard the door open, Paulie lumbering into the room. He let his belly precede him, making a statement more eloquent than words.

'Well?' he asked, fishing in his pocket for a cigar stub and clamping it between his teeth.

'About as we expected,' Duncan replied, topping up his own glass and pouring one for Paulie, who took it with a nod of acknowledgement.

'How much does he know?' Paulie asked.

'Enough. Not all of it, but enough.'

'I'd hoped Morgan's kid would get to him, boss,' Paulie said, tone like a disappointed child on Christmas morning. 'Thought I'd told him enough to put him off his guard, make him think Morgan wasn't a threat.'

'Ah, but young Connor is smarter than that, isn't he? Must be what Jen sees in him.'

Paulie shifted his stance. 'And what about Jen? What do we do there?'

MacKenzie looked at Paulie for a long moment. Knew that if he gave the word, the man in front of him would go after Connor Fraser that very moment, and not stop until one of them was dead. But not tonight. Not yet.

'We wait,' MacKenzie said. 'Fraser wants to come for me, fine. He has a piece of the picture now, that's all. Let him keep Jen happy. If that changes or he starts asking the wrong questions, we'll revisit it. But for now, we leave him be. OK?'

'Aye,' Paulie said, draining his glass in a mouthful. 'For now.'

CHAPTER 73

Morning came to Stirling, grey and listless, a lot like Connor was feeling. He rose early, ran through some stretches to rouse himself, took in as much coffee as his body could handle without the shakes kicking in. Showered and inspected himself in the mirror, the bruise where Morgan had head-butted him blossoming like a perverse flower on his cheek. He'd have to do something about that. He sent Jen a quick message apologising for his absence and asking her to meet later that day. The response was quick, warm and just a little flirtatious – enough to tell him that MacKenzie was keeping his word and not mentioning anything to her.

Yet.

Connor felt thoughts crowd in on him then, tried to calm them. He'd sleepwalked into this relationship, the nights Jen staying becoming more frequent and relaxed as they slipped into a familiar routine. Then she had helped him with his gran's files, which had fostered a great intimacy between them. But was that what he really wanted? Especially now, with all he knew about Jen's father.

He grunted a humourless laugh. Families. He was hardly one to talk.

He made a mental note to call in on his gran when he was done at the police station, then got changed and left, sending Ford the location of the café he wanted to meet at. Their conversation was brief and perfunctory, Connor explaining that he had no intention of telling

Ross anything of what he had learned about Dean Barrett, Paulie, Duncan or Ford's involvement.

'Doesn't matter anyway,' Ford had said, the rings under his eyes as dark as his coffee. The man had obviously been up most of the night. 'The doctors doubt DCI Morgan will ever regain consciousness now, and as for me, well . . .' He shrugged, let the sentence trail off.

Connor said his goodbyes, headed for Randolphfield. Gave his statement to an impassive Ross, keeping it factual and, as promised, devoid of any mention of Ford. He felt no real guilt in that omission, wondered what sort of man it made him that he didn't.

An hour later, he was free to go and he left, pausing on the steps of the station to ping Donna a message.

Inside now, just waiting for Ross, she replied. *Need to get out of here as soon as, publisher wants to talk to me about the book. Could be big. And you still owe me a quote. X*

Connor smiled at that, the memory of her kiss on his cheek glowing in his mind, like an ember. *Will give you one over a drink. We've earned it,* he typed. Stopped for a moment. Considered. Then hit send. Fuck it. Too late now.

He pocketed the phone, headed for the car. Time to see the other woman in his life.

CHAPTER 74

Ida began busying herself the moment Connor arrived, the flat becoming a maelstrom of cups, cutlery, cakes and sandwiches. Connor tried to help but she waved him aside as she shuffled around the kitchen area. 'You'll just get in my way, son,' she said, as she made a pot of tea. 'Have you seen the size of yourself lately? Barely leaving enough room for me in here as it is. Just you sit yourself down, tell me what you've been up to, though by the look of that cheek of yours, it's not been anything healthy.'

Connor smiled, took a seat at the kitchen table. He remembered it from the house his gran had lived in: it was a large drop-leaf item, rich oak polished to a high shine. The place mats that were dotted across it were the same as Connor remembered too, vinyl rectangles with depictions of wildlife scenes on them. Seeing them here, in this sheltered flat, gave Connor a strangely paradoxical sense of the familiar and the alien.

'So, come on, then,' Ida said. 'Don't keep an old woman waiting. What's been happening?'

He told her as she worked, keeping as much of the detail out of it as possible. He had been working on a big case, but that was mostly over now. There were a few things still to iron out, but the majority of the work was done. He omitted any mention of staring down the barrel of a gun or fighting for his life, though after what his dad had told him, he wondered how alien such topics would really be to his gran.

She finally stopped fussing around the kitchen, took her seat across the table from him. She seemed more herself today, no confused pauses, no slight defocusing of the eyes as she drifted for a moment or a name suddenly escaped her. But, still, there was something, some nervous energy that she was exuding, like she was singing a familiar song in the wrong key.

'And what about this young lady you've been seeing, Jennifer? What about her?'

Connor took a deep breath. Good question. 'Not a lot to say,' he answered, as his gran poured him a cup of tea. 'With everything that's been going on at work, I've not had much time to see Jen, really.'

'Aye, but you had time to see your dad, didn't you, son?'

The bluntness of the statement stopped Connor dead. He stared up at his gran, who returned his gaze. No anger, no anguish, just those eyes, eyes he now recognised as his father's, staring back at him. Waiting.

'Gran, I, eh, I'm sorry about all that. Yes, I saw Dad. And I'm . . . sorry I stirred everything up. I had no idea that . . .'

'That was sort of the point, bonny lad,' Ida replied, turning her cup on her saucer softly. And for the second time in as many moments, Connor didn't know what to say. Bonny lad. She hadn't called him that for years, not since he had been a boy. To hear it now, after all this time, was like an echo from the past.

'What did your dad tell you?' Ida asked. And in that moment, Connor knew that her whole performance in the kitchen had been a delaying tactic, her way of buying time and building up the courage to ask that one simple question.

'Just that his dad wasn't a nice guy,' Connor said, his tongue feeling thick and alien. He had faced killers and madmen, had guns pointed in his face and knives plunged into his body, but nothing was as intimidating as the cool, even gaze his grandmother was giving him now. 'He said things came to a head after he brought his report card home, that he stopped Campbell hurting you. That he left after that. I, ah, I did a little checking. I know he ended up in Dundee.'

Ida blinked once, a small smile stretching her lips. 'Aye,' she said. 'Your dad was a lion that night, Connor. He saved my life, I'm sure of that. Your grandfather was an unhappy man, you know. He hated

271

the way his life had turned out, so he turned that hatred on those he thought had helped build a cage around him. He was vicious and cruel and spiteful, and I hated him for what he did to your dad.'

'What he did?' Connor asked, mind reeling. 'What?'

Ida sighed, adjusted her glasses. Picked up a pen that was lying beside her cup and held it between her index and middle fingers, like the cigarettes she had given up when Connor was a child.

'He changed him, Connor,' she said at last. 'Your dad was a sensitive, caring young man. But what his father did changed him, calloused some part of him that only wanted to express itself. After that night, he was never the same. He became even quieter than he had been when his father was around, introverted, made an effort to stay away from all the things that had brought him joy before that. So he stopped painting and writing, started to study the sciences and practical subjects. He became obsessed with medicine, and the thought of helping people. Oh, don't get me wrong, it gave him a good life. But I'd love to kill his bastard of a father for what he did.'

Connor started, as though he had been electrocuted. In all his years, he had never heard his gran swear, or speak in a tone that was so flat and devoid of emotion. A tone, he realised, much like his own.

'Dad said Campbell got in touch once,' Connor said. 'Did he ever try again?'

Ida gave Connor a smile that told him she had been expecting this question, reached into the pocket of her cardigan. 'This is what I was looking for when I fell like an eejit,' she said, sliding a tattered old envelope over to him. 'It's a letter Campbell sent to me about eight years after he left us.'

Connor took it, confusion galloping through his thoughts. 'Go on,' Ida said. 'Read it. You've come this far.'

Connor unfolded it, the paper feeling too fragile and delicate in his hands. Read.

My dearest Ida,

I wanted to write to you and clarify a few things. I am so, so sorry for what I did all those years ago, for the pain I

*inflicted on you and Jack. I have no excuse, other than
I want the best for the boy, want the best for both of you,
and when I feel things are going awry, I lose my temper.
The life of an artist is no living for a boy, and I hope
Jack will see that.*

*I am living comfortably in Dundee. My address is at the
top of the letter and, when you have come to see that I
only ever had your best interests at heart, I would hope
to see you both. Perhaps you can come and visit me, or
perhaps I will come home and see you. I don't have a lot
of money, but I will send what I can when I can.*

With all my love and forgiveness,

Campbell

The letter was signed and dated at the bottom, the signature an ostentatious scrawl.

Connor folded it, laid it on the table between him and his gran.

'See what I mean? Spiteful and cruel, blaming your dad for what happened that night. That's why I didn't want you looking into this, Connor. No good comes of it.' She reached out, took the letter and put it back into the envelope. 'He never wrote again, never made good on his wee threat to visit us. I suppose I should have got rid of this, but I wanted his address, wanted to know where he was. Does that make sense?'

Connor nodded, thoughts crashing through his mind. Why had his dad told him Ida had burned that letter? 'Look, Gran, I'm sorry,' he said. 'I'm sorry I started all this, sorry I ...'

She held up a hand, shushing him. 'Leave it be, bonny lad. You're a curious soul, always have been. Your mother was the same, always wanted to know the answer to everything. Your dad can be like that as well. But now you know. Your grandfather was a nasty, petty little man, best forgotten, OK?'

'OK,' Connor said, relief flooding through him as his gran smiled and the woman he knew emerged on her face.

'Good,' Ida said. 'Now have a sandwich, son. Big man like you needs to keep his strength up, especially when you've got a young lady to introduce me to.'

Connor piled sandwiches onto his plate. He had no real appetite, but the last thing he was going to do was insult his gran by not eating the food she had prepared. Especially after what she had just told him. He took a bite of a cheese and pickle sandwich, the taste bringing back childhood memories of afternoons spent with her. And, again, there was anger. His gran had looked after him, effectively been a surrogate parent, and someone had laid hands on her. The injustice gnawed at him, soured his memories. All those years, and how much pain had his gran hidden from him behind a smile, a hug or a kind word?

He was just reaching for his cup when his phone beeped in his pocket. He gave his gran an apologetic look, then pulled the phone out. Felt a pang of confused worry when he read Robbie's name on the caller ID.

'Robbie, you OK?' he asked, turning away from his gran and curling himself around the phone.

'Aye, boss, I'm fine,' Robbie said, sounding clearer, more focused than he had the previous day. 'Just getting ready to head home, but there's a bit of a stooshie here at the hospital, and I thought you should know.'

'Oh,' Connor said, even as the thought whispered in his mind. It was inevitable. He knew what Robbie was going to say next, was already plotting his next move.

'Yes, boss. Seems you didn't hit Morgan hard enough last night. Just heard from one of the cops here. They uncuffed him when he was going to the toilet, so he took the moment to batter his police guard and the nurse. He's escaped.'

CHAPTER 75

After meeting Fraser at the café, Ford had started walking. He had no real idea where he was going, but was seized by the need to move, try to process what he now knew.

Following the incident at the steading, a full search was ordered on Morgan's home in North Queensferry. It was a small, neat bungalow in a cul-de-sac not far from the railway station, its elevated position giving a commanding view out over the Forth and to the bridges that spanned it. As the most senior officer in the area, Ford had co-ordinated the search of the house.

He wished to God he hadn't.

On the surface, it was just another home. Unremarkable furniture, a clean, functional kitchen with cupboards that were half empty, a living room dominated by crowded bookshelves and a television that looked as if it had last been used in the late nineties. What first struck Ford was the lack of personality in the place: everything was functional, but there was nothing other than the books to give any feel for the character of the person who lived there. There was only one picture in the living room, a small portrait of Dennis Morgan's wife, Carolyn. Ford had never met her, but he knew she had died in 2002. The police family had closed ranks around Morgan at the time, but Ford had heard the whispers – depression, therapy, suicide. Had that been what had driven Morgan to kill? The sudden loss of his mother? Or was there a simpler answer? That he was simply born rotten, and struck when he saw the opportunity?

The answers were waiting for Ford in a room at the back of the property. It was a small room that had been converted into an office. As with the rest of the house, it was neat, ordered, dominated by a large table wedged up against the far wall and bookshelves that covered every other available space. Most of the books were what Ford would have expected – political history and reference books. But there was one bookshelf next to the desk that was dominated by psychology texts – books about depression, self-harm and the treatment of sudden trauma. Interspersed with these were books on criminology, anatomy and one book that stabbed a shard of ice into Ford's guts. *Inside The Mind of a Serial Killer – What Drives The Monster To Kill?*

Ford snapped on a pair of latex gloves, closed the door on the other officers who were combing through the property. Took the book off the shelf, leafed through it, Dennis Morgan's words from all those years ago echoing through his mind: *Two is only one short of three.*

The book was made up of profiles of various killers, Hindley and Brady, the Wests, Dahmer, profiling each killer and giving theories on what had turned them into murderers. The book was heavily annotated and highlighted, Post-it notes marking certain sections and pictures, mostly generic shots of where the murders had taken place.

Ford sat heavily in the chair, spun it slowly to face the desk. Knew he was breaking protocol, found he didn't care. Michael Morgan was a killer, and his father had manipulated Ford into helping protect him. Ford needed answers, didn't care how he got them.

He pushed back from the desk, considered it. Tried the top drawer on the left-hand side of the desk: locked. Stared at it for a second. Here was another line. Was he prepared to cross it?

Made a decision, reached into his pocket and pulled out his Swiss Army knife. Selected a blade, wedged it into the drawer and levered it down. As expected, the drawer sprang open easily, standard desk locks being there more for decoration than serious security.

In it was a plain A5 notebook, leather-bound, held closed with an elasticated strap. Pages bulged from it as though it was an over-filled sandwich. Ford lifted it from the drawer, laid it on the desk. Took a breath, removed the strap, flipped it open.

It was some kind of diary, written in the same small, neat handwriting that filled the textbook Ford had just found. On some pages there were angry drawings in red biro, childish scrawls of animals with blood gushing from wounds, doodles of knives and other weapons. He flipped through it slowly, not wanting to touch it too much, knowing he was making a mistake, but unable to stop. Found a page and started reading.

I don't know why I'm this way. It's just always been there, a blank spot. I look at Mum and Dad and I try to be what they want me to be. I try to be the good son, try to live up to the name Dad gave me (even though I hate it). But there's something missing. Something that I only understood was missing when I found that cat when I was coming home from school. It was weaving around the road, dragging itself. It hurt to look at it, the shape was just . . . wrong. I think it had been hit by a car or something — the back end was all twisted, blood dribbling from its mouth. I followed it for a while, it wasn't moving fast. When I reached for it, I swear I was only going to pick it up to try and help. But it clawed at me, and before I knew it, my hand was around its throat. Squeezing. Its eyes were bulging and it was thrashing as hard as it could, making a sound I'd never heard before. And that's when I knew. When I looked into its dying eyes and felt it thrash for its life, I knew this is what I'd been missing.

I snapped its neck and dumped the body in a bush. Had to play it cool with Mum and Dad — they wouldn't have understood why I was smiling.

There were further entries detailing Morgan's hunt for other prey. Cats were his favourite as they 'roamed free and their owners waited longer to raise the alarm'. Ford flipped through, his disgust rising. But then, in the centre of the notebook, spread over two pages, was another entry. At the top of the page, there was what looked like a passport picture of Carolyn Morgan, carefully taped in place. But, unlike the rest of the entries, the writing here was large, jagged, untidy.

Angry.

She died today. Selfish bitch. Came home from school and found her at the kitchen table in a puddle of pills. Stupid cow had used the butcher's knife to open her wrists. What the fuck am I going to cut my chicken with now? There was so much blood. I knew she was having problems, could see the same emptiness I feel in her eyes. But she always tried to hide it. Guess she got tired, like I do. But there was so much blood, and her eyes were empty, glassy, staring across the table as if she was trying to check it was level. Dad lost it when he got back, grabbed me, pushed me out of the house. Called his pals. I told him it was OK, I was fine. What I didn't tell him was I wished I'd been there to see her do it. But I know one thing now. I will be there to see someone die, one day. I want to know.

Ford shuddered, flicked through the pages. Found more entries, the same cold, analytical prose. Had Morgan known what his son was, the malignancy that was growing under his nose? He found his answer in the last entry of the diary.

So today's the day, my coming-out party. I tried to be careful, but Dad found out quickly enough. He recognised the girls from that reception we went to at Parliament. Suppose it was stupid of me to track them, but they were so alive when I saw them in Edinburgh, glowing with that pride and happiness that I just don't get. I wanted to understand it. Wanted to take it away from them, cut it out of them. So imagine my delight when I found them at the uni in Stirling. I was *only there for a lecture for the day, looking at maybe transferring closer to home. And there they both were, in the student union. It was Fate.*

Dad asked me if I remembered the girls, so I told him. I guess I was just tired of lying, of hiding myself. I almost felt sorry for him. After all, I'd just kicked the stilts out from under his world, shown him what I'd done with the name he'd entrusted me with. I've wondered about that. Michael Dennis Morgan. Giving me his name, was it an act of love, or a branding of property? He cried, said it would be OK. That he would sort it. Give me an alibi. And then the threat. That if I ever did it again, he would kill me himself. I think I might take him up on that offer. One day.

Ford closed the diary, centred it on the table as he tried to collect his thoughts. Any psychologist would make quick work of it – Michael Morgan was a psychopath. Unable to feel like other people, he had tried to understand himself. On the outside, he had been the perfect son, the high-achieving academic. But on the inside he had been diseased, rotten, twisted. A killer in the making, the pressure growing until it had to be released. He had fixated on Jessica and Rhona, struck when he saw them again.

And Dennis Morgan had covered it up, using Ford to help him do it.

Ford had left the house, driven home. Head spinning. There was enough in that diary to convict Michael Morgan a hundred times over. But what did that mean for his dad? And what did that mean for Ford himself?

He had spent a fitful night wrestling with this thought. Met with Fraser, then stumbled out of the café in a sleep-deprived haze. Was still thinking about it when his phone went, Connor Fraser calling.

'Fraser, look, I—' he began.

'You heard yet?' Fraser asked, a hardness in his voice stopping Ford dead in his tracks.

'No, what?'

'Michael Morgan just escaped the police guard at the hospital in Fife. Donna will be safe with Ross, but I wanted to check in on you, just in case.'

Ford took a breath, mind flashing back to the night before and the last lines in the diary he had found.

If I ever did it again, he would kill me himself. I think I might take him up on that offer. One day.

'He won't come for me,' Ford said. 'I know where he'll go.'

'Tell me,' Fraser said, impatience in his voice. And in that moment, Ford knew two things. He knew Connor Fraser was going to stop Michael Morgan, no matter what the police did.

And he knew he was going to help him.

CHAPTER 76

'You sure about this?' Connor asked, as he drove out of Stirling, heading for Larbert and the Forth Valley Hospital.

Ford nodded, not taking his eyes from the road, as though he was willing the car to go faster. 'Yeah,' he said, thinking back to his last conversation with Michael Morgan. What was it he had said about his dad? *Maybe it's best Dad doesn't wake up at all.* The diary had told Ford that Michael Morgan felt some sort of perverted debt to his father. And if this was the end of the line, Michael Morgan would make sure he paid that debt in full.

Connor said nothing, opening the car up as they left Stirling behind and hit the backroads. From what Ford had been able to ascertain, Michael Morgan had feigned a need for the bathroom and overpowered a police officer who would now, no doubt, be facing some awkward questions. Shortly after this, a taxi driver stumbled into the hospital, clutching a wound to his head and shouting, 'Some bastard just nicked my taxi.'

A description of the taxi had been circulated, and Connor found himself checking vehicles on the road as he drove. Ford seemed convinced that Michael Morgan would make his way to Larbert and his father and, after his confrontation with him in Culross, Connor knew the man was capable of killing again. He had seen it in his eyes when he had dragged himself from the floor, blood spouting from the head wound Sanderson had inflicted. No hesitation, no doubt. Just focus on the task in hand.

'OK,' Connor said. 'You've got officers covering anywhere he might go, and the description of Morgan and the taxi he stole has been distributed. But how do you look for one man in a hospital dealing with hundreds of people? You can't lock the place down, and his dad is in the critical care unit, which is behind a security door. So how is he planning to get to him? And, if he is heading to the hospital, how do we find him?'

Ford stared out at the road, muscles in his jaw twitching and flexing, as though he was chewing on Connor's words, and finding their taste unpalatable.

'I don't know,' he admitted at last. 'But I'm sure this is where he's heading, Fraser. You didn't see that diary of his. The man needs help. He said Dennis threatened to kill him if he ever struck again, but he also said his dad helped him, kept him out of trouble. So I've got to ask, how many other crimes did Dennis help him cover up, how many other blind eyes did he turn? If his dad wakes up, there's a good chance he'll be brain-damaged. Dennis Morgan would hate that. So Michael will think he's doing his dad a favour by ending his suffering. And . . .' he shuddered, ran a hand over his face '. . . and it'll give him the chance to see what he missed with his mum.'

They made the rest of the journey in silence, the weight of what Ford had said making further conversation impossible. But as he drove, Connor was unable to dismiss thoughts of his own father, Jack. Smashing a bottle over Campbell Fraser's head, staring down at the man who had made his life a living hell, prepared to die to protect his mother. The thought filled Connor with a mournful rage that fuelled his need to find Michael Morgan. His dad had often counselled him to watch for his temper, but today Connor wanted nothing more than to release it.

They got to the hospital, made their way to the security office, which was adjacent to the A and E department. A uniformed officer was waiting for them there, poring over the CCTV feeds that flashed up on a series of screens dotted along the wall of the room. At the control panel, a harassed-looking security guard tried to keep up with the police officer's requests, images dancing off the lenses of glasses that had probably been fashionable sometime in the late eighties.

'Anything?' Ford asked, ignoring the officer's quizzical glance at Connor.

'Eh, no, sir, nothing,' the officer said. 'No sign of the vehicle that's been described, no one fitting Morgan's description either. As for DCI Morgan, as you know he's in the critical care unit, and we've got an officer stationed there now per your instructions.'

'I thought I said to get him moved?' Ford asked.

The uniformed officer shrugged, concern turning his features pale. 'Sorry, sir, we were advised not to do so by the medical team. He's still in a very serious condition, and they've not got enough available beds to move him to.'

'Shit,' Ford muttered, rubbing at his forehead. Had he been wrong, was it possible that . . .?

A sudden squawk from a radio on the uniform's shoulder startled Ford from his thoughts.

'Back-up to critical care, back-up to critical care!' a breathless voice cried from the radio, the static on the line accentuating the panic. 'We have a hostage situation. Repeat, we have a hostage situation!'

Ford turned and headed for the door, Connor stopping him with a raise of his hand. 'Wait,' he said, turning to the security guard, who was now as pale as the reflections in his glasses. 'Show me the entrance to critical care. Let's see what we've got.'

The guard flicked a few switches and an image of a corridor appeared on the main screen in front of him. A typical long, narrow hospital corridor, unremarkable except for the trail of smears on the floor leading to the entrance to critical care. Connor cursed internally. Of course, he had given Morgan the perfect disguise when he had hit him. After all, what was a more natural sight in a hospital than someone hurt and looking for help? What had happened? Morgan had somehow managed to slip into the hospital, got his broken nose bleeding again, then wandered the hallways, head down. Made his way to the critical care unit, asking for help. Whoever had answered the intercom to the unit had either buzzed him in to offer assistance or come out to get him. Either way . . .

'Show me inside,' Connor said. 'Dennis Morgan's room.'

'We don't have cameras in the rooms,' the security guard said weakly. 'Only the main areas.'

'Then show me the internal corridor,' Connor snapped.

A few more button flicks and the image changed, looking onto another corridor, shorter this time, with doors dotted along it. One door was flung open, a knot of people standing in front of it, hands across their faces. What were they seeing in there?

Ford gestured for the uniform to give him his radio. 'This is DCI Ford,' he said. 'What have we got in there, son?'

'Sir,' the voice came back, a breathless whisper, as though the officer was talking in a church and not a hospital. 'I'm sorry, sir, he suckered me. Punched me from behind. By the time I'd collected myself, he'd got into the room. He has a—'

'Malcolm?' a voice cut across the officer's, echoing and distant. 'Malcolm, is that you? Why don't you come and join the party? It's all happening here.'

'Tell him I'm on my way,' Ford hissed into the radio, then cut the line.

'Call back-up now,' Connor said. 'Make sure that security door is open for me.'

'Me?' Ford said. 'What do you mean "me"? He asked for—'

'Sir,' Connor said, his voice gentle now, calm. 'All due respect, I'm going to get there a lot faster than you are. He thinks you're on the way, that buys us a little time. But we need to lock this place down, just in case he gets past me. He can't get away again.'

A hard moment of silence. Then Ford nodded. 'Make sure he doesn't get past you,' he said.

***

Connor sprinted towards the critical care unit, his mind running scenarios as he moved. Standard response to an escaped murder suspect, who was presumably armed, in a public space would be to send an armed response unit, probably from Stirling itself. Not that Connor planned to give them a chance to get a shot off.

He got to the door of Morgan's room, still hanging open. Took a deep, calming breath, swallowed the harsh, metallic tang of adrenalin at the back of his throat. Then stepped into the room.

'Connor!' Michael Morgan said, eyes glittering. He was standing beside his dad's bed, a car wrench hanging from his right hand. No doubt a souvenir from the taxi he had stolen to get there. He was wearing a shapeless grey hoodie, the front of which was spattered with the blood that ran freely from his nose.

Connor turned to the uniformed officer who was standing in the room, baton drawn and extended, looking unsure. 'Connor Fraser. I'm here with DCI Ford,' he said.

'Very glad you could make it, Connor,' Morgan said, a dead smile on his lips. 'After all, we've got business to finish, you and I, haven't we?' He gestured to his nose, the smile widening as he did so.

'Fine,' Connor said. 'Let's finish it then. Just step away from your dad and we can—'

The laughter was harsh and cruel, ricocheting off the whitewashed walls of the room. 'Oh, come on, Connor, really? He's the whole reason I'm here. Can't let him suffer like this. And imagine if he did wake up, how disappointed he'd be in me now that I've let our little secret out of the bag.'

Our little secret. An image of his own father darted across Connor's mind, glass bottle aloft, face a sneer of hate. 'So you'd kill your own father?' he asked, eyes locking on the wrench as he judged distances and felt his heart hammer in his chest.

'Not killing,' Morgan said, voice gentle and patient, as though he was lecturing a class. 'Putting him out of his misery. He'll have no life if he does wake up. And he offered to do the same for me. So what type of a son would I be if I let him suffer? The shame? The humiliation? No, better if I end it now.'

Something dimmed and then died in Morgan's eyes, and Connor felt as though he was seeing the man he truly was for the first time. He smiled again, the jagged remains of the teeth Connor had broken glistening and predatory against the smear of blood caked around his top lip, then turned, raising the wrench.

Connor lunged to his left, grabbed the baton from the police officer and twisted it out of his grasp, then spun and surged forward, bringing it up in a slashing arc, hoping to connect with Morgan. Heard a grunt as Morgan stumbled backwards, away from the blow, crashing into a small cupboard unit beside the bed.

'Ah, Connor,' he said as he regained his balance. 'You just don't know when to give up, do you? I should have fucking shot you when I had the chance. I did too. Was watching you and Donna when you visited Sanderson. Was nice of Dad to leave a gun for me, don't you think?'

Connor said nothing, edged his way sideways so he was between the hospital bed and Morgan. Flipped his grip on the baton so it ran up his forearm, like a guard, crouched low, ready. Outside, the sound of sirens grew louder, like a warning of what was about to happen.

As if taking this as his cue, Morgan lunged forward, bringing the wrench up like a club. Connor ducked low, bringing the baton up to parry the blow. Grunted as the force of wrench hitting baton juddered up his arm, numbing it. Kept moving forward, pivoting and crashing a punch into Morgan's side, sending him staggering back, coughing wetly. Even as he fell, Connor followed him, not wanting to give him space to swing the wrench again.

They crashed into the wall, frantically scrabbling, Morgan's sour breath on Connor's face. He tried to push back, get some purchase, but Connor used his weight, pinned him to the wall. Ignored the blows he felt dig into his side as Morgan flailed against him, focused on getting his free arm around the wrench and . . .

An explosion of pain in Connor's arm, white-hot agony lancing through his muscle. He looked down, saw Morgan had sunk his teeth into his arm above where he was holding the baton. Morgan's hand had slapped onto Connor's face, fingers scrabbling up towards his eyes. Connor whipped his head from side to side, but it was no use, Morgan's grip was crazed, vice-like. Morgan drove his fingers forward, the world dimming for Connor as his vision faded and the pressure grew.

The pain galvanised Connor. He took a half-step back, swung the baton blindly, the sound of Morgan's wrist snapping drowned by the clatter of the wrench on the floor. Swapped hands and drove the baton into Morgan's stomach, air and blood exploding from the man's mouth as he doubled over. Connor dropped the baton, caught Morgan's jaw with a vicious upper cut that reignited the agony in his wounded arm as it connected. Morgan grunted, started sliding down the wall. Connor caught him, pinned him back against the wall, drew back his fist . . .

Not killing, putting him out of his misery.

Targeted the nose, ready to drive it back into Morgan's brain, end it. He should have done this back at the house. Saved everyone this. But no time like the present to correct a mistake.

'Enough!' The police officer from whom Connor had snatched the baton had regained his composure, was aiming a can of pepper spray at Connor's face. 'He's had enough. Now put these on him,' he extended his free hand, offering a set of handcuffs to Connor, 'or I swear I'll spray both of you and leave you gagging on the floor.'

Connor's eyes darted between the spray and the cuffs. Easy enough to swat the spray out of the man's hand, then turn, punch into Morgan's throat, collapse his windpipe properly this time, end it now.

You've got bad blood, son.

He closed his eyes, forced the memory away. Then opened them, took the cuffs. Manhandled the semi-conscious Morgan around and snapped the cuffs on, just a little too tightly. Put his knee into the small of Morgan's back and drove forward, Morgan bouncing off the wall and leaving a smear of blood in his wake.

Connor surveyed the room, glanced over to Dennis Morgan, his chest still rising and falling rhythmically in time to the grinding wheeze of the ventilator. And in that moment, looking at the bloodied lump of flesh that was Morgan's son, Connor fervently hoped the old policeman would stay asleep for ever.

After all, if he ever woke up, it would be to a world of nightmares.

CHAPTER 77

Donna stared at the phone, the sudden silence of the flat crowding in on her as she tried to process what she had just heard. After finishing her interview with Ross, she had returned home and, as promised, phoned Debbie Maitland at Frontline PR, the firm that had been handling Sanderson's story and negotiating the book deal. Debbie answered on the third ring, her voice bubbling with the pitch-perfect PR professional enthusiasm that set Donna's teeth on edge.

'Donna, so glad you could call. Are you OK? We've only heard the bare bones of what happened, but you must have gone through absolute hell.'

Donna assured Debbie that she was fine, skirting around the issue as quickly as possible. She didn't want to dwell on the previous night, let the memory of her nightmare vision of Mark become anything more tangible than a fleeting memory. Knew that if she did it would haunt her dreams for ever.

'Good, good,' Debbie had said, in a tone that made Donna wonder if she'd just been sniffing anything in the toilets. 'Well, I'm glad you called, because we've got a little offer. Now that Sanderson has been arrested, the book deal is dead, and we won't be maintaining him as a client. However, all the media coverage you generated has somewhat put us in the spotlight, and we were wondering if you could help us out.'

'What?' Donna asked. 'How do you mean?'

'Well, everyone was impressed with your handling of the Sanderson story. So, we've got a double-header for you, if you will. Write your story, about your encounter with Sanderson and your ordeal at the farmhouse, then come and work with us at Frontline. It's clear you can handle yourself in a crisis, you present very well and, frankly, we need someone like you, who can see a story and maximise it. And your name recognition wouldn't hurt when we're pitching for clients either.'

Donna felt the room crowd in on her, a sudden whining noise filling her ears. And then her mother's voice, soft, insistent: *It's no job for a mother with a young son.* Christ, she could walk away from it all, give Andrew everything he ever wanted.

She ended the call with Debbie in a numbed daze, promised to look over the proposal she was going to email to her. Hung up the phone and sat there, mind racing.

Give it up. Stop chasing the story and be the story for once. No more running into murderers or psychopaths, no more watching the people she loved being hurt and killed. It was tempting, so tempting, and her mother would be delighted.

And yet . . .

She had become a journalist to prove herself, show she could be the equal, and better, of any man. And then, when she had fallen pregnant with Andrew, and Mark had walked out on her, she had rebuilt her career brick by brick, story by story. She was a reporter on a national broadcaster, had the respect of her peers and her pick of assignments.

Could she give that up for a safe, comfortable PR role? Should she?

She stood, suddenly frustrated by the claustrophobic silence of the room. Headed for the door. She would collect Andrew from her parents early, spend the rest of the day with him. Clear her head, hope the answer would come to her.

Somehow.

CHAPTER 78

You're a curious soul, always have been. Your mother was the same, always wanted to know the answer to everything.

Connor was at the gym, the Bach blaring in his ears unable to drown out his gran's words. He was in the free-weights area, glaring at himself in the mirror as he curled a barbell, which was bowed in the middle from the amount of weight he had stacked it with. Every sinew was agony, as though his blood had been replaced with battery acid and his lungs had become a furnace. And still he curled, trying to deaden his thoughts.

He just couldn't leave it alone. After leaving his gran, he had promised himself it was over. That he would look no further. But, still, it nagged at him, the thought of Morgan standing over his dad, ready to kill him to end his misery, spurring him on. His dad had told him in the pub that his gran had burned the letter, so why lie about something as innocuous when he had exposed so many other ugly truths during their conversation?

A curious soul . . .

After his encounter with Michael Morgan, Connor had returned to the flat, cracked open his laptop and gone through the files that Robbie had sent him on his grandfather. All normal and routine: he was a surveyor registered in Dundee, where he had worked till his death in 1974. The death certificate Robbie had dug up stated that Campbell had been found at his home, at the foot of his stairs, neck broken, head cracked open like an egg. The formal cause of death was listed as accidental, with alcohol as a contributing factor. Translation? He had been pissed, tripped and fallen down the stairs.

All fine. Except the death certificate was dated ten days after Connor's gran had received the letter.

And there it was again, the bogeyman that haunted all policemen. Coincidence. Connor remembered the look in his dad's eyes in the pub that night, the sudden, inescapable fear Connor had felt that his father was going to attack him. What was it his dad had said? *No warning. No hesitation. I brained him. He went down like a ton of bricks and, for a minute, I thought I'd killed him. But I hadn't. Unfortunately.*

Connor grunted as he curled the barbell again, arms beyond pain now, retreating to a place of numbness he wished his mind would follow.

Unfortunately.

Was it a coincidence? Or was the thing Connor feared most, the thought he did not want to entertain, the truth? That Jack Fraser had seen the letter, and the veiled threat to return, decided to take matters into his own hands and visited his father one last time? Attacked him and, either intentionally or accidentally, killed him?

He dropped the weight, glared at himself in the mirror. Thought again of someone, anyone, attacking his gran, knew what he would do. He would kill them. No hesitation. No warning. They would die. But would his dad do the same? Again, his gran's words: *That night changed him, Connor.*

The question was, how much?

He whirled as a soft hand touched his shoulder, Jen flinching back, naked fear contorting her face as she jumped away from him.

'Jesus, Jen, I'm sorry,' Connor said, as he pulled out his earphones. 'I was just concentrating, lost in the set.'

'Yeah,' she said warily. 'I can see that. You OK? You were going at it fairly hard there.'

He shrugged. 'Ach, I'm fine,' he said, pulling his face into what he hoped was a reassuring smile. 'Just trying to work out some tension, you know what it's like.'

'There are better ways to do that,' she replied, a smile playing across her face as she reached up and brushed the bruise on his cheek. Connor could see the question form in her eyes, was grateful she didn't ask it. 'You're getting awfully close to overdoing it in here. Listen, I'm done in an hour. How about we get something to eat? My turn to cook for a change.'

'Sure,' Connor said. 'But let's eat out tonight. I feel like getting out for a bit.'

'You'll do anything to avoid my cooking, won't you?' she said. Then she leaned forward, kissed him on the cheek. And in that instant, Connor thought of another kiss, and another promise.

I'll give you a quote over a drink. We've earned it.

'Right, I'll see you when I'm finished,' Jen said. 'And rack those weights when you're done!'

He ticked a salute towards her, watched her disappear into the gym, Duncan MacKenzie's words in his ears now.

Just make her happy, Fraser.

Could he? Would he? Was that really what he wanted? A relationship with Jen and a war with her father? Connor was under no illusions that he was going to war with Duncan MacKenzie: the look the man had given him at his office the other night had told him that much.

He collapsed onto a weights bench, scrolled through the contacts in his phone. Found his dad's number, stared at it. One call. One more call, one more request for a drink. But what would he say? 'Hi, Dad, thanks for coming. Did you kill your old man?' Same again, was it?

He grunted. Pocketed the phone, went back to the weights.

Some questions were better left unanswered.

CHAPTER 79

The wheezing sigh of the ventilator was almost soothing in the silence of the room. Ford took a seat beside Dennis Morgan, felt a pang of jealousy for the man as he lay asleep, unaware of the chaos his actions had wrought.

'You're a fucking bastard, Dennis,' Ford said, the words like an insult to the almost church-like quiet.

He had managed to see Fraser's statement to Ross, knew that he had been good to his word and kept Ford's name out of his investigations and what he had discovered about Morgan covering up for his son. So, unless Duncan MacKenzie decided to come forward, he was in the clear. Barrett wasn't going to be a problem, not with Paulie looming in the shadows.

He grunted a laugh at that thought. In the clear. Yes. He had allowed his own youthful stupidity and eagerness to blind him to the truth, let him follow a senior officer down a path he should have never started on. He had actively participated in the framing of a man for murders he had not committed. And while Sanderson was hardly an angel, that fact burned Ford like acid.

He had been used. Manipulated. And a killer had remained free and eventually claimed another victim when the time was right. What did that say about him as a police officer, as a man? He stood, glared down at his old boss, found that, despite himself, he was unable to hate the man. His son had turned out to be a monster, true, but he

293

was still his son. So he had protected him as best he could, monitored him. It was only when Sanderson was released and the possibility of a new alibi presented itself that Michael Morgan had given in to the impulse to kill again.

He leaned down beside his chair, scooping up his briefcase. Opened it and slid out the notepad that was there. Looked down at Morgan, then pulled out his phone, sent a text to Mary: *Grab a bottle of champagne on the way home, would you? We're celebrating tonight.*

He smiled at the thought of her getting that text. She would question him, needle him for an answer. And he would give one to her. In time. After all, there was no rush. Not now. Soon, they would have all the time they needed.

He sat back down, propped his briefcase on his knee like a makeshift table. Turned the notepad to a fresh sheet of paper and began writing the letter he had spent years composing in his mind.

Dear Chief Constable Guthrie . . .

ACKNOWLEDGEMENTS

For a lot of reasons, this was the hardest book I've ever had to write. So huge thanks are due to Ed James, Derek Farrell, James Oswald, Paddy Magrane, Bob McDevitt, Craig Russell, Mum and Dad, and everyone who attends the scene of the crime for helping me get this one over the line.

Special thanks are due, again, to Louise Fairbairn (@scarletrix), crime fiction champion and blogger extraordinaire, who gave the book an early read-through and the thumbs up when I was lost in the woods. And, of course, thanks to Alasdair Sim, holder of the mighty Red Folder and purveyor of fine whiskies and hellish hangovers, who gave me the all-important nod and verdict (at an appropriate social distance, of course).

To the other three of the Four Blokes – Gordon Brown, Mark Leggatt and, yes, even the Auld Man Douglas Skelton, thanks for keeping me laughing and keeping me working.

And lastly, as always, to everyone who has read any of my books – either by picking one up in a shop, taking it out of a library or downloading it in e-book form – thank you. Writers write because we have to, but readers read the results of that compulsion by choice, and it's always an honour and a privilege to have someone choose to read my work.